THE LONGING

THE LONGING

Age Of Faith: Book Five

TAMARA LEIGH
USA Today Best-Selling Author

ISBN: 1942326084
ISBN 13: 9781942326083

TAMARA LEIGH NOVELS

CLEAN READ HISTORICAL ROMANCE
` The Feud: A Medieval Romance Series
Baron Of Godsmere: Book One, 02/15
Baron Of Emberly: Book Two, 12/15
Baron of Blackwood: Book Three, 2016

Medieval Romance Series
Lady At Arms: Book One, 01/14 (1994 Bantam
Books bestseller *Warrior Bride* clean read rewrite)
Lady Of Eve: Book Two, 06/14 (1994 Bantam Books
bestseller *Virgin Bride* clean read rewrite)

Stand-Alone Medieval Romance Novels
Lady Of Fire: 11/14 (1995 Bantam Books best-
seller *Pagan Bride* clean read rewrite)
Lady Of Conquest: 06/15 (1996 Bantam Books best-
seller *Saxon Bride* clean read rewrite)
Dreamspell: A Medieval Time Travel Romance, 03/12

INSPIRATIONAL HISTORICAL ROMANCE
Age of Faith: A Medieval Romance Series
The Unveiling: Book One, 08/12
The Yielding: Book Two, 12/12
The Redeeming: Book Three, 05/13
The Kindling: Book Four, 11/13
The Longing: Book Five, 05/14

INSPIRATIONAL CONTEMPORARY ROMANCE
Head Over Heels: Stand-Alone Romance Novels
Stealing Adda, 05/12 (ebook), 2006 (print): NavPress

Perfecting Kate, 03/15 (ebook), 2007
(print): RandomHouse/Multnomah
Splitting Harriet, 06/15 (ebook), 2007
(print): RandomHouse/Multnomah
Faking Grace, 2015 (ebook), 2008 (print
edition): RandomHouse/Multnomah

Southern Discomfort: A Contemporary Romance Series
Leaving Carolina: **Book One,** 11/15 (ebook),
2009 (print): RandomHouse/Multnomah
Nowhere, Carolina, 2010 (print): RandomHouse/Multnomah
Restless in Carolina, 2011 (print): RandomHouse/Multnomah

OUT-OF-PRINT GENERAL MARKET TITLES
Warrior Bride, 1994: Bantam Books
*Virgin Bride, 1994: Bantam Books
Pagan Bride, 1995: Bantam Books
Saxon Bride, 1995: Bantam Books
Misbegotten, 1996: HarperCollins
Unforgotten, 1997: HarperCollins
Blackheart, 2001: Dorchester Leisure

*Virgin Bride is the sequel to *Warrior Bride*
Pagan Pride and *Saxon Bride* are stand-alone novels

www.tamaraleigh.com

Special thanks to beautiful reader, Barefoot Believer, who took to heart Everard and Susanna's story and inspired me with these scriptures:

"My beloved is mine, and I am his...This is my beloved, and this is my friend...Set me as a seal upon thine heart, as a seal upon thine arm: for love is strong as death..."
~ Song of Solomon 2:16, 5:16, 8:6 (KJV)

1

Cheverel, England
April, 1160

H IS NAME WAS Judas. Not Judas of the Bible, but a Judas all the same—or so his father believed.

Lady Susanna de Balliol knew better.

Though the blood spoken between the boy and her claimed him as her nephew, the hearts upon which the name of the other was written made them as near to mother and son as they might come. However, for as well as their bond had served her brother all these years by keeping his son out from underfoot—at inopportune times, ensuring the boy was nearly invisible—Alan de Balliol had scorned them both. Or worse.

Now, in the failing light of day but a month following her brother's burial, Susanna slowly inhaled and more slowly exhaled as she and Judas awaited the announcement of whether it was a boy or a girl born to the departed baron's fourth wife.

A boy.

She did not have to be told it in words, for the joy shouted down from the birthing chamber announced it well enough. Feeling herself begin to fold where she sat clasping her hands so tightly she could no longer feel them, she forced herself back in the chair and looked up at Judas where he perched on its arm.

He was but ten years old, though one would not know it to stand him alongside his peers who would fall short by inches. More, they would not know it to look in eyes that were cursed with a greater depth of experience than they ought to be. Alan was to blame for that, though there were others as well. And she did not exclude herself, certain that if she had tried harder, she could have preserved more of her nephew's innocence.

"I have a brother," Judas murmured, no joy in the statement, nor animosity. He was simply wary of how the babe's arrival changed things.

In spite of one hope after another being trampled beneath the ruthlessness of Alan de Balliol, Susanna allowed herself the smallest hope that things would not change for the worse. After all, her brother was dead, and his second son by his latest wife was just that—second. Regardless of Alan's suspicions, he had waited to learn the sex of the child before doing what he had surely longed to do for years. Thus, Judas remained heir.

An obstacle between the newborn son of Lady Blanche and the barony, the voice of worry pecked at Susanna and threatened to upset her sensitive stomach. Such an obstacle would not suit the lady. More, it would not suit the woman's mother who made not the slightest pretense of having a care for Judas.

That loathsome, beak-nosed harpy would wish *her* grandson to inherit the barony, an expectation she had carried high upon her haughty chin since the announcement of her daughter's pregnancy months past. And that made the situation quite possibly dangerous.

"It does not bode well," Judas said.

How she hated that his thoughts were so familiar with her own when they ought to be racing with those things upon which other boys of his age indulged—swords and riding and running and wrestling and all manner of mischief for which he absolutely must be chastised on his journey toward manhood. But for Judas de Balliol, those things were a distant second to survival.

Susanna pulled her hands apart and laid one upon his where it gripped his thigh. "It changes naught, Judas. You are your father's heir."

He raised his eyebrows. "For how long, Aunt Sanna?"

Until it could be proven otherwise. But it could not. Could it?

She squeezed his hand. "I am sure the king will acknowledge you soon." Rather, Queen Eleanor, who acted as regent while her husband was occupied with his lands in France as he had been for nearly two years. "And then you will be Lord of Cheverel. Thus, we continue on as always. We stay the course."

Judas forced a smile that she wished he felt down to his heart. "We stay the course," he said and slipped off the chair arm and crossed to the hearth before which they had sat throughout the endless hours of moaning, screeching, sobbing, and cursing.

He had only just added another log to the fire when the tap-tap-tapping of hard-soled shoes sounded from the stairs.

He straightened and turned as Susanna pushed up out of the chair, both knowing to whom those footsteps belonged.

Lady Richenda bounded into the gravely silent hall, her round face uncommonly radiant. Locating her audience that did not include the servants who paused amid their duties to receive news that was already well known, she took quick, short steps to the hearth and halted before Susanna.

"*I* have a grandson—a large, lusty boy!" Though her smile did not seem capable of further breadth, it defied its limits when she shifted her gaze to the boy beyond Susanna. "Not a sickly bone in his body. Did you not hear those lungs of his?"

They were not merely prideful words, and it was only years of discipline that allowed Susanna to maintain a passive expression despite the distaste that sought to bare her teeth. Hopefully, neither did Judas give the woman satisfaction.

"Congratulations, my lady," Susanna said, ever grateful it was she who looked down upon the other woman whose thick, compact figure placed the top of her head beneath Susanna's nose. "And your daughter? How does she fare?"

With a frown that likely meant Judas had not responded as hoped, Lady Richenda said, "As only a daughter of mine could. Soon she shall be back on her feet and ready to resume her duties as lady of Cheverel and, now, mother to the son of Baron Alan de Balliol."

Whose death made him baron no more.

Susanna inclined her head. "I am glad to hear it." And she was, for she had grown cautiously fond of Lady Blanche during the woman's first year of marriage to Alan. But then Lady Richenda had come to live with them and the influence she exercised over her daughter had changed everything, and only one thing for the better. Alan, who had begun to treat his new wife poorly following their first year of marriage when she had not grown round with child, had become almost genial toward Blanche. All that could be concluded was that he feared Lady Richenda.

"By what name is my brother called?" Judas asked, and Susanna briefly closed her eyes.

The lady's laughter bounced. "Why, he bears the name of Alan." She raised her eyebrows. "He *is* his father's son."

Susanna drove her fingernails into her palms to contain the longing to scratch out the woman's eyes, certain this last barb had gone especially deep beneath Judas's skin. "My brother would be pleased," she said, and it was true, for had he lived, he would surely have gifted his name to the second son long denied him.

Done with the conversation, Susanna said, "I pray you will give our good wishes to your daughter and tell her we look forward to welcoming our new nephew and brother." She turned up her lips, reached forward, and set a hand upon Lady Richenda's arm, a gesture sure to send her back the way she had come.

The breath the woman sucked between her teeth almost whistled. "That I shall," she said and glanced one last time at Judas before turning on her heel.

When she disappeared up the stairs, Susanna allowed her shoulders to lower, then her chin. "I am sorry, Judas. I wish..."

She heard his feet stir the floor rushes and sighed when his arms came around her waist. There had been a time when such expressions of solace and affection were not far and few between, but he had begun to leave them behind, and more determinedly these past months. He had known, as she did, that if Alan de Balliol fathered a second son, the balance of life would be further tipped in a direction that was already too precarious.

Glad her belly was empty, she drew a shuddering breath. "Ah, Judas, I wish—"

"'Tis not for us to wish, but to do," he repeated her words with which they had become self-reliant over the years, then he lowered his head between her shoulder blades.

Susanna wrapped her arms over his, this son of her heart if not her body, and murmured, "So now we keep watch, Judas mine." Feeling his nod, she added, "And we pray."

"Why?" he said so softly that, had she not anticipated the question, it might have been mistaken for a whisper of air come through the window.

"He listens," she reminded him as she found herself doing more often, "even if He does not yet answer as we wish Him to. Believe it, Judas."

"'Tis not easy. I..."

When it seemed his hesitation would know no end, she turned in his arms and lifted his chin. "Tell me."

His lids were lowered, lashes brushing the dark smudges beneath his eyes. Finally, he looked up. "Sometimes I would rather believe He did not listen. Do you not think His silence would be easier to understand, Aunt Sanna?"

She felt a pang in her heart. Often, she had thought it would be better if the Lord did not know what went here below, especially in her younger years before she realized the great number of prayers answered as she had wished them to be. The infant given into her care had thrived despite the loss of his mother, his early childhood illnesses had not proved fatal, that with which he had later been afflicted was now mostly under control, Alan had not sent him away or disowned him, and always—no matter what it cost her—she obtained what they needed to move from one day into the next.

Acknowledgment of that last caused shame to warm her. And for it, she nearly always began or ended her prayers with, *Even if my sins are too great for You to bless me, Lord, I beseech You to bless Your beloved Judas.*

"Do you not think it?" her nephew pressed.

"I have thought it," she admitted, "but ever I remind myself of the prayers that have been answered, which gives me hope that the greatest of these will one day find favor with the Lord." She kissed his brow. "Do not cease praying, Judas, for your prayers strengthen mine." And were surely more pleasing to the Lord than her own.

2

Susanna would not like it. She said it was for her to steal about and listen in on conversations not meant for their ears, but she had not seen what he had seen, and it might be too late to learn the meaning of it if he wasted time seeking out his aunt. More, he was no longer a child. He was heir to Cheverel, and though he had yet to be formally acknowledged and appointed a protector to aid in the administration of the demesne, he was determined to sample as much of his new position as possible.

Convinced it was his right to know, firsthand, the workings of his household, he drew back from the window through which he had seen Lady Richenda pass a missive to one of their men-at-arms who had immediately spurred away from the manor house. Shortly, she reentered the hall and cast her gaze about, but she did not see him where he had retreated into an alcove that had served him well for years.

With a square-edged smile that bespoke satisfaction, she bustled forward and up the stairs.

Judas followed. Measuring his footfalls to avoid the creaks in the steps he had learned to stay clear of long ago, he ascended to the first landing and peered down the right-hand side of the corridor in time to see the door of his stepmother's chamber close—not quite all the way.

Moments later, he stood alongside the door opposite the crack that allowed a glimpse within, that small slice revealing Lady Blanche in a chair near the window, a bundle in the crook of her arm.

"I have done it!" Lady Richenda's voice was more tempered than usual, likely in deference to her grandson.

"Done what, Mother?" Her daughter sounded nearly as fatigued as she had three weeks past when Judas had been summoned to her chamber and she had drawn back the blanket to reveal his brother's face—one he had rarely seen since, as if she feared he would do the babe harm.

"I have done what we spoke of yesterday and the day before and the week before," Lady Richenda said.

Silence fell, and Judas wondered what passed between the two women that should cause neither to speak. Had he made a sound? Did they suspect someone listened at the door?

Much to his disgust, his heart that was already causing a terrible commotion in his chest, beat harder.

Then, blessedly, the conversation resumed. "I wish that you had waited, Mother. I am not yet myself, and I do not know when I shall be. My thoughts are ever escaping and I am so tired. And, Lord help me, I do not understand why I feel such terrible sorrow."

"Need I remind you that your husband is dead? And, for the moment, your son is but a spare?"

For the moment...

Sharp laughter sounded from the younger woman. "That first is not so bad, and sometimes I think the second—"

"'Tis not for you to think, and most certainly not while you are in such a state!"

A shrill gasp sounded. "Mayhap I would not be in such a state if you allowed me a wet nurse! God's mercy, this child drains me!"

And that child began to fuss.

"See what you have done!" The robust Lady Richenda appeared in the crack and, when she disappeared, the bundle was gone from Lady Blanche's arms.

There was nothing more to be learned over the next minutes as Lady Richenda paced back and forth and crooned in a voice so raspy and coarse Judas was surprised that the infant calmed.

"I want a wet nurse," Lady Blanche restated.

"Our Alan is too important to be given into the hands of another, but once his future is secure and all threats to his wellbeing are removed, you shall have your help."

Lady Blanche groaned. "Do you truly believe the queen will grant us an audience?"

Guessing she spoke of the missive just sent, Judas steeled himself for what was to come—that for which he and Susanna had kept watch.

"I have placed all my hope in it being granted," Lady Richenda said. "We must pray it is."

Pray! Judas nearly spat. If her prayers were answered as she wished, then it would be hard to believe her God was the same as his, even though the priest told that one should not question the workings of the Lord.

"Still," Lady Blanche said, "what if she does not reject Judas's claim to Cheverel in favor of my son's?"

There it was, the only surprise being that it was so soon set in motion.

"Though my husband snarled and spat that he could not have beget a child such as that one, never did he outright disavow him. Never did he set the words to parchment."

Judas looked down. Though he knew what his father had believed of him and had felt his sire's disgust on those occasions when others bore witness to his son's gasping and wheezing and writhing, it still pricked in those places that Judas had yet to harden.

"God's teeth!" Lady Richenda erupted, setting the babe to crying. "If your husband had but waited a month to die! A month!"

"As he did not, Mother, what do we do if the queen determines there is naught to prove Judas is misbegotten?"

The tap-tap-tapping of the older woman's feet that not even the rushes could quiet told Judas she was pacing again, doubtless trying to resettle the babe. "Lady Susanna," she said. "I am certain she knows the truth, just as her brother believed."

Does she? Judas wondered. She owned that she did not, assured him she was certain he was born of Alan de Balliol, but—

"If she could be made to talk," Lady Richenda mused.

"You know she will not. She loves the boy."

"Fool that she is," Lady Richenda muttered, then laughed. "Of course, now that you are delivered of a son, the best solution to that whelp's claim to Cheverel is for him not to arise from one of his attacks."

Judas jerked. She wished him dead? *That* he was not prepared for, and it shook him so deeply he felt a constriction about his chest—of the sort that could leave him gasping and flopping like a fish tossed to shore.

Breathe! he silently commanded. *In through the nose. In. Hold. Out through the mouth. Out. Slowly.*

"Unfortunately," she continued, "I have seen fewer of his attacks this past year. And when he is taken with them, always his aunt is there to coax the breath back into him. If it could be arranged—"

"Cease!" Lady Blanche lurched out of the chair, disappearing from view. "God preserve me! There is something very wrong with you, Mother."

As her protest sank in, the dots before Judas's eyes danced away and he drew a slow breath of sweet air. However, his throat stoppered when a sharp crack of flesh on flesh sounded, followed by a cry far different from the infant's.

"Do you or do you not want Cheverel for your son?" Lady Richenda demanded.

A whimper sounded that made Judas reach for the door handle. However, reason prevailed before he could reveal himself. Curling his fingers into his palm, he lowered his hand. As much as he longed to act the lord of Cheverel and aid his stepmother, his interference would not be tolerated. Not yet.

"Hear me well," Lady Richenda said. "You will do what is required to secure your son's future, your future, and mine. Do you understand?"

Lady Blanche cried out again.

Feeling very much his ten years and hating the way they wore upon him, Judas pressed his arms tight against his sides and stepped back from the door.

"Do you understand, Blanche?"

"I understand! Do not! Pray, stop!"

Unmindful of the temperamental floorboards, Judas backed away. Blessedly, whatever sound his feet stirred up was surely masked by the increasingly unhappy babe. More blessedly, he had not the voice to yelp when a hand closed around his arm.

He swung around to face his aunt where she stood on the landing. Eyes wide with urgency, a finger to her lips, she shook her head.

He allowed her to guide him down the stairs. And the rest of it—the walk from the manor house to the bank of the river where she urged him to sit against an ancient oak—was as if seen through a haze.

When he finally lifted his head from her shoulder, she cupped his cheek and smiled sadly, "Judas mine, I wish that you had not listened in."

"Then we would not know what I know." Haltingly at first, then in a rush as emotions gave way to anger, he told all and glimpsed upon her face what he thought was fear. In the end, she assured him there was hope in Lady Blanche's response to her mother's wicked suggestion and reminded him that he mostly had control over his breathing attacks. Thus, she concluded that their only real worry was whether or not Queen Eleanor would grant Lady Richenda an audience.

Judas concurred, though he did not truly. Despite his aunt's continual intervention and because of it—his punishments often falling upon her—his father had taught him well what to fear. And Lady Richenda was to be feared. Still, wishing to give Susanna comfort as ever she gave him, he let her believe she had eased his concerns.

"Sanna?" he said when they rose to start back.

She sighed and met his gaze. "The answer to what you would ask of me is no different from the other times I have answered, Judas—I do not know."

"Lady Richenda believes you do, just as my...father did."

"And, as is often the case, the lady is wrong."

He drew himself up to his full height, for he had never before ventured as far as he was about to. "Then what do you *think?*"

She caught her breath and, as was her habit when pressed to account for the past, gripped through the material of her bodice the pendant upon its slender chain. "What I think," she finally said as she lowered her hand to her side, "is that I have no right to guess at something so far beyond my reach."

He did not want to accept her answer, but he could see he would gain no other. Not this day. But perhaps another day once he raised himself above the weak-kneed Judas de Balliol who had been so affected by what had passed between Lady Richenda and her daughter.

Resignedly, he nodded.

As they walked back to the manor house over which dusk had fallen, they agreed they would continue on as always. They would stay the course. They would keep watch.

3

Cheverel, England
May, 1160

SHE WISHED HE would not look at her with such imaginings in his eyes. Though she told herself she ought to be at least somewhat accustomed to the regard of men who deemed her passing pretty, it was hard to forget she was no longer the plump, splotchy-faced girl who had gone in search of her friend, Judith, that day.

"Aye, I shall keep watch over him," Sir Elias said and bent his head nearer. "But it shall cost you a kiss."

And he would get it, though that was all. "If that is the price I must pay."

He chuckled, winked, and stepped away from her.

She watched him wend among the fenced areas where a handful of men-at-arms and squires practiced at arms. When he reached the farthest area where Judas swung a sword against another of the few knights she trusted—an older man who had been her father's man before her brother's—she turned opposite.

With the crash and clang of blade upon blade sounding behind, her brisk steps making her skirts snap at her ankles, she followed the servant whom the cook had sent to fetch her. Another problem with the menu?

A delivery of foodstuffs that had not arrived? Had Lady Richenda once more put the back of a hand to a kitchen boy?

Vexed that it continued to fall to her to manage the household while Lady Blanche slid from her fifth week post-birth into her sixth, she entered the kitchen some minutes later. It was empty.

She turned to the servant who had fetched her. Discovering the girl had disappeared, she stepped back out onto the garden path by which she had gained the kitchen and called, "Hilde!" and twice more as she strode among the vegetables that would soon find their way into the kitchen.

"Milady?" The cook's head popped up from behind a low-lying bush. "There be somethin' ye need?"

Susanna halted. "I understood 'twas *you* who needed *me*."

The woman sat back on her heels. "Nay, milady. All be well with my pots and spoons, roastin's and stirrin's."

Had she misunderstood the servant? No, the girl had definitely said she was sent by Hilde.

Susanna heard it then—the absence of steel upon steel and grunts and shouts that had receded as she advanced on the manor house. Though diluted, those sounds should yet be present.

She snatched up her skirts and ran for the training field that lay downhill from the manor house.

Please, Lord! she sent heavenward as she flew past the soldiers' barracks, the smithy, the stables. *Protect Judas!*

It was worse than the worst sight imaginable, for never had she seen him in such distress where he lay in the dirt on his back with knights, men-at-arms, and squires gathered around as if the throes of death were a wonder to behold.

Scrabbling at his chest and throat, choking and wheezing sounds issuing from his gaping mouth, legs alternately kicking and stiffening, Judas de Balliol struggled to keep hold of life.

She shouted his name, and the brightly-clothed figure she pushed past caught her arm.

THE LONGING

She stumbled, landed hard on a knee and, as she wrenched her arm to free herself, snapped her chin around and found the impassive face of Lady Richenda above her.

Susanna knew herself to no longer be the fourteen-year-old girl who gasped at any cruel word spoken in her direction, who hunched her shoulders up to her ears at the first sign of physical aggression, but until that moment she had not realized just how far she had risen—though some would say she had fallen.

She came up snarling and swinging and, an instant later, gave expression to the one who so lacked it. Taking no moment to savor the horror, pain, and crimson mist distorting the woman's face, she sprang away and dropped to her knees alongside Judas.

"Breathe!" she commanded as she dragged him up into her arms. "In, Judas, in!"

His dark head lolled against her chest, and she nearly cried out, but then his lids fluttered and there came the thready sound of air being dragged in through his nostrils.

"That's it. Hold it—just a moment."

As he did so, she lifted his lax hand from the dirt, placed it in his lap, and began to trace the sign of the cross upon it. "Now breathe out... out...slowly..."

He parted his lips and exhaled. His next breath was stronger, as was the one that followed. And those who had stood around watching and doing nothing to save him, began to murmur.

She dropped her chin, letting her hair fall forward to curtain their faces. *Thank you, Lord. Thank you.*

Judas's fingers closed firmly over hers, preventing her from tracing crosses in his palm.

She raised her lids and saw he had tilted his face up to hers, the eyes with which he regarded her steady and reflecting none of the sickly fatigue usually present.

"Judas?" she breathed.

He smiled grimly, whispered, "Now we know, Aunt Sanna."

"What?" No sooner did she ask than everything fit painfully, perfectly together. Lady Richenda was responsible for this—had sought to bring about what Susanna had tried to convince Judas that the woman would not do. Indeed, the lady had even tried to hold Susanna back. And Judas had used whatever opportunity had been given him to test his brother's grandmother by meeting cunning with cunning, his ten-year-old heart corrupted by the need to survive.

Something inside Susanna broke, something she knew needle and thread would not put back together. The pieces were too hard, too sharp, too jagged. Thus, the sob that stole from her throat was followed by another, part relief that it had not truly been a near mortal attack he suffered, part grief over his stolen childhood, and—selfishly—part despair that this was her life. For years, her hell had worn the face of her brother. Though his hand had rarely landed a blow to her person, the constant beatings dealt by his hateful words had wounded deeply. But at least it had not been deadly—not like this new hell that wore the face of murder that could take from her the only being in the world who mattered.

She heard Judas's voice and felt his arms come around her, but she could not stop crying no matter the spectacle she made of herself. Not until she heard another voice, one so hated it could not be ignored, did she drag herself out of her insides and back into the dirt of the training field.

"Poor child," Lady Richenda said. "Certes, he must needs rest if he is to regain his strength. Help him."

Susanna snapped up her chin. To the right stood the one who had been thwarted, though perhaps she would succeed another day.

When Susanna saw what her fists and nails had wreaked upon the older woman, it was hard not to laugh. Lady Richenda's veil was askew, upper lip smeared with blood that had not been completely wiped away, and four livid scores ran down her left cheek onto her neck.

"And assist Lady Susanna," she continued. "She is not herself, distraught as she is over her nephew's illness."

The two men-at-arms who stepped forward did so without conviction, as if uncertain of Susanna for her having attacked the other woman. Fortunately, their dragging feet provided the time needed for her to stand on her own and pull Judas up beside her.

"Aunt Sanna?" he said, his shortening of her name in the presence of others revealing how shaken he was. But, then, never had he seen her so reduced by emotion.

She swallowed hard against hiccoughs that, in her youth, had followed a torrent of tears. "I am fine," she said and put an arm around his shoulders. As he leaned heavily against her, his foresight in doing so but another ache to her heart, she set her gaze upon the men-at-arms. "We do not require your aid," she said and drew Judas with her to where Lady Richenda quite impossibly tried to look down her nose at them, squat thing that she was.

"If you ever again…" Susanna drew a deep breath. "…lay a hand upon Judas or me, I vow you will know exactly how *distraught* I can be made to feel."

The lady's eyes widened, showing yet more of the hatred she bore them.

"Test me if you dare, *my lady*." Susanna turned Judas opposite and, picking her gaze over those who had but watched, walked slowly past them.

Only when they were far enough ahead to not be heard by those who followed did Susanna ask Judas, "Where did Sir—?"

"My lady!" someone called.

She pressed her lips closed and continued toward the manor house.

"The boy is well?" asked the one who drew alongside.

She swung her gaze to the knight, identified him as one of the majority who had followed her brother's lead in disparaging Judas over the years. Now he answered to Lady Blanche and her mother, though he and the others would answer to Judas once he was acknowledged as heir. *If* he was acknowledged.

"The *Lord* of Cheverel is well," she clipped, "though we have not you to thank, have we?"

The man's grimace seemed genuine, but she took only slight comfort in it, knowing that though he was not as hard-hearted as some, he would bend to whoever wielded power. And that was not yet Judas.

"I am sorry, my lady. We knew not what to do to help the lad."

And had not even thought to try. However, the older knight with whom Judas had been at practice and the one to whom she was to have owed a kiss had known what to do. And they had not been among those gathered around Judas.

"I left my nephew in the care of Sir Elias and Sir George. Where did they go?"

The man shrugged. "They were summoned by Sir Talbot."

The head of the household knights and securely under the thumb of Lady Richenda. It had all been planned.

Determining Judas could just as well answer her next question, Susanna said, "We are most grateful for your concern, Sir Knight. Good day."

He opened his mouth as if to say more, closed it, and turned aside.

After confirming that Lady Richenda, who followed with a knight on either side of her, remained distant, and once they were past the smithy and the curious regard of those nearby, Susanna said, "How came you to lose your breath, Judas?"

He looked up, and a bit of a smile curled his lips. "You know I did not truly lose it, aye?"

She sighed. "Nearly too late for my heart to bear."

"I thought it best you also believed," he said, then answered, "When Sir Elias and Sir George were called away after you left, I knew something was afoot, but just as I decided to return to my chamber as you would have me do, Sir Morris said he would finish instructing me at swords."

Susanna caught her breath, for though the knight was small of stature, he was quick and wily, so much that his skill at arms was as feared as that of the head of the household knights. Remembering his hard, bruising kiss—one not owed but stolen—and grasping hands, she swallowed bile.

"I was fair certain of what he had been set to do," Judas said, no longer leaning as heavily upon her as they neared the manor house, "and full certain when I saw Lady Richenda at the fence. Thus, I let him push me hard until I felt the air grow thick." He gave a dry laugh. "Then I gave the hag what she wanted."

Susanna gripped his hand tighter. "Judas, I am sorry."

He looked up at her out of eyes that nearly belonged in the face of a wizened old man. "It changes everything."

She inclined her head. "I fear it does, meaning you had best stumble and give me your weight again."

He did not hesitate, for he also knew they would not be watched as closely if he appeared too weak to rise from bed over the next several days.

"I did not expect it to be so easy to claim my reward," Sir Elias murmured as he stared up at Susanna where she knelt beside his pallet. "My lady ought to exercise more caution lest she be thought overly enamored of my person." Smiling sleepily in the light cast by the half moon outside the window, he brushed his fingers across her lips. "In the middling of night...beside my bed...alone..."

As much as she longed to clamp her teeth upon those fingers, she pushed his hand aside and rasped, "You have earned no reward."

He sighed. "I did what I could. Some things cannot be helped."

It was true. Neither he nor Sir George could have refused Sir Talbot's summons, but that did not mean she was in this man's debt. Yet.

Sir Elias eased up onto his elbows, and when his blanket slipped down, she was relieved to see he wore an undertunic. "How fares the boy?" he asked.

She hesitated. Though committed to what she had come to ask of him, still she feared it could be a mistake. Unfortunately, there was none better to aid her. "That depends upon you, Sir Elias."

"Me?"

"Judas and I require your help."

"Another favor?"

She tried not to swallow hard, but there it was. "More than ever I have asked of you, but which, I believe, you are honorable enough to grant."

He chuckled. "Am I?"

"Certes, you have heard tale of what happened to my nephew in your absence and must know 'twas by design. Thus, I ask you to save him from further attempts upon his life."

"How do you propose I do that?"

Catching herself dragging her teeth across her bottom lip, a nervous gesture vanquished years ago, she quickly remedied the habit. "By delivering Judas and me to Wulfen Castle."

His eyebrows soared, and he whistled low. "That is no place for a lady. Indeed, I am told women are forbidden within its walls."

Susanna knew that, but the fortress renowned for training boys into knights was where she would find the one who might be able to alter the dangerous new course set for Judas's life. Whether the man could be moved to do so was another matter.

"And even if you find welcome there, my lady, 'tis a good two days' ride."

"This I know, but it is all that is left to us. Will you take us?"

"If I do," he said slowly, "you know I cannot return to Cheverel. Indeed, it could prove difficult to sell my sword arm to another lord."

"You are assuming Judas will not be awarded his father's title, and I tell you that when he is, your services to Cheverel's new lord will be much needed. And Sir Talbot's will not."

He stared at her, then he began to smile. "It seems you have bought yourself a savior, my lady."

She sighed loudly.

"However," he added, "this favor will cost you more than one of your kisses."

Though her soul jerked, she nearly laughed. Of course it would cost more, but if it saved Judas...

She rose to her feet lest this time he demanded payment in advance and said, "So be it. After you have delivered us safely to Wulfen, you shall have your reward."

Thus, the bargain was struck—a great favor for something far greater than a favor. But that was the way of things. At least in the life of Susanna de Balliol.

Before the sun thought to part the darkness and warm the land, the three of them stole from the manor house that, by all rights—or perhaps not—belonged to the boy who peered longingly over his shoulder until they were distant enough to spur the horses to flight.

4

Wulfen Castle, England
May, 1160

EVERARD WULFRITH, SECOND born of Drogo Wulfrith, was not in the habit of rising three hours before dawn—often two, but rarely more. However, something had disturbed his soul. A dream? A sound? Movement where there should be none? That other sense that could not be called upon but had often proved as valuable as his other senses?

He breathed out, peered at the night-shrouded land through the white mist expelled from his mouth, then pushed off the battlement against which he had braced a shoulder this past quarter hour.

The squires he passed along the wall acknowledged him with one "My Lord" after another and he nodded at each in turn. Noting one who was unsteady on his feet and making an effort to keep his eyes open, he marked it in his mind to discuss with the knight charged with the squire's training the appropriateness of giving the young man a night watch. Age and size were not always the measure by which one moved through the ranks toward knighthood.

As he neared the steps that both descended to the outer bailey and ascended to the roof of the gatehouse, his ears picked up the sound of what, perhaps, that other sense had first known.

Two horses, perhaps three. And four more that rode in pursuit, the latter belonging to the mounted guard that patrolled the castle's bordering wood for occasions such as this.

Everard shouted a warning and was pleased when he saw that already those on the walls were lighting additional torches to illuminate the land before the walls. Changing course, he took the steps two at a time to the gatehouse roof where he found the aged knight who had once been in service to his sister-in-law, Lady Annyn.

"My Lord," Sir Rowan said, then set himself in the space between two battlements.

Breathing in the breeze that skittered across his face and over his shaved head, Everard strode to the battlements to the right of the other man. He leaned forward and caught sight of two horses carrying three riders, next the four mounted guard who would soon overtake them.

Within two hundred feet of the walls, the trespassers were surrounded and held at swordpoint.

Everard smiled at the fearless efficiency of those young men who would soon don spurs and a Wulfrith dagger that proclaimed to all that they were the worthiest of knights.

The words exchanged between the uninvited and the guard carried across the cool air, but they were too distant to make sense of them.

When one of two figures mounted on a single horse struck out at the squire who had edged near to yank back his hood—rather, *her* hood, as told by the voice that berated him—Everard murmured, "That is settled."

It was rare for the uninvited to be admitted to the castle, nearly unheard of for a woman to be let in. *Nearly* since his sister-in-law, Lady Annyn, had found a way in and his own sister had, for a time, needed to be hidden from King Henry.

Though tempted to leave the mounted guard to send the riders on their way so he might sooner set to his morning prayers, Everard held.

"I shall deal with them, my lord," Sir Rowan said when the squires, flanking the trespassers, guided their mounts toward the gatehouse.

Everard neither accepted nor declined, for though he knew his time was better spent elsewhere, his curiosity was roused.

As those escorted forward drew near, he noted the man wore the trappings of a knight—chain mail and sword. The woman who rode beside him with her hood down about her shoulders had the bearing of a lady. Much of her hair, torchlight giving it the cast of a river stirred with silt, had escaped the neck of her mantle and fell around the dark-haired boy who sat on the saddle before her with his face turned up and eyes fixed upon the walls.

"Who goes?" Sir Rowan called as the horses were reined in a few feet from where the uppermost edge of the drawbridge settled when lowered.

The lead squire's gaze first found Everard, but quickly shifted to the one who had called down. "Sir Elias Cant requests sanctuary for the lady, the boy, and himself. He tells they are pursued by those who seek their deaths."

Everard returned his regard to the boy who had yet to move his gaze from the castle walls. He was of a good size, well on his way to manhood. The woman...

Her gaze, intense even in torchlight, grazed his before shifting to Sir Rowan. Guessing she was near the age of thirty, Everard concluded she was the boy's mother. Was the knight her husband? More, was it true someone wished them dead?

"With regret," Sir Rowan said, "we cannot grant admittance. Women are not permitted within our walls."

The lady turned her head sharply toward Sir Elias, gripped his arm, and leaned near. Whatever she spoke, the words were not loud enough to reach those on the walls, but they were impassioned.

Sir Elias nodded and returned his regard to the battlements. "Sir Knight, our situation is dire, for our pursuers are not far behind and our horses cannot carry us much longer."

There was little room for exaggeration in that last bit, for even from such a height, Everard could see that the animals whose breath heaved white clouds upon the night had been ridden hard.

"I see no immediate threat," Sir Rowan replied. "Ride on!"

Once more, the lady appealed to her knight, and with such animation that the boy finally tore his gaze from the walls to attend to the exchange. As the woman settled back in the saddle and raised her face to Sir Rowan, Sir Elias called, "We ask that you deliver a message to Sir Everard Wulfrith."

Everard frowned. He was certain he did not know the lady. Not only had she shown no recognition when her eyes lit upon him, but Wulfen Castle was nearly all there was to his life, especially since it had been mostly given into his keeping following the marriages of his older and younger brothers. Perhaps she simply knew *of* him from a son or brother who had trained here.

"What message?" Sir Rowan demanded.

"We pray he will grant us admittance—if naught else, for the sake of Lady Judith."

Everard jerked. Not even the cruelest blade could have so deeply delved and bled his innards as that name. But his Judith? Judith who had become another man's wife? Judith who was no more?

Realizing he no longer drew breath, he straightened from between the battlements, slowly breathed in, slowly breathed out.

Movement to his left returned him to the present and he looked across his shoulder at the knight who advanced on him—and who was not quick enough to disguise the concern upon his face.

"My Lord?" Sir Rowan halted alongside him.

Discomfited at having slipped into the skin of the young man he had been at twenty and two years of age, Everard expelled his next breath on the words, "Lower the drawbridge."

5

SHE HAD NOT wanted to speak the name. Not yet. But it had accomplished what she had prayed it would, and so quickly that she knew the one whose aid she sought must have been near.

Had he been the silent figure between the battlements? Nay, his face had been too distant to recognize, but she had seen he was bald and Everard Wulfrith had the most beautiful hair a man could have—the envy of many a woman, including herself. Of course, it had been eleven years...

Even so, thirty and three was not so great an age that he would have lost his hair.

"Dismount!" a stern voice ordered above the grind and screech of the lowering portcullis that competed with the rumble and clank of the rising drawbridge.

Having brought her horse to a halt alongside Sir Elias's in the midst of the mounted guard who had escorted them into the outer bailey, Susanna looked to the aged knight who stood before them with hands on hips. It was the same one who had conversed with them from atop the gatehouse. But where was that other one who had stood with him there? More, where was Everard Wulfrith?

Distantly aware of Sir Elias swinging out of the saddle, she swept her gaze over the wall walks that dimmed as the additional torches lit during their approach were extinguished.

Hoping it would cause their pursuers to ride past believing their prey had done the same, she peered into the shadows of the outer bailey. But there was no one to be seen—until a tall figure whose bald head caught moonlight appeared before the raised portcullis of the inner wall that accessed the donjon. And then he was gone.

"Come down, Judas," Sir Elias said where he now stood alongside Susanna.

Grateful he did not reach to her nephew which, no matter the boy's fatigue, would have offended, Susanna drew her arm from around Judas's waist.

Immediately, he dropped down beside Sir Elias.

The reward of her favor near at hand now that the knight had fulfilled his end of the bargain, she was tempted to do the same when he lifted his arms to her, but she reminded herself that if it was possible to put him off, it would not be done with the vinegar of her disdain. Thus, she went into his arms—and groaned softly as her worn, aching muscles protested their unfolding.

"Surrender your weapons," the gatehouse knight ordered as Sir Elias set her to her feet, "and give me no grief!"

"I do not like this," Sir Elias muttered.

"Such precautions are to be expected," she said and reached beneath her mantle to remove the dagger from her girdle.

One of the two young men who had dismounted stepped forward to receive from Sir Elias his sword and two daggers, next her dagger, lastly, Judas's. Then the second young man came behind the first and said, "Raise your arms, Sir Knight."

Grudgingly, Sir Elias complied and the squire ran his hands up and over him. His search produced another dagger, causing the gatehouse knight to grunt.

The young man moved to stand before Susanna, and she saw it was the one she had struck when, refusing to lower her hood for fear of revealing she was a woman, he had done it for her. "My lady?"

Dear Lord, he will enjoy this.

"You jest!" Sir Elias barked, but she shook her head at him and he ground his teeth.

She pushed the mantle back off her shoulders and raised her arms out to the sides. Surprisingly, the young man quickly and impersonally patted her down and, finding nothing more, moved on to Judas.

Empty-handed, excepting the dagger Sir Elias had secreted in his boot, the squire turned to the gatehouse knight. "They are disarmed, Sir Rowan."

The knight nodded and turned away. "Follow me."

"Certes, I hope you know what you are doing," Sir Elias said low as they crossed from the outer bailey into the inner where the donjon rose massively at its center. "As I have warned time and again, the Wulfriths do not suffer fools gladly."

"Then I had best not be a fool."

They were met at the base of the donjon by a young man who appeared to be of an age that would soon see him knighted. Though fully dressed and alert, his tousled blond hair evidenced he had been roused from sleep.

"Squire Joseph," he introduced himself with a curt bow. "I am to show you to your chamber."

Then they would not simply be granted an audience? Of course, it was not yet day, so perhaps they would be made to wait.

The gatehouse knight turned as if to depart, paused, and narrowed his gaze on Sir Elias. "You would do well not to test that one." He jerked his head in the direction of Squire Joseph. "There is a good reason he was sent to you." Then the man strode away.

"I bid you come," the squire said and began his ascent.

Susanna put a foot on the first step only to pull it back at the sound of hooves thundering across the land. They had come...had not been put off the scent...would be near to bringing their prey to ground if that prey had not been let into Wulfen Castle.

Ride on, she silently beseeched as she peered over her shoulder at the walls that showed no evidence this night was unlike any other uninterrupted night. *Pray, ride on.*

"They have gone past," Sir Elias said moments later and took her elbow. "Come, my lady."

She did not want his hand upon her, but the relentless ride—far different from the leisurely pace to which she was accustomed from atop a sidesaddle—kept her from rejecting his assistance. And as he guided her up the steps, each one seemingly taller than the last, she gave him more of her weight.

The great hall they entered was dark and quiet, though not so much that the numerous bodies upon pallets could not be seen and heard. Guessing here were the sons of nobles whose fathers vied to place them at Wulfen, Susanna paused inside the great doors.

"This way," Squire Joseph said quietly and started toward more stairs. Blessedly, they had only to ascend the first flight.

"You are to remain within," the young man said as he pushed open a door and motioned them inside.

Susanna stepped into the chamber, pulled out of Sir Elias's hold, and turned to face the squire. "I must needs speak with Sir Everard. When will he see us?"

He raised his eyebrows. "I know not when *Lord* Wulfrith will see you, but I trust you will find the accommodations acceptable until he grants an audience."

Much depended on how long they would be made to wait, for there was only one bed. Dare she ask more of her host? Of course, if ever there was a time to do so, it was now before *Lord* Wulfrith learned who was under his roof. "I thank you, Squire Joseph, but we require two chambers—providing another is available."

The squire looked from her to Sir Elias. "You are not husband and wife?"

She raised her chin. "Sir Elias is my protector. And friend." That last he was not, but if such a claim disposed him toward delaying his reward, it would serve.

"I shall inform my lord of your request," the squire said. "By what name might I tell him you are called?"

She swallowed. "I will myself tell your lord my name." The better to ensure she gained at least a few minutes' audience.

After a brief hesitation, the squire said, "Very well," and closed the door behind him.

"Now what?" Sir Elias asked.

"We wait." Struggling against fatigue that threatened to make her knees give way, she turned to Judas who stood erect despite a face lined with the exhaustion of two days of hard riding broken only by snatches of sleep. "You must rest," she said and stepped forward to assist in the removal of his mantle.

He drew back and dropped into the chair that sat before an unlit brazier. "I shall wait with you."

She did not argue, for to do so would only cause him to try harder to keep his eyes open. "Of course," she said.

An hour later, the dark still thick outside the window, Sir Elias having carried a sleeping Judas to the adjoining chamber that he and the boy were to share with a household knight, Susanna counted herself fortunate that the savior she had bought had not returned seeking payment. Of course, he had never struck her as being of a foolish bent, and it would not be wise to compromise her while she awaited Lord Wulfrith.

Continuing to ignore the longing to seek her ease in the chair lest the man she waited upon found her asleep, she held out her hands to the glowing, coal-heaped brazier that Squire Joseph had lit for her when he had delivered her pack—no doubt riffled through to confirm it held no weapons.

When would Everard Wulfrith come? And when he did, what would he see? Though tempted to try to put order to her appearance, it stank too much of vanity and concern for what he thought of her. Besides, she already knew what those thoughts were—the same as they had surely been these past eleven years. If he had thought of her at all.

She fingered her face. Finding the familiar, angular planes, she thought how sad it was that her wish to be as slender as Judith had been granted. Not that she missed the padding beneath her skin that had earned her fourteen-year-old self the secondary name of "plump," but she had never wished to be this thin—"gaunt," according to her brother.

The door opened to her right, and Susanna stilled.

Was it him? She had only to shift her eyes to look near upon the one who stood in the doorway, but she could not without first recovering words rehearsed over and over since fleeing Cheverel. Thus, as she rooted around inside herself, she sentenced him to remain unacknowledged.

But it was not a sentence he was willing to serve, for he stepped inside and said, "My lady?"

That voice...

Realizing she still had a hand to her face, Susanna lowered it and looked across her shoulder into eyes that had last looked so near upon her not with suspicion as they did now, but surprise, then alarm.

It was he whose shaved head had reflected moonlight. And it was also *him*.

Hardly able to breathe, she reached to the base of her collarbone against which the pendant rested beneath her bodice and closed her fingers around it.

"You wished to speak with me," Everard Wulfrith said.

He was eleven years older, face grown a bit coarse, shorn of the hair Judith had pulled her fingers through, but he appeared much the same. And though not of the mythical proportions he had seemed to the girl she had been, he was very tall and broad.

He frowned, narrowed his eyes.

"Forgive me for staring so boldly." She released the pendant and turned to fully face him. "'Tis just that you have changed, and yet not so much that I would not know you."

His frown deepened.

Tamping down the longing to drag her teeth over her bottom lip, she said, "But you do not know me, do you?"

"I do not."

No hesitation. No attempt to look nearer upon her.

"Thus," he said, "as I have much to attend to ere dawn, tell me what I can do for you, my lady."

She clasped her hands at her waist. "I require your aid to right a wrong—if a wrong has, indeed, been committed. And methinks only you can tell me that."

His shoulders rose with a long breath that told he exercised patience. "Speak, lady-who-will-herself-tell-her-name."

Wishing the rehearsed words were not lost to her, that she did not have to form from scratch what she must tell, she said, "It has been many years, but you knew me as Susanna de Balliol."

Everard felt every muscle tense. There was that cruel blade again. As it went deeper, he nearly cursed himself for not knowing her. In the chapel where he had gone after ordering the drawbridge lowered, it had occurred to him the boy could be Judith's, the two accompanying him tasked with delivering the long-departed woman's son to the man who should have been his father. But that possibility raised the question of where Alan de Balliol stood in all this. Now, however, the greater question was why that man's sister, the same who had come between Judith and himself, stood before him.

Of course, perhaps this woman who wafted the scent of roses, whereas once it was sweet woodruff that had whispered in the space between her and others, was not Lady Susanna. It would certainly account for the reason she was so unrecognizable. Was a game afoot?

"Am I so very changed?" she asked softly.

Determined to put an end to this farce so he might sooner see her and her companions away from Wulfen, Everard strode forward. He halted so near that she was forced to tip her head back to hold his gaze, giving him the perfect vantage to compare his memories of Alan de Balliol's sister against this woman who called herself by that name.

Her hair was no longer dark blond woven through with strands of lighter blond. It was lightest brown—that of a stirred-up river as he had thought when he had looked down from the battlements. However, the light of the brazier was kind to it, imparting a cast of honey wherever it flickered. Her soft, round face was no longer soft, no longer round, cheekbones prominent as if she did not eat well. Lips that had bowed and flashed pearly teeth each time he had looked her way, knew no curve. And, as also previously thought, she appeared to be of an age beyond the twenty and five she would be.

He settled upon her eyes. They were still the golden-brown of amber. And in them, he saw her. "Susanna," he conceded. "I do not think I have ever known anyone so changed."

She looked down, but not before he glimpsed what he did not wish to believe were tears. And it was good he was not prepared to believe it, for when she lifted her chin, there was no excess moisture. "As you, yourself, can attest, Lord Wulfrith, eleven years is a long time and can much alter a person." Her gaze flicked to his head.

He stiffened. Not at the possibility she believed age had caused him to lose his hair, but lest she hit upon the true cause of its absence. After all, she had seen Judith and him together that day, and he was fairly certain she had heard what had been spoken between them.

He took a step back and saw her shoulders ease. "What do you think I can tell you that will right this wrong of which you speak?"

"The boy with me is Judith's son. He is called Judas."

Everard knew he had not misheard, but still he asked, "Judas?" for who would burden a child with that?

"My brother named him," she said, "after Judith died following his birth."

"Why?" he rasped.

She frowned. "I am thinking I do not need to tell *you*, Everard Wulfrith. But if I do, then perhaps you have already told *me* what I need to know."

Everard knew he was gifted with intelligence alongside the capacity to fight well for his life and the lives of others, but in that moment he felt dull-witted. In the next, he was alert to another's presence.

"I will ask it if you cannot, Aunt Susanna."

As the lady swept her gaze to the doorway, Everard turned to face the boy who stood with a shoulder brushing the doorframe. Alan de Balliol's son was well versed in stealth, having made so little noise in gaining the chamber that Everard had become aware of his presence only a moment ahead of the words that announced it. Though Everard was hardly himself in the presence of this woman, that was no excuse, for such an oversight he would not accept from a knight-in-training.

"Return to your chamber, Judas," Lady Susanna said. "We will speak later."

The boy shifted his gaze to Everard, and in his eyes shone something like accusation. "I know who my father believed you to be."

Rather than indulge him with a response, Everard set about assessing him as came naturally to one who had spent much of his life training boys into men capable of defending their lives and the lives of those it was their duty to protect.

"Judas?" Lady Susanna stepped forward, but the boy held up a hand that made her halt as she drew alongside Everard.

"My father may never have spoken this man's name to me in your hearing, Aunt Susanna, but he told it to me after revealing Lady Blanche was finally with child—and that he would soon have a son."

"You did not tell me." She sounded hurt, as if the boy's silence were a betrayal.

He shrugged. "It changed naught—only let me know the reason you asked Sir Elias to deliver us here."

As the lady and her nephew fell silent, as if there were no more pieces of the puzzle to be tossed about, Everard summed up the boy.

He was a good size that bespoke he was nearer thirteen years of age than the ten required for him to be Judith's son, but that was not enough to dismiss him, for Everard and his brothers had also been of greater height and breadth than their peers. Though Judas de Balliol's bearing was erect, gaze direct, and speech precise, those things could also be explained away, especially in light of the absence of a glimmer or a twitch of playfulness about his face. And then there were the bruises of fatigue beneath his eyes…

If Judith *had* borne him, and Everard had not so distanced himself that first year that he had been unaware it was a son she birthed upon her deathbed, then this boy was likely amongst the emotionally scarred ranks of those who were nearly as difficult to train as the rebellious ones. Of course, Judas de Balliol might number among those who came too late to Wulfen, but Everard would have to reserve judgment until he could look nearer upon him.

A moment later, the opportunity presented itself when Judas stepped forward and placed himself in front of Everard. "My father hated you. Perhaps more than he hated me."

The world was not right, Everard thought as he imagined how black a soul must be to so deeply impress its hatred upon a child, let alone a child of its own making—in this case, an infant given the name of the one who had betrayed Jesus. Everard had known Alan de Balliol to be grasping, self important, and unworthy, but this?

He scrutinized Judas's face that did, indeed, bear traces of one nearer the age of thirteen. But of greater note were his eyes, the depths of which revealed soft spots of vulnerability—rather, humanity. All was not lost. Yet.

Judas pressed his shoulders back. "I would know, did my father have good cause to hate you?"

Everard felt the tug that, if he allowed it, would draw him back eleven years to when he had last held Judith.

"Are you my father?"

It took everything in Everard to contain himself. He had not thought this encounter could take a more twisted turn, but it had done so with such speed he felt the wind of it. Forcing his face to remain impassive, he said, "I am not."

The boy raised his eyebrows. "*Could* you be my father?"

Lady Susanna gasped.

The impertinence! "Boy," Everard growled, "how old are you?"

Though Judas de Balliol's gaze wavered, the rest of him was still. "I am ten. And my name is Judas, not *boy*. So you could be my father?"

Everard realized that, by questioning the boy's age, Judas had assumed it was done to determine if the sin committed with his mother could have resulted in pregnancy.

"All of ten," he clipped, "much too young to be so bold. However, since you are of so few years, I shall answer the question asked twice of me though it was well enough answered the first time. Nay, I could not be your father, no matter your age. And you do your mother, God rest her soul, grave ill to think it."

Judas drew a deep breath and looked to his aunt. "Cheverel is mine."

Only then did Everard realize the boy had been speaking of his father in the past tense, and he knew what it told, even before he looked to the woman beside him.

She met his gaze. "Alan de Balliol is dead, God rest—" She closed her mouth and gave a slight shake of her head as if to deny her thoughts the very words she had denied her tongue.

Things had not been well between her and her brother? Not that it was any concern of his.

"You have what you came for," Everard said. "A day and night's stay I will grant to ensure you and your horses recover sufficiently, and then you will be gone from Wulfen."

Susanna held her tongue, for now was not the time to tell him she did not have all she had come for. As for what he had given her, it depended on whether or not he spoke true. Strange, but she wished he lied, for her brother had not deserved a son like Judas. But then, did Everard Wulfrith?

She smiled tightly. "I thank you, Lord Wulfrith. And now, I would like to rest." *Ere I fall at your feet.*

He inclined his head, stepped around Judas, and did not look back.

As his footsteps receded, she settled her gaze upon her nephew. "So now you know."

He shrugged. "Perhaps."

Dear God, is the last of my sweet Judas slipping away that he should be nearer yet in thought to me?

Heart aching, she reached forward—and almost drew back for fear the gesture of affection would be deemed offensive. But he allowed her to tuck behind his ear the lank of hair that had fallen into his eyes. Her little boy was not completely lost to her. Not yet.

6

HOW SHE COULD have slept so soundly to find that when she opened her eyes it was once more nearing night, she did not know. Not that she had not needed the dozen or more hours of sleep after the merciless flight from Cheverel, but she had long ago learned to sleep lightly and in snatches the better to watch over Judas. Was it because it felt safe here, so distant from the place that had ever been her home?

Not wanting to move from where she lay on her stomach, she slid her gaze from the unshuttered window through which late afternoon sunlight fell, to the platter of food that had been left on the bedside table. Her belly grumbled—thankfully, not in a way unreceptive to sustenance—and she nearly reached for something to settle it. However, the longing to return to sleep was too great to resist.

"Safe," she breathed and closed her eyes.

Are you? Believe it at Judas's peril.

She sat up and looked around the chamber. She was alone as she had been in the earliest hours of morn after Judas had returned to the room he shared with Sir Elias. But surely he was next door—

She abandoned the bed, so swiftly that she nearly tripped on the sheet that came with her. Ignoring her aching muscles, she kicked her feet free of the cloth and lunged across the room. Shortly, she rapped her knuckles on the door of the chamber beside hers.

"Judas!"

No answer though, in truth, she did not allow much time in which to give one before thrusting the door inward. A bed and two pallets, all three empty.

"Dear Lord," she breathed and stepped back into the corridor. If the din that met her ears had been present moments earlier, she had not heard it. Though she told herself the boisterous sounds had nothing to do with Judas, it was the same she had told herself when she had awakened years past to find her five-year-old nephew absent from his bed beside hers. After exhausting her search abovestairs, she had ventured to the hall. There she had found Alan and his men gathered around Judas who stood with arms folded over his chest as he looked warily from one drunkard to the other, shrugging and shaking his head when they put to him questions about the betrayal of Jesus by the one with whom he shared a name.

Susanna told herself that such a thing would not happen at Wulfen Castle, then she ran. She knew she was barefoot, knew she wore only a chemise, knew her hair was too loose, but she did not care. However, the dozens upon dozens of boys and young men streaming into the hall did care, for as she sprang off the last step, their eyes stuck to her and feet faltered.

She searched among their faces. And there, on the far side of the hall, was Judas beside Sir Elias.

Thank you, Lord.

Judas took a step forward as if to gain her side. And halted. As he stared uncertainly at her, Sir Elias bent his head to her nephew and said something, then the knight strode toward her.

"Be about your duties!" a deep voice commanded, setting into motion those who had stopped to stare.

Before Susanna could search out the speaker, Everard Wulfrith placed himself in front of her as if to shield the others from the sight of her. He was angry. She saw it in his glittering eyes and the set of his dirt-streaked jaw, but it seemed not the kind of anger to which she had grown accustomed in her brother's household. His appeared to be more of the disapproving sort like her father had turned upon her, rather than the sort that warned punishment would not come near to fitting the crime.

"For this," he said low, "women are not welcome at Wulfen. Now return to your chamber."

She drew a deep breath and blinked her eyes wide when struck by the thick smell of unwashed, sweat-doused bodies that was certainly not exclusive to the man before her. Without thinking, she lifted the back of a hand to her mouth and nose.

Everard Wulfrith smiled grimly. "Yet another reason—the easily offended sensibilities of a lady. 'Tis good you leave us first thing on the morrow."

She lowered her hand. "I am sorry. I was concerned about Judas. But as to our departure, I would speak to you on that. There is more that must needs be—"

"There is not."

She swallowed. "But I—"

"My lady!" Sir Elias halted alongside their host and nodded over his shoulder. "As you can see, Judas fares well."

She glanced at where her nephew continued to watch from afar. Though hurt that he hung back, she understood. After all, she was unapproachable on two fronts—a woman in a place where none were allowed, and one who did not present as a lady in her state of dress. And there was poor Judas, surrounded by peers for whom he was surely too much of a curiosity as it was.

"Return to your chamber," Everard Wulfrith said again.

Sir Elias stepped nearer. "Allow me to see you abovestairs, my lady."

Before she could decline, for she would not have Judas left unattended, Everard Wulfrith clipped, "Stand down, Sir Elias. That the lady not further add to the unseemliness of her behavior, she will take herself abovestairs."

Overlooking what was behind his objection to Sir Elias serving as escort, especially as he was right to be concerned with how it might be perceived considering her appearance, she said. "I shall, Lord Wulfrith, but first I would request another audience—"

"Go."

There would be no moving him, she realized as she stared into eyes that were mostly pupil, ringed by a fine line of the grey-green that had made her heart flutter so many years ago.

Knowing she would have to await another opportunity—or make one—she pivoted and, rebelling against appearing to have been sent away like an errant child, measuredly ascended the stairs.

7

If NOT FOR her determination to speak with Everard Wulfrith, even if it meant once more sullying his hall to seek him out, Susanna would not have changed into fresh clothes with it so near unto night. Once she had tended to her ablutions, made all the easier by the washbasin Squire Joseph delivered following her departure from the hall, she had donned a fresh chemise and bliaut and worked a comb through her hair until it was manageable enough to be plaited.

Now she waited and, from time to time, eyed the supper viands that had replaced the cold ones to which she had earlier awakened. She knew she ought to eat, but as the minutes counted themselves into hours that drew nearer the morn when Judas and Sir Elias and she would be ejected from Wulfen Castle, more and more her nerves picked at her and pained her belly.

She rose from the chair before the brazier, crossed to the door, and opened it to once more attend to the sounds that rose from that place she was not welcome. It seemed the dining was done, but there were yet numerous voices and bursts of laughter, indicating the night was not near enough its end that those below would soon seek their rest. And still Judas and Sir Elias had not returned abovestairs.

She closed the door and began to pace. If Everard Wulfrith did not come to her this night, she would go to him. She had seen the curtained wall behind the dais in the hall and knew the lord's solar lay behind it rather than abovestairs. Thus, she would have to negotiate the hall once all were abed and do so without awakening its numerous occupants. Fortunately—in a manner of thinking—she had learned enough of stealth these past years that she stood a good chance of reaching her destination. And then...

She pulled her braid over her shoulder and began to worry at the crossed tresses, their smooth courses from one hump to the next soothing her. What words would reach Everard Wulfrith? How much needed to be told to gain his aid?

A knock sounded.

He had come! After a moment of foolish vanity, during which she wished she had a mirror with which to check her appearance, she hastened across the chamber. Containing the impulse to throw the door wide, she eased it open.

"Sir Elias!" She looked left and right of him. "Where is Judas?"

"He wished to remain in the hall. It seems the knight who first denied us entrance to Wulfen knows how to spin tales of sword and spear and bow. Judas is entranced."

She took a step toward Sir Elias. "You left him alone?"

"Hardly alone, and certainly not lacking protection."

"What do you mean?"

"It seems Lord Wulfrith has taken an interest in him—at least, from a distance."

"Make sense, Sir Elias!"

He gave a crooked smile. "He watches Judas—as he did much of the day while we were out about the castle grounds."

Susanna caught the inside of her lip between her teeth and, heart beating faster, pondered the reason Everard Wulfrith showed interest in a boy he was determined to send out from the safety of his walls. Did he see Judith in him? Perhaps himself? Regardless, there was hope in that.

"You are thinking we may not be set out on the morrow," Sir Elias said.

She returned him to focus. "That is my hope."

He nodded. "We shall see, hmm?"

"Aye."

Silence fell, one that made her long to push the door closed, but she knew her business with him was not finished. And it could be—done with now and forever...

Or another day, perhaps one that will never come. After all, there are worse things than not keeping one's word.

Still, she would have to give him something. Knowing she would be a fool to yield anything behind a closed door, she stepped forward, causing him to step back, and pulled the door closed behind her. She leaned against it and raised her gaze to his. "Now, I suppose, you wish to collect your reward."

He raised his eyebrows and took back the step he had given away.

Unlike some of the others with whom she had bargained in the past, he did not hungrily descend upon her, allowing her to rise to her toes and press her mouth to his. Then she dropped back to her heels.

His brow furrowed. "Come, Lady Susanna, you know I was promised a greater reward than that."

She curled her fingers into her palms. "Wulfen Castle is hardly the place to...It would be unseemly..."

What looked to be hurt passed over his face. "You think that was the bargain struck—that I deal in the currency of a lady's virtue?"

Of course that was what he had meant, for it was certainly what the others had meant, forcing her to move on to the next bestower of favors once they became dissatisfied with mere kisses.

Sure there would be teasing in his eyes, Susanna searched them. It was there, but not so deep as to be mocking or cruel, and she found herself wondering if he truly believed she yet had virtue about her. After all, he had to know he was not the only one to grant her favors. She had seen the looks exchanged between knights, did not doubt they talked amongst themselves. And lied.

She swallowed hard, asked softly, "Is that not our bargain?"

THE LONGING

"It is not."

Though she knew she should not be so ready to believe him, she felt warmth bloom in her breast that always seemed cold except in the presence of Judas. But as she felt a smile move onto her mouth, it occurred to her he might find her unworthy of greater intimacy. After all, she was no beauty, and the mirror denied her would only show her to be several years beyond her true age. Good for a kiss, but that was all?

"I am not so dishonorable as that," he said, and she knew her face reflected more than ever she allowed it to.

Did he speak true? It was but a matter of honor? She momentarily closed her eyes, and when she opened them, he wore a slight smile. "Then what did you mean when you said your aid would cost more than a kiss?"

"More than one of *your* kisses. *That* is what I said."

"Oh."

"Oh," he repeated, then bent his head and set his mouth upon hers.

As always when granting such favors, Susanna squeezed her eyes closed so she would not be made to suffer the memory any more vividly than was necessary and clenched her teeth lest the one who collected on their bargain sought to further violate her mouth.

However, when Sir Elias's kiss deepened, she did not protest. She was too grateful and too surprised that she did not taste bile—more, that the kiss was almost enjoyable. And she might have allowed herself to experience it a bit longer if not that she heard the sound of feet upon the stairs.

Judas? She tried to pull her head back, but it was against the door, and so she turned her face in the direction of the stairs and said, "Cease, Sir Elias."

"One of *my* kisses," he breathed and pressed his lips to a spot beneath her ear.

The footfalls sounded louder, foretelling it was only a matter of moments before whomever they belonged to appeared. She slid her hands to the man's shoulders and pushed. "Pray, Sir Elias, cease!"

He pulled back, but not before Everard Wulfrith bounded onto the landing.

The scene was surely one never before played out at Wulfen Castle, but even more than it offended for the stain cast upon its walls, it offended for the heinous act perpetrated against the lady who pleaded for an end to it.

Everard did not remember the last time he'd had occasion to put all of his body behind an assault, but there was something satisfying about smiting the one who had retreated only upon realizing the lady was no longer at his mercy. Through the unfamiliar haze of rage, Everard savored the feel of fist meeting bone, the shout of pain, the strain of throat muscles beneath his forearm—

"Nay!" Hands dragged at him, sank nails into his arm. "Release him!"

—the wheeze of breath denied, the blood that ran from nose and split lip, the bulging, alarmed eyes—

"Everard, do not!"

The use of his Christian name by the one who smelled of roses pierced the haze, and he snapped his chin around and narrowed his eyes on the woman who pressed near his side, trying to pull him from Sir Elias. "He sought to ravish you!" he growled.

"He did not!" Amber eyes wide, she shook her head. "I vow, he took no more than I willingly gave."

Revolted that she made such an unseemly claim and bothered that she should need the man so much, he said, "You speak false. I heard you plead with him—"

"Because *I* heard you upon the stairs!"

Everard's breath ground to a halt, and he looked closer upon her, noting her mussed braid, swollen mouth, and the flush of color across her cheeks that imparted a youthful, appealing glow to her otherwise gaunt features. Did she speak true? For this she had entreated the knight to cease?

Whether or not it was so, in that moment he recognized that he who did not lose control had done so—and not because he faced life-threatening circumstances that were as close as one could come to justifying such behavior.

He wrenched his forearm from the man's throat and stepped back, breaking Lady Susanna's hold on him.

As Sir Elias bent forward, braced his hands on his thighs, and drew loud, strained breaths, the lady laid a hand to the knight's back. "You are well, Sir Elias?"

He nodded, but it was some moments before he straightened. Putting his back to the wall, he met Everard's gaze and raised a staying hand. "The lady speaks true," he croaked, then drew the back of that same hand across his nose and mouth. "I meant her no harm."

Of course she spoke true, even if she did not, for the man was surely not so foolish as to reject the lifeline thrown him.

Sir Elias glanced at his crimson-smeared hand. "God in Heaven, I heard you Wulfriths were a fierce lot, but—"

"I assure you, that was naught," Everard growled. "And you would do best to take yourself far from my sight."

The man considered Everard, then looked across his shoulder at Lady Susanna.

She inclined her head. "Go."

"You are sure?"

"Aye."

Wiping at his bloodied face, the knight pushed off the wall. "I will not be far," he said, and Everard heard the challenge in those words that were in direct opposition to the warning just given. Sir Elias was fortunate it was not the youngest of the Wulfrith sons he faced, for Abel would have found it more difficult than Everard to suppress the impulse to see how much more intimate the knight would like to become with a fist.

Everard watched the man stride the corridor, listened to the sound of his footfalls upon the stone steps until they were swallowed by the din of those in the hall, then he set his gaze upon Lady Susanna where she stood before the wall against which he had slammed Sir Elias.

Lashes shadowing the tops of her cheeks, she stared at the floor and gripped one hand over the other at her waist—so still, it was as if she did not breathe. Then her gold-touched brown eyes were upon him.

"I beseech you to accept my apology, Lord Wulfrith." She took a step forward. "Now, might we speak of—"

With a single stride, he set himself over her. "Scarcely clothed, you come into a hall brimming with young men whose minds should be upon a hundred different things before thinking near upon a woman. But that is not enough. Barely out of sight, you further insult my hospitality by engaging in a tryst hardly befitting a lady and upon which anyone could have happened—if, indeed, it was a tryst."

He caught the flicker of feeling in her eyes, next a tightening about her mouth as if she were determined to keep her lips closed against the truth of what he had heard and seen.

Everard felt a tightening about his own mouth. "For this," he said, "women are not welcome—or allowed—at Wulfen. I should never have let you in."

She swept her tongue across her lips. "Aye, you should have, even if only for Judith's sake, she who would be grateful for what you have done for the son she—"

"I will *not* discuss her with you."

"I do not ask that you do. There are matters more pressing, namely Judas's safety. To grant me the audience I begged is the reason you came to me, is it not?"

"Certes, I did not come for the same reason Sir Elias did."

The catch of her breath was slight, but then she glanced toward the stairs. "Is this where you would have us speak?"

For propriety's sake, Everard was tempted, but those knights who held chambers on this floor would soon make for their beds. Unfortunately, though his solar where he conducted private business would not place them in such close quarters, Susanna de Balliol would have to pass through the hall to reach it since he had no intention of revealing the hidden passageways. And, having already determined it best not to further expose those of Wulfen Castle to this woman, much of the whispered talk over supper having been of the lady who should not be here, it would have to be her chamber.

He pivoted, thrust open the door, and stood aside.

As she stepped past, she paused and lightly touched his sleeve that was flecked with Sir Elias's blood. "If you do not see to that, 'twill stain."

He looked to her hand upon him, and she immediately removed it and crossed to where a washbasin was set near the supper viands Squire Joseph had delivered to her. The latter appeared untouched, and he guessed here was the reason she was so gaunt. Remembering the plump girl from years past, he wondered if she intentionally starved herself to attain a more pleasing figure or if a lack of appetite made her eschew sustenance. Regardless, he did not think it recent behavior, for not only was the skin of her face firm, but the hollow look about her told that it was years in the making.

Susanna kept her back to Everard Wulfrith for as long as possible, wetting and wringing the hand towel the better to compose herself out from under his painfully observant gaze. Everything depended on what she would tell. Thus, her words must be carefully chosen to rouse compassion and a sense of responsibility—even if Judas was not of his loins. After all, the boy's lot had been cast as a result of what this man had sought to take from her brother.

She turned and crossed the chamber to where Everard Wulfrith had positioned himself just inside the doorway, extended the dampened towel.

He gave it a dismissive glance. "You have your audience, Lady Susanna. Tell what you would that I might attend to more pressing matters."

Suppressing the impulse to rebuke him, a not so difficult undertaking considering the practice she'd had with her brother, she said, "There is naught more pressing than Judas, Lord Wulfrith."

He raised his eyebrows.

As she regarded him, she acknowledged he was more changed beyond the absence of hair that the abundance of stubble told was by choice. The Everard Wulfrith she remembered had been pensive, at times overly solemn, but still there had been lightness about the young man with whom she had been...

Besotted. That was what the beautiful Judith had said, though it had not been said unkindly.

Before memories of that day could unfold, Susanna focused more intently on Everard Wulfrith whose impatience she sensed as tangibly as she had felt his distaste when she had declared Sir Elias had taken no more than she had willingly given—a pronouncement she had determined to let stand, for it was not only true in this instance, but she was certain it would serve Sir Elias and her no better were she to reveal the starting place of their kiss. Whether she engaged in trysts or bargained with her body, neither reflected well upon her.

"Speak," Everard Wulfrith said so sharply she nearly jumped.

"Life has been difficult for my nephew. His name ought to tell you that."

No response.

"The day after Judith birthed him, she died."

There—some swift-footed emotion in his eyes.

"My brother was distraught over her death, then angry. The more he looked upon his son who was born a very good size from a man not of great stature, the more he questioned if the babe was, indeed, his—and began to believe Judith's death was God's punishment for her terrible sin." She replenished her breath. "Though the morning-after sheets had been hung out following their wedding night"—

Emotion again, but just as quickly gone.

—"he determined she had tricked him, that she had not come to him a maiden. Thus, he concluded that the babe delivered barely nine months after the nuptials was more likely yours than his."

She thought Everard Wulfrith might reaffirm that he could not be the father, but he remained silent. "However, he never denied Judas, at least not by way of ink and parchment, for of his three marriages, Judith was the only wife to produce a child."

She pondered if there was any benefit to elaborating on Judas's suffering, not only of how poorly he had been treated but of the breathing attacks that had caused her brother to further scorn the boy. But as tempted as she was to try to arouse sympathy in that direction, she more feared that if Judas was this man's son, he would be less inclined to claim him, perhaps as repulsed as Alan.

"And so, until my brother had another heir…"

She crossed to the bedside table where yet another platter of viands had grown cold and dropped the towel beside it. She considered the bread, pinched off a crust and, rubbing it between her fingers, watched the crumbs fall into the congealed stew that had earlier smelled fragrant.

"Therein lies the dilemma," she said. "A month following Alan's death—"

"How did your brother die?"

She turned and the remainder of crumbs dropped from her fingers to the rush-covered floor. "He was hunting and took down a boar. However, it was not dead as thought and caught him unawares. He finished it, but not before receiving mortal wounds." Only now, when it was known the lengths to which Lady Richenda would go to see her grandson made heir did Susanna count it a blessing that her brother had met such a horrible end. Had there been any possibility of foul play, Lady Blanche's mother might have tried to place the blame for Alan's death upon those she wished to be rid of—Judas and Susanna.

"Continue," Everard Wulfrith said.

It was a moment before she found her place again. "The dilemma we face is that, a month following Alan's death, his fourth wife delivered a son, and now she and her mother seek an audience with the queen that Judas might be declared illegitimate and set aside in favor of her child."

"Then 'tis an audience with Queen Eleanor you ought to seek, Lady Susanna, not me."

"There are two problems with that which sounds so simple to you. The first is that Judas overheard the mother of Alan's widow suggest his death would be the easiest way to see her grandson made heir." She could not tell him it had played out upon the training field, for he would want to know the means by which her nephew's life was to have been forfeited. "The second problem is you."

His lids narrowed. "Me?"

"Though I do not believe Alan revealed your name to his wife or men, you are the reason there is a question of whether or not Judas is a de Balliol."

"The *only* reason?" he said low and deep.

She knew he believed it was she who had carried the tale to her brother, just as Judith had first believed, but she would not waste her breath in self defense when the air was better spent on Judas.

"If you know for certain you cannot have sired Judas, then we shall seek an audience with Queen Eleanor to defend his claim to the barony, but we cannot do it alone."

He said nothing for a long moment, and when he did, he once more stood over her. "What do you suggest?"

She had to tilt her head back to maintain eye contact. "Exactly what you think. Far too many of my brother's retainers are under the control of Alan's widow's mother and would surely stand witness to his disparagement of Judas, and especially his fondness, while full up in his cups, for proclaiming he had been cuckolded."

Anger darkened Everard Wulfrith's eyes, banishing the color to the farthest reaches, but she was not fearful, for she knew it was not directed at her. He saw the cruelty and injustice of what she told, and whether it so deeply affected him because it had been done to a child of his own making or a child innocent of what his father had believed of him, it mattered not. She had him.

"You will do it?" she asked. "You will bear witness that you could not have fathered Judas? That he is a de Balliol?"

The color began to return to his eyes, and when he blinked, the black of his pupils no longer dominated. "What makes you believe the queen will take my word over that of your brother's men?"

"I have not forgotten the dissent between your family and King Henry whilst you supported King Stephen's claim to the throne, but I also know there are few families King Henry holds in such high regard as yours now that he has your fealty." How she wished he would not stand so near, that his eyes did not probe so deep.

"What do you gain from this?" he asked. "Why do you care so much what happens to the boy?"

The question was so ludicrous that she nearly laughed. "He is my nephew. More, he is as a son to me, all that is left of my friend, Judith——"

"Friend!" The anger had returned, but this time it was not directed at one beyond his reach.

Refusing to retreat, she said, "Aye, friend. She did not have to ask me to watch over her son, but it was the last thing she did ere she died, and I have done it as best I could."

"Then for her and her son, you sacrificed your own happiness? Never wed?"

His question was more unwelcome than he could know. But this was not the route she wished their conversation to travel.

"Perhaps as a means of atoning?" he pressed.

Susanna curled her fingers into her palms.

"Too late, would you not say? Judith *is* dead."

The cruel bite of her nails would not stop her words from crowding the space between them. "'Tis not *I* who must needs atone, Everard Wulfrith. *You* are the cause of this misery, and you will right the wrong."

He drew his head slightly back. "Will I?"

Her right hand came up, but she stopped it before he could—and he would have, his reflexes a step ahead of the slap she longed to land to his immovable face.

As she stared at his splayed hand that had arrested its own course near her own, he said, "I will not." Then he pivoted and strode toward the door.

Dear God, what have I done?

Susanna flung herself across the chamber and grasped his arm as he stepped into the corridor. "Forgive me, Lord Wulfrith. I am but frightened for my nephew."

He looked at her hand upon him. "Another spectacle, Lady Susanna?"

Whatever it took…"If you truly loved her"—she winced at the shake in her voice—"you would save her son, even if 'tis true you could not be his father."

His lids narrowed. "It *is* true. No matter your pretty words about a past that is best left buried, I am under no obligation to Judas de Balliol—or you—to stand before the queen and declare myself incapable of having cuckolded one of King Henry's barons."

Pride. Of course that was it, though it certainly was not all. Susanna gripped his arm tighter. "I beg you, do not turn your back on Judas. He is only ten!"

"And he is not my problem."

Feeling her color drain, Susanna released his arm and gripped the door frame lest her knees gave out from under her.

Something like concern lined his face, but then it smoothed away. "Eat something." He jutted his chin in the direction of the table. "You are too gaunt and shall need your strength for the morrow's ride."

Gaunt. As Alan himself had been fond of pointing out once "plump" no longer served.

"Good eve, Lady Susanna." He started to turn away.

"I will do anything," she whispered, "whatever you ask of me." And however he wished to interpret that…

Not well, she saw when he looked across his shoulder, then he was striding opposite.

She closed her eyes, gripped the doorframe so hard her bones ached. *Do not buckle. Deep breath. Now turn. One foot before the other. Close the door. One foot before—Very well, rest. Only for a moment.*

When she finally opened her eyes where she leaned back against the door, they fell upon the untouched viands Everard Wulfrith believed would give her strength, which was true if she could keep it down. Still, it would not be the kind of strength she needed. And she resented it where it sat cold and stale and stomach-turning.

It was not plump Susanna de Balliol who lunged across the chamber. It was not gaunt Susanna de Balliol who wrenched the platter from the table. It was Susanna de Balliol who had only one thing in the world to lose—Judas. It was that one who threw the platter across the room. That one who did not flinch when it and the goblet of wine and food-stuffs crashed against the door. That one who sank to her knees, hunched forward until her head nearly touched the rushes, and tried—so very hard—to pray to God who seemed in no mind to heed the groaning and cries of a soul as sinful as hers. Not even for the sake of His beloved Judas.

8

He did not expect to find Sir Elias within an arm's throw of his fist, but the man was near the base of the stairs, reclining against the wall, pressing the back of a hand beneath his nose as he watched those in the hall.

Regardless of whether or not the woman abovestairs had spoken true about what had gone between her and this knight, still Everard felt the prickle of dissatisfied knuckles. Fortunately, it was such an unfamiliar sensation that he recognized it as unbecoming of a Wulfrith knight, especially in light of the distance that now stood between Sir Elias and Lady Susanna.

Not until he was two steps removed from the knight did the man look around, his lack of startle evidencing he had heard Everard's descent. Though there was a wary light in his eyes and tension about his shoulders, he did not appear to have retreat in mind. Of course, they were within sight of those in the hall, and there was a measure of safety in that. A *measure*.

Everard halted alongside him. "Certes, you take chances you should not, Sir Knight."

The man lowered his hand, revealing the damage Everard had inflicted—swollen and purpling nose and lip—and shrugged. "I have heard that before. Indeed, I am not without the scars to prove it." He glanced up the stairs. "I wager she has allowed you to think the worst of her."

"Allowed?"

The man opened his mouth, but snapped it closed as a crash of metal against wood sounded from above.

Everard peered up the stairs, listened for more of the lady's temper to find its ease, and once again reflected that, for this, women were not welcome within these walls. He returned his gaze to Sir Elias. "'Twould seem the lady is displeased with the audience granted her."

The man frowned. "You are certain that was of Lady Susanna's doing?"

"There are no others abovestairs," Everard clipped, then picked up the thread the man had let unravel, just as he had done in telling that the lady had allowed the worst to be thought of her. "What makes you think it could not be her?"

The knight glanced toward the hearth where Judas de Balliol stood back from the others who boisterously encouraged Sir Rowan to regale them with another tale. "Are the Wulfriths as honorable as I have heard told?" he asked, then gave a sudden laugh. "Well, by those who do not count themselves your enemies."

Everard knew he should not pursue this conversation, that his time was better spent calling an end to this day that would begin the candle burning toward the next when the boys and young men resumed their training in the dark before dawn. Still, he said, "'Tis as we strive to be."

"As do I, though..." Sir Elias pressed a hand to his nose again, eyed the bit of blood he came away with. "...I seem prone to failure."

Everard, who rarely lacked evidence of being well supplied with patience, wondered if, at last, he was coming to the bottom of it.

"Since giving myself in service to Alan de Balliol three years past," Sir Elias continued, "I have become acquainted with Lady Susanna, and never have I known her to throw or break things no matter how difficult her circumstances."

Though Everard was tempted to question how difficult those circumstances could have been—hers a privileged life as the pampered daughter of a baron and the fondly regarded sister of the brother who had inherited their father's title—he did not. Despite how adept she was at churning an anger so rarely churned he had almost forgotten he possessed such depth of emotion, he was not blind or insensitive. Whatever the root of her circumstances, they were well enough written on her thin, unsmiling face and in eyes that no longer danced with light and mischief.

"Most stoic, she is," murmured the one who, whatever his purpose, seemed inclined to defend the lady he believed he knew well.

"How well *do* you know her, Sir Elias?" Everard pointedly put to the knight who had returned his regard to the boy he was charged with watching over.

Sir Elias looked sidelong at him. "You speak of our kiss." It was of good benefit to him that he did not smile or leer. "It was not our first, though methinks you would have it be our last."

Everard's knuckles prickled again. "I care not what goes between you and the lady providing it does not go within my walls."

The knight shrugged a shoulder. "Then 'tis good we depart on the morrow. We do, do we not?"

As told by the platter flung against the door abovestairs. Though inclined to confirm what had already been determined, Everard's own question had not been answered. "You said she allowed me to think the worst of her."

Sir Elias put his back to the wall, swiped at his nose, and crossed his arms over his chest. "She will not like that I speak of such things, but if it gains whatever she seeks and which, I wager, you are unwilling to give, it is as much in my best interest as hers."

Everard nearly asked what the man's best interest was, but…One question at a time.

"Such is the way of Lady Susanna," Sir Elias continued. "Even when 'tis clear she is not in the wrong, she is loath to defend herself. Rather, she saves up her defenses for another." He jerked his head in the direction of Judas de Balliol. "It is for him she does it—and other things."

Everard did not like the sound of "other things," but he set the question behind him. One at a time.

"I would not say Baron de Balliol was cruel to the boy, but—"The knight snorted. "Aye, cruel fits, though I have seen worse."

Once again, Everard felt his anger churn.

"Most times it was not bad, but when the wine and ale flowed..." He nodded. "...one would not believe the boy was of the baron's loins, and the more de Balliol imbibed, the less he believed it himself and the louder he cursed and claimed to have been cuckolded."

But what of when Judith had yet lived? Had her husband suspected he had been cuckolded? Had he treated her ill as her body burgeoned with child? The knave had named her son Judas—Judas!

"That does not seem to sit well with you, Lord Wulfrith," Sir Elias murmured.

Neither did this knight whose narrowed eyes witnessed emotions Everard was unaccustomed to making an effort to suppress. Clearing his face, he said, "Do you intend to tell me in what way Lady Susanna allowed me to think ill of her?"

"She took the blame for our...indiscretion, did she not?"

Refusing to yield to his knuckles, Everard flexed his hands. "Your face tells otherwise."

"Ah, well, there is that." The man touched his swollen nose. "However, that misunderstanding she did set right. Ne'er was she in danger of ravishment. I do have more honor about me than that."

Everard let an impatient breath slide out between his teeth. "I grow weary, Sir Elias—"

A cheer shot through the hall, and he turned his head and looked upon those entertained by a piece of Sir Rowan's tale that very likely involved the edge of a blade. It took a more practiced eye to discern if Judas, who continued to stand at the outskirts of the group, was as moved as the others, but there was a lean to his body, tension in his bearing, and a widening of eyes that told he wished to draw nearer.

Before Everard had gone abovestairs and found Lady Susanna dishonoring his hospitality with a tryst, he had observed the boy and concluded Judas de Balliol was, indeed, one to be watched. On the surface, he appeared mostly harmless, but he was far too watchful to be trusted. There was something sly about him. However, if it was true what Lady Susanna and Sir Elias told of his upbringing, it was to be expected. And corrected if he was to one day rank among men worthy of knighthood.

Everard returned his gaze to Sir Elias and discovered he had become the observed. "Which misunderstanding did the lady not set right?" he prompted.

"She let you believe she is wanton, did she not?"

Everard waited.

"She is not wanton, Lord Wulfrith."

"Then what?"

"Desperate—in a world beaten in and out of shape by men."

Desperate was not entirely unexpected, but that last was, especially as it was spoken by a man. Again, Everard tried to take the knight's measure, but Sir Elias seemed ever shifting, one moment as if something inside him was trying very hard to be honorable, the next as if that something was not powerful enough to battle his baser, self-serving side. Why? Might he have deep feelings for Susanna de Balliol?

It was not something Everard was inclined to ask, as it had nothing to do with him, and yet he said, "Do you think yourself in love with the lady?"

Sir Elias dropped his head back against the wall and seemed to consider it. "I have thought I could be, but I do not dare, for methinks she may be too...broken."

Concern pushed its way through Everard's resistance. "Broken?"

"Aye, I have seen what such desperation can do to a woman—beat her down so that what remains of her unplucked petals is too bruised to stay long upon the stem."

Again, a peculiar choice of words. "You sound more a poet than a knight, Sir Elias."

He looked momentarily away, gave a short chuckle. "I do. But then, I am a man without a sword." He spread his hands, looked pointedly at his belt. "Alas, not even a dagger."

"They shall be returned to you on the morrow upon your departure."

The knight nodded. "As told, Lady Susanna's circumstances have been most desperate."

"When I knew the lady, her circumstances and prospects were desirable."

"How long has that been?"

"Eleven years."

"Ah." Sir Elias's eyes went up to the side. "'Twould be about the time her brother wed Lady Judith, a woman I am told was most beautiful."

Once again, they were back to a place Everard did not wish to be. And, doubtless, this knight also suspected him of having fathered Judas.

"What has desperation done to Lady Susanna?" Everard clipped.

The man pressed the back of a hand to his cut lip, drew a sharp breath, and grimaced. "Though I am tempted to speak false, Lord Wulfrith—and with good cause, hmm?—I will tell you that I was promised far more than a kiss to deliver Lady Susanna and her nephew to Wulfen."

Everard felt all of his being go still as his mind reached back to the unanswered question of those *other things* the knight had said the lady did for Judas's sake, then farther back to her desperate plea—that she would do anything he asked of her. He had not wanted to believe it was as it had sounded, but it fit. She was in the habit of bargaining with her body and this knight—

Feeling his knuckles again, Everard moved toward Sir Elias who quickly descended a step and thrust a hand forward as if that might ward off another beating. "I did not intend to collect on it," he said. "This I vow."

A burst of laughter brought Everard back to himself, and he silently thanked Sir Rowan whose tale had prevented him from behavior most unbecoming—at least, in this setting.

He drew a deep breath. "What *did* you intend to collect, Sir Elias?"
The knight slowly lowered his hand.

"You said it was as much in your best interest as the lady's to speak
of such things," Everard pressed. "If not greater intimacy with the lady,
what, Sir Elias? What is in this for you?"

The man sniffed up a thin line of blood. "Once Judas is acknowledged as de Balliol's heir—and you seem of no mind to claim him as
your own son—I am to be elevated to the head of household knights.
That I very much want, Lord Wulfrith."

There—the measure of the man. And yet, Everard could not say his
motivation was entirely dishonorable. He inclined his head. "Then make
ready to depart Wulfen on the morrow ere first light. I wish you—and
Lady Susanna—Godspeed on the journey ahead." He stepped past him
and began the descent of the final steps to the hall.

"After all I have told," Sir Elias said, "still you will not aid her?"

Everard looked over his shoulder. "I am mostly inclined to believe
you speak true—that 'tis not merely a ploy to gain my cooperation—but
it changes naught. My duty is to Wulfen and the young men I am charged
with growing into knights, and here I shall remain. Good eve, Sir Elias."

He turned forward and, as he struck out across the hall, called,
"Seek your beds!"

As expected, the young men stood and hastened toward the piles of
pallets upon which they would gain their night's sleep—excepting Judas
de Balliol who moved stealthily along the walls toward the stairs and
over whom Everard grudgingly acknowledged regret. If the boy was not
already ruined by the desperately debased Susanna de Balliol, he soon
would be.

He thinks me a wanton, a trollop, a harlot. And I do not care.

That last was a lie, and one should never lie to one's self. Susanna did
not *want* to care, for there was no way to take back the words with which

she had offered herself to him even more easily than she had agreed to what she had believed Sir Elias required of her. Such a fool she was, for only minutes earlier Everard Wulfrith had forcefully declared he had not come for what Sir Elias had.

Not that. Never that. She was not and never would be a Judith. Did not and never would possess power capable of bending a man to her will. Could not and should not have hoped there.

"Oh, Judas," she whispered, "forgive me for not being more worthy to gain the Lord's blessings for you." The breath of a sob, but one of many over the hours she had knelt amid the rushes, fleetingly warmed her knees through the material of her skirt. That bit of heat in a chamber grown cool was so welcome that she let another sob escape. But that was all, for having long ago spent her tears upon God, she had finally lost the strength to hold her body together while it strove to shake itself apart. She was done with such expressions of misery. It was time to do something.

But what? There was nothing to be done that she had not already attempted. With dawn's approach, they would be put out of Wulfen Castle. In air colder than that which now clamped itself around her shoulders and clung to her back, they would ride to...

"I do not know," she whispered, though it would have to be wherever Queen Eleanor could be found. London? Southampton? Dorset? What if when they found her, she would not grant an audience? What if she had already recognized Lady Blanche's son as heir?

She groaned, a sound so pitiful she thought she might retch.

What good has wallowing ever done, Susanna? Do something!

"Naught to be done," she muttered.

Arise!

Slowly, she uncurled her hunched back that had stiffened so deeply that the sound of her unfolding did not require silence in which to be heard. And the ache...Not only in her muscles and joints but crowding her head and stabbing at the backs of her eyes.

Tightening her throat against a whimper, she settled back on her heels and peered at the darkened chamber through thinly narrowed lids.

Arise! Now!

She edged around to the left, reached to the bed, and pressed nearly numb hands to the mattress. It was pathetic how difficult it was to raise herself to standing—as if she were four score and five years of age. Breathing hard, shivering harder, she braced herself a long moment and swallowed against the parched tissues lining her throat.

If only she had not subjected the wine to her fit of temper. But there was water.

Moved by a desperate fear that she would dry up and be of no use to Judas, she patted her way around the foot of the bed, took what she hoped would require only one step but required two to reach the long table against the wall, and groped for the wash basin. She nearly upended it, causing the water with which she had earlier set herself to rights to splash her hands.

Teeth chattering, she slid her fingers into the cold depths, scooped up a handful, and put her mouth to it. She did not taste the dross. She tasted blessed wet. And thrice more before she returned to the bed and eased down upon it.

She hurt—so deeply she longed to let fatigue drag her away from here. But the respite would be brief, and Judas would be no better for it. Thus, despite the seeming hopelessness of gaining God's intervention, she would pray.

"If only there was one more worthy of seeking blessings for Judas," she whispered.

But there was only the sinful Susanna de Balliol. Even at Cheverel, she had mostly been alone in praying for him, for Alan had refused the local priest admittance to the manor house following Judith's death. From that time forward, spiritual guidance was found exclusively at the little church in the nearby village, and visits there were limited to the attendance of services in the presence of guests of high rank and those rare occasions when Alan was away from the demesne. For that, Susanna had come to rely upon personal prayer rather than the intercessory prayer of a priest. Though she believed God did attend to her prayers for Judas, ever she was aware they suffered from the taint of the one who spoke them. Hence, the disclaimer.

"Even if my sins are too great for You to bless me, Lord," she prefaced the prayers yet to come, "I beseech You to bless Your beloved Judas."

9

*I*F NOT FOR *the son who should have been yours as well, do it for me. Only ever me...*

Everard set his mind against the voice he did not wish to hear any more than he wished to hear the answer that had come to him time and again in this place that wore out a man's knees. But there she was again, so near he imagined it was not a draft near his ear but her sweet breath.

For me, Everard.

Having an hour past spared his body further abuse by abandoning the altar before which he had knelt, he sat forward on the bench against the side wall, pressed his elbows hard into his knees, and gripped his head in his hands.

Only ever me...

He opened his eyes, but the deep shadows in which he sat were nearly as conducive to memory as the dark behind his lids. Like shutters thrown wide, that day returned to him, more vivid in sight and scent, taste and touch, hearing and hope than he had allowed in eleven years.

"Judith," he murmured.

She laughed, drew slightly back upon the bench they shared, and regarded him out of eyes as starry as the night sky. "*Beloved* Judith. If 'tis true what you feel, that is as you should call me, is it not?"

He smiled. "Beloved Judith." He reached up, slipped a hand inside her veil, and drew forth a thick, blond tress. "I love your hair," he said and slid his fingers through it.

Again, she laughed. "My hair? Yours is much finer, Everard Wulfrith. Indeed, 'tis what first caught my notice the day we met."

"Aye?"

She made a face. "You know it, just as you know all the ladies long to do as I do, even dear Susanna."

He frowned. "Susanna?" Though she bore the title of 'lady' and was only three years younger than Judith, she was younger yet in terms of maturity.

"Aye, 'tis clear she is besotted with you, though not as much as I." She leaned near and pushed her fingers into his hair. "'Tis softer than my finest bliaut—so soft methinks I would like to wear it."

Everard knew that already they trespassed one upon the other more than they should, but her touch and words stirred him, and it would be just a kiss. He angled his head and moved in until their lips nearly touched. "Tell me I may, beloved Judith."

"You may," she whispered, then it was she who came the last bit and touched her mouth to his.

He kissed her. Tasted and breathed her in.

"Promise me," she said against his lips.

Everard opened his eyes and looked into hers. "Whatever you would have."

Her fingers in his hair slid higher, gripped his scalp. "Promise your hair will only ever know my hands—no other's."

He chuckled. "And if I do?"

"I will go away with you."

Then she would break her betrothal to Alan de Balliol? Chest feeling suddenly full, he said, "Only ever you, Judith," and recaptured her mouth.

It was with great effort and the reminder that he had years and years to better know her kisses, that he finally pulled back.

When she made a mewl of disappointment, he drew her hands from his hair and kissed the left, then right—and sensed a presence that did not belong in this place with his beloved and him.

He swung his chin around. There, on the garden path, stood Alan de Balliol's sister. Unmoving, leaning slightly forward as if she had suddenly arrested her advance. Color high in her round cheeks. Mouth and eyes wide as she looked between the two of them.

Judith sprang to her feet. "Susanna!"

The girl threw a hand up as if to ward them off, took a step backward, turned, and ran.

When she disappeared around a hedge, Judith looked up at Everard who had risen beside her. "She is my friend. She will not tell."

"She is also his sister," he said, "but regardless, it changes naught."

Judith's gaze wavered, and he tensed at her nod that seemed less than certain.

He lifted her chin. "Fear not. You are mine."

"Alan—"

"Will soon be in your past. I give you my word."

Her smile was tremulous. "You would do anything for me, Everard Wulfrith?"

"Anything, beloved Judith. You have but to ask."

As that vow, made by a man little more than one score aged, resounded through the one who was now one score and thirteen, Everard felt the fight go out of him.

Dragging his hands down the sides of his shaved head and across his cheeks and jaws, he sat back.

Guessing it was near the hour when all of Wulfen Castle would rouse to start the day with mass that would be followed by pre-dawn training exercises, he settled his gaze upon the low-burning candles at the altar and turned his thoughts to Susanna de Balliol—she whose trespass that day in the garden had caused him to rigorously hone his senses so that never again could any steal upon him.

He sighed. As hard as it was to do what he knew he must, it was the right thing, and he ought to be grateful for the decision, for he was not— and did not ever wish to be—one who allowed emotions to overrule the knowledge of right and wrong. What was asked of him would open him wide, allowing the eyes of others to peer into those places he did not wish light to shine upon. But for Judith he would do it.

He stood, crossed the chapel, and exited. However, when he reached the chamber given to the woman he did not want at Wulfen, he found the door open and the torchlight from the corridor showed it was empty.

His alarm was only momentary, for he knew what it meant. As instructed on the night past, Sir Elias had made ready to depart before first light. If they had not gone already, they would soon. And he would have to ride after them.

Everard strode down the corridor and descended the stairs to the hall where the boys and young men were beginning to rise from their pallets.

"My lord!" Squire Joseph called.

Near the great doors, Everard turned. "Why was I not told our visitors had departed?"

The young man blinked. "I am sorry, my lord. When you said last eve that I should rise early to see them from their chambers, I understood it to mean you did not wish your morning prayers disturbed by their departure."

He had understood right. "When did they leave?"

"But minutes ago, my lord."

Then they might yet be within the walls. "See to your duties," he said and hurried through the door another squire opened for him.

As he stepped down into the inner bailey, the great chains of the drawbridge rent the silence—the sound of descent rather than ascent, meaning there was no need to run. The portcullis would not be raised until the drawbridge's journey was at its end and a final check was made of the land before the walls.

He passed from the torchlit inner bailey into the outer. Ahead and to the left, facing outward before the portcullis, were three mounted horses, and standing alongside the largest of the mantled figures was Sir Rowan who ceased conversing with Sir Elias the moment he caught sight of the one who advanced upon them.

When the last of the chains let out and the drawbridge settled to the ground with a great thump that rolled like thunder beneath Everard's boots, Sir Rowan called, "My lord!"

Sir Elias looked around. Even in the dim, shuddering light of torches, there was something about the turn of his mouth that told he did not believe Everard had come to wish them Godspeed. "The extra mount for the boy is much appreciated, Lord Wulfrith," he said.

Everard had ordered that it be provided for Judas to speed their journey, but now—

"That is, of course, if one is needed," Sir Elias added.

Everard claimed the space vacated by Sir Rowan, noted the knight's battered face looked little better in the dim light than it had on the night past. "'Tis not needed, for you are not leaving Wulfen—not this day."

The knight raised his eyebrows.

Everard shifted his gaze past him to Judas who looked almost small and vulnerable upon so large a horse as he peered at the lord of Wulfen Castle. Everard inclined his head. "Dismount and return the horses to the stables."

As the boy and knight complied, the woman on the far side remained unmoving. Though her face was turned toward Everard, it was too deeply shadowed by her hood to confirm she was pleased by the turn of events. But she must be.

Everard skirted the horses and halted alongside her. "I have said you may dismount, Lady Susanna."

Her expression no more visible as she looked down upon him, she said, "Why have you changed your mind?"

For Judith. "For Judas," he allowed, for it was also true. He looked to the right where the boy and Sir Elias followed Sir Rowan in leading their horses toward the stables. "Methinks *he* may be worth saving."

He did not hear her sigh, but as he returned his gaze to her, he saw the plume of her long, slow exhale. However, sharply contrasting with her relief was her grip upon the saddle's pommel—so tight her arm trembled.

"I thank you, Lord Wulfrith." Her voice was not much more than a whisper.

Bothered by his inability to read her expression, Everard said, "You may wish to save your thanks until you know the conditions under which you will be allowed to remain at Wulfen." Doubtless, she would be far from pleased.

"Anything you ask," she said.

He narrowed his gaze on her—a useless endeavor. But even if her face could be seen, something told him it would not reflect what she had earlier implied. "'Tis good we are agreed," he said and, though the side of him that had cause to dislike her was tempted to leave her to dismount on her own, he reached to her.

She made no move to lean toward him but continued to hold tight to the pommel.

"Lady Susanna," he prompted.

"Forgive me, I…" A pitiful sound escaped her, her hand dropped from the pommel, and she fell forward over the horse's neck.

Though Everard would later question whether or not she had been in any real danger of tumbling to the ground, he lunged forward and pulled her down into his arms.

As he settled her against his chest, her hood dropped back and torchlight cast the shadows of her lashes across the tops of her cheeks and lit a face so nearly bloodless he might have thought her dead if not for her breath upon the air. What disquieted him nearly as much was her weight. As thin as she was, he would not have expected it to require much effort to bear her, but not as little as this—and less even if not for her thick mantle and gown. Whatever Susanna de Balliol's sins, fleshly or otherwise, she was not well.

Knowing what had unfolded before the portcullis had been in view of many of those upon the walls, Everard resented the spectacle that had surely distracted the young men from their purpose. And for this— always this—women were not allowed at Wulfen.

As he strode toward the inner bailey and the donjon beyond, he glanced once more at the one he had let in. Judas was worth saving, but Lady Susanna…

As Sir Elias said, it was likely too late for her.

10

It was a feeling not unlike being borne upon water—the uncertainty of rising and falling over restless waves and the fear that when next one fell, they would go under. And not come up again.

Seeking to assure herself she was not in water, that she would not drown, Susanna told her lids to open. They refused and her body rose and fell again and she felt the prickle of water upon every inch of her skin that portended it would soon sweep over her and fill her nose and mouth. Thus, she promised herself she would but look out upon the waterless world for only a moment. Her eyes agreed and lids creaked open.

Above her, a ceiling. Left and right, the posters of a bed. In the doorway, a wavering figure that wavered no more when it disappeared. She would not drown. Not this day.

Her lids lowered and she nearly went adrift again, but the question of Judas pried her consciousness wider. "Where?" she croaked out of a mouth so painfully dry she thought drowning would not be so bad if she could only wet her lips and tongue before dying.

She forced her eyes open to narrow slits. The room was not the same as the one she had first been given—

She gasped.

When had she left that chamber where she had flung viands and drink against its door? This day? The day past? All she knew for certain was it had been before Everard Wulfrith appeared in the outer bailey and said her nephew might be worth saving.

Answered prayer. Nearly too late, but answered despite the sins of the one who had groveled for Judas to be blessed. Thus, the man who had refused to give aid had been moved to change his mind. As if unaware of the urging of God—or unwilling to acknowledge it—he had said he did it for Judas, but if he did it for anyone, surely it was for Judith. What did that say of a man who, with eleven years behind him, violated the castle's edict that no women were allowed within and gave shelter to the son of a man he surely hated?

That he had loved and might still love the woman who had become her brother's wife...

Susanna sighed over something she had once hoped to attain herself, and which was too late to attain now.

Emotion filled her throat and she tried to unblock it, but it hurt to swallow.

She whimpered, turned her head to the right, and was grateful the bedside table was in that direction so she did not have to expend the strength to look opposite. The dagger she had surrendered upon entering Wulfen Castle lay there, but it was of no interest in light of the cup she had hoped into existence. Not caring what it contained providing it was wet, she turned onto her side and, with a shaking hand, reached for it. Her fingers fell short. With effort that dizzied her more than any amount of wine had ever done, she edged nearer. But still the cup exceeded her reach, and she thought that if she were not so dry, she would cry.

"Please," she whispered and shifted toward the mattress edge. It was too much. Once more overwhelmed by the feeling of being upon water, of it sweeping over her, her quaking hand and straining fingers dropped to the table and she heard something fall to the floor.

Not the cup...

When she broke the surface, she could not say how long she had been under, only that her thirst was worse and she did not care to whom the approaching footsteps or voice belonged. All that mattered was the cup and, blessedly, when she opened her eyes again, it was still on the table.

Gripping the mattress edge, she dragged herself higher up the bed. The tip of one finger grazed the cup's base, and a sob escaped her. It was as if someone played a cruel game, giving her hope for something that would ever be just out of reach.

And that someone was here, pulling her hand away, placing himself between her and the cup, raising her up, settling her against something firm and so warm that she only then realized how cold she was. All that had mattered was her thirst. And now there was no hope—

"Drink," he said, and she felt the rim of a cup against her bottom lip, caught the scent of wine, and saw the red depths beneath her nose.

Yet more cruelty? Placing it within reach only to snatch it away?

She raised her chin and startled to find it was Everard Wulfrith against whose side she was pressed where he sat upon the mattress—his arm around her waist supporting her, his hand offering the cup, his body that smelled of earth and toil, his grey-green eyes frowning into hers.

"Drink," he repeated.

For fear he would, indeed, snatch it away, she brought both hands up, clasped them over his upon the cup, and gulped as much as she could draw into her mouth.

"Slowly," he said, easily overpowering her to lower the cup.

She started to protest, but then the rim was against her lips again, and he said, "Slowly, Lady Susanna, else you will not keep it down."

She tried, but time and again he had to pull the cup away and draw his thumb across her bottom lip to prevent droplets from falling upon her bliaut.

He could not have liked the amount of time it took to drain the cup, which surely seemed as long to him as it did to her, but finally the last drop was had and he set the cup on the table.

She tilted her head back against the bulky muscles of his arm and shoulder and peered into his face. "More," she whispered.

He lowered his gaze to hers, and she thought that she was almost as near to him as Judith had been that day in the garden. The garden...

"That is enough drink for now," he said.

...where *besotted* Susanna de Balliol had come upon the lovers. And from whom she had fled. "I wish I had not seen it," she murmured and lowered her lids over eyes that burned. "Would that I had not."

Wondering what she spoke of, Everard stared into her pale face until her chin dropped and head fell against his shoulder.

Thwarted. Still, he conceded that what he had come to settle between them could be done later. After all, if she truly wished his help, it was already settled. She but needed to know what was required of her.

As he started to ease her out of the crook of his arm, he caught a glint of silver and followed it to the chain that slanted across her collarbone. He knew he trespassed, but he drew it forth and an oblong pendant slid from the neck of her bodice. The scent of roses that hovered about Susanna de Balliol grew stronger, and he did not need to locate the catch to know the pendant contained crushed petals. His mother wore a similar necklace on occasion.

He turned it in his hand and was surprised—and disturbed—by the thought that roses, with their deceptively soft petals that made one forget the thorns, did not suit this woman. Rather, sweet woodruff that had once scented the air around her—

Chastising himself for letting his thoughts loose, he lowered the pendant.

Sir Rowan appeared in the doorway. "My lord?"

Though relieved the knight had not shown himself moments earlier, Everard was discomfited that the man had witnessed the haste with which his lord had moved to aid the lady. Of course, what man of honor would not have done what he had, for she had so far extended herself to reach the cup that she had nearly tumbled out of bed.

"Sir Rowan?" he said as drew his arm from around her and gently settled her upon the pillow.

"You would have me tell Squire Joseph to wait on the food?"

Everard drew the coverlet over the lady who, despite the room having been warmed by the day's sunshine coming in through the open window, had been so chill where she leaned against him that the heat his body had generated from hours of training had quickly cooled.

"I will tell him myself," he said—and instruct him to see to the lighting of the brazier though it was rarely needed during daylight hours at this time of year.

He stood from the bed, bent and retrieved the sheathed dagger from the rushes where Lady Susanna had surely knocked it in her quest to reach the cup, and set the weapon on the table.

As he crossed the chamber, he reflected that only once since his knighting at Wulfen had one of the tower rooms lodged a woman—his sister, Lady Gaenor, when it had been necessary to hide her from King Henry who had ordered her to wed Baron Christian Lavonne. In the end, the king had his way and Gaenor had spoken vows with their enemy-turned-ally. Blessedly, what could have been a miserable marriage was quite the opposite. It seemed a miracle, but all of Everard's siblings had wed well, and he rejoiced in their happiness and the children born to them. That path, however, was not cut for him, and he had determined he would remain keeper of Wulfen Castle until it was time to pass the privilege to one of his nephews. And then...

Then he would grow old alone.

Halting before Sir Rowan, he glanced across his shoulder at where Lady Susanna lay so still. "When next she awakens," he said, "send word."

The day had dimmed—yet another day in which she had barely been present since her arrival at Wulfen Castle. Guessing the one who had earlier summoned Everard Wulfrith remained nearby, Susanna lay unmoving and tried to take stock of her state before the lord of Wulfen Castle once more appeared.

She was thirsty, though not as painfully as before. Hungry, so severely that she as much feared filling her belly as leaving it void. Weak,

though her bones no longer felt as if without substance. And her head...
It did not ache at the mere opening of her eyes, but that did not mean she
would not feel as if stabbed when she moved.

She drew a deep breath, rolled onto her back, and silently gave
thanks when her discomfort proved relatively mild.

As expected, the doorway was not empty. There was the older
knight who had initially refused Judas and Sir Elias and her entrance to
Wulfen and who had also been present to send them away.

"My lady," he said.

By what name was he called? Rowan?

"I shall send for food and drink," he said. "Is there anything else you
require?"

Whether or nor she required Everard Wulfrith, she guessed he
would also be sent for. And though the weak side of her wished to delay
their talk, she needed to know the conditions that would allow Judas
and her to remain at Wulfen Castle—more, how he intended to save her
nephew.

She shook her head.

The knight turned away. Almost immediately, his retreating footsteps sounded as if they descended rather than traversed a corridor, and
she realized he was already upon the stairs. She swept her gaze around
the walls. Was this a tower room? Likely, since such a room would further distance her from Wulfen's young men. Too, though the door stood
wide open, there were no sounds to be heard from the hall below.

Belly rudely grumbling over its vast emptiness, Susanna assured herself food was coming—as was the man who had held her so she could
drink. But she did not want to think about that, for it had felt achingly
good to be in those arms even though they belonged to a man who surely
hated her more than he pitied her.

Not liking the thought of being vulnerably flat on her back when he
returned, she levered onto her elbows and, after another bout with the
sensation of being borne upon water, raised herself to sitting and scooted
backward until her shoulders met the wall.

Knowing she must look a mess, she peered down her front. Her gown's bodice was rumpled, but of greater concern was the pendant that lay upon it. She tucked it beneath the neck of her garment and pulled the coverlet up under her arms. Then, putting her head back against the wall, she dragged fingers through the snarls of her hair until it was ordered enough to braid. However, as she began to section it, she abandoned the idea. Not only did it require too much effort, but she had no ribbon with which to secure it.

She dropped her hands into her lap and surveyed the room—bed, bedside table, chair, side table with wash basin and the pack that held the few items she had taken from Cheverel, and a brazier.

That last made her frown, for it was lit in daylight, something rarely required during late spring.

Of course, when last she had awakened, she had been terribly cold. And Everard Wulfrith had surely known it when he had helped pour drink into her and wiped her mouth to save her the humiliation of dribbling upon herself.

Susanna caught her breath, reflected that the task she had set herself would be easier if the man Judith had loved presented no proof he had ever been as Susanna's adoring fourteen-year-old self had viewed him.

She shifted her gaze to the narrow door to the left behind which, she hoped, a garderobe lay so that she might relieve her bladder after Everard Wulfrith had come and gone. Next, she considered the bedside table and wished a cup of wine there that would be of more use than her dagger.

She reached to the weapon and was grateful her hand did not quake as violently as it had when she had earlier failed to bring the cup to hand. Had Judas's and Sir Elias's weapons been returned to them as well? Of course, her dagger was exclusively used to render meat of a size easily chewed.

Footsteps again. Of ascent rather than descent.

She clasped her hands in her lap.

Everard Wulfrith entered, and his gaze immediately fell upon her. However, rather than approach her, he positioned himself beside the doorway as Squire Joseph came behind bearing a platter.

Noting that the lord of Wulfen was freshly clothed as she did not think he could have been earlier when the scent of his body had revealed he had not expected to draw as near her as he had done, she turned her regard upon his squire who kept his gaze averted as he set the platter on the table beside her.

"Good health to you, my lady," the young man said and turned on his heel.

Too soon, Susanna was alone with Everard Wulfrith, Sir Rowan absent from the doorway.

Busying her eyes with the contents of the platter—bread, cheese, slices of fowl, and a cup of wine whose pale red depths told it was well watered. Grateful for that last since she needed all of her senses about her, she lifted the cup and forced herself to sip from it as it had been impossible to do earlier without Everard Wulfrith's aid. Throughout, she felt his stare.

She returned the cup to the platter and looked across the chamber. "I am much better," she said the first thing that came to mind, then the next, "How long did I sleep?"

He raised his eyebrows. "Since this morn when the abuse to which it would seem you regularly subject your body proved too much and you collapsed atop your mount."

She had, hadn't she? Feeling her face warm, she wondered what had come afterward. Had he—

"Twas good I was there to pull you down, else you might have found your end beneath your horse's hooves."

Imagining herself senseless in his arms, of being carried by him, she felt herself flush deeper. "I am sorry I was such a burden."

He frowned. "Hardly. You are not much more than bones barely covered in skin."

His words cut, though she did not think they were meant to be cruel. And even if that was his intent, his observation was nearly the truth, for it was many years since she had eaten for the enjoyment of taste. Her belly was so often in a state of agitation that she had learned not to stuff it full and to limit herself to only a few bites of foodstuffs heavy in spice and floating in fat. It rarely ended well when she indulged.

"Regardless," she said, "I thank you."

He jutted his chin at the platter. "Eat."

Happy for the excuse to look elsewhere, she determined it was best to start with bread. If it stayed down, she would venture further.

As she broke off a piece, she asked, "What of my nephew?"

"He is well."

Though tempted to ask *how* he was well—with what he had occupied his day—Everard Wulfrith's tone suggested his answer was sufficient. More, though, instincts honed by time and adversity told that she need not fear for Judas's safety while he was under this man's protection. Of course, on occasion, instincts had failed her.

"Eat, Lady Susanna."

She blinked at the bread that was fast turning to crumbs upon the coverlet, hurried it to her mouth.

"And listen," he said.

If not for the seriousness of what she knew he would tell, she might have smiled at him having waited until her mouth was full before beginning what he surely did not intend to be a conversation.

"Here are the conditions with which you shall comply if you wish to remain at Wulfen Castle. This chamber is the limit of your reach. Should I permit you outside it, you shall do so in the company of an escort. Agreed?"

Only the scant space between these walls. She swallowed and reached for the drink to aid the bread in its journey to her belly.

"You have but to nod, Lady Susanna."

She cleared the lump in her throat. "Then I am to be a prisoner."

His brow lined. "Call it what you will, I will not have you further distracting the young men who are here to train, not gawk. However, do you find confinement too distasteful, you are welcome to leave."

Of course she would agree. Consoling herself that her stay in the tower room would not be long, for surely he would see to the matter of Judas's inheritance quickly, she said, "I agree."

"I expected you would. Now eat."

She broke off a smaller piece of bread the easier to swallow it.

"Next," he said, "no one comes to this chamber without my permission, including Sir Elias."

Then the knight would also be allowed to remain at Wulfen? It was surely as he would wish to do since he could not return to Cheverel until Judas was lord.

Her next bite of bread going down with little difficulty, she nodded, said, "Excepting Judas, of course," and reached to the platter again.

"*Not* excepting Judas."

She was glad her mouth was not full, for she would have choked. She snatched her hand away from the platter. "I will not be allowed to see my nephew? Why?"

"Not only do I believe it best to limit your influence upon the boy, but such is what is required of all who—"

"*My* influence?"

"Aye. *Your* influence."

She sat forward, the sudden movement momentarily blurring her vision. "You make it sound a bad thing."

"It is, Susanna de Balliol."

"Explain yourself, Lord Wulfrith!"

His mouth tightened. "I speak of the influence of a woman who uses her body to gain favors."

Her belly clenched and face and neck were swept with the numbing sensation of lost color. He knew the truth of her encounter with Sir

Elias in the corridor, meaning the knight had revealed their bargain. In her defense? There seemed no other cause for him to do so. Still, it was nothing for which to be grateful.

"All the more reason you cannot be allowed to move freely among our young men," Everard Wulfrith said.

As if she might attempt to seduce boys who did not yet practice the treachery of men but would soon enough learn it. Just as this man who as good as called her a Daughter of Eve—inherently sinful and inferior—had learned it.

Control yourself, entreated the sound side of her that acknowledged how badly she needed his aid. *After all, is there really much difference between a woman who freely consorts with a man not her husband and one who allows intimacies only for the sake of gain? Both unseemly. Both sins.*

"Eat," Everard Wulfrith said—one too many times.

She inhaled sharply, told herself to stop, but could not. "One might think you had never done something you should not with a woman you should not," she snapped.

This time it was his breath heard around the chamber.

Foolish, Susanna! If you could hold your tongue with Alan de Balliol, surely you can hold it with Everard Wulfrith who, despite his condemnation of what he does not understand, has shown you more kindness these past two days than your own brother did these past eleven years.

As she stared at the man who had not drawn any nearer since coming within, whose face had hardened and color had risen, she feared all was lost, that he would quit the chamber and put them out of Wulfen.

She moistened her lips. "Forgive me. 'Tis just..." She shook her head. "You know not what you ask. Judas is like a son to me."

Though she thought some of his tension eased, she felt his struggle to remain within when he clearly wished to be without. "Regardless," he finally said, "I do not ask it. I require it. However, if it comforts you, know that there would be few, if any, opportunities for Judas to come to you here. He will be far too occupied."

She blinked. "With what?"

His gaze flicked to the platter. "Eat."

The price of an answer...

This time, she chose a piece of firm white cheese. And wished she had not, for it had a sharp, potent taste she would have quickly cleared from her mouth were she alone.

"On the morrow," Everard Wulfrith continued, "Judas shall begin training with the others. Hence, another reason to separate the two of you as all our young men are separated from their mothers when they undertake the journey toward manhood."

"I did not bring him to you for training. That he already receives at Cheverel."

"He will receive it here as well."

"But we will not be long at Wulfen."

Annoyance grooved his face. "You are wrong. Though I shall soon send a missive requesting an audience with the queen to defend Judas's claim to Cheverel, I do not expect we will receive an answer any sooner than a month hence. Indeed, it could be several months. But for however long it proves, I will not allow your nephew to sit idly by when he can benefit from our training."

A month. Perhaps several. The realization of how long she might be confined abovestairs made the bile rise. And even more she regretted the cheese.

"Therefore," he said, "all that remains is for you to agree to my conditions."

At her hesitation, he said, "This morn, you told you would do anything. This is the anything you must do, Lady Susanna, for 'tis everything."

She dipped her chin. "I agree."

"Good, then we begin." Once more, his gaze shifted to the platter. "Now eat and be done with it."

She loosed a short, defeated laugh. "Do you not tire of telling me to eat and drink?"

His lids narrowed. "I do."

She sighed. "Again, I am sorry, for though I would accommodate you—indeed, I wish I could—I cannot eat any more."

She startled when he strode forward, pressed her back more closely to the wall when he leaned over her, caught his scent that was far different from the odor of his body when he had come earlier.

"If I must, I will feed you, Lady Susanna, for I have had enough of your swooning and sickening."

As she stared up at him and imagined him making good his threat, her belly twinged in a way entirely different from the rousing of bile. "'Tis not defiance that makes me refuse," she said, "nor any silly female whim, Lord Wulfrith. It is fear that I will mess the rushes, for I do not feel well."

"Neither would I if I starved myself as you do."

"I do not starve myself." At least, not intentionally. "Sometimes my belly troubles me, making it difficult to keep food down, that is all. But I give you my word that, when it settles, I shall eat more."

He considered her. "See that you do," he said and pivoted.

He was leaving? Unsettled at the prospect of the confinement that stretched long before her, she called, "Lord Wulfrith?"

He halted in the doorway but did not turn back.

She did not know what to say. *Was* there anything to say? Likely nothing that would change his mind regarding how she would spend the next month or more at Wulfen Castle. But there was something she wished to know. "How much have you hated me these eleven years?"

He turned. "I have hardly thought of you at all, Susanna de Balliol."

As she had thought might be the case. "And when you have?"

"In the beginning, 'tis true I hated and more deeply when I heard of…her death."

"And now?"

"I have learned hate is destructive to one's self. Though, at times, it can be exquisitely so, I do not indulge—at least, not for long."

"I am glad. But still you do not like me and never shall, am I right?"

"Very likely. After all, it is not possible to know if 'twas loyalty or jealousy that guided you that day."

Susanna drew a hand up her chest and closed her fingers around the pendant beneath her bodice. She knew what he believed she had done—the same Judith had first believed—but what did he mean by this? "I can make no sense of what you say."

"Loyalty to one's family, I understand well, Lady Susanna. Jealousy that is of such strength as that worked upon Judith…" He shook his head. "…not even from a girl not yet a woman."

She longed to defend herself, to tell him it was neither, but as he said it was impossible to know if what he believed she had done was driven by loyalty or jealousy, he certainly would not believe that her only crime, and for which she had paid year after year, was betraying her brother—disloyalty to her own kin which should have earned *her* the name of Judas.

"Good eve, Lord Wulfrith," she said and was relieved when the doorway emptied of his height and breadth. Now if only she could empty herself of him.

11

SUCH A SCENE was not tolerated in the great hall, though certainly it occurred outside it, most often upon the training field. They were lusty young men, each vying for a place among the others as they strained toward manhood. Here, however, they were expected to behave nobly, with restraint and manners. This eve, they had not.

Even more of a surprise than finding his hall in a shambles when he returned belowstairs was the one at the center of it all. Judas de Balliol.

The boy strained against Sir Elias's hold, thrusting his body toward the one held by Squire Joseph—Squire Charles, recently elevated from the standing of page, though that honor could be reversed.

Knowing whatever had caused the altercation would not have if Wulfen's knights had been present, rather than gathered in the barracks as they often did before the evening meal, Everard tried not to begrudge his men the well-earned break from their charges.

"What is this?" he shouted as he strode forward.

The excited voices of those surrounding the combatants quieted. Judas de Balliol, however, remained heedless.

"Say it again, knave!" the boy barked. "Say it and I will knock another tooth down your throat!"

It was no idle threat, Everard acknowledged as a path quickly opened for him. Though it was impossible to know the extent of damage to Squire Charles's teeth, his mouth being a bloody mess, something had surely gone missing.

"Be about your duties!" Everard ordered, and the onlookers scattered.

As he drew near the combatants, he looked from the young squire who no longer required Joseph's restraint, to Judas who yet required Sir Elias's.

Everard had sensed that emotions ran fast and deep beneath the boy's quiet exterior, but though he loathed the means by which such feelings had been plowed into one so young, he was encouraged. He liked this glimpse of Judas's passion nearly as much as the vulnerability he had seen in his eyes—providing, of course, the boy had been sufficiently provoked to act as he had done against one who was several years older than he. And that was quite possible where Squire Charles was concerned.

Everard halted near the two, nodded at Joseph who promptly released Charles, then Sir Elias who hesitated. Rightly so, for Judas continued to strain, gaze fixed on the one from whom he wished to take more teeth. And he might have succeeded if not that Everard caught him by the neck of his tunic as he sprang past.

Hoping the boy could summon enough dignity that he would not have to be dragged from the hall, Everard said, "Charles, come!" and pulled Judas toward the dais beyond which the solar lay.

Just when he thought the boy would disappoint him, Judas stopped struggling. Of his own accord, he landed his feet hard to the dais and crossed its span alongside Everard who released him only after they stepped into the solar past the heavy curtains Squire Joseph flung back.

"There." Everard pointed to the large table across the room. "Sit."

Rubbing at his neck where the tunic had cut into him before he had reclaimed his dignity, the boy crossed to the table and dropped into the nearest chair.

"And you," Everard told Charles who had entered behind.

Dragging his bloody mouth across the shoulder of his tunic, the squire tramped forward and took the seat farthest from Judas.

Everard followed but remained standing between the two. "In as few words as possible, Squire Charles, explain how I can leave an ordered hall and return a quarter hour later to find it a den of chaos."

The young man glanced at Judas. "It was not—" He dragged his words to a halt, grunted. "Apologies, my lord, it began with me."

That lesson—to admit responsibility for his actions—had been the hardest for Charles to learn, so much that, on occasion, he still slipped. Everard was pleased he did not do so this time.

"I do not like the way he skulks about." Charles jutted his chin at Judas. "Nor that knight who follows everywhere after him. And his name—Judas, he who betrayed our Lord, Jesus Christ. It portends ill."

Judas rose so abruptly his chair teetered.

"Sit!" Everard commanded.

Tension in every line of his body, he slowly lowered to the edge of the chair.

"Are those the words that earned you a bloody mouth, Squire Charles?"

The young man held his lord's gaze with difficulty. "They are the words I speak now."

"What words did you speak *then?*"

His jaw shifted. "I said his father must have hated him to give him so vile a name."

Everard's insides tightened. He had hoped Judas's attack upon the squire was provoked, but not in that way. "I am surprised you have your head about you, Squire Charles. Recite lesson one."

The young man opened his mouth, frowned, and shot his gaze to the one who had bested him. "Forgive me, my lord, I do not see how it applies."

Everard looked to Judas. "How many years have you, boy?"

Judith's son drew a sharp breath, obviously as offended at being called "boy" as when Everard had chastised him for his impertinence during their first meeting. But that was what he was and would be until he learned there were places one did not dispense retribution, Wulfen's hall being among them.

"I am ten winters aged," Judas begrudged.

Everard returned his regard to the squire whose wide eyes reflected shock at the great disparity between them. "*That* is how it applies, Squire Charles."

The color of shame crept into the young man's face. It was one thing to fall to a peer, quite another to fall to one considered well beneath him. "I did not know," he strangled.

"Now you do. But we shall save apologies for later when reflection allows them to be better meant." He gestured for the young man to rise. "In the meantime, think well upon lessons one and six."

"Aye, my lord." He inclined his head and strode past.

"Squire Charles!" Everard called as the young man neared the solar's curtained entrance.

"My lord?"

"I am pleased you have learned lesson three well."

"I thank you, my lord."

As Joseph drew the curtains aside to allow the squire to pass into the hall, Everard looked around and found Judas watching him, interest brightening eyes that had previously been full up with anger. But before the boy asked the question, Everard knew what it would be.

"What are these lessons? One...three...six?"

Everard lowered into the chair beside him. "Lesson one: prey not upon those weaker than one's self."

"I am not weaker than that knave." Judas thrust a hand forward, the knuckles of which bore traces of Squire Charles's blood. "'Tis his blood upon me."

"In your case, that is so, but it has not been so with others, though Squire Charles makes good progress." Everard gave that a moment to sink in, then continued. "Lesson three: take responsibility for one's actions. Lesson six: think one's words through ere spilling them."

Judas became lighter about the mouth, and it appeared he might even smile.

Curious, Everard watched him more closely. "Those are among the lessons Squire Charles must learn ere he earns his spurs and can, by all rights, call himself a man."

The boy nodded. "They sound much like my aunt's lessons, though she does not number them."

Everard could not let that slip past unexamined, for in order to counter Lady's Susanna's influence, he would need to know its extent. "What lessons are those?"

The boy considered him. Considered him some more.

"Tell me these lessons your aunt has taught you," Everard said more sharply. And should not have, for Judas's face closed up as if shutters had been thrown over it.

Everard grabbed hold of his patience and regretted, as he had often done these past days, that the tolerance he ever had well in hand should waver in the face of Susanna and Judas de Balliol.

"You make it difficult to help you, Judas."

The boy put his head to the side. "You have not said how you intend to do so."

Patience. "I shall send a missive to the queen requesting an audience so that I may stand witness to your claim to Cheverel."

He nodded. "As you should."

Everard stiffened, but he tempered his next words, for though anger was the means by which to coax some into opening themselves wide, it seemed more likely to close up Judas tighter. "You have much to learn about respect."

The boy shrugged. "I know how to feign it. That is sufficient."

As taught by his aunt? "Then you choose not to feign it with me."

Annoyance flashed across the boy's face. "You do know 'tis not a favor you do me in agreeing to support my claim? If you are my father, you owe it to me to set things right. If you are not, still you owe it to me."

Past the ire sparked by the boy's words, Everard grudgingly acknowledged the truth of what Judas said. No matter that he had never done more than kiss Judith, those kisses shared with another's betrothed had led to this day.

He sat forward. "This is the last time I shall say this. You were formed from de Balliol blood, not Wulfrith. Though that you have come seeking my help is evidence I bear much responsibility for the place in which you find yourself, it is not because there exists a possibility you are my son. You, Judas de Balliol, are rightfully born, not the result of a man cuckolded. Now you must needs begin behaving as the rightful lord of Cheverel."

There. More spots of vulnerability in the boy's eyes. And a sheen of tears he was not quick enough to conceal with the lowering of his gaze.

"That is settled, hmm?" Everard asked.

He jerked his chin.

"Good, then here is your first lesson: address one's betters with respect. And that begins with me, your lord."

Judas's chin snapped up. "A lesson? *My* lord?"

"Aye. While we await word from the queen, you will train here at Wulfen, beginning on the morrow."

"I did not come here for training."

As Lady Susanna had pointed out. "Regardless, you will avail yourself of all we can impart during your stay. And, I vow, you will be all the nearer to becoming a man."

Judas stood. "Where is my aunt? I would speak with her."

"You will not."

"Why?"

Everard stood and looked down upon him. "You are now under my protection, not a woman's, and I say you are done hiding behind your aunt's skirts."

Anger again, glittering in the boy's eyes.

"You must learn to exercise self control," Everard said. "Indeed, that is lesson two."

The boy took a step back. "You think I do not know how to control myself? Be you assured, I do. I simply choose not to when it suits me."

Just as he chose not to show Everard respect. "And when does it suit you not to control youself?"

"When my actions are justified, and I know it likely I will prevail."

Everard frowned.

"I have learned when to stand and fight and when to walk away no matter how much I long to hit something very hard."

Another lesson taught by Lady Susanna? "As you longed to hit Squire Charles when he besmirched your name?"

Judas's nostrils flared. "I know well what the name stands for and why it was given me, but I am done with being made to feel ashamed. If Squire Charles and others wish to believe my name is who I am, all the better, for they put themselves at great disadvantage if they think to know me by way of five letters."

Everard did not smile, though he was tempted. In some matters, anger was, indeed, a way to coax the boy out of himself—just not where Lady Susanna was concerned. If Everard read him right, Judas was bent on protecting the one who had raised him. Not much more than ten, but only in years.

Everard inclined his head. "Well said, Judas de Balliol, and that will be all."

The boy frowned. "What of my aunt?"

"This conversation is at an end. Now go and, while you make ready for supper, think on all we have discussed, for on the morrow your training will be far different from anything you have experienced."

It was clear he wished to argue, but he pushed his shoulders back, turned, and crossed the solar.

There was one more thing. "Judas!"

The boy turned. "My...lord?"

Near enough. For now. "Tell Sir Elias I would speak with him."

The boy nodded and slipped into the hall.

As Everard awaited the knight's arrival, his thoughts drifted to where he did not wish them to go. Though they had done so throughout the day, he had turned them back for their promise to disturb him. Now, however, they slipped past his defenses and he saw again Lady Susanna strain to reach the cup, heard her sob when she could not.

Sir Rowan had been there, could as easily have been the one to raise her up and put the cup to her lips, but Everard had thought nothing of it until it was too late. As he had held her, he had searched for the lie of her, but it had not been there to find and he had accepted she truly was unwell. And then the words she had whispered...

I wish I had not seen it. Would that I had not.

What? That day in the garden when she, far different in appearance from the woman who had come to Wulfen, happened upon Judith and him? Was that what she wished she had not seen? If so, better yet had she not carried the tale to her brother.

Still, Everard regretted that when he had later returned to the tower room and she had pressed him to explain the reason for limiting her influence upon the boy, he had revealed the knowledge gained from Sir Elias that she bargained with her body. She had paled further, looking so stricken he had feared she might once more lose consciousness, but then came anger. When she had flung open the door to Judith and scattered his own sins between them, his anger had risen to meet hers. Thankfully, he had pushed it down, denying himself one more thing to regret where Susanna de Balliol was concerned.

At the sound of footsteps upon the dais outside the solar, Everard looked around. A moment later, Squire Joseph admitted Sir Elias.

The knight took one stride within. "Lord Wulfrith," he said as the curtains fell into place behind him.

"I will not keep you long, Sir Elias, for there are few things you must needs know about your time at Wulfen."

"Aye, my lord?"

"A missive shall be sent to the queen requesting an audience to prove Judas de Balliol's claim to Cheverel. While we await a response, the boy will receive training alongside those in our charge. Hence, he shall sleep in the hall amongst the pages. If you insist on keeping watch over him, as is not necessary within these walls—"

"Is it not?" Sir Elias interrupted. "You saw what happened this eve."

Everard raised his eyebrows. "The boy more than held his own, Sir Elias. I assure you, it was noted by the others, none of whom would make such use of my hall as Judas did."

The man's mouth tightened.

"As I was saying, if you choose to keep him under watch, you will do so from a good distance to avoid the appearance of coddling that ill-favors him amongst his peers. However, know that I would prefer you spend your time being useful to me."

Sir Elias's lids narrowed. "In what way?"

"I do not yet know the extent of your skill at arms, but as someone saw fit to knight you, it must be adequate. Thus, I would have you aid upon the training field where, of added benefit, you may more easily serve Lady Susanna's purpose of ensuring Judas's wellbeing."

After a long moment, the knight said, "I see no reason not to accept."

"Good."

"And Lady Susanna? Where is she in all this?"

"Abovestairs, well out of sight for the duration. But do not think to find her in the chamber where you last saw her. I have moved her else-where to ensure she causes no more disturbance among those to whom my first duty lies."

The man's brow furrowed. "She is a prisoner, then."

It was the same as the lady had concluded. "Necessarily so, for my only other option is to return her to Cheverel. And, if you are as fond of her as you seem to be, you will agree this is the better course."

With a disgruntled air, the knight nodded and departed.

Everard closed his eyes and rubbed them, ignoring the temptation to grab an hour of rest before the evening meal was served. Resenting that his sleep had been nearly non-existent these past nights, he took up parchment and quill. First, he composed a missive to the queen, then one to his older brother to warn him that his presence at Wulfen Castle might be required earlier than expected. When—if—Queen Eleanor granted an audience, the keeping of Wulfen would fall to one of Everard's brothers. Though the youngest, Abel, was due in less than three weeks, he might be gone again by the time an answer was received.

After setting his wax seal to both missives, Everard leaned back, gripped his temples to relieve the tension, then dragged his hand over his scalp. And paused over the bristles beneath his calloused fingers.

He did not mind the keen blade he applied as often as twice a sennight, for it had become habit these past eleven years, so much that he rarely thought upon what had driven him to shave his head that first time. But then Lady Susanna had burst in upon his life.

Had she guessed the reason for his shorn hair? If she had heard as much as Judith and he had feared, it was likely. In which case, she surely laughed at him, for it had been a dramatic gesture, even for one aged twenty and two.

Everard drew his hand away, and this time when his thoughts drifted, they went to the day following Lady Susanna's blunder in the garden.

It had not been easy to get Judith alone, for Alan de Balliol was taking no chances. Though the wedding was to have been held in three days' time, that morning it was announced it would take place that very day.

Everard had knocked two guards senseless in order to steal Judith away, but when he had entered her chamber, she had not received him as expected. Her reddened eyes evidenced she did not wish to wed the man chosen by her father, but she said, "I cannot go with you, Everard."

"You can, and you will." He pulled her near. "You love me, do you not?"

"I do, but marrying Alan is a promise I must keep."

"That is your father's promise."

"It is as good as mine, for even if he supported me in breaking my betrothal, never would he accept you."

"Because the Wulfriths side with King Stephen."

"Aye."

Everard's resentment welled. How was it possible politics could wield more power than love?

Judith smiled sorrowfully. "My family shall ever support Duke Henry's claim to the throne, as do the de Balliols. Thus, it would be folly to allow my heart to travel down a road different from the one it has long been set upon."

"Judith—"

"Enough!" She pulled free, fumbled in the purse upon her belt, and thrust her hand forward.

He stared at it, not wanting what she wished to return though she had vowed she would never remove it from her person.

"Take it." She opened her fingers. In it lay the brilliant ruby he had pried from the hilt of his Wulfrith dagger weeks earlier as proof of his love.

He returned his gaze to hers and saw no wavering there. She was first the good, self-sacrificing daughter, second the woman who loved him. "'Tis yours," he said, "want it or nay."

She lowered her hand to her side. "I shall never stop loving you, Everard."

He clenched his fingers into his palms to keep from taking hold of her, kissing her, trying to persuade her to do what she would not be persuaded to do.

Swallowing hard as if so great an effort might clear the tears from her eyes, she reached up. "There will be another whose hands know what mine have known." She pulled her fingers through his hair. "As there should be." She rose to her toes, touched her mouth to his, and dropped back on her heels. "Farewell, Everard."

He had gone and, hours later, watched from the bordering wood as the sounds of the wedding celebration rose above the walls and assaulted his ears like clanging anvils.

When he had returned to Wulfen Castle, it was with a clean-shaven head and no word of explanation—his secret longing. But possibly secret no more.

She had said she would eat more, and she had. But it was not much. And now Squire Joseph stood at the door with more viands.

"My lady?" He raised his eyebrows, glanced past her into the chamber.

Susanna did not wish to appear ungrateful, but she hesitated before stepping aside so he could carry the tray within. As he did so, she looked to the knight upon the landing.

Sir Rowan inclined his head, and she was relieved to see no evidence of offense upon his aged face. Earlier, when she had finally risen from bed to avail herself of the garderobe, he had stepped to the threshold—no farther—and asked if he could be of service. She had declined and all but closed the door in his face. Though she might be little more than a prisoner, it did not seem much to ask to be afforded whatever privacy could be had.

Squire Joseph returned to where she stood, now bearing the first tray of foods from which Everard Wulfrith had threatened to feed her. "Cook has also prepared a draught to aid in digestion," he said. "He tells that you ought to drink it some minutes before eating."

Susanna blinked. "I thank you. And Cook." Only after the squire stepped past and started down the stairs did she realize there was another whom she ought to thank—Everard Wulfrith, for the draught was surely his doing.

Tightening her grip on the door handle, she dropped her chin to hide how painfully moved she was by the kindness once more shown her— and by a man who surely believed her unworthy of such consideration.

"Lady Susanna?"

She startled to find Sir Rowan's hand upon her arm, lifted her head to see if his face could be as easily read as others' who sought something for something—or those who sought something for nothing. There was no gleam in his eyes, no quivering nostrils, no grin about the mouth. And there was nothing forceful about his grip.

"May I help you to the chair?" He nodded at where she had earlier pulled it near the bedside table when she had kept her word to eat more. It was far too near the bed.

"Do not fear me," the knight said. "I am certain Lord Wulfrith gave it much thought before appointing me as your…"

She looked back at him, wondered at the sheepish look that did not fit the man who had refused to admit a woman to Wulfen. "As my jailer?"

He shrugged. "I suppose I am that, but it cannot be helped in a place where women are as rare as a rose in winter."

Rare but not entirely unheard of? "Then I am not the first Daughter of Eve to breach Wulfen's walls?"

He pulled his chin back. "Daughter of Eve? I have always thought Sisters of Mary a more fitting name for men's other halves."

Again, he surprised, for it seemed most men preferred the derogatory reference to women over that which bestowed upon them the virtues of the Virgin. Those at Cheverel, especially her brother, had certainly been fond of equating women with the one believed to have been man's downfall.

Cautiously warming toward Sir Rowan, she asked again, "I am not the first Sister of Mary to come within Wulfen's walls?"

There, a slight grin and a glimpse of teeth that was not at all wolfish. "You are not, my lady."

Though Susanna longed to know more of what he alluded to having an intimate knowledge of, she did not think he would further enlighten her. "I would have you assist me to the chair if still you do not mind," she said.

He took a firmer hold on her arm and drew her across the chamber.

"I thank you," she said as she lowered onto the seat.

He turned to the bedside table, retrieved the cup from the tray, and handed it to her. "Before you eat," he reminded.

She did not like the smell of the liquid, nor the taste, but the promise of relief from the roiling at her center made her drain it to the drop.

Sir Rowan relieved her of the cup. "Give it a few minutes, then I would suggest the meat pie ere it cools further." He started back across the chamber.

"Sir Rowan, shall I always find you outside my door?"

He peered across his shoulder. "That depends upon Lord Wulfrith—and the reason you ask."

Meaning if she intended mischief, she would ever be under the eye of whomever was set outside her chamber. Despite how considerate Sir Rowan seemed to be, she did not like that, for it made her state of imprisonment all the more suffocating.

More, though, it stole from her the opportunity to test the limits of her prison walls. Not that she meant to defy Everard Wulfrith—at least, not openly. Somehow, she must find a way to at least see Judas from a distance.

"Good eve, my lady," Sir Rowan said.

"And you, Sir Rowan."

He closed the door, and she leaned forward and chose the warm meat pie he had suggested. Unlike the draught, it smelled wonderful. And yet, her second bite was no less bland than the first. Was it her, or did Wulfen's cook lack skill in the art of spice? Regardless, the half of it that she swallowed stayed down.

12

HE HATED THIS, though he was better than most of the pages whom, he determined, would become increasingly familiar with his back—at least during this accursed pre-dawn exercise when he was made to run the wood. Providing he proved as accomplished when it came time to demonstrate his skill at arms, it was his face with which the others would become familiar.

Such imaginings drove Judas onward and, despite the stone-weighted belt about his waist, it was not long before he began to over-take even the squires.

What think you of this? he silently put to the man whom he longed to pass though he knew he would not likely come within sight of the one who had twice denied fathering him. If what Lord Wulfrith spoke was true—

I hope it is. I do. Far better de Balliol blood than Wulfrith. After all, had Alan de Balliol been cuckolded, would not his conduct toward the child birthed by his wife have been justified? Would not his scorn and cruelties have been his due? Though Aunt Susanna would not agree, it seemed a good reason for Judas to wish himself a de Balliol. Otherwise, he would have to rethink his hatred of the man who had named him, might even be compelled to pity him. And that he did not wish to do.

Of course, there was another reason it was preferable to be a de Balliol, and that was Cheverel. Once he was lord, no one could ever again make him feel inferior or sling his name around. All he had suffered would not be for nothing, the price paid in full. And Aunt Susanna...

He growled in remembrance of Lord Wulfrith who believed her nephew hid behind her skirts. That had stung, the anger Judas had made no attempt to hide earning him lesson two—exercise self control. And he would. He would bide his time, and when the opportunity to seek out his aunt presented itself, he would take it. And Lord Wulfrith could wallow in his ignorance.

Nearing two dark figures ahead who were of a size that told they were also squires, Judas pumped his arms and legs harder and nearly shouted with triumph when he passed between the two and heard them groan.

Though those ahead were too numerous for him to make it all the way out front, he would pick off as many as possible and, if nothing else, Lord Wulfrith would regret that Judas de Balliol was not his son.

As he passed another squire, he heard rushing water and picked out bits of light reflected upon the great fall that poured into a shimmering pool below. Realizing it was a ravine he ran alongside, he felt his heart surge and chest constrict. However, when a closer examination of the ground revealed he had more than ten feet between him and the steep edge, the constriction eased. Still, he knew not to push himself further, and would have maintained his pace had he not heard the approach of those he had passed—and who would surely laugh once they returned the humiliation he had visited upon them.

He reached his legs farther, swung his arms more vigorously, and veered right. Ahead, visible in the bit of light that evidenced the sun thought hard on returning to the sky, were the figures of those he had yet to overtake where they negotiated the uppermost portion of the river before it dropped off and fell into the pool below.

'Tis shallow, he assured himself, but the thought of the slippery rocks to which he must set foot made his chest constrict again.

"Ah, nay," he huffed. It would not happen here. He would not suffer that shame. Easing back, he ground his teeth when the squires ran past with jeers and laughter.

Judas glanced over his shoulder to confirm no others were near and went left where he paused on the far side of a tree, braced his hands on his knees, and silently talked his breath back under control. When his chest eased, he straightened and considered those now fording the river—all of smaller stature that confirmed he would not be the first page to reach the training field before Wulfen's outer walls, and certainly not ahead of any squires.

On the morrow, then, he told himself and lunged forward.

He knew those colors. They did not bode well.

Swinging his gaze from the banners of those who had been intercepted by Wulfen's mounted guard, Everard squinted against the sunlight that sought to obscure his search of the training field. There—Sir Elias striding toward Judas who had paused in taking down a wooden post with a two-handed sword. The knight knew what this portended and, as he had acted quickly, Everard less begrudged Sir Elias's decision to continue to watch over the boy.

After signaling for Wulfen's knights to resume training their charges, Everard glanced one last time at Judas and Sir Elias, silently approved their leisurely retreat that would draw less attention, and returned his sword to its scabbard. He nodded at Squire Joseph to do the same.

Normally, he positioned himself before the drawbridge to receive those who came unannounced to Wulfen while training commenced outside its walls. However, to provide distraction for the two who would soon slip beneath the portcullis, he swung himself over the fence and, followed by Joseph, strode forward to meet the contingent that numbered six.

Shortly, flanked and fronted by Wulfen's guard, the riders reined in before Everard where he stood with hand upon sword hilt.

"My Lord Wulfrith," said the patrol's lead squire who was only months from earning his spurs and a Wulfrith dagger to mark his passage into manhood, "these knights hail from Cheverel under the command of Sir Talbot who would make an inquiry of you."

Having already taken measure of the riders, Everard was unimpressed with their restless ranks. More, he was unimpressed that it was two days since they had ridden past in the earliest hours of morn in pursuit of those whom Wulfen Castle harbored. Whatever trail they had followed had grown cold here, and only now they returned. It was a poor reflection on their worth, but welcome.

He returned his gaze to Sir Talbot, not only known by his position at the fore of his men but his visage. Eleven years had lined the skin and loosened it about the jaw, but not so much that he was unrecognizable. Of benefit, there seemed no recognition in the eyes with which he regarded Everard. And not necessarily due to a shaved head. More likely, it was because, in serving Judith's father that first year following his knighting, Everard had simply been *Sir* Everard and his acquaintance with Alan's man had been but a glancing one across a distance—excluding the day of the wedding when Everard had stolen upon the knight and knocked him senseless in hopes of carrying away Judith. The only real question was whether or not the man's lord had ever revealed the name of the one who had thought to take his betrothed from him.

Everard jutted his chin. "Make your inquiry, Sir Talbot, for I have much with which to occupy myself during the hours of sunlight that remain."

The man's mouth tightened. "My men and I have ridden hard many days now." Unexpectedly for a man as sturdy as he appeared to be, his voice had a nasal quality and was languid as of one who has drunk too much but is still conscious of the need to form intelligible words. "Perhaps you will allow us to quench our thirst and break our fast in your hall?"

"With regret, I will not, Sir Talbot, for as you surely know, Wulfen Castle is exclusive to the training of England's finest knights. Thus, visitors are not welcome for the distraction they breed."

When a murmur of dissent arose from Sir Talbot's men, Wulfen's mounted squires—and Joseph beside Everard—made adjustments to their postures and hands in preparation for the commencement of hostilities. And further adjusted themselves as a sharp-eyed wiry knight issued a curse so vile that if ever the Lord wished to make an example of a blasphemer, he would surely begin with that one.

Sir Talbot snapped his chin around. "Sir Morris, keep your mouth about you else I shall keep it for you!"

The recipient of the rebuke narrowed his eyes and stared at the one to whom he answered.

"My apologies, Lord Wulfrith," Sir Talbot said. "As for the hospitality you are unable to extend"—he shrugged his shoulders, then his mouth—"a pity, for who would not like to see up close that of which so many speak but few have laid eyes upon?"

Everard raised his eyebrows. "Wulfen is a castle much like any other, Sir Talbot. 'Tis what we do here that makes it noteworthy."

The knight nodded. "I will not keep you much longer. My purpose is to inquire if you or your men have seen or heard of a knight who passed through these parts within the last two days—a Sir Elias Cant. He would have been in the company of a lady and boy."

"I have had no such report," Everard said.

"You are certain?'

Normally, Everard would have pointed out that none came near Wulfen Castle without notice, as evidenced by the patrol that had intercepted Sir Talbot and his men. However, upon the morning in question, Wulfen's guard had no longer been outside the walls, having escorted the pursued within. Thus, Sir Talbot and his men had ridden past unchecked.

"I am beyond certain," Everard said with umbrage due one who is questioned who should not be. "Naught goes within or without of which I am not made aware."

"Again, my apologies, Lord Wulfrith. I press you only because the trail was warm at the village that lies but three leagues distant and, shortly thereafter, went cold."

"Perhaps, Sir Talbot, you ought to consider that those you seek doubled back the better to..." Everard smiled wryly. "...elude you? Or do I make an assumption I should not?"

"You assume right. The traitorous knight abducted a lady and her nephew from Cheverel, and I have been charged with bringing him to ground."

So that was to be the story. Everard pitied Sir Elias who, at best, would find it difficult to sell his sword arm to another lord if Queen Eleanor denied Judas's claim. At worst, the man might find his neck in a noose.

Everard inclined his head. "Then I wish you Godspeed."

"I thank you for your time," the knight said, then he signaled to his men and turned his destrier.

Wulfen's guard urged their horses aside. However, when Sir Talbot and his men struck out across the land, the squires followed to ensure their unwelcome visitors did, indeed, depart.

"That is done," Everard said. "For now." He looked to the young man beside him. "What make you of this, Squire Joseph?"

"I know not all the circumstances, my lord, but I am thinking the situation might have proven dire for the lady and boy—and certainly Sir Elias—had you not granted them sanctuary."

Sanctuary. Everard's thoughts stumbled over the word. Was that what he had given them? Though Wulfen Castle was hardly a monastery or convent, it seemed so. Of course, it was more of a prison for Lady Susanna, but such bars were necessary where she was concerned. As for Squire Joseph's conclusion, he saw what Everard saw. Had Lady Susanna and Judas been captured, it was likely they would not have been returned to Cheverel—at least, not alive, for who better to blame their deaths upon than Sir Elias who was said to have abducted them.

"You are thinking right, Squire Joseph." Everard turned on his heel. As he strode toward the fence and the training field beyond, he pulled his gloves from beneath his belt and slapped them against his thigh.

This was an even more dangerous game than Lady Susanna had led him to believe, and if one's pieces were not moved without much thought, and the opponent's pieces not taken without due consideration, the board upon which it was played could become a bloody mess.

13

THE DAY COULD get no longer. Worse, on the morrow there would be another, and another after that, and—

Cease, Susanna! You make it no better with your pacing and muttering. You have been given time, have you not? Time Judas and you might not have had. Time otherwise filled with fear and riding hard in hopes of reaching the queen before your pursuers reached you. Time in which to fail—perhaps mortally. Now do something with that time!

"What?" she asked of walls she was certain had moved nearer in upon her since she had awakened hours ago.

She turned quickly around, but there was nothing here with which to occupy herself while she waited for word of how Judas fared on his first day of Wulfen training.

Suddenly light of head, wishing she had been more temperate in her movements, she splayed her hands out to her sides. When she once more settled into her center, she crossed to the window and peered out at nothing—at least, not anything that could hold her interest, for she had been placed in a tower room at the back of the donjon. She had a view of the bordering wood, those who patrolled the inner and outer walls, and the garden below that serviced the kitchen.

"Naught," she muttered, then turned, leaned back against the shutter, and closed her eyes. "Lord, I am grateful that you have blessed Judas.

I am. I just…" She dropped her chin to her chest and closed her hand over the pendant beneath her chemise. "I can hardly breathe."

"Lady Susanna?"

She snapped her head up.

Sir Rowan stood in the narrow wedge of doorway. "My apologies," he said. "I did knock."

She dropped her arms to her sides and stepped away from the window. "I am sorry I did not hear." She raised her eyebrows questioningly.

"Squire Joseph has brought your nooning meal."

More food. "I thank you."

He stepped inside, pushing the door wide to allow the squire to enter behind him.

The young man acknowledged her as usual, swapped the new tray with the old that had been a simple morning repast of bread and cheese, and withdrew.

Susanna eyed the offering, a small trencher filled with some sort of stew, a cup that surely contained the draught that had been of good benefit to her sensitive stomach, and a goblet of wine.

Well, here is something I can do—eat. Though if this meal proved as bland as last eve's, she would be fortunate to stretch the activity to a quarter hour.

"Is there anything you require, my lady?" Sir Rowan asked.

"Company," she quipped. "Of course, I may not be allowed that."

He put his head to the side. "If I will suffice, I will sit a while."

She opened her mouth to accept, closed it, considered him more closely. Since being ensconced here, she had not felt threatened by him, and not simply because he was at least of an age her own father would be were he yet living. Beyond the man's gruff front, there was something kindly about him, and if her judgment failed her in that regard, she had but to consider it was Everard Wulfrith who had appointed him to watch over her. But beyond the issue of her safety, there might be more than company to be had from him.

"I would like that, Sir Rowan."

He inclined his head, stepped into the corridor, and returned a moment later with a stool she had not realized he kept on the landing. But then, she had not been outside this chamber. Yet.

As she crossed to the chair beside the tray, Sir Rowan set his stool near the foot of the bed, keeping a good five feet between them.

Susanna drank the draught first, retrieved the platter, and set it on her lap. While she waited for the medicinal to begin its work, she smiled lightly and said, "It seems you never leave your post, Sir Rowan."

His mouth lifted, but she caught the slight narrowing of his lids that revealed her nonchalance had not found its mark any better than on the night past when she had asked if she would always find him outside her door.

He cleared his throat. "It only seems that way, my lady, for I have the same needs as any other living being."

She lowered her gaze to the platter. Though she had considerable practice at schooling her face to reflect only those emotions she wished it to reflect, she was finding it more difficult to achieve at Wulfen. In the muscles of her face and eyes—even in the wish of her fingers to knot into fists—she could feel the twitch of feelings best kept hidden. Assuring herself that once she recovered from this nasty bout of what Everard Wulfrith called "swooning and sickening," she would be herself again, she mulled the knight's words. When did he see to his needs? While she slept? More, was there another who relieved him during that time?

Choosing her words carefully, she said, "I am sorry."

"For what, my lady?"

"That you, a knight, are made to watch over me as if you are a nursemaid."

He gave a short laugh that held no taint of bitterness that might have been of use to her. "There was a time I would have minded performing such a service—even been offended—but I am mostly content, for my days are winding down."

"What say you?"

"As you can see…" He peered down his seated figure. "…my youth is long gone, as is my middle age. Thus, providing I can yet be useful to my lord, my pride is best set aside."

"You do not look to be of a great age," Susanna said, and it was true.

He chuckled. "You flatter me, my lady."

That was true as well. She dipped her spoon in the trencher, took a bite, and sighed.

"'Tis not to your liking, my lady?"

"It does not taste bad. It just has little taste. 'Twould seem Wulfen's cook is not…" *Do not offend, Susanna.* "Well, he is not very generous with his spices."

The knight peered nearer upon her meal. "I do not find his offerings lacking. Indeed, I would say he is openhanded with spices as befitting those for whom he cooks."

Is it me, then? Has something dulled my sense of taste?

She started to suggest he sample her meal, but caught the sound of someone ascending the stairs. Hoping Everard Wulfrith brought word of Judas, she swept her gaze across the chamber as Sir Rowan rose from the stool.

The doorway was filled by the man she had hoped for. Garbed in what appeared to be a fresh tunic though it was the middling of day and there were surely more hours of training ahead, he looked from Susanna to the knight. "What goes, Sir Rowan?"

She bristled at the suspicion in his voice. Not that he did not have reason to suspect something was afoot…

"My lord, I but keep the lady company whilst she partakes of her meal."

"As I asked him to do," she said. "I did not think you would mind."

Everard Wulfrith stared at her.

"The lady and I were discussing spices," Sir Rowan said. "She does not think Wulfen's cook is generous enough with them, and I argued to the contrary."

Inwardly, Susanna cringed. She was fairly certain Sir Rowan meant well, but it made her sound ungrateful.

"Lady Susanna is correct." Everard Wulfrith stepped into the chamber. "Where *her* food is concerned."

Understanding dawned upon Susanna, but Sir Rowan more quickly voiced his own. "Ah, the draught."

His lord halted alongside him. "I would speak with the lady alone."

"Aye, my lord." Moments later, the knight closed the door behind him.

Everard Wulfrith came the rest of the way, so near that Susanna had to put her head back to hold his gaze. As he looked down upon her, she wished she had done something more with her hair than comb her fingers through it. Rather than leave it loose and limp about her shoulders, she should have, at least, donned a veil.

"My apologies if the viands are not to your liking," he said. "However, in consideration of the stomach difficulties from which you said you suffered, Cook was instructed to omit spices from your food."

As much as she longed to retreat behind her lids and gather herself back into the one person who required but one thing of him, she braved his disapproving gaze and wondered how she could dislike a man who had not only wronged her more than she had ever wronged him but now imprisoned her, and not dislike him at all when he showed so much consideration. And this was no small thing, for the cook had too many mouths to feed to spend time altering food for one person. It could not sit well with him.

Fearing tears, she determined she would get the apology out of the way and move on to a subject nearer her heart. "Forgive me if I seem ungrateful, Lord Wulfrith. I am not. Though ashamed to admit it, I am but slow-witted." She drew a deep breath. "Tell me, how fares my nephew?"

"He shows potential, but there is much work to do whilst he remains at Wulfen."

"Oh." She was surprised, for Sir George and Sir Elias had told her that her nephew made good progress, especially for one of so few years.

"Eat, Lady Susanna."

Again! She looked to her hand that hovered alongside the spoon she had not realized she had released, took it up again, and slipped a spoonful of bland meat and vegetables into her mouth.

Everard Wulfrith pivoted and strode to the stool Sir Rowan had left behind. He seated himself, put one foot on the bottom rung, the other on the floor.

"Judas has no specific strength as I can yet discern," he said, "though it was reported to me that throughout much of his run in the wood this morn—"

"Run?" Susanna recalled her nephew's younger years when he had most easily succumbed to breathing attacks while overexerting himself with too much stretching of the legs. "What has that to do with a knight's training?"

Annoyance gathered Everard Wulfrith's eyebrows. "'Tis foundation, Lady Susanna. Thus, it has everything to do with a knight's training." He dropped his gaze to the trencher and did not continue speaking until, once again, she slid the spoon in her mouth. "Though your nephew gained ground on nearly all the other pages and passed a good number of squires, he could not maintain his pace and was among the last to come in."

Had he lost his breath? Certainly not to Everard Wulfrith's knowledge. Perhaps Judas had felt an impending attack and eased back. Or, as suggested, he had been unable to maintain his speed.

"You cannot take another bite until you swallow that one, Lady Susanna."

Feeling her face warm, she swallowed and snapped, "I am not a child."

He did not gainsay her, but neither did he apologize. "The good of it," he continued, "is that he has determination and the desire to prove himself. The bad of it—"

"Bad?"

"I knew him to be forceful, disrespectful even, but last eve he attacked an older boy."

The spoon dropped from Susanna's fingers into the stew, causing flecks of gravy to dot her hands. "What?"

"It surprises you?"

"Of course. Judas can be roused, but he is mostly a gentle soul. Is he well?"

"He is. 'Tis the squire who will feel that encounter for some days to come."

Susanna shook her head. "I cannot believe he would attack another. Though, perhaps, if greatly provoked..."

"There was that. The squire took offense at your nephew's skulking about and Sir Elias's hovering. I believe it was disparagement of Judas's name that pushed him to strike the young man."

Now she understood—or nearly so, for Judas had always controlled himself when a drunken Alan or one of his men entertained themselves with such taunting. Now it was happening again.

Somehow, Susanna remembered to lift the platter from her lap before standing. Without a care for the din, she all but dropped it on the tray, then whipped around to face the man who sat unmoving. "This is your Wulfen training?" She stepped her feet wider to counter the sway in her legs. "These are the sort of young men you train up to be England's *finest* knights?"

He inclined his head. "They are. And they can greatly offend. Wulfen is not merely for well-heeled young nobles, Lady Susanna. Indeed, its training is of greatest benefits to those who are rough, even raw. Whenever possible, and it is usually possible, we reshape them into worthy young men."

"I see naught worthy in one who belittles another for a name not of his choosing!"

"The matter has been dealt with, and both are contrite—"

"Both?" She took a step nearer him. "For what has Judas to be contrite?"

His mouth tightened. "For loss of self control. For fouling my hall with behavior unbecoming of a knight in training."

Susanna's hands hurt, the fists at her sides so tight she only then realized that she, herself, was losing control. And she must not.

She released her breath, turned, and dropped to the edge of the mattress. "I beg your forgiveness, Lord Wulfrith." She stared at her hands as she forced them open, then she pressed her palms together between her knees. "I cannot help being protective of Judas. He has endured much."

"For this—"

"For this," she muttered. "Aye, I know. For this, women are not allowed at Wulfen."

And that, Susanna. Why do you insist on beleaguering him? There has to be an end to his patience, and you do not want to be standing near when he comes to it.

She lifted her head and only then realized how close she was to him, that she had but to reach to the side to touch his knee. Not that she wished to.

Pushing her shoulders back, she met his eyes that were ever too watchful. "The only explanation I can offer for Judas's loss of self control—the only one I can think of—is that he must feel safe here. Ever before, he suffered such slights from those with authority over him. Men."

"I am aggrieved to hear that, though not surprised. As told, Wulfen is of good benefit to those who lack proper upbringing."

"I did not say he—" This time, she stopped herself from defending Judas, and not only because she did not wish to test Everard Wulfrith.

Noting his raised eyebrows, she sighed. "You are right. His was not a proper upbringing." Though she had tried.

After a long moment, he said, "There is a matter of greater import we must discuss, that which brought me to your chamber."

Susanna's heart lurched. "Aye?"

"I had expected that if Cheverel's knights were to pause at Wulfen to inquire after Judas and you, they would have done so before now, but this morn they rode upon the training field outside the walls."

Her throat nearly closed up. "Did they see Judas?"

"They did not. Sir Elias was quick to deliver him back inside the walls."

Relief nearly bent her over. "What did they say?"

"Quite the tale—that Sir Elias abducted you and your nephew."

Fingers starting to curl inward again, she squeezed her palms flat between her knees. *Dear Lord, do not let that knight pay a high price for aiding Judas and me.*

"As I am sure you understand, Lady Susanna, there is much to be read into such an accusation, and none of it bodes well—for any of you."

What he spoke was true. It was not just Sir Elias for whom such a tale could prove dire. And she should not be surprised, for Lady Richenda had already shown she was not above seeking Judas's death.

Feeling suddenly cold though the heat of a brazier had not been necessary to keep the chill from her this day, she asked, "Was it Sir Talbot who led them?"

"It was. They were six strong, among them a Sir Morris."

Again, she should not be surprised, and yet the name made her shudder and took the straight right out of her back. Where she bent forward, she distantly heard the creak of the stool, felt the brush of a leg against hers.

"My lady?"

"I am fine." She shuddered again. "Pray, give me a moment."

The mattress gave on one side of her, then the coverlet was drawn around her shoulders.

Sir Morris. That scourge upon the earth. He who had not only come the nearest to ravishing her but had so forcefully engaged Judas at swords that it had been beyond believable that her nephew had nearly lost his breath to such an extent he might have died.

Hands gripped her shoulders, large and warm through the coverlet. "Susanna?"

It was not only the concern in that most welcome voice that brought her back to him but that he had eschewed her title. Raising her chin, she found Everard Wulfrith's face before hers where he had lowered to his haunches.

She swallowed hard. "I vow I shall not swoon again. I will not."

Did he wince?

"'Tis obvious this Sir Morris is dangerous," he said, "but to what degree? What do I not know?"

Seeing no reason to elaborate on the sins of only one, Susanna said, "They are all dangerous. Wh-what did you tell Sir Talbot?"

The concern upon his face was displaced by a frown but, blessedly, he left that most vile knight in the mud where he belonged. "It could be said I lied, for I told I had no report of a knight traveling with a lady and boy."

"Do you think you were believed?"

"I do, though the truth of it depends on whether or not your brother ever revealed to his men the name of the one whom he believed cuckolded him."

"I never heard evidence of it. Indeed, he could not bear…"

"What?"

She dragged a hand from between her knees, gripped the pendant beneath her bodice. "Your name was not to be spoken—ever." To attest to that, she had a small scar upon her right cheek from where her brother's ring had sliced her the one time she had forgotten. Hence, she had been surprised to learn Alan had revealed the Wulfrith name to Judas. But then, during those last few months of his life, he had been happily drunk, as opposed to unhappily drunk, relishing that soon he would replace the son he denied.

"That is good," Everard Wulfrith said. "Now tell what else I need to know, Susanna."

Still he eschewed her title, and though she knew she had no right to a flutter of pleasure, it made itself felt—right there, beneath her hand that held tight to a reminder of him. "What else?" she whispered.

She could not be certain, but she thought he growled. "I speak of what you and Judas are not telling me. There is more, and I would hear it."

There were only two things she consciously withheld from him, and what did it matter that one attempt on Judas's life had already been made? What did it matter that it was not she who had revealed the kiss in the garden? Sir Talbot's lie that Sir Elias had abducted Judas and her was evidence enough of the mortal danger Judas faced. And she was surely too much maligned by what Everard Wulfrith had witnessed between Sir Elias and her in the corridor for him to believe that Judith and he were responsible for their downfall.

"You are right," she allowed, "there is more, but naught that changes what we require of you."

This time she was certain he growled—just a moment before he closed his eyes and dropped his chin.

Susanna stared at the multitude of short, dark blond hairs that bristled his scalp. If there had been any doubt Everard Wulfrith was no longer capable of growing a full head of hair, there was none now. Indeed, if he did not soon take a sharp blade to it, he would not much longer present as bald-pated.

She loosed the pendant, reached.

With a heavy sigh, he lifted his head. "Susanna—" His eyes that had been destined for hers, narrowed upon her extended fingers.

Only then realizing what she did, she snatched her hand back and looked hard upon it where she caught hold of it with the other in her lap.

Oh, you are pitiful to think you can go there, Susanna. You are no Judith.

As he straightened, she lifted her gaze just enough to watch the unfolding of his legs.

"I shall trouble you no longer, Lady Susanna," he said gruffly.

Lady Susanna...

"When you are ready to reveal what you deign not to tell, send Sir Rowan with word." He turned toward the door, paused. "Your food grows cold—"

"Do not!" She thrust her chin up, glared into the narrowed eyes he swung to her. "Do not, or I shall scream."

He considered her, then took up the stool. Moments later, he closed the door behind him.

Susanna lay back upon the bed and felt a burn in her belly as she saw again her hand reach toward him so she might touch hair that had only been for another to touch...

"Only ever Judith," she breathed.

It was not a dream, but the memory was just as feverish and, like those night travels, was viewed behind her closed lids where she lay upon the bed wishing for sleep so the day would be done sooner.

The memory sharpened, pulling her in. And back.

"Susanna?" Everard Wulfrith's voice, part amusement, part disbelief, made Susanna falter where she wove among the garden's plants.

"Aye, 'tis clear she is besotted with you"—the voice of the one she sought—"though not as much as I."

Susanna halted alongside a thick hedge of rosebushes that had more thorns about their stems than petals and tried to make sense of the conversation into which her name had been inserted. It was true she was besotted with Everard Wulfrith, but surely Judith was not. She must be in one of her teasing moods.

"'Tis softer than my finest bliaut," Susanna's friend said, "so soft methinks I would like to wear it."

Wear what? Susanna frowned amid the silence that was so complete she dared not swallow lest she was heard.

"Tell me I may, beloved Judith."

Beloved...

Judith's whispered something was followed by more silence, then she said, "Promise me."

"Whatever you would have."

"Promise your hair will only ever know my hands—no other's."

"And if I do?"

"I will go away with you."

Susanna stumbled back, grabbed hold of thorned stems to steady herself, hardly felt the sharp points penetrate her palm. She could not have heard right. Judith was betrothed to Alan.

She shook her head, certain she misunderstood what was happening on the other side. A jest! That was what this was. They had heard her approach and but played with her.

"Only ever you, Judith," Everard said.

Beginning to smile over how gullible she was, Susanna hurried forward and turned off the pathway onto the next. And halted so abruptly she nearly toppled forward.

On the bench ahead sat Judith and Everard, their mouths upon one another's.

No jest.

Everard drew back. Smiling, he pulled Judith's hands from his hair and kissed each one. Then his head came around and eyes stopped on Susanna.

Judith jumped up from the bench. "Susanna!"

Susanna threw a hand up as if the pitiful gesture might ward off the truth of what she saw, then turned and fled. But not to her brother. Never to Alan.

Unwilling to relive any more of that memory now that she understood what she should have understood sooner, Susanna opened her eyes. "Oh, Judith," she whispered, "still he mourns you. Still no other hands have known his hair. A good husband he would have made you."

She rolled onto her stomach, pressed her face into the pillow, and cried.

When a knock sounded some time later, she sat up and wiped her face with handfuls of the coverlet. Certain another tray of food was about to be delivered, wondering how she might fight the temptation to send it flying, she rose and crossed the room.

"Aye?" she asked, easing the door open just enough to look upon Sir Rowan without revealing much of her face.

"Apologies, my lady, I would but know how you fare."

Cringing at the possibility he had heard the muffled sound of her misery, she fumbled for an explanation and found the one nearest the truth. "You will think it silly, Sir Rowan, but I am afflicted with too much time in which to do naught but think. Of course, you are no less afflicted, are you?"

"I am mostly at peace, my lady. Thus, I more often find comfort in my thoughts than affliction."

If only she could be at peace…

"If you but tell me what would offer the best distraction, I shall ask Lord Wulfrith if I might deliver those things to you."

He would do that? More, would Everard Wulfrith? In the next instant, she almost laughed. Of course he would—providing her requests were not perceived as a threat to his young men. Thus, she asked for a psalter, quill, ink, and parchment. And though she feared she would be thought greedy, she also asked for a chess set in the event Sir Rowan might once again be prevailed upon to provide company.

"I will do what I can," he said. "If you think of anything else, I shall be here."

"I thank you, Sir Rowan." She closed the door, leaned back against it, and listened as she must do if she was to learn of the man's comings and goings.

14

"Ah, Sir Morris..." Sir Elias mused. "I thought 'twas him with Sir Talbot." He looked closer upon the man beside whom he was seated at the high table. "I will tell you what I can, but so I might know what needs to be told, may I ask the reason you single him out from among those who rode upon Wulfen?"

Everard inclined his head. "I am disturbed by Lady Susanna's reaction to mention of his name." And since she would not elaborate, he had decided to enlist the aid of this man whom he had invited to join him at meal.

"I wager she did not react well," Sir Elias said.

"She did not."

The knight glanced at Judas whose page duties this eve included refilling pitchers of wine after the attending squires divided their contents between the goblets throughout the hall.

Guessing the knight wished to confirm the boy was out of earshot, Everard waited. And did not like that when the man looked back at him, he was slow to answer as if deciding what to tell and not tell.

"She has good cause," he finally said. "One night, shortly after I arrived at Cheverel three years past, Baron de Balliol let the wine flow freely and most of his men shed what few manners they had." He raised his eyebrows. "I believe it fair to say such behavior would not be tolerated at Wulfen from boys, let alone full-grown men."

"Sir Morris was in his cups as well?"

The knight shook his head. "Not so much, nor was I, for I knew to be cautious in a household with which I was not yet familiar."

"Then?"

"Something about Sir Morris bothered me. He was too watchful, as if he awaited an opportunity that might present itself as his lord grew increasingly inebriated. Thus, to keep my mind off the wine I denied myself, I made a game of observing him."

"And?"

"Lady Susanna came belowstairs so discreetly that had I not seen his attention settle upon her, I do not know I would have noticed her—she can be that quiet. He followed her to the kitchen. And I followed after."

Everard tensed. Another bargain made? An arranged tryst out of sight of her brother?

"He had her backed into a corner, and she had only a cup with which to defend herself."

Everard frowned. "Defend herself?"

Sir Elias smiled wryly. "That knight is not one with whom she would ever have bargained, Lord Wulfrith. Ravishment was Sir Morris's intent."

Everard felt his ire rise against the man who had this day cursed the Wulfrith lack of hospitality, next a stab of remorse at having been so ready to interpret the situation as he had done. "You interceded," he said.

"Nay, that was her brother—after I brought the matter to his attention."

Everard leaned nearer the man. "You left her there?" he said between his teeth. "You had best explain yourself, Sir Elias."

The knight shifted in his chair, glanced around. "I assure you, there was time, Lord Wulfrith. Too, the lady is quick, and though I have never given her cause to strike me, I have seen and heard tale of what she can do."

Further evidence she was no longer the compliant, guileless girl whom Judith had believed would not reveal what had happened in the garden. The acknowledgement caused Everard's thoughts to slide backward to Judith's insistence that her friendship with Susanna was of greater depth than the girl's kinship with her overbearing brother. Had he known how wrong she was, he would have taken her from her father's home immediately following the incident and before her family could remind her of her duty to them. A mistake that could never be remedied.

"Though Baron de Balliol could not walk a straight line," Sir Elias wrenched Everard back to the present, "his appearance in the kitchen was all that was required to end Sir Morris's assault."

"All? Did not your lord beat the man for attacking a lady—his own sister?"

Sir Elias shook his head. "I imagine that is as a Wulfen-trained knight would do, but de Balliol? Though the lady's bodice was torn, he accused her of tempting his men—named her a Daughter of Eve—then returned to the hall and finished drinking himself senseless."

Everard swallowed hard to contain his disgust. What had turned de Balliol against his own sister that he could be so cruel and unmoved? Her affection for and defense of the son he rejected?

"That Sir Morris remained in his service," Sir Elias continued, "ought to inform you of the state of the household in which Lady Susanna raised Judas."

Worse and worse, and little of it from her own lips. Because of pride? Shame? Resignation? Or, as this man had told two nights past, did she merely save up her defenses for when they might be needed for Judas?

Sir Elias drained his goblet, set it aside, and waved away the squire who hastened forward to refill it. "I know you cannot think much of me for not personally defending her honor that day, but I will not be as Lady Susanna and let a smudge upon my character become a stain. I was cautious, aye, but from that day forth, I have stayed as near her nephew and the lady as possible, granting whatever favors I can so she has little need of turning to others for favors."

Everard frowned. "You make your—shall I call it protection?—sound almost chivalrous, Sir Elias."

The knight turned a hand up. "Almost is better than not at all, hmm? And I did deliver her to your walls with Cheverel's men fast upon our heels."

So he had. Such a curious man. "Still you deny that you love her?"

"I care for her, that is all."

"Why? Especially if she is as broken as you believe her to be?"

The knight leaned back in his chair. "There is something very beautiful about brokenness." It was said with near reverence. "The longing to put something back together again, to see it restored no matter how many cracks might forever mar its surface." He blinked, sighed. "Forgive me, Lord Wulfrith. 'Tis a weakness of mine."

Recalling when the knight had spoken of a woman's desperation and unplucked petals too bruised to remain upon the stem, Everard thought again that Sir Elias sounded more a poet than one bred to swing a sword.

"You are a curious knight," he said. "Indeed, sometimes I wonder if you are a knight at all."

If he had expected the man to look chagrined at having his manly profession questioned, Everard would have been disappointed. But he was more disposed toward the smile that ran up the corners of Sir Elias's mouth. And not at all surprised when the man changed the subject by asking, "You have sent your missive to Queen Eleanor?"

Everard settled back and looked around the hall that evidenced they were near meal's end. The squires and pages who had served other squires and pages and knights with decorum befitting a nobleman's hall were beginning to remove empty platters and goblets, those who had emptied them talking amongst themselves.

Satisfied that, even with a woman within Wulfen's walls, all was as it should be, Everard said, "I sent the missive this morn."

"So now we wait."

He looked sidelong at Sir Elias. "That is one of the things we do."

"There are other things?"

"We prepare Judas to stand before a queen and convincingly assert his claim to his father's lands. And, perhaps, we ought to send someone to Cheverel to take measure of the effect of the boy's absence."

After a long moment, Sir Elias said, "I am glad Lady Susanna would not be dissuaded from seeking your aid, Lord Wulfrith. If Judas has any hope, it seems to lie with you—a man not his father."

Not of a mind to mull whether or not that last was spoken with sincerity, Everard said, "I shall do my best by him," then stood and called an end to the meal. Amid the clamor, he strode the back of the dais and stepped past another of his squires who held aside the curtain between hall and solar.

Absently rubbing a hand over his heavily stubbled head, he crossed the floor and noted the cleared surface of a table positioned before the hearth between two chairs. As with the other items he had agreed Sir Rowan could deliver abovestairs, the chess set was gone. He would not likely miss it, though, for despite his love of the game, he rarely had time to indulge. Indeed, it was hard enough to find time to shave, especially these past few days, as surely noted by Susanna—

He halted in the center of the room, drew his hand from his head, and closed his fingers into his palm as what he had not wished to examine determined to examine him.

If the lady had not previously guessed at the reason for his bare scalp, he was certain she did now. But almost more disturbing than her possession of knowledge none other possessed was that she had reached out to him. Had he not looked up, would she have ventured nearer? Would she have touched him? And why? She could no longer be besotted with him as Judith had said she was all those years ago.

Everard shook his head, then crossed to the table against the far wall. There, he took up the keen blade he had not applied in over a week and scraped the bristles from his face, then his scalp.

15

I<small>F SHE DARED</small>...

Susanna tapped the parchment with the quill's dry, ink-darkened tip, slid her gaze down the days she had listed and alongside which she had made notations. Any of the seven days of the week would do, for Sir Rowan's comings and goings were fairly consistent—all within a half hour.

One hour before midnight, when she was believed to be well asleep, he departed and did not return for six hours, during which he surely sought his own rest. But those dark hours were the only time that no guard stood outside her door. Though Sir Rowan departed three times during the day, to eat and relieve himself, another kept watch. As told by the voice, that other was Squire Joseph.

"So...night," she murmured. "*If* I dare." And she longed to, for it was now eight days since Everard Wulfrith had come to her tower room with word of Cheverel's knights. In all that time, the only tidings she had of Judas were from Sir Rowan who was kind enough to inquire after him but had no firsthand knowledge of her nephew. All he could say was that he progressed well. But that was not enough, no matter how hard she tried to be content.

In the next instant, she heard boots on the stone steps outside her door. It did not fit the schedule, being much too late in the morning and not near enough the nooning hour for the delivery of a tray of viands. Nor was it approaching a time when Squire Joseph relieved Sir Rowan.

Heart making mischief beneath her ribs, Susanna set the quill alongside the stoppered ink pot, slid the inked parchment beneath the half dozen sheets with which she had been provided, and hastened to the chair set before the small table whose surface was covered by a large chess board. As she seated herself, a knock sounded.

"Enter!"

It was the lord of Wulfen who stepped inside and closed the door. However, he did not present as he had done those times he had previously come to her. His broad shoulders and muscular torso and legs were clothed in the finest garments—a white tunic embroidered around the neck with threads of silver and red, its sides pleated, its front slit from hem to just below the waist such that the dark red hose beneath were visible; a wide, heavily tooled baldric worn over the right shoulder and reaching down to the opposite hip where a sword was fastened; a studded belt draping his hips and upon which hung a sheathed dagger whose hilt was jeweled; lastly, cuffed leather boots.

Even in the absence of hair, Everard Wulfrith was most handsome.

"Do I meet with your approval, my lady?"

She swept her gaze to his, then sat back from the chess set that was to appear to have been her focus before his entrance. "Forgive me for staring. Not only did I not expect one who has not brought word of my nephew in over a sennight"—

Careful. It will do you no good to acquaint him with the depth of your frustration.

—"but I am awestruck by your finery."

"Ceremonial garb," he said dismissively, and strode forward.

Though curiosity bid her ask him to elaborate on the ceremony he had attended, or would be attending, Judas came first. Unable to offer him a seat across from her since Sir Rowan had taken his stool with him following their last game, she peered up at him from beneath the edge of her veil where he came to stand near the table. Noting his smooth scalp appeared to have recently met with a blade, she asked, "How is my nephew?"

His intense gaze lingered over her face, swept her bodice and lap, paused upon her hands that curled over the table's edge.

Now that she was the one scrutinized, she was more grateful for the basins of heated water that had been delivered to her on the day past so that she might wash her hair. She was also glad she wore her best bliaut that, with several of her other garments, had been returned to her this morn, freshly laundered—yet more kindness and consideration that, despite the answer thus far denied her, allowed her to say with some lightness, "Do I meet with *your* approval, my lord?"

His eyes settled upon hers. "You look much improved, my lady."

"I feel much improved."

"I am told you eat well."

Not only owing to the draught, but that the fare tasted less bland as she grew accustomed to it. "And I am told Judas makes good progress." She raised her eyebrows. "But whereas you have proof, I have none."

"Your nephew fares well." He shifted his regard to the chessboard. "As expected, Wulfen has been good for him. Though, also as expected, he presents a challenge."

She tensed. "Still your young men taunt him?"

Moving his gaze chess piece to chess piece, he said, "They do not. Though I am sure some are tempted, your nephew proved he is not of a mind to turn the other cheek."

No longer. "Then?"

Relinquishing his fascination with the game, he looked back at her. "I do not think it would surprise you to know he has a penchant for sneaking about. Three nights past, he was caught in the kitchen after all were bedded down—"

"That is not so bad. He was but hungry."

"Hungry or not, 'tis not permitted, and this he knew."

Deciding that, in this instance, it could not hurt to rouse sympathy for Judas, she said, "Neither was it permitted at Cheverel, but it was necessary."

"In what way?"

"It was not always fitting for him"—*or me*—"to eat at table with my brother."

Something like anger flickered in his eyes, but he said, "Of greater concern are Judas's attempts to steal abovestairs—to search you out."

Susanna felt a pain in her heart. Was Judas frightened? For himself? For her?

"As he is adept at stealth—a definite strength—twice he has made it abovestairs unchallenged. Unfortunately for him, he is not able to go missing for long before his absence is noted."

Oh, Judas mine, take heart. Surely some far away day we will laugh over this.

Though she knew it would sound like a feeble excuse, she said, "He has never been separated from me for more than a few hours. These nine days cannot have been easy for him."

As if she had not offered an explanation, he continued, "And then there are the lies he is quick to tell to avoid punishment."

She swallowed. "What kind of punishment?"

Everard Wulfrith's brow lined. "Appropriate punishment, I assure you. Running laps around the training field, longer service at table, mucking out stables, hauling bathwater."

She contained a sigh of relief. "I thank you for your forbearance, Lord Wulfrith. All I can offer by way of explanation is that Judas does what he must to survive."

"He does not have to do those things at Wulfen."

"I am sure you are right, but he does not know that."

"Then he must learn. Or perhaps it would be better said he must *unlearn* what you taught him. They are your lessons, are they not?"

Shame crept over her. She lowered her gaze, with it her chin, only then realized how sore in the neck she was from peering up at him. "I can only say it seemed right at the time"—she feigned interest in the chess pieces—"and that my...lessons served Judas well even if they no longer do." She looked up. "You did say stealth is a strength of his?"

A corner of Everard Wulfrith's mouth lifted, and she was heartened by the waning of his censure. "I have never seen one so young take down game at such close range. Indeed, many well-seasoned knights are incapable of moving as quietly and holding still as long."

Then all those years of walking lightly around Alan, noiselessly slipping in and out of spaces occupied by him and his men was good for something other than keeping unearned punishment at bay.

"Too, your nephew is very fast on his feet."

Once again, she tipped her head back. "When last we spoke, you were disappointed with his speed—said that he was one of the last to come in from the morning runs."

"Surprisingly, he has quickly learned to pace himself. These last three days, he has made the training field not far behind the most experienced and fit squires."

And, it seemed, with none the wiser that he had ever suffered from breathing attacks.

Judas will be fine. Better than fine.

Feeling tears, she looked again to the chess board. "I am glad you bring me good news with the bad, Lord Wulfrith."

"The bad is tolerably bad, Lady Susanna. Your nephew but requires clear expectations, respect for authority, and firm guidance."

"I thank you for all you do for him." Throat tightening further, she determined it best to change the subject. "Just as I thank you for making the passing of days more endurable by providing me with the means by which to while them away."

Everard Wulfrith was slow to answer, as if not ready to move from talk of Judas, but he said, "'Twould appear you make good use of ink and parchment."

She glanced at him, followed his gaze to her right hand upon the table's edge. Her thumb and first two fingers were stained with ink—that which had been used to plot Sir Rowan's absences from outside her door. Heart bumping against her ribs, she said, "I fear I am not as careful as I should be."

"I have much the same result when I write in haste. What words do you pen, my lady?"

Bump. Bump.

"Thoughts, ideas." She shrugged.

"No poetry?"

Had she laughed, the sound would have been bitter. "Surely you know I am no longer as fanciful as once I was." When she had thought herself a woman though others thought her still a girl, when she had first awakened to the feelings of a hopeful heart, when many were the words she had penned in imitation of those sung by troubadours.

"So you are not," he said with what sounded almost like regret, then he returned his attention to the chessboard. "This game you play against yourself?"

"Aye." *The light and dark sides of me.* "Though Sir Rowan is kind enough to challenge me from time to time."

"Then I must needs have another chair delivered to your chamber."

Susanna felt a flutter of happiness, not only because the older knight would be more comfortable when he joined her, but Everard Wulfrith had once more gifted her with kindness. "I thank you in advance," she said.

He nodded, stepped to the table's edge, and reached. "May I?"

"Do, for that side of me cannot find a way to protect my king without sacrificing my queen."

He replaced one piece with another and set the dark, defeated piece alongside the board. "And so your queen is saved. Pawn takes knight."

Susanna leaned forward. It was true, her white king was no longer in jeopardy of being parted from his queen. "I did not see that."

"Seemingly insignificant pieces"—he tapped the triumphant pawn— "often wield great power by their ability to be easily overlooked."

"'Tis unfortunate that is not true off a chess board," she mused, "that it could be so in life." As she sat back, the light coming in through the window happened upon the dagger on Everard Wulfrith's belt, drawing her eye to the sparkling, jeweled hilt.

"But it is so in life," he said, "as you have proved in taking control of the game by moving three pieces out of reach of Cheverel—Judas, yourself, and Sir Elias."

It was a kind thing to say and worth pondering, but before Susanna could think further on it, she noted an absence of sparkle upon the dagger's hilt where there should be much. The empty socket was the right size, and the alternating pattern told that the missing gem was likely a ruby.

She lifted a hand to her bodice and gripped the pendant through it.

"My lady?"

She met Everard Wulfrith's gaze. "Forgive me, but did you know a gem is missing from your dagger?"

He jerked, though the movement was so slight that had she not been watching for a reaction, she would have missed it. The easy lines of his face tightening, he drew back from the table. "I have stayed too long and neglected my real purpose for seeking you out," he said.

Wishing she had not spoken of the missing gem, dreading what his real purpose was, she asked, "Which is?"

"This morn, Squire Joseph and Squire Niall completed their night vigil in the chapel. Thus, the great privilege of knighthood is to be conferred upon them. I thought you might like to watch."

She startled. "But women are not allowed—"

"Out of sight of our young men. If you are interested, I shall have Sir Rowan escort you to the rooftop to observe the final part of the ceremony that, at Wulfen Castle, is held before the donjon steps."

She nodded with more enthusiasm than she had felt in...She did not know how long. "I would very much like that." To stand beneath the heavens. To see land and sky on all sides of her. Above all, to see Judas, even if only from a distance. "I thank you."

"I shall tell Sir Rowan." He turned on his heel.

"Lord Wulfrith?"

He looked over his shoulder, and there was something like wariness in his eyes, as if he thought she might further inquire after the missing gem.

"Have you had word from the queen?" she asked.

"It is too soon for that."

True, for though it seemed months, hardly a fortnight had passed. "Then we know naught of my brother's widow's request for an audience with Queen Eleanor."

"We may soon, for after the newly knighted Sir Niall departs Wulfen and before he begins his year of service in the household of his new lord, he will pause at Cheverel and beg a night's lodging. I anticipate that, within a sennight, we will have word of the state of the De Balliol demesne."

Nearly overwhelmed by the lengths to which Everard Wulfrith was willing to go for Judas, Susanna silently thanked the Lord for his intervention, then said, "I am glad we came to Wulfen."

"And I am glad you have given Sir Rowan no grief."

In short, that she had caused no further trouble since being exiled to the tower room. That she had not yet done what she longed to do—and could do now that she was certain of the hours when no one stood guard over her.

Realizing he awaited a response, she cleared her throat. "You thought I would?"

"I know not what to think of you, Susanna de Balliol. I know only that there is a woman within my walls who should not be here and hope you do not make me regret it any more than already I have." He dipped his head. "Good day."

The door closed behind him, then came the murmur of voices, followed by descending footsteps.

Though Susanna rarely spent prayers upon herself, holding them in reserve for Judas, she dropped her head back and whispered, "Lord, help me be content to remain here in this room that I might not give Everard Wulfrith more cause to regret my presence. Give me peace over Judas, alongside strength. Amen."

She reached to her neck, caught hold of the chain, and pulled the pendant from her bodice. The small, egg-shaped cage was formed from tightly woven silver wire, though not so tight that the scent of crushed rose petals could not be perceived.

"I know whence you came," she whispered. "I know where you belong."

Near the base of the stairs and out of sight of Sir Rowan, Everard paused in the dim light and ran his mind's eye over what had transpired in the tower room. Though deeply unsettled when Lady Susanna had noted the absence of what had not graced his dagger's hilt for eleven years, in truth, he had been unsettled before then. And he did not understand the reason.

He felt no attraction for her—could not possibly—and yet something about her had moved something within him. Just as strange, the movement had not been unfamiliar. It was as if felt before, though certainly he had never acknowledged it.

As he had looked upon her, almost lovely in her crisp gown, veil falling about a face softly framed by tresses that shone as if having been combed and combed again, he had not seen the girl he had known but the woman who did not wish herself to be known. Though still she could not be said to look well, the gaunt edges of her face had softened, there had been an occasional glimmer in her eyes, and lips whose natural state seemed to be compressed, had begun to curve. Thus, it was not only interest in the chess game that had often caused him to look away from her. It was this…

What, Everard Wulfrith?

He did not know. All he was certain of was that it should not be and it distracted him from more important things.

Hearing his teeth grind, he shifted his jaw to ease its ache. Then he retrieved the torch he had earlier set in a wall sconce, bent, and worked the catch. With a soft click, the hidden door swung inward.

He stepped onto the narrow stairway built into the donjon's walls, reseated the door, and began his descent.

This day, two more worthy young men would go forth to defend family, people, lands, and country. *That* was what his thoughts were best spent upon, not the missing gem, and certainly not Lady Susanna.

16

It was a peculiar feeling—as if, in crossing the threshold for the first time since Everard Wulfrith had carried her over it, she ought to stretch her arms and legs like one released from a space so cramped that the only fit for it was to hug knees to chest. Silly, really, but she was tempted.

"The roof access is this way," Sir Rowan said and turned to the left.

With his back to her, Susanna considered the stone steps to the right. However, there was not much to appraise, for the single torch in its wall sconce did a poor job of casting out shadows. Still, there was comfort in knowing that somewhere below those stairs lay the great hall, and somewhere in the midst of that, Judas could be found during mealtimes and at night when he made his bed there.

"My lady?"

She lifted her skirts and hurried forward. However, she did not have far to go, for it was not much of a corridor. Halting alongside Sir Rowan, she peered up the ladder fastened to the wall that ascended to a square door in the ceiling.

"I will have to trust you are capable of negotiating it unaided," he said, "since it would not be fitting for me to climb up after you. Too, the door is of a good weight."

She nodded. "I require no assistance."

He stepped forward and, with the creaking of aged bones, scaled the ladder. Several rungs from the top, he worked the bolt free and raised the door whose hinges made little protest as it was laid back upon the roof.

From out of a wispy blue sky, daylight streamed into the corridor and settled warmly over Susanna.

Sir Rowan, having completed his ascent to the roof, knelt beside the opening. "Keep your skirts clear, my lady."

She hitched them up, tucked the hem into her girdle to prevent the material from catching beneath her feet, and climbed to where the knight gripped her arm and assisted her the remainder of the way.

Once her feet were firm upon the roof and her hem lowered, Susanna was tempted to whirl about. It felt almost forever since she had been out of doors, and to be so on such a beautiful day...

Savoring the view that could not possibly be better from anywhere else—the castle's beautiful stone walls, the land before it, the wood beyond, and all that sky—she said, "Oh, I have missed this." She breathed deep. "I do not know how it can be, but the air here is not the same as that which comes through my window."

Sir Rowan chuckled. "Come, my lady."

She did not begrudge his hand upon her arm that guided her across the great expanse of roof, the corners of which were all fit with doors like the one Sir Rowan and she had come through—just off center of the tower rooms below.

He drew her between two battlements and said low, "The ceremony has begun."

Leaning into the embrasure alongside him, Susanna gasped at the sight. Though the center of the wide donjon steps was clear, both sides were lined with Wulfen's knights-in-training, all crisply garbed. As told by their size, the squires occupied the right-hand side, the pages the left, though there was one among the latter whose height was better suited to the right.

"Judas," Susanna breathed, "he is there."

"And, as told, well," Sir Rowan murmured.

She could not confirm that from this distance, but she had to believe it was so.

"My lord," a voice rose amid the silence, "I present Squire Joseph Marveaux, most worthy candidate for knighthood."

Loath to abandon her nephew, though she had but the top and back of his head to look upon, Susanna slid her gaze to the dark-haired knight who stood upon the lowermost step on one side of the blond-headed squire, then to a red-headed knight on the other side. The former held a sword, the latter a shield.

"Come forth, Squire Joseph," a familiar, resonant voice drew her regard to where the lord of Wulfen and two older men stood on a dais erected before the steps. Everard Wulfrith's figure and face she could well enough see, and as when he had come before her in the tower room, she was struck by his presence.

"Do you know the symbolism, my lady?" Sir Rowan asked as Squire Joseph approached the dais, followed by the two knights.

"I have never witnessed a knighting ceremony, so I know not."

"The white vesture worn by Squire Joseph symbolizes purity, the red robe his nobility as well as readiness to be wounded in defense of Church, country, lord, women, children, the poor…"

Susanna smiled. "All that?"

"And more, such as old men like me." He jutted his chin at the scene below. "Now the sword and shield, both having been blessed by the priest, will be passed to the lord of Wulfen."

And so they were once all three ascended the dais.

"Who are the men on either side of Lord Wulfrith?" Susanna whispered.

"The squires' fathers, for it is rare that one's sire does not attend Wulfen's knighting ceremony, even if 'tis a second or third son. It is this moment, you see, their minds have bent toward since first they held their infant sons."

Sorrow swept Susanna, and she looked again at Judas. It would never be so for him. Had Alan lived, even had he secured a place for his son in another lord's household for training, she did not believe he would have appeared for the momentous occasion. Indeed, following the birth of his second son, knighthood would not likely have figured into Judas's life, for her brother might well have committed his first-born to the Church so that he would never again lay eyes upon him.

"Both have traveled a great distance to be here," Sir Rowan continued, "though others have traveled farther yet—a few from France."

"France?" Susanna frowned. "Is not Wulfen exclusive to training up warriors to defend England?"

"Mostly, but as our king has vast lands on the continent that must needs be defended—Normandy, Aquitaine, Gascony—exceptions are made." He returned his gaze to the scene below where Squire Joseph had lowered to his knees before the lord of Wulfen. "Now the Oath of Knighthood, the breaking of which is seen as a crime against God that can lead to eternal damnation."

The words of Everard Wulfrith and Squire Joseph that resounded around the bailey were comprised of all manner of promises to be kept as the knight ventured through life, including devotion to the Church, loyalty to one's lord, defending those unable to defend themselves, conducting one's self honorably, and being charitable.

At last, the oath was spoken and a reverent silence descended that Susanna expected was set aside as a time for prayer—until shattered by the crack of a hand upon Squire Joseph's cheek.

She gasped, jerked back from the embrasure.

"Forgive me, my lady." Sir Rowan caught hold of her arm and steadied her. "I should have warned you of what was to come."

Vaguely aware more words were being spoken below, Susanna said, "You knew Lord Wulfrith would do that? For what? Has he determined Squire Joseph is unworthy to be knighted?"

"Quite the opposite. He is worthy beyond most of those knighted throughout England."

She shook her head. "I do not understand."

"The slap represents the crossing of the threshold between boy and man. Though some who conduct the ceremony merely tap the squire upon the shoulder with the flat of a sword, Lord Wulfrith stays true to tradition which is believed to be the best means to impress upon one who is newly knighted the seriousness of his vows."

It was hard to believe, and yet she knew Sir Rowan would not lie.

"Take heart, my lady, Squire Joseph and Squire Niall, and all those who came before and will follow after, anticipate the dubbing with great longing. Indeed, it is hoped the blow will be sufficiently hard enough to cause swelling and a bruise that proclaims to all the young man's newly attained status."

"It seems barbaric."

Sir Rowan shrugged. "'Tis the way of warriors."

Susanna leaned into the embrasure again and saw that Squire Joseph—now Sir Joseph—had gained his feet and was being fitted with sword, shield, and spurs. When the two attending knights stepped back, Everard Wulfrith extended something.

"The Wulfrith dagger," Sir Rowan said, "given to those worthy enough to be knighted here."

And jeweled, Susanna saw when Sir Joseph turned and held the weapon aloft, inviting sunlight to play among the facets adorning the hilt.

"By many, as highly esteemed as their sword," said the knight as a cheer rose from the gathering.

Susanna did not have to look near upon it to know that the dagger seen to be missing a gem this day was also a Wulfrith dagger—held in such high regard, and yet for love of Judith, it had been despoiled.

Emotion surging through her, she swallowed convulsively.

The remainder of the ceremony, during which Squire Niall was knighted in the same manner, complete with the resounding slap, passed by in something of a blur. Then, with much revelry, the knights, squires, and pages converged upon the new knights.

Eager for a better view of her nephew, Susanna did not move from the embrasure, and Sir Rowan did not ask her to, as if he understood her need to make this indulgence last as long as possible.

Judas moved to the outskirts of the gathering—alone—but her sorrow over his solitude receded when he turned to watch the others and she saw his face. He appeared alert and interested, and she thought there might even be a curve to his mouth. Too, though his bearing was erect, it was not so stiff as to appear ill at ease.

Everard Wulfrith had said Wulfen had been good for her nephew, and though this was not much proof, it settled her some.

"He looks well," she murmured.

"He is."

Susanna sighed. "I suppose now I must return to my chamber."

"Soon. There is one more thing you must needs see."

Curious, she swept her gaze over the gathering, and her eyes quickly picked Everard Wulfrith from the press of bodies. As she watched, he made his way through the throng and, shortly, gained her nephew's side.

"There," Sir Rowan murmured, just as Everard Wulfrith raised his gaze up the donjon and settled it on Susanna.

So unexpected was his acknowledgement that she nearly jumped back, as if for fear of having been seen though he had said she might watch.

Next, he bent his head near Judas, and she tensed lest her nephew once more received correction for one of the challenges he presented. However, there seemed nothing morose about the boy's face when he lifted it, and even across the distance she could see how wide his eyes were when they found her between the battlements. Then he smiled.

She caught her breath, for it was no forced smile, no tolerant smile, no bitter smile. It came much too fast and bright to be mistaken for anything other than genuine, and she wondered when last she had seen him wear such an expression. Too, even from here she could see that the dark smudges beneath his eyes had lessened considerably.

Thank you, Lord!

Heart wonderfully full, she smiled back and raised a hand.

Discreetly, Judas returned the gesture, keeping his arm at his side and bending his hand from the wrist.

"'Tis time you return to your chamber," Sir Rowan said.

She looked at him where he had stepped back from between the battlements—and realized this was the thing he had said she needed to see. What he had not said and might not even realize, was that Judas needed it as well, even if only to keep him from seeking her abovestairs.

In that moment, had Everard Wulfrith been near, Susanna was not sure she could have contained her gratitude and resisted flinging her arms around him. And for that, it was good he was well out of reach.

Hoping to show her appreciation with another smile, she looked back at him, but his gaze did not await hers. Neither did his figure, for he strode toward the donjon steps.

Wishing his withdrawal did not feel like loss, Susanna once more looked upon Judas. His smile yet present, he inclined his head before following the others who took their cue from their lord.

"Now they feast," Sir Rowan said.

Susanna watched until her nephew went from sight, then turned away. "I am much heartened, Sir Rowan, as, I am sure, my nephew is. When next you see Lord Wulfrith, would you tell him I am grateful for what he has done?"

"I shall, my lady." He started back across the roof and, as she followed, she focused her senses so that, for however many days of confinement lay ahead of her, she would be sustained by these memories.

Too soon, she found herself back in her tower room. In possession of a promise from Sir Rowan that he would join her for a game of chess this eve, she watched the door close behind him, then crossed to where her sheets of parchment were stacked upon the side table. She nearly retrieved the one that listed Sir Rowan's comings and goings. However, it required no further mulling. She had gained what she sought—a glimpse of Judas and assurance he was well. Everard Wulfrith had given her that and, hopefully, would again. Thus, she would honor his wish that she remain abovestairs.

Her next thought made her press her teeth into her lower lip. The roof *was* abovestairs. And who would be any the wiser if, in the middling of night, she ventured there to take in the star-dotted sky? Providing, of course, she could work the bolt upon which Sir Rowan had expended some effort and the door did not prove too ponderous to set back without sending it crashing down and alerting those who patrolled the walls. Still, the possibility of discovery twisted her stomach. After all Everard Wulfrith had done for Judas and her...

Remembering when he had stood over her and the chess board, she closed her eyes and saw him in his fine tunic, hose, and boots, saw him looking as near upon her as she had looked upon him, saw him go from almost amiable to tightly guarded at mention of the missing gem, saw him peer up at her from the inner bailey and direct Judas's attention toward her. And knew what it would be better not to know.

Once more, like the foolish girl I vowed to never again be, I am besotted.

"Nay." She shook her head, turned a hand around the pendant. "I am not." She but ached for Judith's loss of so great a love, that her friend's decision to comply with her family's wishes had denied her knowledge of how deeply she was loved in return, that the heart which had too soon stopped beating had surely been broken.

"If one could live without a heart," she whispered, "better it torn from the breast ere ever it knew love. If not that...Aye, if not that—"

She gave a sharp laugh. It sounded like poetry, though far removed from the hopeful, fawning words she had once penned. These words, so lacking the possibility of redemption, ached.

Still, she was tempted to set them down in ink—for Judith's sake, she told herself, certain the feelings that assailed her were but a reflection of what her friend must have experienced over the loss of Everard Wulfrith.

As she stared at the parchment, she struggled to ignore the longing to fill the hours with the scratch of a quill and a trail of curvaceous ink. She could not.

Thus, perched on the edge of the mattress, writing instruments set out on the bedside table, she began to write. And though the feelings she sought to express in words were slow to be painted upon parchment, when she closed her lids with the lowering of the sun, the ink told a story—one she persuaded herself belonged to another.

17

Cheverel, England
June, 1160

TALBOT DID NOT like being under the thumb of a woman. But then, what man did, other than those with mush for spines? Unfortunately, his association with Lady Richenda had become more necessary with each passing day since he had first betrayed his lord a year ago. Indeed, there were times his spine felt so limp that he wondered how he remained upright. Never before had he felt less like a man. The only consolation, if there was any, was that even his lord had been wary of her. Were there a way to go back, to drag himself out from beneath her clawed thumb, he would. But it was too late. If she was to be believed, he had much to lose.

She spun around, not unlike a child's top, he thought, her middle extending well beyond the width of her upper and lower body. She even wobbled a bit before finding her center. If not for the reason he had asked to speak to her abovestairs, he might not have been able to suppress his secret amusement. He might have laughed.

Lowering the hands she clasped against her mouth, she wrinkled her heavy brow and said, "And only now you think of this, after the wretch has availed himself of a meal and a night's lodging at my expense?"

Her expense. His gorge convulsed. "As told, it was the Wulfrith dagger—that which is awarded to those knighted at Wulfen—that fit it together."

And might never have fit had he not downed so much ale on the night past. Faced with the choice of stumbling up what had seemed hundreds of steps to his chamber and sleeping in the chair before the hearth, he had chosen the latter. Thus, when Sir Niall had been the first to rise from his pallet in the hall shortly after dawn and had gathered his belongings for departure, Talbot had silently watched—not out of interest, but a means of delaying when he, himself, must rise and test the weight of his aching head.

It was then he had seen what was in the young man's pack, though its appearance was brief as it was displaced to make room for the thin blanket that had warmed Sir Niall throughout the night. There was no mistaking the Wulfrith dagger, for it was a thing of such beauty, worth, and significance, that those who possessed one proudly displayed it— most certainly in the company of other nobles. And yet, at Cheverel, it had been kept out of sight.

The suspicion roused by that had thrown a line backward in time that Talbot had set his hands to and followed to Wulfen Castle where Lord Wulfrith, the giver of such daggers, had denied all knowledge of those whom Talbot and his men had pursued. Sprawling in the chair, gaze narrowed upon Sir Niall, Talbot had followed the line farther back to when Alan de Balliol had travelled to the home of his betrothed, Lady Judith, previous to their marriage. It was there that Talbot had first laid eyes upon a Wulfrith dagger.

The annoyingly childish patter of Lady Richenda's feet alerting him to her approach, he returned her to focus a moment ahead of the appearance of her snapping fingers beneath his nose.

"Where are you, Sir Talbot?" she demanded.

He nearly stopped himself from speaking the truth, but the effort would only increase the pounding in his head. "Unfortunately, I am here with you, *my lady*."

She startled, but her surprise quickly rearranged itself into flared nostrils and bared teeth. "Careful, Sir Knight. I make a much better ally than an enemy."

And he had danced at the end of her puppet strings long enough to know that to be true. "That you do."

She regarded him long, then shook her shoulders out. "I ask again, how is it possible that one who has long enjoyed the privilege of being head of Cheverel's household knights, only now recognizes this Everard Wulfrith as the same one who was in service to Lady Judith's father?"

He drew a deep breath that made the backs of his eyes ache. "As told, I did not know his name eleven years past, only that he was a Wulfen-trained knight. On the few occasions I was in his presence, he remained at a distance, the most notable thing about him the dagger upon his belt. Too, whereas he is bald today, then he had much hair."

She snorted. "Still, it does not speak well of you."

He was glad he had not mentioned that, as he had looked down upon the lord of Wulfen from atop his mount, the man's decidedly unfamiliar face had, for a brief moment, not been as decided as thought. Something had niggled at him, and then no more. Until this morn.

"Well, at least you are not entirely inept." Lady Richenda turned and pattered across the floor rushes. "Better now than not at all."

As he entertained all manner of dark imaginings about a fitting end for the woman, she paced, steepled her hands, and tapped her fingers together. "I think you are right," she finally spoke. "Even if the lord of Wulfen is not the one who cuckolded my son-in-law, though I am inclined to believe Judas was fathered by that vile, ungodly miscreant"—

And here Talbot stood, making her contempt toward Everard Wulfrith truly laughable.

—"the fact that he knew Lady Judith and Lady Susanna...that Susanna and Judas were last seen near Wulfen..." She nodded. "...that this young knight pauses at Cheverel and conceals that he earned his spurs at Wulfen, surely to spy upon us..." She grunted. "I am of a mind to have you *detain* this Sir Niall."

"I would advise against it, my lady. As he but shared a meal and stretched out upon a pallet for the night, there is naught of consequence for him to report to Lord Wulfrith."

"Ha! So says one who is so in love with his ale he had to sleep below-stairs among the rabble last eve."

He loathed that it should be true, but still he did not think Sir Niall had gained anything of value, especially since there was little of value to be had. They awaited the queen's summons, and that was the end of it.

Lady Richenda made a face. "Aye, 'tis probably best to let the knight go so they continue to believe we are oblivious, rather than alert them to our intent."

Talbot stiffened. "What intent is that, my lady?"

She raised her eyebrows. "Now that we know where to find Judas and that wretched aunt of his, what intent could there be but to gain entrance to Wulfen Castle?"

He did not know why he should be surprised that she reached so high, for in doing so, it was not her blood that would spill. "Lady Richenda, one does not easily—if at all—gain entrance to Wulfen. More, one does not cross the Wulfriths. If it is true Lady Susanna and the boy are under their protection, time is best spent putting your efforts into preparing for Queen Eleanor's summons to prove your grandson is Cheverel's true heir."

That pattering again, and she once more stood before him. "I am not in the habit, nor will I ever be, of allowing others to decide my fate, Sir Talbot."

Her fate. Always *her*. What about Lady Blanche and her babe?

"At least, not whilst I have arrows in my quiver. And since it now has arrows aplenty, I see no reason the queen should be bothered over this matter." She poked his chest. "You know where the boy is. And this time, you will not let him slip away."

Was there no reasoning with her?

She poked again—hard—and he whipped his hand up and turned it around hers. "'Tis a dangerous game you play, my lady."

She lifted her chin higher. "*We* play, Sir Talbot. That is, if you wish your son to be lord of Cheverel."

This was her favorite string to jerk, reminding him of his betrayal on a night much like the night past when Talbot had left loyalty and good sense at the bottom of a tankard. That night, Alan de Balliol had brimmed with anger that, as usual, his sister and son had not been spared—nor his wife—and so, goblets and tankards had also brimmed. And Talbot, in seeking to find a place to sleep off all he had imbibed, had happened upon Lady Blanche who had been in need of a shoulder to weep upon.

The sight, smell, and touch of her mother making him want to retch, he thrust her hand away and turned his back on her. "You say he is mine, but I do not know that, just as you can not."

She laughed. "You think my son-in-law capable of fathering a child? How many times did he wed? Four! How many children did he produce? None, for even he did not believe it possible—consider Judas, hmm? Thus, how likely was it that, after you gave in to temptation with his wife, he finally got a child on her?"

Lord, I wish he were not mine, for he will make a murderer of me.

"You know the answer, Sir Talbot. And no matter the danger, you will play the game, for a good father always does right by his child."

Her feet sounded across the floor, the door opened, and she said, "We are finished."

He pivoted and strode forward. As he passed her squat figure, she said, "If it pains you to do it yourself, send another. It matters only that it be done."

18

Wulfen Castle, England
June, 1160

THE BOY WAS good, and yet it seemed he held back—that he chose to go only so far with his training at arms, which hardly fit one who had a difficult time containing his pride at coming in ahead of his peers during morning runs.

Here, upon the training field, Judas ventured near the edge of his effort and ability, but never close enough to excel. It was as if he so feared going over the side that he would not test how wide and firm that edge was. In battle, such caution might be warranted, but not at Wulfen, for here his life did not hang by a frayed rope, and if blood was shed, as did happen during training, it would not be mortal.

Judas de Balliol required another lesson, this one more easily demonstrated than recounted.

Though Everard mostly left the pages' training at arms to the knights to whom each was assigned and their attendant squires, he jumped the fence and shouted, "Cease!"

Immediately, the squire who had backed the boy up against the fence jumped aside, turned his quarterstaff, and thumped its end to the ground. "My lord." He snapped his chin in deference.

Judas was slower to react, but after watching Everard's advance, he pushed off the fence and lowered the iron-tipped end of the pole that stood more than a foot taller than he. "My lord." He inclined his head.

Everard halted before him, glanced at the half dozen pages who sat the fence awaiting their turn with the squire. "You must push yourself harder, Judas."

Face flushed and beaded with exertion, the boy frowned. "I do my best, my lord."

"I do not think you do. I believe there is more within you that could better defend your position and change your side of the fight from defense to offense."

Everard saw resentment flicker in Judas's eyes, though it was not of the strength it had been previous to the knighting ceremony five days past. "As told, my lord," he said, "I do my best."

"Then I shall show you how to do better."

What next came and went in Judas's eyes looked more like fear, but Everard had no intention of humiliating him with assurances he would come to no harm. "Squire!" he said and held out a hand to Judas's opponent.

The young man crossed his lord's palm with his quarterstaff.

Everard closed his fingers around the pole, beckoned with it. "Come."

Judas followed him to the center of the field where Everard turned to face him. Not surprisingly, many of the others in the separate fenced areas paused to take note of what their lord intended with one who was not yet a squire.

"Attend to your own training!" Everard bellowed before returning his attention to Judas. "Assume the proper stance, Page."

For a moment, he thought the boy would refuse, but he slowly turned his body so that his forward hand and forward foot faced his opponent, then set his feet the proper distance apart and readied his weapon.

"Begin!" Everard lunged.

Judas fended off the first blow, the next, and just barely the one after that, the result of which was that he lost a good measure of ground as he was driven back toward the fence.

"Press forward," Everard demanded. "Put your weight behind it."

Judas complied and countered a downward blow by raising his quarterstaff horizontally overhead—the perfect defense, as told by the crack of wood upon wood that resounded around the field.

"Swing harder!" Everard demanded.

He swung harder.

"More swiftly!"

Teeth bared, spit flying, the boy slammed his pole against Everard's. And again, and again as they moved left and right, forward and backward across the field beneath the gape-mouthed regard of the pages upon the fence rails.

"Watch my eyes, the lean of my body, my feet. Anticipate!"

Breathing hard, Judas slid his foremost hand lower and narrowly missed forfeiting the flesh of his knuckles.

Then, once again, Everard drove him back. One step...two...three...

"Give me more, Judas!"

The boy's eyes widened, shoulders rose and fell heavily, but though he continued to deflect the blows, all was defense now. Unless he could be roused to test that edge, he would once more find himself against the fence.

"Imagine I am trying to kill you," Everard growled as he feigned a hit to Judas's face. "Imagine your next blow is all that shall keep me from succeeding—but one misstep and your life's blood is spilt, your last breath drawn."

Judas did not have to imagine it, for his throat was closing up, lungs beginning to strain, those terrible, degrading sounds sliding over his tongue and past his teeth.

Not here. Pray, not here. Not before all!

"Halt!" another shouted.

Sir Elias? Was that him? He would know what to do. He knew…
what…how…

Judas felt a grip on his upper arms, felt himself being lowered to
the ground, realized he had lost the quarterstaff when his splayed, slick
palms tasted the air denied his lungs.

Dear God, I need breath! Just one. Down deep.

"…a breathing attack," Sir Elias's voice drifted to him as Judas began
to strain and jerk.

Then came Lord Wulfrith's voice amid the murmuring all around.
Harsh. Angry. So near it was possible he was the one supporting Judas.
But then, he had been the closest, the one ordering his pupil to give
more.

I should not have. I knew I should not have.

Everard choked down his anger and turned his attention to getting
the first breath back into the boy—that which seemed always the hardest
to come by. Having settled Judas against his chest, he said as calmly as
possible, "Ease yourself. Hear me? Ease yourself as best you can, Judas."

The boy's lids fluttered, eyes shifted side to side.

Everard laid the flat of a hand just beneath Judas's ribs. "Breathe in
here—through your nose, if you can. Hmm?"

Blessedly, there came the wheezing sound of air being forced past
the constriction.

"That's it," Sir Elias said where he had lowered to his haunches beside
Everard. "Hold it. Now slowly out."

It was some minutes before Judas breathed normally again, and
though the others upon the training field feigned disinterest, Everard
knew nothing had escaped them.

He relinquished Judas into Sir Elias's care with the order to see him
abed for the remainder of the day, but as he turned away, Judas said low,
"I am sorry, Lord Wulfrith."

Everard looked over his shoulder.

Eyes moist in his pale face, the boy said, "I did not want you—
anyone—to see that."

Everard raised his eyebrows. "Mayhap they would not have had I been informed you suffered such an affliction."

"I thought I had it under control."

Likely he had, but then he had been ordered to give more and pushed himself to a place he had surely known he should not go. Everard frowned. "The morning of your first run, you suffered the same?"

Color feathered his cheeks. "Nearly, but I knew to stop."

The reason he had been so far ahead only to come in so far behind. "Lesson six, Judas de Balliol—once you know the true reach of your ability, let no man push you past it."

"Aye, my lord."

"Lesson seven, let pride not be so powerful as to be the death of you."

Judas nodded.

"Sir Elias"—Everard captured the knight's gaze—"you and I will speak more on this later." As would Lady Susanna and he, though he kept that to himself knowing the threat would not sit well with Judas and liking too much that, since seeing his aunt upon the roof, the boy had not tried again to steal abovestairs.

"Aye, my lord," Sir Elias said, and he and Judas started across the training field.

Everard dragged a hand down his face and released the breath he had thrust deep. Though he longed to go directly to the donjon and confront Lady Susanna about what she had withheld, he determined it was best to return the training field to a semblance of normalcy. After ordering the squire who had engaged Judas at quarterstaffs to resume his work with the pages, he went to stand against the fence to the right of the boys who perched upon it.

However, it was not their facility at arms that occupied his thoughts. It was Judas's affliction. The boy was not the first Wulfen knight-in-training to suffer such fits of breathing. There had been another, one whose training had been a year behind Everard's. Though Merrick's fits had been rare, enough had been witnessed over the years so that those of Wulfen had learned how best to aid him when he could not control them himself. And now he was dead these past seven years, though not from loss of breath. The murder of another had been his downfall, though the circumstances and the sacrifice of his own life to save the sister of his victim—the same who had wed Everard's brother, Garr—had been his redemption.

Everard tried again to focus his attention on the page who struggled to fend off the squire's blows, but what had happened here would not let him be. Nor his guilt. Though he told himself it was misplaced, his actions had caused Judas to be taken with a fit, one that had revealed the boy's secret shame to all. And could have meant his death.

Ah, Susanna, what else do you hide from me that would be better known?

"I only ever tell tales of great men to those of Wulfen, but there is one of a woman who was not much more than a girl when my story commences. You would like to hear it?"

Susanna smiled, leaned toward the knight who occupied the chair on the other side of what remained of their chess game that had ended in her victory—with much consideration from her opponent. "Most ardently, Sir Rowan."

So began the tale of a girl whose brother, a squire destined for knighthood, was murdered. And as Sir Rowan spoke of the events of the day when the young man was returned home and his cold body laid out upon a table, there seemed genuine sorrow in his telling and he cleared his throat several times.

"And then Lady Annyn discovered the rope burns around her brother's neck and knew his death to be no accident as told by the great lord whom the young man had served. Thus, she determined that one day she would have her revenge upon this lord whom she believed was responsible for her brother's death."

"Was he?" Susanna asked.

Sir Rowan frowned at her. "You wish me to spoil the tale, Lass?"

Lass…She caught her breath at being so fondly named as she had not been since before her father's passing.

"Eh?" the knight pressed.

She shook her head and he continued, telling how the young woman trained for years in hopes of exacting her revenge and, when she was ready, cut her beautiful hair and donned the clothes of a squire in order to gain entrance to the great lord's castle—a fortress forbidden to women.

Susanna gasped. "Wulfen Castle?"

He raised his eyebrows. "However, this lady in boy's disguise soon discovered its lord was not the beast she had believed him to be. Thus, when given the opportunity to slay him, she could not. While the one who had taught her weaponry and stealth waited for weeks in the wood for her to bring word that vengeance was had, she was unveiled and taken captive. And that one in the wood—we shall call him Sir Knight— sought to free her by sending an arrow through the great lord who held her. But, alas, Sir Knight was captured as well and, with the lady, borne to another castle where they were imprisoned in a cell while the great lord recovered from his wound."

Feeling the hard edge of her seat where she had scooted nearer the knight, embarrassed that she should behave so like a child, Susanna shifted backward. "Go on, Sir Rowan."

He told that the lord's mother had taken pity on the young woman and provided her with a chamber in the castle while Sir Knight was left behind and soon took ill.

"By Lady Annyn's charms and devices, she persuaded the great lord to show Sir Knight grace and he sent his physician to tend her man. While Sir Knight recovered, Lady Annyn and this great lord grew in affection toward one another and the lady determined he was too honorable to bear responsibility for her brother's death—that it must be another. And so, defying Duke Henry—"

"Ere he was king," Susanna said.

Sir Rowan inclined his head. "Defying Duke Henry who had ordered Lady Annyn to wed the most loathsome man in all of England, the great lord wed her himself."

"Oh! Do troubadours sing of this? Know they the tale?"

A smile rose to the knight's mouth. "If they knew it, they would sing of it, my lady, but discretion was exercised, for what king in waiting—and so powerful one as Henry—would wish it known how neatly his plans were foiled and how loath he was to act against so great a lord as that who claimed Lady Annyn for his own?"

Susanna frowned. "But that cannot be the end. Still you have not told who murdered her brother."

"Ah, the revelation."

"Aye?"

"That most loathsome man in all of England? He came with the king to claim his bride and, when he discovered she had wed another, his anger was immense."

"What did he do?"

"There was naught he could do before so great a lord as that who had wed his betrothed. And that might have been the end of it, but all started to unravel when the loathsome one noticed a knight who attended this great lord—"

"What shall we call him?" Susanna rasped, once more on the edge of her seat. "He must have a name, else I will become confused."

"Sir Merrick, he who after his knighting by this great lord, remained in service to him. And who knew things no one else knew and was rightfully feared by the loathsome one."

The pieces were beginning to fit well, but she asked, "Sir Merrick knew of the murder?"

Sir Rowan drew a deep breath. "Indeed. He was present."

"What?"

"'Tis so. He was there, though he told that he had not realized death was the intent of the game they played with Lady Annyn's brother and he would have stopped it had he been able to."

"They—Sir Merrick and that other one whom Lady Annyn was to have wed?"

"Aye. They served the great lord alongside her brother, and they did murder him by hanging."

Susanna caught her breath. "For what reason?"

"He knew that the one who would become the most loathsome man in all of England had betrayed their great lord. Thus, the young man could not be allowed to reveal that betrayal."

"And Sir Merrick? You said he was not able to stop the hanging."

Sir Rowan nodded. "He sometimes could not breathe properly, and that night he was so afflicted that he was incapacitated."

Susanna stared at Sir Rowan, her own breath lost. She had heard there were others beset with the same sufferings as Judas, but this was as near as she had come to verifying it.

"So," Sir Rowan continued, "Sir Merrick met the loathsome one over swords and aided in saving the life of Lady Annyn, for which he yielded up his own life."

Susanna drew her bottom lip between her teeth. "Is it wrong that I should be sorry for him?"

Sir Rowan was a long time in answering. "So long as you are not sorry that his opponent was also slain."

"By Sir Merrick?"

His mouth curved slightly. "'Twas another who dealt the killing blow, but Sir Merrick made it possible."

She was not happy another person had died, but considering the man's sins, neither could she be sorry for his death. "It seems fitting that so vile a being should die, for now he can harm no others."

Sir Rowan sat back in the chair. "And there, in all its sorrow, glory, and circumstance, ends my tale."

"All of it is true, is it not?"

He nodded. "Thus, salted with much regret and much relief."

"And you were Sir Knight?"

Another nod.

"Lady Annyn was—is—one of the Sisters of Mary whom you told came within Wulfen's walls before me?"

"Aye. Now she is the wife of the eldest Wulfrith brother."

That made Susanna happy. Out of something terrible and painful had come something wonderful and joyous.

"They love?" she asked softly.

"Lady Annyn and Baron Wulfrith? Most assuredly," he said, and yet the sorrow that had hovered over him in telling of the death of Lady Annyn's brother returned.

Susanna reached across the table and closed a hand over his that rested alongside the chess pieces banished from the board. "You miss her."

"I do. She was almost like a daughter."

"Do you never see her?"

"My life is at Wulfen, hers is at Stern Castle. Thus, I have determined to be content with tidings of her well being and that of the children she has given her husband."

She squeezed his hand. "Is it enough to determine to be content, Sir Rowan?"

He raised an eyebrow. "Far better than unabated sorrow."

His words verified her suspicion that there was more to the tale of Lady Annyn and that it had to do with the character of Sir Knight, but she knew he had told all he would tell.

"I thank you for the game—more, the tale, Sir Rowan. Both have brightened a day that, otherwise, would have been dull."

"'Twas my pleasure, Lass—"

Almost at the same moment, they each turned their head toward the open doorway whence issued the pound of feet upon stairs.

Sir Rowan pulled his hand from beneath Susanna's and stood. She did the same, straightening just as Everard Wulfrith crossed the threshold.

Mouth grim, tension all about him, he halted.

He is angry. What have I done now?

The answer that flew at her nearly made her gasp. But surely no one had seen her upon the roof at night. She had been heedful, had stayed low near the battlements lest she was glimpsed between them.

"My lord," Sir Rowan acknowledged him.

As Everard Wulfrith looked from the knight to the table to her, from one to the other again—as if gauging the distance between them to determine if there was more to their meeting than a game of chess—she gave thanks his advance had been heard. Had he come upon her with her hand covering Sir Rowan's, he would have suspected something was afoot. Though it had been an innocent gesture meant only to comfort, it would have boded ill.

Feeling resentment rise, Susanna counseled herself against taking offense, reminding herself he would have good reason to suspect her motives since he knew she was not averse to trading a favor for a favor. Too, she must not forget all the kindnesses he had shown her, especially that of five days past when he had gifted Judas and her with proof that the other was well.

Hating the silence, she said, "Sir Rowan has shared the story of…" She let her words trail off, wished she had thought them through before speaking, for she doubted Everard Wulfrith would look kindly upon her being privy to his family's history.

However, Sir Rowan said, "'Twas the tale of Lady Annyn Bretanne."

Everard Wulfrith's frown tightened. "Though I cannot say I approve, Sir Rowan, I cannot begrudge you the telling of it since 'tis your story as well. Too, it is rather convenient since one of the players in that tale has something to do with what I have come to discuss with Lady Susanna. Sir Merrick did figure into it, did he not?"

"Indeed, my lord." There was a question in Sir Rowan's voice.

"Good." The lord of Wulfen's long legs carried him forward, and he placed himself over Susanna such that she had to lift her chin high to hold his gaze. "I speak of that knight's affliction," he said gruffly, "one shared by another who is amongst us now. One who, by his silent tongue and that of Sir Elias and your own, did collapse beneath the weight of that same affliction—a terrible showing that could have been prevented had I been told he suffered from such."

A chill went through Susanna, and she took a step back, coming up against the table so hard that several chess pieces toppled and fell to the rushes.

Gripping the table's edge on either side of her to steady herself, she struggled to recall what was required to send forth speech and finally said, "Is Judas—?"

"He recovers."

Thank you, Lord!

She swallowed. "Where is he?"

"Resting. Sir Elias keeps watch over him."

She let her shoulders drop, then her chin to her chest.

I was not there for him—am not there for him now. Is he frightened? Does he need me?

A hard finger and thumb gripped her chin, lifted her face. "Why was I not told of his ailment?"

She glanced at Sir Rowan who stood motionless and watchful. "It..." She jerked her shoulders in a feeble shrug. "...did not seem necessary. He mostly has it under control."

"Mostly! *Mostly* does not cover what just happened upon my training field and under my instruction." He put his face so near hers that she felt his breath across her every pore. "Believing he held back, I took up the quarterstaff and told him that he needed to give more. I pushed him harder, demanded more, and he gave more—so much that he lost his breath and would have dropped to the ground had I not caught him."

Susanna closed her eyes, wished the truth of it was that Judas had feigned another attack. However, though such a ploy was acceptable at Cheverel where most were acquainted with his affliction, he would not want those of Wulfen to know of his weakness.

She lifted her lids and found the eyes above hers hard and glittering. "Sir Elias was near? He gave aid?"

"He *and* I. As told, Sir Merrick suffered from the same."

And so he had known what to do. "Forgive me for not speaking of it. Judas was ever made to feel ashamed of his fits, and here..." She drew a deep breath. "Surely you understand, Lord Wulfrith, that he would not wish anyone to know of it."

"Yet they know now when but a word to me might have averted the attack and saved him his pride."

"Aye, but then also—" Remembering they were not alone, she glanced at her guard.

Everard Wulfrith followed her gaze, released her chin, and stepped back. "Leave us, Sir Rowan."

The older man turned and, moments later, closed the door behind him.

"Also?" Everard Wulfrith wasted no time bringing her back to what she had left unspoken.

She took a step away from the table, clasped her hands at her waist. "I feared that if Judas was, indeed, your son, you would be so ashamed to learn he suffers from breathing attacks that you would refuse to acknowledge him as being of your blood, just as..."

Say it, Susanna. There is no lie in it.

"...my brother was ashamed to own Judas as his son."

Movement at Everard Wulfrith's sides drew her gaze to hands that had closed into white-knuckled fists. "Almighty! I have enough sins of my own without others putting theirs upon me!" He swung away, strode hard across the chamber, strode back.

Eyes boring into hers where he once more stood too near, he said, "I do not know what else I must do to convince you I am not of the ilk you think I am, Lady Susanna, but as God is my witness, had I sinned with Judith and had Judas been born of that sin, for naught would I deny him. Naught!"

It was as she had begun to believe, but as she peered up at him, she finally accepted he was too honorable to have lain with Judith. Though it was a relief to finally believe, it was also an ache, for Alan's misbegotten suspicions had denied him the blessing of knowing and loving his own flesh and blood. "That saddens me," she whispered.

His hands descended to her shoulders. "What say you?"

"I know I should not be aggrieved that Judas is not your son, but I am."

His nostrils flared. "You would prefer I had cuckolded your brother?"

"Nay! 'Tis just all those times that Alan did not know I watched him, when he stared long and hard at Judas, as if searching for himself in the boy...He did not know—never knew—he was looking at the son he longed to see. A terrible loss for both of them." She felt tears in her throat and eyes, but did not look away. "Too, though I would not wish sin on anyone, I believe that had you fathered Judas, he would have a worthy sire."

As her words slid through Everard, he told himself to let them pass without further consideration, but he pulled them back to make sense of them. Sincere though they had sounded, he struggled to believe she held him in such high regard as to wish his blood, rather than her brother's— and hers—flowed through the boy.

Who was this Susanna de Balliol? And why did he care so much? Why did he want the tears in her eyes to dry? Why did he wish those in her throat to ease? Why did he long to coax a bow from the sorrowful turn of her lips? Why did he yearn to more deeply breathe in the scent of her and test her mouth beneath his?

"My lord?" she breathed.

There was a question in her eyes that should not be there, and he was to fault for it. He should not have drawn so near, should not have touched her, should not have looked upon her as he would never have believed he could.

"Forgive me." He set her back from him. "All was long ago said that should be said. Now I will bid you good day." *And get myself to the chapel for prayer.*

However, before he could turn away, she said, "I would like to see my nephew."

"And I would like to accommodate you, but I believe it best to stay the course, especially as he is well enough that he shall soon return to training."

"I beseech you—"

"For this, Lady Susanna," he said more sharply than intended, "women are not allowed at Wulfen. Do not waste your breath, nor my time, asking for what I will not give." He crossed to the door, paused. "Is there anything else you hide from me that I ought to know?"

She shook her head. "Naught that matters. Naught you would believe."

He did not like her answer. More, he did not like that, just as much as he wanted to know what was behind it, he longed to use it as an excuse to linger.

He pulled open the door and strode past Sir Rowan and down the dim stairs.

19

Sɪʀ Rᴏᴡᴀɴ ᴡᴀs two hours gone. And now, just past the middling of night, all would be abed. At least, she prayed it was so.

She peered down her ill-clad figure. Though covered modestly enough, garbed as she was in her thickest chemise, her lack of a bliaut would be unseemly were she caught. Unfortunately, there was no hope of moving undetected around the donjon encumbered by the rustle of thick skirts. If she was to reach Judas in the great hall where he bedded down, this was how she would do it.

Which you should not do.

She knew she should entrust Judas to the Lord, but in this she was weak. She had to see for herself that he was well. Hopefully, Everard Wulfrith would never know what she did.

"Everard…" She closed her eyes and saw again his face above hers, felt the moment she had thought he might kiss her. And, as she had done time and again since he had departed, wondered if it had only been imagined. Reason told her it was foolishness born of singular longing, but still there was a *mayhap*. Ever a *mayhap*.

Susanna fixed her grip on the candle that would light her way and opened the door. As when she had thrice before ventured onto the roof, all was dark outside her chamber except for the light she brought with her. All was quiet. But unlike those other nights, she turned right, rather than left, for on the latter side there was nothing beyond access to the roof. She did not know what, exactly, lay to the right, but wherever it led and by what passages it coursed the donjon, it was certainly the way down.

The steps, a dozen rising up from the landing below, were solid and in good repair, and she quickly descended—only to find herself in another short corridor with a wall before her.

She turned, certain she had missed an opening onto another corridor, but there were only walls and stairs up to her chamber. Her thoughts bounced around but soon settled on the answer to this riddle. Set somewhere in these walls was a hidden door, the only access to her tower room.

Certain it would not take long to discover it since it was most likely built into the outer wall and its span was short, she set herself to the task. However, no matter how often she walked the corridor, passing candlelight over the stone joints of the outer walls and inner walls, certain air from an unseen crack would cause the flame to sputter, no matter how intently she slid her fingers over the joints, there was nothing to indicate the presence of a door.

The floor? It seemed unlikely, but she searched its every inch. To no avail.

"Think," she muttered where she stood in the center of the corridor. "As surely as you draw breath, there is a way out of here."

But which way? Certainly not the obvious and less obvious, meaning the obscure and more obscure. There was no doubt Everard and Sir Rowan used these steps, for she often heard their feet upon them. But perhaps they did not use all of them.

She thrust the candle before her. The surfaces of the three lowermost steps were fairly smooth, but those thereafter were not.

Susanna ascended to the first of the worn steps and passed her candle close to the wall. The flame sputtered.

"There you are." She set the candle on a step up from where she stood and slid her fingers down the narrow crack. Twice she missed the door's catch as she worked her way around the perimeter, but on her third try, she found it in the lower right corner. With a click and a scrape, the door swung inward and released a cold breath of air.

Wishing for the warmth of her bliaut, she retrieved her candle and stepped onto a narrow stairway that could not be an easy thing for a man the size of Everard to negotiate.

Though her imagination prepared her for all manner of disturbing encounters—immense spider-adorned cobwebs, scuttling and squealing mice and rats, dead and disintegrating things, slimy, weeping walls—the steps were relatively clear of vermin and debris. The same could be said of each of the three landings and their flights of steps that followed. And then there were no more, only a passageway that extended beyond the reach of her candlelight. Fortunately, it appeared she did not need to venture farther, for her searching eyes found another door right off the steps.

Standing before it, trembling with chill and fear, she pressed an ear to the crack and listened. If there was sound, it was stuck on the other side. Heart knocking stoutly as if also at a door it wanted badly to go through, fear stirring up bile, she reminded herself she was near Judas. Indeed, he might be right on the other side.

She sank to her haunches and found the catch. Before releasing it, she extinguished the candle whose light could reveal her before any sound she made. Doused in darkness, she set the candle to the side with the command that she not forget it upon her return abovestairs—a grim journey in the absence of light.

Holding her breath, she worked the catch. The door opened toward her with no resistance or sound and, blessedly, a whiff of warm air. She straightened and peered around the door into more darkness, but not so much that she could not identify it was a tapestry before her, dim light penetrating its weave.

Please be of the glowing embers of a fire in the great hall—just enough light to guide me, not enough to be seen.

Grateful she had chosen her chemise well, not only for its thickness but its earthen color that was less likely to be noted than one of white linen, she stepped through the doorway. There were no rushes here to rustle beneath her feet, though surely there would be plenty on the other side.

Lightly running her fingers across the backside of the tapestry, she moved toward the pale strip of light that marked the edge of that which concealed the entrance to the hidden passageway. Without incident, she reached it and peered around it.

The room was immense, but it was no great hall. And as she identified the furnishings lit by the embers of a fire that no longer flamed, her heart lurched so violently it hurt.

Swallowing bile, she stared at the large bed that lay between her and the curtained wall that let into the great hall.

'Tis the solar. Everard's bedchamber.

No one had ever dared enter his bedchamber unbidden, but here someone was. He would nearly wager his life upon it, though it was only that other sense—that which came and went as it pleased—that had roused him from sleep and bid him close his hand around the dagger's hilt beneath his pillow.

Engaging his other senses, upon his face he felt cool drifts of air amongst the warm, smelled and tasted their mustiness. And knew whence it came—*and* who was within before he even caught the scent of roses that was too slight to redeem the air freed from the hidden passageway.

Containing the impulse to demand his night visitor show herself, he eased his hand off the dagger, peered across the solar at the shadow-shrouded tapestry, and waited for the lady's slight figure to slip from behind it.

There—more movement than form. With little to differentiate her clothing from the shadows, she chose her steps well, exhibiting more stealth and foresight than he would have expected. But then, Judas was nearly a master of stealth and, it seemed, among the lessons imparted by his aunt were those in how to move about undetected.

As Everard watched Susanna, he noted she made no sudden movements, her breathing could not be heard, and even the sound of rushes beneath her feet were so slight as to be mistaken for the hiss and sigh of the dying fire. Too, the course she set brought her perilously close to the bed where she had to know he slept, and he was certain she did so to avoid the greater risk of passing through the glow of firelight.

Step by gentle step, with the greatest evidence of her presence that of the scent of roses, she drew near the foot of the bed where Squire Werner, Joseph's replacement, slept on a pallet.

Anticipating she would tread upon the young man, Everard was tempted to put an end to her night excursion. However, there seemed more benefit in discovering just how far Susanna de Balliol would go in grinding their agreement underfoot. Too, when the squire found himself rudely awakened, it would be a good lesson for one who must learn to sleep lightly to protect his lord and himself.

But there was no rude awakening, for she paused just past the right-hand bed post, surely a step away from the sleeping squire, and he heard the slow release of her breath that ended on words spoken so low he might have been convinced they were his own in his head, for he was certainly thinking them.

"For this…" she whispered, then cautiously skirted the pallet, moved toward the curtains, and took with her the scent of roses.

He knew then what she sought. As he had denied her access to Judas, she had determined to break their agreement and seek her nephew herself. It angered him, and yet it also moved him that she so loved the boy she risked wrath and being set out of Wulfen to see for herself that he was well. And so he let her go, though he knew that if her foray into the hall failed—her presence revealed—disorder would ensue.

When she reached the curtains and slipped beyond them, he rose from the bed. He was not surprised when no cry issued from his second squire who slept outside the solar and who was also in danger of being tread upon.

Shortly, he drew back the curtain's edge. It took a moment to locate Susanna, for just as she had done in his solar, she knew to keep to the deepest shadows where flickering torchlight was loath to go.

It seemed she was also gifted with another sense, for it was not long before her furtive search amid the gathering of pages upon pallets came to an end and she bent low and did not rise again. She had found him.

Susanna pressed her lips to keep joy from spilling from them as she strained to make out her nephew's features that were deep in shadow, but not so deep that she did not know him and could not see the hair tossed across his brow. She heard his breath move smoothly in and out, and beneath the hand she laid to his chest, felt its strength.

Thank you, Lord!

And now she should go, for she had what she sought and might sleep secure in the knowledge that Judas was well as Everard had told.

She lifted her hand from his chest, only to impulsively sweep the hair off his brow.

A moment later, scant light glittered in his eyes and he whispered, "Aunt Sanna?"

"Shh." She touched a finger to his lips. "Sleep again, Judas mine."

"Lord Wulfrith told you?"

Lest their whispers roused those nearby, she bent nearer and put her mouth close to his ear. "Aye, and I should not be here, but I had to see for myself that you are well. You are, hmm?"

Thankfully, his response was a nod that would not carry.

"I must needs return to my chamber." She kissed his cheek. "Sleep sweet."

She sensed he wished to talk, but when he nodded again, she straightened. With a heart much relieved but heavy, she retraced her steps.

The solar was as quiet and still as she had left it, and as she traversed it, she exercised the same caution that had earlier allowed her to pass through it undetected. This time aware of where the squire slept, she did not pass as close to the foot of the bed as she had done before, but near enough to avoid the glow of embers and to note that the shadowed figure upon the mattress appeared to have not moved since she had first slipped past him.

At last, she was behind the tapestry, then returned to the hidden passageway with the door once more secured behind her. Though she knew it best to return to her chamber without delay, her relief at what she had accomplished was so great she was nearly weak. Thus, after retrieving the extinguished candle, she felt her way through the dark to the steps, sank down on the lowermost one, and silently thanked the Lord for guiding her to Judas and back again.

She nearly asked forgiveness for not keeping her word to remain abovestairs, but not only were God's blessings best saved for Judas, she did not truly regret what she had done. Fortunately, Everard would never know.

20

"I SHALL NOT GO again. I will not risk it. All is well."

These things Susanna told herself as the day after the night she had stolen through Everard's bedchamber slipped past and then another, and she found herself in the middle of the third day without word from the lord of Wulfen as to how Judas fared now that all knew of his affliction. Was he taunted? Further isolated? Abused?

All Sir Rowan could report was that her nephew appeared to be well. But that did not mean he was, for he was accomplished at putting on a face few could see past unless he wished them to. And how could she forget the tale told of Lady Annyn's brother who had been hanged by fellow squires? For this and the turning of her stomach that cook's draught could not sufficiently settle, Susanna had this morn sent a missive to Everard by way of Squire Werner who brought her meals now that Squire Joseph had departed Wulfen.

Pray thee, come to me, she had written. *I would have word of Judas.*

That was hours ago.

She paced, cast off her veil, and worried her fingers through her hair until the numerous strokes to which she had subjected it were long forgotten. Then she dropped facedown across the bed, letting her feet dangle over the side.

"If you do not come," she muttered, staring at the door, "I will go again. I will risk it. By my own eyes I will know all is well." She did not mean to lower her lids for any length of time, but her eyes were so tired they stung.

That was how Everard found her when she did not respond to his knock.

Disturbed by the sight of her where she lay across the middle of the bed, hair strewn about her face and shoulders, lashes casting feathery shadows upon her pale cheeks, lips softly parted, he knew he should return to the hall where the others partook of their midday meal. However, though he had not wanted to answer her summons, he was here now. Too, this day he had received tidings from Sir Niall, and it would be remiss of him not to share with Susanna what had been learned of Cheverel.

In this instance appreciative of Squire Werner's inefficiency that had prevented him from accompanying his lord abovestairs—likely, he was still assembling the tray of viands—Everard turned back to Sir Rowan.

"As the lady must needs be roused from sleep, relieve my squire of the tray when he delivers it and send him on his way." He would not have the impressionable young man see her thus. Indeed, even a man not so young should not see her laid out in such disarray.

The knight inclined his head. "Aye, my lord."

Leaving the door open, Everard strode across the chamber to the far side of the mattress upon which her head rested. And discovered, up close, she was even more comely.

The observation gave him pause, for still he did not want to be attracted to Susanna de Balliol.

But he was. And if he was yet more honest, he had felt the tug the first morning he had let her within his walls and come to her chamber. She had surely heard the opening of the door, but as if gathering the courage to face him, she had remained unmoving in the glow of the brazier. Though he had thought her too thin and hardly in the bloom of youth, he had also thought her lovely. Then she had revealed her name, and he had seen the girl in the garden who had flown to her brother with the tale that had torn Judith from him.

However, with nearly every encounter since, that girl receded, so much that three days past he had nearly kissed her. It was that temptation, more than his anger with her inability to hold to their agreement, that had kept him from the tower room these past days. And he had excused the delay in bringing word of how Judas fared by reminding himself that her greatest worry had surely been allayed by her excursion to the hall.

She sighed, and he thought she might awaken, but she turned her face opposite, revealing the flushed cheek that had been pressed to the mattress. She looked as if she belonged exactly where she was—as he imagined one's bride would look the morning after the wedding nuptials. And that carnal, unbidden thought returned him to a conversation of two and a half years past.

As he and his eldest brother had stood upon the wall watching their youngest brother, Abel, retreat from the training field where he struggled each day to regain skills lost in battle—much for the love of a woman—Garr had spoken of the lengths to which a man would go for such love and said he believed Everard would go as far, if not farther. Everard had dismissed the idea, certain he would never again feel anything approaching what he had felt for Judith.

And I do not, he told himself. He was attracted to Susanna and, in some ways, admired her, but that was all.

Knowing Squire Werner would not be much longer in delivering her tray, he said, "Lady Susanna?"

She stirred.

"Awaken, my lady."

Her lashes fluttered. Then, with a sharp breath, she gathered her knees beneath her and sat back on her heels. "Lord Wulfrith!"

He frowned, for she looked even more appealing as she stared wide-eyed at him past the hair tumbling across her face. Turning aside, he said over his shoulder, "Put yourself in order," and crossed to the table upon which sat the chessboard.

"I thank you for coming," she said, and he heard the mattress sigh and the rushes rustle as she stood from the bed.

"I apologize for not calling upon you sooner." He began returning defeated chess pieces to their light and dark squares. "But I trust you knew your nephew was well tended and suffered no lasting ill effects from his attack."

The sounds of her movement ceased, and he wondered if she considered owning to the truth. Finally, she said, "Aye, but still I worried."

And had determined she would see for herself. "I would have you know," he said, "Judas resumed his training the day after and, throughout, has not been lacking the close, albeit discreet, regard of Sir Elias and myself."

"I am heartened to hear it." She moved again, her footsteps telling that she approached, then passed behind him. "And the others? How do they behave toward him?"

He had hoped she would not ask. Peering over his shoulder, he saw her retrieve her veil from the floor.

As she straightened, she glanced at him. Finding him watching her, she averted her gaze and began brushing the gossamer material. "I should not have been so careless. Now 'tis stuck through with rushes."

Everard lifted the chessboard, crossed to the side table, and set it alongside the writing instruments he had sent her—ink, quill, parchment. His hand brushed the latter, causing the sheaf to shift and reveal small, beautifully worked writing along the lower edges of two parchments tucked beneath the others. One read: *Wednesday-an hour ere midnight.* The other: *for the days and nights of longing are long.*

Then Susanna was beside him, shoulder brushing his forearm as she swept the parchments together. "Why have you moved the chessboard here?" she asked in a rush that bespoke her disquiet at what he might have glimpsed.

And to what *had* he been privy? The former was an accounting, and knowing of the night she had ventured out of her chamber, he did not doubt it was the means by which she had determined the best time to do so. Thus, it had been no impulse that had caused her to trespass upon his bedchamber. It had been planned, and well before he had brought word of Judas's breathing attack. Though he knew she was no longer a sweet, innocent girl, this further evidence of what the years had wrought might have angered him if not for the latter piece of writing. A sennight past, when he had asked if she penned poetry, she had denied it, claiming she was no longer fanciful, but he was fairly certain the words that mourned the length of days and nights were in that vein.

He glanced at the parchments she had resettled farther along the table, then looked to her. Gaze wary, bits of rushes yet gracing her hastily donned veil, wafting the scent of roses, she stood too near for comfort. And for that, he was grateful it was his habit to submit to soap and water and don fresh garments after long, sweat-soaked mornings.

Deciding there was no gain in revealing what he had learned from her writings, he returned to the matter of the chessboard. "As I have foregone sitting at table with those of Wulfen in order to answer your summons, my lady, I shall eat my midday meal here. Hence, we have need of a table." It was true, though what he did not tell was that he also wished to ensure she ate, for Sir Rowan had reported her appetite was waning though she continued to take the draught.

"Of course." She gestured at the table. "While we await your squire, would you tell me more of Judas—how the others behave toward him?"

That last he preferred not to address since he did not wish to worry her—and the answer might give her cause to once more brave the hidden passageway—but twice now she had asked it and he did not think it would go away without a lie.

Once they were seated across from one another, he said, "There have been two altercations, one during the morning run through the wood, the other upon the training field."

She sat forward. "Judas?"

"Be assured, your nephew—"

He caught the sound of Squire Werner's emergence from the hidden passageway and nodded toward the door.

Her brow smoothed, and she sat back.

There followed a lightly spoken conversation between the squire and Sir Rowan and, shortly, the knight appeared bearing the viands, some of which yet wafted heat despite the distance from the kitchens to the tower room.

With regret at having reduced the knight to such servitude, Everard motioned him forward.

Sir Rowan lowered the tray to the table. "Should I close the door, my lord?"

"Nay, the lady and I speak of naught that cannot be told in your hearing."

The knight inclined his head and withdrew. A few moments later, the sound of his feet on the steps told that he had removed himself from directly outside the chamber. Doubtless, he would wait upon the landing below.

Everard returned his attention to Susanna and was pleased when, without prompting, she retrieved the cup containing the draught and put it to her lips.

"As I was saying," he continued, "your nephew is capable of teaching lessons of his own. Thus, I do not believe either of those who sought to test him—one of the same age, another a few years older—will bother him again."

She lowered the cup. "How badly was Judas hurt?"

Everard leaned over one of two trenchers that contained rabbit poached in a wine sauce thick with onions. "That is the thing—your nephew bears not much more than scratches and a few bruises."

"Truly?"

He dipped a spoon in his trencher. "Upon my word."

She finished the draught. "What I do not understand is how these altercations can occur if Sir Elias and you keep watch over him."

Famished, the breaking of his fast this morn too many hours past and the day as arduous as any, Everard allowed himself several mouthfuls of tender rabbit before responding. "They occurred because we permitted it," he said and, before she could protest, continued, "What you must understand about training boys into men is that, as much as possible, they must make their own way—account for themselves, defend themselves, prove themselves. To remove that opportunity does them great disservice, making them appear weak and breeding in others resentment, disrespect, and scorn that serves far worse than any cruel words or beatings. To wit, those who set themselves against your nephew have learned to respect him and his abilities rather than one who intervenes on his behalf."

Beneath her regard that remained troubled, he took another bite, then asked, "Still it does not make sense?"

At her hesitation, he said, "Consider this, when it comes around— and it will—that a grown man must defend family and home, is it better he set to it knowing he is capable of doing so without aid, or that he wait upon help that may never come?"

She slowly nodded. "It makes sense to my head. But my heart..." She shrugged. "I could not do what you do."

"Nor are you expected to. You have done your part by raising a boy worthy of knighthood training. Be content with that."

Her head bobbed. "This from one who believes I am a bad influence?"

He had said that, but as the hidden things of Susanna and Judas came to light, the less inclined he was to believe it—certainly not as intently as before. "I was harsh," he said, "and for that I apologize."

She blinked. "I thank you, Lord Wulfrith."

The bits of gold in her amber eyes brightening, affecting him in ways it should not, he shifted his attention to her trencher. It remained untouched. However, he held his tongue and scooped up another spoonful of his own meal.

"I thank you again," she said.

He raised an eyebrow.

Her lips bowed. "For not commanding me to eat."

"Forsooth, I was much tempted."

"Aye, you were." She filled her own spoon with rabbit that appeared to be poured over with a lighter sauce and seemed to suffer a complete lack of onions, obviously in consideration of her stomach.

Deciding it best to let the conversation be while they ate, more to ensure she had no cause to lose whatever appetite she had than to alleviate his own hunger, Everard returned to his trencher.

Nearly a quarter hour passed before they spoke again, and only when she set her spoon down with what seemed finality. She had not eaten all—far from it—but neither had she nibbled.

Everard lifted his goblet and, as he carried it to his mouth, said, "Some good has come of exposing your nephew's affliction."

Susanna, who had been marveling at how well her stomach behaved, drew her hand back from her own goblet. "How can that be?"

"Squire Charles, the same who taunted Judas about his name and, for it, lost a tooth, now appears to be of a mind to befriend him."

Though she wished it was something to rejoice in, it alarmed her. Not that she did not want her nephew to have friends, but it was not as easy as that.

"You seem as uncertain as Judas," Everard said.

It struck her that she was becoming even less adept at hiding the expression of her feelings from him. "I cannot help questioning the young man's intentions, just as my nephew cannot. As you already know in some regards and surely suspect in others, those of my brother's household were not often kind to his son. Indeed, even friendship genuinely extended could be withdrawn once one learned it was wiser to show no affection for a boy shunned by his own father."

Everard broke his stare, rubbed his eyes. "I guessed as much. Just as I suspect your brother did not treat you well, Susanna. Is that not so?"

Her breath stopped, not only from his conclusion but that he addressed her informally, the same as he had done when she had reacted poorly to the news that Sir Morris was among Sir Talbot's party that had paused at Wulfen, the same as he had done all those years past before he had come to believe her to be the instrument of his loss.

He pushed his hand up over his shaved head. When he returned his gaze to hers, there was something raw in his eyes, as if he suffered.

And she did not doubt he did. Though he did not ask after Judith, his thoughts surely went beyond Judas and Susanna to the woman he had loved and, knowing what he now knew of life at Cheverel, imaginings of how Alan had behaved toward his wife during their short-lived marriage.

Susanna struggled against the need to reassure him, for she did not think her efforts would be appreciated. But she could not let it be. "Lord Wulfrith, hear me. You should know that though my brother could be cold toward Judith, he was not cruel. Truly, he was not. And when it was known she was with child, it seemed as if their marriage—"

"I did not ask after her," he said sharply. "I asked after you."

"But—"

"I will not speak of her."

She lowered her gaze. Was his anger directed solely at her? Or did some of it extend to Judith?

Susanna's friend had spoken little of him during her nine months of marriage to Alan, but when her infant son had been laid in her arms—in the midst of her cooing and marveling over the bits of blond hair that would later grow dark—she had murmured, "Now that I have you, no longer shall I wish I had let him take me away." And then she had removed the pendant necklace and held it out to her friend. "I shall wear this no more."

Hope had fluttered in Susanna's breast, only to be stilled when the jolly midwife lost her smile, announced there was too much blood, and told Susanna to take the babe.

Was some of what Everard felt for Judith anger? That though he would have defied all, risked all, to make her his own, she had rejected him? Might he believe Judith had not loved him as he loved her?

Susanna drew a hand upward, pressed it to her midriff to keep it from venturing higher and laying hold to that which evidenced Judith's great love for this man. How she wished she could share it with him, for it might ease whatever pain remained of his loss were he to know he had not been forgotten, that though Judith had done her duty, she had not undertaken it lightly. But Susanna feared he would not be receptive to it coming from her, and so she lowered her hand to her lap.

And jumped when Everard reached across the table and lightly gripped her chin. "Judith is gone," he said solemnly. "Naught can be done for her now. What matters is what can be done for Judas. And you."

She stared into his eyes, could hardly breathe, for she was too aware of his warm skin against hers, the rough pads of his fingers, the quiver of her lower lip upon the edge of his thumb.

With a deep breath that further broadened his shoulders, he released her chin, picked a rush from the edge of her veil, and sat back. "Methinks we ought to speak of other things."

"Other things?"

"This day I received tidings from Sir Niall."

Forgetting the heat and sensation of his touch, she sat straighter. "What news have you?"

"He was granted a night's lodging at Cheverel and observed that the household is under the control of your brother's mother-in-law"—

Lady Richenda.

—"as well as Sir Talbot, the same who rode upon Wulfen a fortnight past."

That did not surprise her. Following Alan's death, Lady Richenda's partiality toward the head of the household knights had become something more, and Susanna had known an agreement had been reached between them even before Sir Talbot had done the lady's bidding by summoning the two knights in whose care Judas had been left the day he had feigned a breathing attack.

"What of my brother's widow, Lady Blanche? And her babe?"

"Present as well."

Susanna was relieved, for no matter her circumstances, she wished no misfortune upon the lady, nor the babe who was as much her nephew as Judas. All she wanted was for what rightfully belonged to Judas to remain his.

"Thus," Everard continued, "just as we have not been granted an audience with the queen, we can assume they also await a summons."

"Was there talk of Judas—if they still search for him?"

"None in the hall, though Sir Niall learned from the blacksmith that the tale of Sir Elias's abduction of Judas and you has spread throughout Cheverel, and that most believe both of you are victims of mortal ill."

Susanna pulled her bottom lip between her teeth. "Which could prove useful if Judas falls into the hands of those who seek to steal Cheverel from him."

Everard moved as if to sit forward, and she thought he might once more reach to her, but he pressed back and curled the fingers of his hand upon the table into his palm. "Fear not. The boy and you are under my protection and shall remain so until his inheritance is secured."

She frowned. "Then you believe the queen will find in favor of Judas?"

After a long moment, he said, "I think it more likely than that she will not."

"And if...?" She did not want to ponder the alternative, but she must prepare for it. "If she denies my nephew's claim to Cheverel, what then?"

"He will have a place here at Wulfen." Everard's lack of hesitation evidenced he had already considered the possibility. "And when his training is complete, he shall make his own way as a knight whose services are highly sought after."

Though the thought of being parted from Judas nearly broke her heart, it was gratitude that brought tears to her eyes with such force she had to look down, for it was well known that nobles vied to place their sons and heirs at Wulfen. "I thank you, Lord Wulfrith—more than ever you will know."

"I am glad to do it for Judith's son. But what of you, Susanna? Have you considered what you will do if he is denied?"

There was nothing to consider, for there seemed only one course available to a lady of twenty and five who, possessing no dowry, had no prospect of marriage. Staring at the pink ovals of her nails, she said, "As Cheverel is my family's home, I shall return there."

It would be a sorry existence beneath Lady Richenda's rule, but surely it could not be much worse than all the years she had been subject to Alan's authority. If she could make herself useful to Lady Blanche, there was hope her life would have some meaning, that the days and nights would not stretch intolerably long, that moments of happiness might even be found—perhaps with little Alan. Of course, how likely was it she would be entrusted with the care of the one who had displaced Judas?

She felt her tears quicken.

You will not cry! Certainly not over something that may never come to pass. She closed her eyes. *Please Lord, do not let it come to pass. See Judas given what is rightfully his.*

"I will leave you now, my lady."

She jerked her chin up, met Everard's gaze, quickly looked away in hopes he had not seen how wet her eyes were. "Of course, Lord Wulfrith. I have kept you too long." She stood and, feigning concern over her wrinkled skirts, smoothed her hands down them.

Out of the corner of her eye, she saw him pivot toward the door. Only then did she return her gaze to him. A moment later, he went from sight.

When she heard his voice and Sir Rowan's, she drew the pendant from her bodice and watched it unwind upon its chain, the movement causing the scent of roses to waft upon the air, though not with the intensity of weeks past. It was time to replace the dry, crushed petals—

"Nay." She closed her fingers around it. That time was past, the pendant's purpose spent. Or soon would be. "If I dare…"

The chapel had not been his destination, for there was much to be done in preparation for the arrival of his younger brother, Abel. And yet here he stood before the altar, more thoughtful than prayerful as he tried to order his thoughts so that he might turn them into prayer.

He clenched his hands. More often than not, he knew where he stood with himself, conscious of his emotions and their origins. However, since Susanna had come to Wulfen, he had encountered tangles and knots in his consciousness, so intricately woven and tightly drawn that he sometimes felt as if he had stepped out of himself into another man. It was certainly what he had experienced when he had gone to the tower room an hour earlier and acknowledged his attraction to her.

That had been but the beginning, for it was he who had moved the conversation from Judas to her in advancing that her brother had not treated her well. He had been as taken aback by his query as she had seemed to be and struggled to make sense of his feelings, but hardly had he begun than she spoke in defense of her brother, and that had led to Judith.

His response had been harsh, though not only because he did not wish to discuss the woman he had lost. He had truly wanted to know more about Susanna, but without the shadow of Judith or any other falling over her. Just Susanna.

Remembering what he had done, he splayed the hand that had lifted her chin as he had sought to explain his reason for refusing to speak of Judith. It had not seemed to be his hand, not his thumb that had felt the tremble of her lower lip, not he who had tried to distance himself from his own response by picking the rush from her veil.

He might have succeeded in detaching himself if he had not felt compelled to ask what she herself would do if the queen refused Judas his inheritance. Staring at her bent head, he had longed to ease her worry but had told himself he had nothing to offer her—a lie, and for that he had quickly departed.

The truth was that she would not have to return to Cheverel, for he could appeal to his mother or sisters to make a place for her in their households. Unfortunately, that would require an explanation. More, on the rare occasions he visited, he would find himself in the presence of a woman who represented a past he ought to put as firmly behind him as once he had done.

Everard shoved a hand over his raspy scalp that evidenced it would soon be necessary to take a blade to it again, then lowered to the kneeling bench. He was much in need of prayer, though not in the matter of what the Lord would have him do about Susanna de Balliol—at least, not with regard to ensuring she had a choice as to whether or not she returned to Cheverel.

21

SHE WISHED SHE could blame it on impulse, but she had given it enough thought to know that what she planned was imprudent and another breach of her agreement with Everard. After all, there were other ways to achieve the same end. But this way...

By the light of the candle she had set upon the stair, she considered the square of folded linen she had bound with a pale blue ribbon made soft by years of securing the ends of her braids.

Aye, this way it would be done and, henceforth, she would not have to think on it again. Too, she could ease her concern, slight though Everard's assurances had made it, over Judas. And it was not as if she had not managed it once before.

Ignoring the small voice that told her it was not too late to turn back, she released the catch.

She had returned, though so deep was the sleep he came up out of that he did not awaken to her presence until she was partway to the bed.

Easing the hold he had taken upon the dagger beneath his pillow, he watched as she drew nearer than she had done before. Indeed, it seemed this time the bed was her destination rather than the mere negotiation of it in order to reach the curtained entrance.

Amid shadows thrown by the canopy overhead, made all the more secure by the limited reach of the dying fire, Everard saw Susanna's dark figure advance, breathed in air that was absent the scent of roses unlike the last time she had come within—and all those other occasions he found himself in her presence. Then she was alongside the bed.

She stood unmoving as if searching him out where he lay at the center, the breath that sustained her so softly drawn that only if one listened well might they hear it.

He did not want his thoughts to venture where next they went, but then they were there, suggesting she had come to bargain between the sheets. Immediately, he rejected the idea, not only because she would be foolish to reveal her knowledge of the hidden passageway and more foolish to do so with his squire sleeping mere feet away, but because it did not fit the woman who made him lose sight and control of his emotions. True, Sir Elias had told that exchanging favors was her way, but not with him.

She bent, and when he caught the sound of a hand sliding across fabric, he considered he might be wrong about her and that she did, indeed, seek his bed. But then she straightened and turned away.

As on that first night that she had ventured through his chamber, she went around the bed, carefully picked her way across the rushes to the curtains, and slipped into the hall. This time, he did not follow, certain she would seek out Judas to assure herself he was well and quickly return to her chamber as she had done before.

In the meantime, he searched a hand across the bed to determine if she had left evidence of her reason for venturing so near. He found nothing. But as he pondered her behavior, it occurred to him the sound he had heard might have been of something being slid between the bottom, wool-stuffed mattress and the top feather mattress.

Three minutes could hardly have passed before Susanna retraced her steps, went behind the tapestry, and closed herself inside the hidden passageway.

Everard dropped his legs over the side of the bed. Moments later, he drew from between the mattresses a cloth folded around something small and hard.

He crossed to the hearth that lent its glow to revealing what Susanna had risked much to leave behind—surely to be found when she was gone from Wulfen. He loosened the lightly knotted ribbon, pushed aside the layers, and felt a blow with the weight of eleven years behind it.

"Almighty," he rasped. In sharp contrast to the white cloth it lay upon, crimson facets captured the light within the chamber. Still, the ruby's brilliance paled compared to how brightly it had shone the day he had given it to Judith as proof of his love.

How had Susanna known it belonged to him? Merely a guess from when she had noticed his dagger was missing a gem? That seemed unlikely, and yet he did not believe Judith would have told her of the gift, not the girl who would have run to her brother with tale of it just as she had done with tale of the kiss. Perhaps Judith had been careless in her keeping of the gem and Alan de Balliol had discovered it and wrung the truth from her...

Everard closed his hand around the ruby and tried to calm his roiling, but he wanted answers. Now.

Do not, he told himself as he strode across the solar. *This is not who you are.*

He pulled from the top of his clothes chest the clean tunic his squire had laid out in preparation for the early morning run.

Think first, act second, he heard again one of many youthful lessons as he dragged the garment on over his head.

Then he was advancing on the tapestry. Shortly, he ascended the hidden stairway in unshod feet and utter darkness, having given no thought to footwear or a torch. Not that either was needed, for he knew the way well.

When he came out onto the steps that led to the tower room, he felt a swirl of tepid night air that evidenced Susanna had left her window unshuttered and door ajar. However, before he reached the landing above, he realized her chamber was not the only way by which air entered. Almost as forcefully, it blew in through the door that accessed the roof. Knowing that was where he would find her, he did little more than glance into the room in which a single candle flickered wildly in its struggle to remain lit.

Quickly, he climbed the ladder. Though he expected to see her the moment he emerged, for the night was endowed with a good moon hindered only by sheer, swiftly moving clouds, she did not immediately come to notice, and when his gaze did find her, the reason was apparent. Back turned to him, garments of a color as bland as the battlements before which she knelt, head bowed, she sat back on her heels. And that sight, regardless of whether or not she was at prayer as she appeared to be, calmed him sufficiently that he did not approach as forcefully and thoughtlessly as he would otherwise have done.

Standing amid the restless air that tugged at his garments, moaned around and over the castle walls, and caused the long grasses of the meadow and leaves of the trees to chatter amongst themselves, he strained to catch Susanna's murmured words of supplication. However, he heard no sound about her, and the only movement was the shifting of her unbound hair. He stepped forward.

Fool! Susanna berated as she stared at the pendant she had emptied of its rose petals when she had removed the ruby from its center. *Never could it have been as easy as it seemed—possibly once, not twice. Not with a man like Everard Wulfrith. Fool, fool! You dared to ease an ache you could only guess at so you might indulge in the childish, dimwitted belief of unrequited love. You risked what did not need to be risked, what could have been left for another day when his goodwill no longer mattered, or even a day that never came. And all this after you agreed to his terms and he showed you naught but consideration. If you are set outside these walls, it will be by your own hand. And Judas—*

Nay, he was safe. He would not be made to pay for her sins. And that was all that mattered.

She closed her fingers around the pendant and, when footsteps revealed Everard was nearly upon her, said, "You were not asleep." Unlike Judas who, this night, had not roused when she had kissed his untroubled brow.

She sensed Everard's hesitation, but still he came. Head lowered, having not moved since catching the creak of the ladder when panic had dropped her to her knees, she saw his hosed legs and bare feet come alongside her.

"I *was* asleep." His voice was harsh. "But just as your trespass awakened me three nights past, it awakened me this night."

She squeezed her eyes closed. She was surprised and yet not that he had known of her first foray through his bedchamber, for it better fit his character that he had not visited her the day following Judas's breathing attack to assure her of her nephew's well-being. After all, since she had verified it herself, it had not been necessary. But why had he ignored that first trespass and not this one? Had he discovered what she had left behind? As much as she hoped it was not so, that the linen square remained hidden between his mattresses, it was a thin hope.

The hand he thrust forward brushed her hair. "How did you come by this?"

A hope so thin he had seen right through it...

As she did not need to look upon what he proffered, she returned her gaze to what she cradled in her own palm—that which had secreted the gem for nearly eleven years. "Judith entrusted it to me."

He expelled a word that was not an oath but sharp enough to sound like one. Then he closed a hand around her arm, pulled her to standing, and set her back against the battlement. "*That* is a lie."

She lifted her chin and, past the hair flying into her eyes, braved his grim, moonlit expression. "No lie. Ere her passing—"

"I do not believe you!"

She felt her own anger stir beneath the layers of years, sensed it seeping and rising through her as it had done when Lady Richenda had tried to steal Judas's breath.

Calm, she counseled. *Do not make this any worse than it already is.*

In a voice far from level, she said, "You do not have to believe what I say for it to be so."

"It is not so. Never would she have trusted you—"

"Had I done what you think I did, she would not have let me so near her. But she believed different because she knew different."

She heard his teeth grind. "You are saying you did not carry tale to your brother of what you saw in the garden?"

"That is the truth."

He stepped so near that she startled. "I will not be taken in by your deceit, Susanna de Balliol. Mayhap Judith was, but not I."

Bind thy tongue. Do not loose it!

But Susanna did not heed Susanna. Hands curling so tight she felt the pendant's every curve in her palm, she said, "Aye, Everard Wulfrith, I am a creature of deceit, perhaps even more than you think, for I sought and embraced deception to gain what Judas and I needed to survive where we were not meant to survive."

She saw uncertainty flicker across his face, but anger was soaking her through and she could not stop the words that vied to reach her tongue ahead of all others. "You asked if there was anything else I hid from you that you ought to know. There is not, certainly nothing that will make a difference where Judas is concerned, but perhaps you ought to know what these eleven years have held for me."

She filled her lungs full, not only for the words she intended to send forth but to ease the tightening about her throat and chest. "Thieving. Lying. Ever watchful. Ever wary. Creeping and keeping to shadows. Bargaining kisses and caresses that made me want to retch and scrub my skin raw 'til it bled. Fending off ravishment that was thought my due for allowing my body to be so sinfully used." She gave a sharp laugh. "Even my brother believed it was my due, for he did little more than scold Sir Morris when he…" She shook her head. She had not meant to speak as far as that.

Everard took a step back.

It was then, with the silence broken only by the play of the wind, that she noticed how lightly clad he was in tunic and hose—a match for her chemise that was far more suited to being abed than being alone with a man. Not that she had anything to worry about where Everard was concerned.

"Susanna," he said, and she thought there was a note of urgency in his voice where there had been condemnation, "here is not the place for such a conversation—"

She jerked her arm out of his hold. "I have not yet told you how I first learned to use my body for gain. You will like this." She did not truly believe that, but there was something satisfying about freeing those words from the depths of bitterness. "The night of the day that Judith breathed her last, my brother, drunk with ale and grief, announced his son would not bear his name, that he would, instead, be known as Judas. Judas, the betrayer! When I spoke out against such cruelty, he took offense and..." Should she tell him Alan had backhanded her with such force she had been knocked to the hearth?

She drew a breath that shamed her for all its shuddering. "He had me put outside the walls. It was winter's end, but still the nights were cold, and I had no mantle. Worse, Judith's babe was in his cradle and there was no one to answer his cries—certainly no one who would answer them as they needed to be. And so I struck my first bargain with the man-at-arms who delivered me outside the walls, the same who had many times looked at me as one should not look upon any woman."

Her belly churned. "In exchange for stealing me back inside, I let him kiss and touch me. And kept my supper down until Judith's babe was safe in my chamber."

As might be impossible to keep down now had she recently eaten. Feeling the telltale burn in her throat, she swallowed hard and the bile returned to where it belonged.

She tried to read Everard's face. However, it told nothing of what he thought of all she had revealed, for it was just as grimly set, if not more so. Likely, he believed she yet lied, and it incensed her.

This time it was she who stepped near. "Ask it, Everard Wulfrith. Ask it, and I will answer no matter how fiercely you name me a liar."

His jaw shifted. "Why did your brother behave toward you in such a manner?"

She nodded. "That is the question, though only because you have laid upon me a burden that is of my own making only in that I saw what I should not have and did not act as was expected of me. And so I say again, 'twas not me who carried tale to Alan about that day in the garden."

Realizing her voice had risen again and how close she was to tears, Susanna tried to urge herself down from the heights of outrage. But her world was out of kilter, and though tempted to steady herself by leaning back against the battlement, she hated how weak it would make her appear and, instead, widened her stance.

"Now the next question," she pressed onward. "If I did not tell him, how did he learn of what went there?"

"I am listening."

"Good, for here is the answer. From an upper window above the garden, Alan saw Judith and you. Just as he saw me, the sister whose duty it was to alert him to his betrothed's betrayal."

Inwardly, Everard jerked. He wanted—and did not want—to believe her, the latter for the selfish reason he would hate himself if he had so misjudged and wronged her.

"Unbeknownst to me," she continued, "Alan waited for me to prove my loyalty was first to kin, but I failed him." A small sound escaped her that might have been a sob. "He was so enamored of Judith that I did not wish to see him hurt, and though I had heard her agree to go away with you, I did not believe she would defy her family. Thus, I determined my brother need never know of her indiscretion. And Judith...I would not say Alan was cruel—not then—but he had been heavy-handed with his first wives, and I wished to spare my friend knowledge of that side of him."

The indignation that had brought Everard abovestairs ebbed further as moonlight revealed that her moist eyes now brimmed with tears.

"And my reward?" Her voice cracked. "The sister of whom Alan had been fairly fond was deemed a traitor and subjected to contempt reserved for those who misplace their loyalty. Thus, I—not my nephew—am the Judas of the de Balliols."

Remembering what he had said weeks ago when she had asked how much he had hated her all these years—that he would not likely ever have a care for her since it could not be known if it was loyalty to family or jealousy of Judith that had guided her the day she had revealed what she had seen in the garden—Everard felt his insides twist. It was possible she lied—

"'Tis true Judith's trust was denied me, for no matter how often I proclaimed my innocence, no matter how poorly my brother behaved toward me, she would have naught to do with me. Then, a month following the marriage, Alan summoned me to his solar. I hoped we might reconcile, but he was not of that mind. He said he would never forgive me for putting Judith before him and, since I loved her so well, he had broken my betrothal so I might remain at Cheverel as her lifelong companion."

Susanna's breath was coming faster, as if her legs, not her words, ran a great distance.

"Faced with a loveless, childless life in the household of a brother who hated me, I cried and pleaded, but he would not be moved and ordered me from his sight. I found Judith in the corridor. She had been listening at the door and heard enough to accept that I had not revealed her. She said…" A small sob escaped Susanna. "…she was so very sorry."

Everard's hold on eleven years of believing ill of this woman slackening, he clenched his hands and felt the ruby dig into his palm.

Dear Lord, how I have wronged her!

When she swayed, he once more reached to her. "Susanna, let us go inside."

"Nay!" She jumped back and came up against the battlement, slapped at his hand when he tried to turn it around her arm, cried out when something dropped to the roof between them with a metallic jangle, fell to her knees and began searching for what she had lost.

Everard knew where to find it, for its sound told all. He lowered to his haunches, scooped it up, and saw it was the pendant necklace he had looked upon when she had been so weak he'd had to raise her up and hold the cup for her to drink. It no longer wafted the scent of roses, for it had been emptied of its petals.

Gripping it by its chain, he held it out to her. "I have it."

Her head came up sharply. As frantic as she was, he expected her to snatch the necklace from him. Instead, the hand with which she reached stilled, and she stared at the pendant as the wind moved it side to side. Then, as if she had come to the bottom of her righteous anger, she shuddered. And when next she spoke, her voice was faint as of one too weary with the world to make much effort to be heard. "I nearly left that for you as well."

Everard frowned. "As well?"

She closed her fingers around the pendant, drew it to her chest, and scooted back against the battlement. "The pendant was a gift to me from my father. I gave it to Judith so she might more discreetly keep upon her person the ruby with which you had gifted her."

Then the gem had not been consigned to some forgotten corner as he had thought it might be. "She told you I gave it to her?"

Susanna shook her head. "Not in words, but I knew it had to have been you, for she was ever bringing it to hand, sometimes so thoughtlessly it was a miracle Alan did not notice."

Everard closed his eyes and dredged up the ache of loss Judith had also felt. The keen edges that had cut him that first year of losing her to Alan de Balliol and then to death were rounded now, the sharp pain reduced to a dull throb. And he was grateful, for there had been a time when a day had not passed without him feeling as if he were bleeding out.

"Should I stop?" Susanna asked softly.

He lifted his lids. "I would have you tell the rest of it."

When she nodded, he rose and stepped forward. As he lowered beside her, she looked across her shoulder. That he could pick the sorrow from her eyes told him he was too near, but he did not move. Nor did she.

"I begged Judith to hide the ruby," she said, "but she would not. Once, my pleading so angered her that she declared she almost hoped Alan would see it and know its meaning. But then she discovered she was with child." A small smile turned Susanna's lips. "My brother was so pleased that he began to treat her more kindly and with consideration, and Judith started to warm toward him—not much, but enough to hope their marriage might be mended by the babe growing in her."

She sighed. "Still, she would not set aside your gift and, more than ever, I feared it would be discovered. For that, I offered her my pendant. There is a hinge on the back and a clasp on the front that allows the top to be parted from the bottom so it can be filled with petals and its wearer made to smell as if she walks among flowers. Amid crushed petals, Judith hid the ruby so she could wear it near her heart and..." She returned her gaze to Everard's. "...never would my brother know you were there between them."

Between them—as if he had made a cuckold of Alan de Balliol. He had not, but what he had done was still wrong. "She should not have," he said harshly, "just as I should not have refused the ruby when she tried to return it ere her wedding."

"Nevertheless, it gave her peace. Thus, throughout most of her pregnancy, things were better between my brother and her."

As Susanna had tried to tell him when they had shared a meal on the day past.

"Had Judith not died, I think it possible she would have become content wed to my brother, for though she had little time with their son, she seemed so hopeful when she held him. And Alan..." She shrugged. "I believe he must have loved her as much as he was capable of loving another, and I have thought, perhaps, it was simply easier to blame her death by childbirth on you rather than hold himself accountable for any part of it. And so he named his son Judas, and every day he grew more certain your eyes were the ones that looked back at him."

So many missteps. So much injustice. Such pain where there should have been joy. Everard opened his own hand and watched the crushed white cloth slowly unfold to reveal the ruby. "And now you return this to me. Why, Susanna?"

As the wind lifted her hair, she considered the gem. "All these years, I have worn it near my own heart where it did not belong, but when I saw where it did belong—that it had been taken from your dagger—I wished to return it so you would know she had kept it. That she had not forgotten you." She looked up. "You believe it, do you not?"

"I do."

Her shoulders eased and she dropped her head back against the battlement. "I am glad."

Everard did not know how to say what needed to be said to begin to make amends for having wronged this woman, and as he struggled for the words, she said, "So now you know what you need not know, and whether or not you believe what I have told, I do not care."

That he did not believe. "Do you not?" he said.

Silence spilled out of her, then a sigh. "Aye, that is a lie. And the truth? I do not want to care."

"Why do you?" As soon as he asked it, he knew he should not have, that the question laid a path to a place he should not go with her.

The tears that had cleared Susanna's eyes returned, though he caught only a glimpse of their sparkle before she lowered her gaze to the pendant. "Eleven years is a long time to pay for betrayal." Her voice was tight, tremulous. "But even longer to be thought ill of by the man whose indiscretion led me to betray my own brother."

Remorse sank hooks into Everard, and deeper yet when the wind shifted the hair across her face and he saw the glistening trail of the tear that had coursed her cheek.

She shook her head. "Though I know I should not care what you think of me or the things I have done to make it through one day into the next, I care far too much. When I came to you for help, that is all I wanted, for you to aid Judas. I did not want to like you as once I had—"

She gave a soft, scornful laugh. "As ashamed as I am to admit Judith was right, I was besotted with you, Everard Wulfrith."

He did not understand his hands that wanted what good sense told him he did not want—to pull her to him and wipe away her tears. More, he did not understand the longing to kiss her when the only thing he ought to ask of her was forgiveness.

"I thought you might have heard her say that," he said gruffly.

She turned her face to him. "That and more." She swept her gaze to his head that denied the wind the frolic her unbound tresses did not. "Only ever her hands," she whispered. "No other's."

Everard had never known himself to be incapable of movement when movement was necessary and, in this moment, it was imperative that he distance himself. He should not be alone with her, in the dark, hands clenched so they would not reach for her. This was about Judith and him. Not Susanna and him. Was it not?

"I am sorry," she said, and he stiffened to hear her speak words that ought to sound from him. "I am sorry she is not here with you." Her breath caught, once more on a sob. "I know you loved her well, and it cannot be easy to have me reminding you of all you have lost. But at least now you know—I hope you know—that I also loved Judith and neither family loyalty nor jealousy made me betray her."

Everard knew, almost wished he did not, for he could not stop himself from doing what he did next. Distantly aware of the cloth falling from his hand, he turned to Susanna, brushed back the hair dancing across her face, and set his palm to her moist cheek. "I know," he said, "and 'tis I who am sorry for all the years you were made to suffer for my lack of discretion, for what you had to do to abide beneath your brother's roof, for every wrong I have done you by thought, word, and deed."

The eyes she lifted to him were bright and searching, then they were spilling tears that wet his fingers and ran down his hand. Behind them came soft sobs that set all of her trembling, harder ones that made her shake.

"Susanna," he groaned and pulled her to him and wrapped his arms around her.

She curled into his chest and cried, not like a woman who has learned to temper such expressions of anguish, but surely how he imagined a girl, pained by the first breaking of her heart, would weep—as, perhaps, Judith had done the day she sent him away, committing the nine months that remained of her life to Alan de Balliol.

"Forgive me," he said and felt one of Susanna's hands rake his chest as she fiercely gripped his tunic as if for fear of falling.

Lord, how do I remedy this? How do I make amends for a trespass that laid ruin to her life as it seeks to lay ruin to Judas? Eleven years! How can she stand to be so near me? How can she not hate me? How do I fix what I have torn asunder?

22

SUSANNA HELD TIGHT to Everard where he had drawn her onto his thighs. It was happening again, something breaking inside her just as when Judas had feigned a breathing attack that had made her realize how corrupted his young heart was by the need to survive. And, as then, her sobs were part relief, part grief. Relief that, at last, her truth was told and believed. Grief that, for all the guilt-induced comfort offered her, it would not change the course of her life.

Still, she wanted to remain in this moment, the better to remember in years to come of how it felt to have strong arms around her that were only for the holding, not the taking—no favor for a favor. Merely comfort.

Remember, she told herself as she pressed her face to the firm, muscular chest and breathed in Everard with each gasp that shook her. *Remember.*

He let her cry, and it was not until she was softly hiccoughing against his tear-dampened tunic that she became aware of his hand moving over her shoulder and upper back, occasionally pausing to gently knead her tense muscles. No man had ever touched her this way. Likely, no man ever would again.

Remember, Susanna. It will make the cold nights warmer.

She tilted her face up.

Everard's own face was raised where he had settled his head back against the battlement, and though she could not see his eyes, she guessed he watched the thickening clouds chase one another across the moon and sky.

As she stared up at him, trying to think of what to say, she realized she did not want to say anything lest it mean the end of his embrace.

But then he lowered his chin, and his eyes found hers. He smiled, though it was a sorrowful turn of the lips. "Better?"

She was—as much as was possible. "Aye."

He opened his mouth as if to say something further, closed it.

"What is it?" she asked.

A long moment passed, then he said, "I have been thinking of Sir Morris—the things I would like to do to him of which, I am sure, God would not approve."

In the anger she had spilled all around him, she had said too much, but did he believe more had happened between her and the knight than actually had? "I thank you for wishing to defend me, but you should know that he only tried to ravish me. He did not—"

"Only!" His hand stilled upon her shoulder, gripped it as if he might shake her. "*Only*, Susanna? Truly, have you such little regard for yourself?"

The tension his touch had eased began to return. "I did give my brother's men cause to think—"

"Mayhap think, but not act. There is no excuse for that knave's behavior." Though the intensity of his gaze could not be seen, she felt it. "When a woman says 'nay,' it is 'nay.' There is no 'aye' in it."

The tears with which she had thought she was done once more threatened her composure. However, she tamped down her alarm with the reminder it would be no great loss considering how little composure she had left. After all, what dignity was there in perching upon his lap and being unable to bring herself to pull back from where she leaned into him? None. But there was contentment.

Oh, pray, remember this, even when you grow old and your mind is not right and death is a breath away. Here is the good of the world you will leave behind. Here. With he who loved Judith.

"I will not have you excuse such behavior," Everard said. "You will not take the blame for a man's depravity. Do you understand, Susanna?"

It would be easy to be offended by any man making a demand of her—indeed, she had often suffered such offenses at Cheverel—but not this one who ordered it for her sake, not his own. "I understand." She lowered her chin. "But still it does not absolve me—"

His hand moved up over her shoulder and neck, curved around her jaw, and lifted her face. "'Tis between God and you. Ask His forgiveness and it will be given, and you need never again feel guilt, just as you shall never again feel you must give any man what is not his to take—regardless of what the queen decides."

But if Judas was denied, it would be worse for her when, having no place to go, she was forced to return to her family home. Of course, with her nephew safe at Wulfen and only herself to fend for, it would not be necessary to bargain, would it? She could survive whatever was denied her, need only protect herself—

The memory of Sir Morris's near ravishment flashed through her. Alan would not be there to stop him, nor Sir Elias who could never return.

"If Judas is set aside," Everard continued, his breath warm amidst the air that continued to stir about them, "he will remain at Wulfen as I have told. And I will secure for you a position with my mother or one of my sisters."

It took a moment for his words to knock her anxious thoughts off their path, but when they did, she could only breathe, "What?"

"You will not return to Cheverel, Susanna."

Regardless of the state of her composure, she did not want to cry again. However, the effort required to contain her tears once more made her tremble. "I would that all men were like you, Everard Wulfrith. But you stand alone."

"I do not. 'Tis just that you have been in the wrong place, and I am sorry I put you there."

It was what she had accused him of doing, and there was truth in it, but she wanted to be beyond that, for the bad of her past to stay there, for it to have no place in her present or future.

"How many others, Susanna?"

She caught her breath. She knew what he asked, but she did not want to discuss it, not now with his arms around her, hand upon her jaw, thumb against her lower lip—all of which somehow made her feel clean rather than dirty as when she was touched as she did not wish to be.

"I beseech you," she whispered, "do not ask that of me."

"I do not mean to shame you. I but wish to know how deeply I have wronged you."

Were he any other man, she did not think she would believe him, but she did not doubt that the burden of what she did not wish to tell was intended to be borne upon his own shoulders—yet more guilt.

"There is only one thing you need know," she said. "Though I may never be versed in what goes between a man and a woman on their wedding night, were I, that part of me most treasured by my husband would be his and no other's."

He tensed, the opposite reaction she had hoped for.

She reached up and laid a hand over his upon her jaw. "Let that be enough, Everard. Ease your conscience."

After a long moment, he said, "You are saying you forgive me?"

There was no reason to hesitate, and yet she did, for his words were ones she had never expected to hear, just as she had thought he would never believe her innocent of carrying tale of a forbidden kiss to her brother.

"That is what I am saying. I forgive you."

When the silence grew uncomfortable, she added, "Please know that I am grateful for all you are doing to make things right for Judas. Regardless of what happens, I can ask no more of you than that."

Softly, he said, "Can you not?"

What did he mean? Though moonlight knew well her upturned face, it was mostly denied his that was bent toward hers. Thus, there was nothing definite to be read upon his face. "I do not understand," she said.

He slid his hand from beneath hers and over the backs of her fingers. "Your hand is cold," he murmured, then drew it upward and touched his lips to her fingertips.

For a moment, Susanna could not breathe. A moment later, air was again denied her as his mouth moved to her palm and warmed it with a kiss.

She gasped. "Everard?"

He raised her hand higher, pressed his lips to the inside of her wrist where he surely felt the pulse fed by a heart that beat so forcefully it hurt.

She shuddered, told herself this was not happening, that only a dream could make it so.

He lowered her hand, but though she was certain he had come to the end of whatever possessed him, he bent his head, angled it, and set his mouth so near hers that there was hardly enough space between them for the wind to pass.

"May I?" His voice was deep, low, and all of her felt as if caressed by it.

She wanted to agree, to grant him an unearned kiss, but should she not first understand why he wished to kiss her, Susanna de Balliol?

"Why?" she said and, in forming the word, her lips brushed his and a sharp, quick sensation moved through her that dropped her onto the edge of something wonderful that required but a single step forward into...What?

"May I?" he said again, leaving her question unanswered.

It matters not. Just remember this.

"Aye."

His lips touched hers, opened upon hers, and Susanna sighed into him.

It was only a kiss, and when it deepened and his hands pushed through her hair and fingers gripped her scalp, it was still only a kiss. He asked no more of her, left the rest of her untouched, and yet it was like nothing she had felt—sweet, yet more than sweet; safe, yet, perhaps, not safe at all, for she longed to step over that edge into the something wonderful that beckoned.

As when she had laid a hand over his that cradled her jaw, she gave only cursory thought to what she did next—reaching up and pressing her hands to the sides of his face, then curving them up over his scalp. But there was nothing to slide her fingers through, stubble only, and it thrust upon her the memory of the promise made to Judith that her hands alone would know his hair. Only ever hers, the woman he had never stopped loving.

Susanna opened her eyes that she had surely closed out of habit—always seaming them tight so that sight would not strengthen the memory of what she did with those who did for her—and peered at Everard's deeply shadowed face. His lids were lowered, and she recalled he had denied her an answer as to why he wished to kiss her. But the answer would be easily found were she honest enough to look where it lay.

She drew a breath of Everard, impressed upon herself this memory of how it felt to be held and kissed by him beneath a moonlit sky with the careless wind their only witness, then pulled her head back. "We must stop."

She sensed his bafflement, but he did not try to hold her to him when she pressed backward and out of his arms.

Settling to her knees alongside him, she lowered her head and tried to talk herself down from the feeling of loss that sought to overwhelm her.

"You are right," he said.

She raised her head. "As told, forgiveness is yours." The wind swept hair across her face. "There need be no atonement."

Where he leaned against the battlement, she saw his lids narrow, and then he sat forward. "Atonement, Susanna? What say you?"

"'Tis not required. I want no part of it."

"You think that is why I kissed you? To atone?" He closed a hand over her two that she clasped in her lap. "I did it because I wished to, and not for the first time. Surely you know I nearly kissed you the day I brought word of Judas's attack?"

Then it had not been imagined. He had wanted that intimacy then, even before he knew she was innocent of what he had long believed—

But therein lies the truth. Do not make more of this than it is, for you will only know greater hurt.

The truth was that Wulfen Castle was without women, and though Everard had more honor than any man she had known, he had desires like others of his sex—surely enough to tempt him to seek intimacy with one of whom he believed ill.

"Aye," she said, "I thought, mayhap, 'twas what you wanted, but I am acquainted with men's needs, just as I am aware of the remorse you feel. This night, when I said I could ask no more of you than what you are doing for Judas, did you not question if I could, indeed, ask more?"

He did not answer.

"And then you sought to kiss me, to give me—one who was once besotted—more than what was asked of you." Again, her throat tightened and, determined she would not cry again, she breathed deep. "Whether or not you realize it, Everard, you kissed me to ease your conscience. And I do not want that."

"Susanna—"

She pulled her hands free of his. "I know where your heart belongs. Though, perhaps, here in the dark, you can tell yourself I am her when your arms are around me, there are too many hours of daylight in which you will see that I am simply Susanna. And I do not wish to be simply anything to anyone. Methinks there would be more ache in that than in being nothing."

She pushed herself to standing and, as the cool night air tossed her hair and chemise about, said, "Providing you continue to apprise me of how Judas fares, you need not worry I shall venture into your solar again. Henceforth, no matter how discontented I am with the length and breadth of my confinement, I shall strive for contentment."

She started to turn away and paused. She did not want to use his remorse for gain, but if she did not ask one thing of him, she feared she would fail at even the striving for contentment. "I hope you will not take measures to prevent me from coming to the roof at night, for it makes the days tolerable and I…" She shrugged. "I can breathe here."

"I will grant you that," he said solemnly.

She inclined her head, then crossed to the door and began her descent of the ladder.

When she was gone, Everard turned his gaze to the cloud-swept heavens and dragged his resistant thoughts back over what had passed between Susanna and him.

He had been deeply affected when she had tried to ease his conscience by assuring him she did not yet know a man as fully as a woman on her wedding night would know her husband. Though relieved to learn she had not had to sacrifice her virtue, he had sensed despair, as if she were resigned to a lonely life without husband and children. But then, it was realistic, for her betrothal had been broken and eleven years had passed that placed her beyond the usual marriageable age, especially for one who did not possess a dowry capable of securing a desirable marriage contract.

And he was responsible, the acknowledgment of which had surely caused him to imply she could ask more of him than helping Judas lay hold of Cheverel. But what had he been offering? And why had he denied that atonement was the reason for the kiss when it had to have been that?

Had to have been? It was not guilt that nearly made you taste her mouth several days past. Recall that you yet believed jealousy had caused her to run to Alan de Balliol.

Desire, then? Only a man's needs as she herself had concluded? He did not think so, and yet what else—?

He shook his head. Questioning his motivations, words, and behavior was becoming too much of a habit. He knew who he was, what he wanted, why he wanted it, what he did not want, why he did not want it. And yet Susanna de Balliol wreaked havoc on his ordered world.

"For this, women are not allowed at Wulfen," he muttered and gained his feet.

As he did so, he heard the soft jangle of the necklace as it landed upon the rooftop. Realizing that, as Susanna had emptied her sorrow within his arms, she must have dropped the pendant between them, he bent to retrieve it. It was then he remembered what else had been forgotten while he held her.

He searched his gaze over the rooftop, but though he expected the ruby's appetite for light to quickly reveal its location, he caught no sparkle. All he found was the pale cloth in which Susanna had wrapped it. Strangely, though he knew he ought to be alarmed that the symbol of his love for Judith was missing, he felt something different. Relief?

Whatever it was, it was distant from what he had felt upon discovering Susanna had left the gem in his solar. That Judith had kept it upon her person while she carried Alan de Balliol's child, while the two of them had moved toward reconciliation...

It had bothered him to learn that, and he had regretted that he had not allowed her to return the ruby the day of her wedding as she had surely foreseen it was best to do. Had he known it would ever be between her husband and her, a constant reminder of a love lost, would he have accepted it?

He feared not, for that foolish young man had not wanted to be forgotten.

Everard pushed a hand up over his head, felt the rasp Susanna's fingers had felt, remembered that soon thereafter she had ended their kiss—as if Judith had slipped between them. And she had, much like the ruby had come between Alan de Balliol and her.

Leaving the gem to its fate, he strode forward and, shortly, halted outside Susanna's chamber. Though he told himself his excuse for entering was only an excuse, he pushed the door inward and stepped into darkness.

In the absence of the sound of her breathing, he guessed she held her breath. "Fear not," he said, "I but return your necklace."

"I thank you," she whispered.

He crossed to the chess table and set the pendant and chain in the center of the board, then returned to the doorway and looked over his shoulder at the shadowed bed. "I will make it better for you, Susanna," he said. "This I vow."

He stepped into the corridor and closed the door.

23

She stared at the clothes. It could not portend well. Could it?

Loosening her tongue from the roof of her mouth, Susanna raised her gaze to Sir Rowan who held the bundle out to her. "Why?"

He smiled lightly. "Do not be anxious, Lass. This is a good thing."

"I do not know how that can be—why Lord Wulfrith would wish me to dress as a man. Did he say where he is taking me?"

"As told, for a ride. You have been too long indoors."

Merely a ride? Or the pretense of one in order to quietly remove her from Wulfen—and Judas? Not that she believed Everard would set her outside the walls to fend for herself, but that did not mean he had not decided to send her elsewhere, perhaps to his mother or one of his sisters as he had assured her last eve he would do if Judas's claim to Cheverel was denied.

Sir Rowan stepped forward, set the clothes on the mattress, and placed a hand on her shoulder. "My lady, you will have fresh air, the sun upon your face, and companionship that, I am sure, is more compelling than mine. And mayhap you will even have occasion to see your nephew ere you return here."

Judas. To see him among his peers and witness for herself that he flourished...

"You are certain I will return?"

"A ride, Lord Wulfrith said, not a journey that requires you to take your belongings with you. He but wishes you to don these garments so you may more easily pass unnoticed through the castle."

It sounded true. And when Everard had returned her necklace, he had promised he would make things better for her. Had he meant this? That she would be allowed to leave her room? To mount a horse merely for the pleasure of it?

Feeling an uncertain thrill, she glanced at the bundle. "Very well. Lord Wulfrith will come for me?"

"Nay, I am to take you to him in the stables."

"I will not be long."

He withdrew and closed the door.

A quarter hour later, dressed in chausses, tunic, and boots, and having worked her hair into a single braid that fell down her back beneath the short mantle draped over her shoulders, Susanna stood at the center of the room.

It did not feel right to be dressed as a man, especially in chausses that settled too closely upon her legs, denying her the modesty and femininity afforded by skirts. In contrast, the tunic was loose, providing none of the support of a fitted bodice. As for the boots, they were thick and heavy, affording no grace with which to appear as if one glided across the floor as she had been taught a lady must do.

Loath to show herself to Sir Rowan, she tugged at the tunic and smoothed the chausses. As she was not beautiful like Judith, she required the trappings of a lady—bliaut, chemise, slippers, veil—to set her well apart from men. Now, not only did she lack those things, but she would be meeting Everard without benefit of the dark as there had been last eve.

A knock sounded. "My lady?"

She blew a breath up her face, stepped forward, and opened the door. "I am ready." She averted her gaze so she would not see his dismay over her appearance.

"Well," he said, "I suppose 'tis better than to flaunt that a lady remains within Wulfen's walls."

She looked up. "What say you?"

"Methinks it unlikely you will pass for a boy, even with the hood over your head."

She glanced down her front. "I feel like a boy."

"Feeling like and looking like are different, Lass." He turned to the wall sconce and retrieved the torch.

Wondering what he saw that she did not, Susanna followed him down the steps.

She could not know if Everard had told Sir Rowan of her middle-of-the-night wanderings, for the knight made no mention of it as they negotiated the hidden passageway, and he spoke only to tell her to heed her footing.

When they came out from behind the tapestry into the solar, she was surprised by the sunlight streaming through the upper windows. All that had been in shadow or dimly lit by glowing embers on the two occasions she had ventured here was now clearly seen. The chamber was impressive, and not even the long table set around with chairs and the enormous postered bed where twice Everard had watched her trespass upon him, could diminish its size.

"Cover your head," Sir Rowan said.

As he set the torch in a sconce near the curtains that separated the solar from the hall, Susanna drew the hood over her hair and pulled it forward to shadow her face.

Passing through the hall presented no difficulty, for there were few about. The inner bailey was the same. However, as evidenced by the din that rose above the walls and grew louder with each step, the outer bailey was a different matter.

Though she kept her head down as she followed Sir Rowan, she felt the curious regard of pages, squires, and knights and was relieved when, at last, they entered the stables.

Everard was within, standing before a silver-gray stallion and a white mare. He was not dressed as fine as he had been for the knighting ceremony, but his tunic and chausses were crisp and clean, and upon his belt was a sword and dagger—the Wulfrith dagger, its hilt still absent the ruby. When would he have the gem reset?

"Lady Susanna," he said, "I am pleased you accepted my invitation to ride."

Realizing she had halted just inside the doors, allowing Sir Rowan to advance without her, she raised her gaze to Everard's. She hated that her face warmed when their eyes met, but no matter what had been behind his kiss, there was no forgetting it. But then, she had not wanted to, had told herself again and again to remember. And she would, even to the detriment of her heart.

"The clothes look to fit," he said, then added, "somewhat."

Suppressing the impulse to cross her arms over her chest, she glanced left and right and, seeing no others, pushed the hood off her head despite the inner voice that chastised her for giving in to vanity. "'Tis good to be outside, Lord Wulfrith. I thank you for the consideration."

He inclined his head, then called over his shoulder, "Judas!"

She gasped, and again when her nephew stepped from a stall to the left, then she was hastening over the earthen floor, grudgingly grateful for the absence of skirts that would have hindered her stride.

Moments later, her arms were filled with her beloved boy.

"Aunt Sanna," he protested, though not so vigorously she was prevailed upon to release him, and then his arms were around her as well.

"Judas mine," she whispered into his hair. "I am beyond glad to see you." She knew Everard might think it unseemly that she was so moved considering her night visits to the hall, but she could not help herself.

Too soon, Judas grew restless and pulled back.

Reluctantly, she allowed him to step out of her arms.

"Though I have been much occupied," he said, "I have missed you, too."

Suppressing the temptation to take back the step separating them and cup his face in her hands, she said, "You look well. I do not think I have ever seen so much color in your face." And the dark smudges beneath his eyes were almost gone.

"Most of my time is spent out of doors."

"Indeed. You are pleased with your training?"

He pressed his shoulders back. "I am becoming a man."

She tried to turn the small sob that escaped her into a laugh, but it sounded so pitiful. Feeling her color rise again, she cleared her throat. "Of course you are. And how do you like those with whom you train?"

He shrugged. "Some I do not like, but others are not so bad. Forsooth, I think..."

"Aye?"

He tensed but, before she could grow alarmed, she noticed the corners of his mouth tugged as if he might smile. He leaned near. "I think I have a friend, Aunt Sanna."

Susanna felt a ray of happiness. "Tell me."

"He is older and, though I did not like him at all when we first came to Wulfen, we are getting along better."

Her happiness wilted at the likelihood he spoke of the squire who had taunted him about his name and whom Everard had said now seemed of a mind to befriend him. "What is his name?"

"Squire Charles."

The same, then. If not that Everard was surely watching and listening, Susanna would warn her nephew to be wary of the young man.

"I did not trust him when he first tried to befriend me," he continued, "but he has defended me several times since my breathing attack, and on the day past, he told me he had an older sister who also suffered from such attacks."

She blinked. "Oh?"

"Aye." His brow furrowed. "She died."

A chill swept Susanna. "I am sorry to hear it."

After a long moment, he said, "You worry too much about me, Aunt Sanna."

She smiled wryly. "'Tis called love."

He looked disconcerted, as if she had shouted the words in the presence of his peers, but then he grinned and said, "I know it well." Then, as if eager to turn the conversation lest she pulled him to her, he said, "I am glad Lord Wulfrith is taking you riding."

"As am I."

"'Tis time, Judas," Everard said.

Susanna felt a spurt of annoyance. However, gratitude quickly doused the emotion, for he had made it possible for her to talk with Judas in the light of day.

"I must return to practice," her nephew said.

"Of course."

Though she hoped he would give her a parting hug as he would have done a year ago, he hurried past her and she peered over her shoulder to watch him exit the stables. Then he was gone, followed by Sir Rowan.

Susanna looked to Everard and, once more discomfited by her state of dress, crossed to where he stood alongside the mare. "Beyond words, I thank you."

His eyes held hers. "I am pleased to have made you happy."

Was she happy? Was this lightness—this sense of well-being—happiness? It had to be.

"Methinks Wulfen has been as good for you as it has been for Judas," Everard observed.

Realizing she had not guarded her expression, she eased the smile from her mouth and said, "For that, I also thank you."

He inclined his head. "You are ready to ride?"

She looked down her front. "As you can see, I am dressed as a man."

"I hoped you would not mind. Though I do not doubt most will know 'tis a lady who passes by, I thought it best to be discreet so our young men are not too long distracted."

"It seems a most effective means."

He raised his eyebrows. "Not as effective as I had hoped, but it will have to do."

Knowing he must have sensed her disquiet over her appearance, Susanna did not take to heart the unspoken compliment. Stepping near the mare, she said, "I shall require your aid."

Everard set his hands to her waist, and though she tried to turn away memories of the night past when she had more intimately known his touch, she felt her pulse race as he lifted her into the saddle. His hands did not linger, and yet their warm imprint remained as he took up the reins and passed them to her.

"Your hood," he reminded her.

While she settled it over her head, he strode to his own horse and swung into the saddle.

Shortly, she urged her mount behind his into the outer bailey where she more deeply felt the regard of those present now that she was in the company of their lord.

Peering out from beneath the hood, she picked her gaze over the young men who practiced at swords, daggers, and spears upon the inner training field and marveled at the sight of so many who would one day stand before Everard Wulfrith to be knighted. But Judas was not to be found there. However, when they rode onto the drawbridge, she saw the training fields outside the walls were more crowded and guessed that here, among the scores who grunted and shouted as their weapons clashed and clanged, she would find her nephew.

She was still searching for him when her horse stepped off the drawbridge and she came alongside Everard.

"To the far left," he said with a jut of his chin.

Squinting against the sun that slowly rose toward the nooning hour, she located Judas and smiled. Then frowned.

Advancing on one who appeared to be of an age that would see him don spurs before long, Judas wielded a sword, something she had regularly witnessed during his training at Cheverel. What was not familiar was his stance.

"Why does he hold an arm behind him with his hand tucked beneath his belt?" she asked.

"Notice 'tis his left hand that swings the sword."

So it was. "Has he injured the right?"

"Nay. Though knights in training are taught to wield a sword with the favored hand, a dagger with the lesser hand, it is of good benefit to ensure the latter is also skilled in the balance and coordination required to swing a longer, weightier blade."

She looked sidelong at him. "Lest the favored hand be injured."

"You are perceptive, my lady. We implemented the training nearly three years past after my younger brother, Abel, suffered grievous injuries during a battle and his favored hand was permanently damaged. It took over six months of rigorous training to make his left hand as strong and deft at wielding a sword as his right had been. Thus, that same facility is now required of our charges."

Susanna watched as Judas awkwardly parried his opponent's blow. "It looks difficult."

"It is, but he makes good progress."

She continued to stare at her nephew who appeared capable of defending himself despite movements that lacked finesse and self assurance. Only when she felt the intense gaze of another did she look away and search out the source. She found it in the person of Sir Elias who stood well back from Judas. Knowing he would not be able to see her smile of acknowledgment amid the shadow of the hood, she discreetly raised a hand.

He inclined his head.

"We should ride," Everard said.

She glanced at him. Had he seen—and disapproved of—the exchange between her and the knight?

"I expect my brother, Abel, this afternoon," he said. "Thus, I would like to return well in advance of his arrival."

Unsettled by the tidings, she wondered how Abel Wulfrith would react when he learned his brother had let a woman into Wulfen. Of course, perhaps he was not meant to know, and for this—to be certain Susanna was out of sight—Everard wished to be done with the ride before his brother came unto the walls.

"Of course. I shall follow."

He waved her forward. "I prefer that you ride at my side."

There went her heart again, leaning so heavily toward him that it felt as if it strained against her breastbone. "I would like that."

As they spurred their horses over the land before the castle, their advance moved the warm, still air, and she had to release the saddle's pommel to grip the hood closed.

"Let it go," Everard called to her.

She looked at him and, when he nodded, allowed the hood to fall down around her shoulders.

Over the next quarter hour, they sped across the open ground and, for the first time since she was a girl, she rode merely for the joy of riding. Indeed, it was more exciting now, for never had she managed such a brisk pace other than during the flight from Cheverel when all she had felt was fear of being overtaken, relief as each league passed without event, and fatigue. As then, she did not ride sidesaddle, but this time no skirts hindered her and she did not share her mount with Judas.

Everard veered toward the trees and, as they neared, slowed. "We can continue on," he said, "or start back by way of the wood. The latter will allow us to pause at the waterfall if you would like to see it."

Susanna knew she should soften her expression of pleasure, but she did not. "I would very much like to see it."

He moved his gaze over her face, said, "You do not know how lovely you are, do you, Susanna de Balliol?"

She lost her smile. He did not speak true, for she was nothing approaching lovely and, garbed as she was, there could not even be pretense of it. She forced a laugh. "And you do not know how kind you are, do you, Everard Wulfrith?"

He lifted an eyebrow. "What I see has naught to do with kindness."

Guilt, then. Atonement. Even if he did not know it.

Determined that she would not bring ruin to their outing by arguing, she said, "I would see the waterfall now."

Few words passed between them as they negotiated the trees, and then none at all once the sound of falling water reached them.

In and out of the slants of sunlight and overarching shade they guided their mounts. Throughout, Susanna attended to the smell of moist earth and fragrant plants, the crunch of leaves beneath hooves, the scuttling of things unseen, the sight of woodland creatures running up trees and flitting hedge to hedge and branch to branch.

The waterfall was a long time in appearing, but when she caught sight of it, the reason its sound had carried so far was evidenced by its height and breadth.

She gasped. "'Tis beautiful!"

"I thought you would like it."

Some minutes later, downstream from the pool into which the thickly ruffled veil of water poured, Everard's hands were once more upon her waist as he lifted her from the mare.

Lest he notice her color was on the rise, she kept her chin lowered until he released her and stepped aside.

"On the ridge above," he said, "is a path our young men often take during pre-dawn runs."

She considered the vegetation-strewn wall that rose up on the other side of the stream. "'Twould be a bad tumble should one draw too near the edge."

"Aye. For that, all the senses must be engaged."

"Have many fallen?"

"It is a rare occurrence but, for those who do not heed their senses, it is not so sharply inclined that they suffer much more than a broken bone."

She almost laughed. "I suppose that is a comfort."

Everard took up the mare's reins, then the stallion's, and turned away. As he led the horses to the bank of the stream, Susanna crossed to a great oak and leaned against it.

He soon joined her and also settled his back to the tree. "When the upper portion runs shallow," he said, looking to the falls, "the young men traverse it and descend to this side before making their way back to Wulfen."

The thought of Judas up there amid the rush of water caused her heart to lurch. "Even shallow, it must be treacherous," she said.

"Right before the fall it is, but the crossing is made well back from the edge so that, at worst, a dousing is the price paid for careless footing—and bruising, as weighted belts are worn to increase strength and stamina."

She put her head to the side. "It makes me almost glad to have been born female."

He swung his gaze to her. "Almost?"

Wishing she had not said that, for she wanted no more of his guilt, she sighed. "I exaggerate. Like many women, I envy the freedom of men—at least, those privileged enough to dictate the terms of their own lives so they need answer to no one." Men like her brother.

Everard turned his body toward her and set his shoulder to the tree. "Everyone answers to someone, Susanna, even the king who stands to make enemies out of allies if he abuses his power. And, if he should be foolish enough to turn all those sword arms against himself, still he answers to God—as we all do."

He was right, but that raised another matter that she knew she should not dwell upon. Before she could push it back down, she heard herself say, "Why do you think God so often takes years and years to ask questions of those who owe Him a great debt of answers?"

Everard was silent so long that she thought he did not intend to venture a guess. "Perhaps," he finally said, "He but gives us time to ask the questions of ourselves so that, in answering them, we have the opportunity to right our wrongs before we are made to stand before Him. Time to atone."

It was not easy to hold her eyes to his, so strongly did she wish to look away, but she forced herself to stare into those grey-green depths. And wait.

He drew a deep breath. "I know I did wrong eleven years ago, Susanna. Though Judith was promised to another, I was arrogant enough to believe that, having been born one of those privileged enough to dictate the terms of his own life, I could claim her without consequence. Thus, though she discouraged my attentions and said she liked your brother well enough to do her duty to her family, I determined that I would convince her otherwise. And I thought I had. But in the end, she went the way she had said she would."

What he told was far more than what Susanna had waited for—almost too much honesty, for never had she expected him to share such private emotions and matters regardless of how deep his need to atone. What did it mean?

"When she sent me away," he continued, "I was hurt and angry and did not believe I needed to answer to anyone for having loved her. Only after I learned she had died from childbirth did I begin to ask questions of myself and loathe the answers—so much that I nearly set Judas and you outside my walls."

She pushed her fingers into the crevices of the bark at her back to keep from laying a hand upon his arm. "But you did not," she said.

His smile was grim. "Prayer. When I avail myself of it—humble myself—always I know the course to take. And this course was a steep one to set my feet upon, not only because you, a woman I believed had betrayed her friend out of jealousy, demanded that I set things right, but because it meant acknowledging that my indiscretion had reached so far into the life of Judith's son that I could be the ruin of him." He heaved a sigh. "I am glad I was wrong about you, Susanna, but the blow is heavier yet knowing I caused you to suffer all these years."

She swallowed. "I have said you are forgiven, and though I am glad for the freedom you have granted me, if it is but a means of assuaging your guilt, methinks it better for both of us had I remained in my chamber."

He nodded slowly. "I do feel guilt, for I am not without conscience, but this is more than that, just as what happened between us last eve was more than guilt or desire."

She stopped her breath, wondered how talk of the training of squires had landed her back on the roof beneath a night sky with Everard's arms around her.

"I still cannot say why I kissed you," he said, "but I know I did it as much for myself as I did it for you. And that 'twas you I held, not the memory of a woman I once loved."

As on the night past, Susanna felt a flutter of hope, but that part of her grounded in survival rose up and demanded she see this for what it was—dangerous hope that could be dashed upon rocks capable of breaking her. Whether it was guilt or desire or both that had caused him to act as he had on the night past, whether it was known to him or unknown, she must accept that she had no future with him beyond what he could do to help Judas.

Though her knees felt weak, she pushed off the tree. "We should not speak further on this."

Everard watched her distance herself, told himself it was wise for her to do so, for each time he drew near her, it was harder than the time before to pull away. Forsooth, he did not know what he felt for Susanna, nor could he be certain how much of what he felt was because of Judith. But as he had told her, it was not merely guilt or desire, for those alone would never had caused him to open himself up to her as he had done— as he had not done with anyone, not even his brothers.

Wondering where he went from here, and knowing it could not be any place that might cause her further hurt, he shifted his gaze from where she walked downstream and looked to the horses that grazed on the lush grass along the bank.

When a quarter hour passed and Susanna continued to grow distant, he retrieved the stallion and mare and followed. As he neared, she bent before a group of low-lying shrubs, out from under which spread bright green ground cover dotted with white flowers.

She surely heard his approach, for she called over her shoulder, "Sweet woodruff."

He halted in back of her and watched as she plucked the tiny, star-shaped blooms from their tender stalks. The scent, not unlike fresh cut hay, and yet much more than that, stirred a memory.

She picked a few more, then peered over her shoulder and said, with what sounded like apology, "I know 'tis common and has not the beauty of other flowers, but I have always been fond of their delicacy and, especially, the scent."

"I know."

She blinked. "You do?"

He released the reins and lowered to his haunches beside her. "It is that which floated about you when you were a girl. I am guessing you filled your pendant with its petals and leaves."

Her face tightened, fingers closed around the blossoms.

Regretting that he had once more made her uncomfortable, he shifted his regard to the ground cover. "Forgive me. 'Tis just that I have an unnatural sense of smell, one that sometimes seems as much a curse as a blessing."

"Then you have smelled roses upon me since my arrival at Wulfen."

"I have. 'Tis how I confirmed it was you who entered my solar that first time."

She lowered her chin and opened her hand to consider the blossoms. "And now you are wondering why roses when I favor sweet woodruff."

"It does raise the question."

After a long moment, she said, "When Judith wore my pendant, she preferred roses, and when she returned it to me ere her death…The scent reminded me of her, so much that sometimes it seemed as if she were beside Judas and me."

"You truly loved her."

She jerked her chin. "I did. And I shall ever miss her."

Dear Lord, she has lost so much.

He picked a blossom from her hand and carried it to his nose. "'Tis a better scent for you," he said and, so she would not think he believed her unworthy of the more lavish rose, added, "Sweet. Clean. Pure."

Her head came up sharply, and he saw her eyes were bright with tears. "You think such words fit me, Everard Wulfrith? You who saw me with Sir Elias, who knows *that* was not just a kiss?"

He knew he should not touch her again, but he released the blossom and slid a hand along her jaw. "What I know, Susanna, is that I am not the only one who struggles with guilt. And just as you would have me released from mine, I would see you free of yours—that you make peace with God and be done with it as I said you should last eve. Ask forgiveness and put it behind you."

In the curve of his hand he felt her swallow. Lowering his gaze past the temptation presented by her mouth, he settled it on the smooth column of her throat and, when she swallowed again, caught the glimmer of the chain at the neck of her mantle.

She startled when he hooked a finger beneath it, pulled slightly back when he drew the empty pendant free of the tunic.

He turned it in his hand. "Aye, sweet woodruff. It fits you, Susanna." He lowered the pendant and straightened. "We should start back."

She nodded, opened the purse on her belt, and shook the handful of woodruff into it.

It took little time to confirm the saddles were properly cinched, and then Everard once more lifted Susanna into the saddle. He handed the reins to her, and that was when he felt a presence that did not belong— one not of the wood though that was where it crouched.

More heavily aware of the sword and dagger upon his belt, he turned, searched his gaze over the ridge above, and picked out and dismissed all sound and movement that did belong in this place.

"What is it?" Susanna asked.

Nothing that could be seen or heard. Perhaps nothing at all. And yet the presence persisted. Upon their return to Wulfen Castle, he would send a patrol to scout the area.

"Naught," he said, not wishing to alarm her, and strode to the stallion and mounted.

Not until they were out of sight of the waterfall did his senses settle—all the more reason to believe he had not imagined there was something back there. Rather, someone.

As he and Susanna rode side by side and the trees began to thin and allow glimpses of the land before the castle, his senses rose up again. However, this time they were borne along by the sound of hooves quickly covering ground. At the edge of the wood, Everard reined in.

"Who do you think 'tis?" Susanna's voice was tight with worry.

Keeping his gaze fixed to the far left where they would soon appear, he said, "Likely my brother, come earlier than expected." It was as he hoped, for though he had wished to speak to Abel about Susanna before introducing them, discomfort was preferable to her fear being realized with another visit by those from Cheverel.

Shortly, four riders on three horses came into sight, and there could be no doubt that the man at the center with the boy in front of him was Abel.

"My brother," Everard said and looked across his shoulder at Susanna. "Let us meet him."

As he started to urge his horse forward, she said, "Would it not be best to allow him to pass so we might return once he is within the walls?"

He raised his eyebrows. "He might as well know of you sooner, rather than later."

Susanna felt her heart lurch. "You are sure?"

"You have naught to fear. Now let us show ourselves ere they are past us."

She nodded and drew the hood over her head.

"That is not necessary," he said.

"Even so, I shall wear it."

Everard looked like he might object again, but a glance at the riders made him urge his horse ahead.

She followed but remained at his back.

No sooner did they come out from among the trees than the riders veered toward them, and it seemed only moments before they reined in before Everard.

Susanna knew immediately that Abel Wulfrith was the one who shared his mount with a boy, for though his face bore a deep scar, he had Everard's eyes, broad cheekbones, and strong jaw. And nearly as deep a voice when he said, "Such a welcome I did not expect, Brother."

"Such an early arrival *I* did not expect," Everard rejoined, then the two drew alongside and clasped arms—and for those spare moments, Abel Wulfrith's gaze fell upon Susanna, probed the depths of her hood, and travelled down her and up again.

She remained unmoving, only to startle when he grinned.

"'Tis good to see you," Everard said as the brothers drew apart, then he leaned toward the boy who could not be more than seven or eight years of age. "And you, John. You have grown quite a bit. Indeed, I wager 'tis not a wooden sword you swing these days."

The boy grinned. "Father has given me a real one. The edges are dull, but only for now."

"I look forward to seeing all he has taught you." Everard returned his attention to his brother. "How is your lady wife?"

"Helene is quite well."

The boy snapped his chin up. "Can I tell him, Father?"

Abel Wulfrith smiled. "You may."

"I am going to be a brother, Uncle Everard, and Father is going to be…" He frowned. "…a father again."

Everard chuckled. "I am glad to hear it." He looked back at his brother. "Most glad to hear it."

"I thank you." Abel Wulfrith eased his destrier aside and nodded at the riders behind. "As told in my missive, I am accompanied by Baron Lavonne's newest knights, Sir Otto and Sir Rainald."

Everard inclined his head. "You are welcome at Wulfen."

"My lord," the men acknowledged him.

"However," Abel Wulfrith said, "as *not* told, I do not yet know who accompanies you, Everard. Will your companion not come out from under yon hood?"

Once more falling beneath the gaze of the youngest Wulfrith brother—and the others of his party—Susanna closed her hands tighter upon the reins and wished it had not been decided that sooner was better than later.

Everard turned in the saddle, smiled reassuringly, and beckoned her forward. "This is a guest of Wulfen," he said as she nudged the mare alongside his.

At his nod, she lowered the hood.

No surprise rose upon his brother's face, only what appeared to be amusement.

"Lady Susanna de Balliol," Everard said, "my brother, Sir Abel Wulfrith."

"Sir Abel," she said, and winced at how small her voice sounded.

The younger man drew near, peered down at her, and mused, "Now this is most curious, Brother."

"As is your lack of manners, *Brother*," Everard said.

Sir Abel arched an eyebrow at Susanna. "He is right, of course. Forgive me, my lady. My only excuse is that this is not a moment ever anticipated. Indeed, I would not even have dreamed it."

"Abel!"

The recipient of the growl grinned. "That is not to say I do not welcome it. Forsooth, I take great pleasure in meeting you, Lady Susanna, and I look forward to knowing more about Wulfen's unusual guest."

Susanna detected no sarcasm in his tone, but still she was wary. "I am glad to meet you as well, Sir Abel."

He looked past her. "It seems we have much more to discuss than thought, Everard."

"We will talk at Wulfen." Everard urged his horse forward.

As Susanna did the same and moved past his brother, she heard the boy say, "Father?"

"Son?"

"I remembered not to speak before thinking."

"I am pleased." Abel Wulfrith's voice carried easily as he came behind Susanna. "Now, what are you thinking?"

"Did you see she is dressed as a boy?"

"Aye."

"But still she is a girl."

"Very much so."

"A girl...at Wulfen," John said, slowly, distinctly, as if to make his father understand the seriousness of the matter.

Susanna nearly smiled.

"There most certainly is a girl at Wulfen, John."

"But girls are not allowed here."

"That is true. However, rare exceptions are made, and I am sure your uncle has good cause to grant Lady Susanna admittance."

Susanna considered Everard where he rode several lengths ahead, wondered if he was also privy to the conversation.

"Do you think she is like Aunt Annyn?" John asked.

Remembering Sir Rowan's tale of the lady who had stolen into Wulfen and shown she was as adept at wielding arms as men, Susanna let the smile onto her lips.

"Nay," Sir Abel said. "Methinks this lady is very different from your aunt."

Susanna tensed, then firmly told herself his words were not meant to insult, for she had not sensed any dislike of her person. Too, he had to know she could hear them.

"Is Uncle Everard going to marry her?"

She startled so violently she knew her reaction was not lost on any who looked her way.

"Now that is a good question." There seemed a smile in Sir Abel's voice. "We shall have to ask him, hmm?"

He could not know there was nothing amusing in the suggestion, that it was so unthinkable it made her nose prickle.

She prodded the mare to greater speed so she might lose their conversation beneath the beat of hooves. When she came alongside Everard, he smiled. But it was a strained smile, one that almost made her wish she had not joined him for a ride—almost, for there was comfort in the woodruff he had remembered about her and thought more fitting with its sweet, clean, pure scent.

Oh, Everard, I wish I were merely besotted, but I do love you. And I am sorry for it.

Side by side, they rode on Wulfen Castle and, when they drew near, she once more donned the hood. And prepared herself to return to the tower room.

They were here—had been here when Sir Talbot had circled back to inquire of the lord of the renowned stronghold if he'd had word or sight of a lady and boy in the company of an errant knight. And that hulking bald man had denied it and refused to admit those from Cheverel within the hallowed walls of Wulfen Castle.

"Arrogant, deceitful, God-forsaken liar," Morris muttered where he sat with his back against the tree as he had done for the past quarter hour.

Not that he was afeared. He was merely wary. And he had cause to be, for he had made no sound that could be heard above the great fall of water, nothing that would have caused Everard Wulfrith to turn and search out the ridge. But search it the knave had done, as if he had another sense about him as it was said some possessed.

Likely by way of the devil, he assured himself, for he did not care to envy any man anything he himself could not own. That way lay helplessness and worthlessness as keenly honed as any blade that had ever sliced through flesh and bone, and he'd had enough of that from the sire who had openly lamented that his third son was cursed with his mother's slight build—had said Morris would have been better born a girl.

"Poltroon," Morris spat, then wrenched his thoughts forward to his present circumstances and decided it would cost him nothing to give God a nod for drawing him to the waterfall this day and hour.

You did well, Lord. I thank You for favoring me.

Not that the Almighty had been in a hurry to do so. Two days and nights Morris had spent in this wood, pacing and cursing at being unable to draw near enough the castle to determine if Judas de Balliol, who was far more deserving of a father's disgust, was among those who trained at Wulfen. More frustrating was this morning's exercise, a run through the wood that, had there been a better moon to identify the boy, would have allowed Morris to draw near enough to drive a blade through his heart and be far gone before the body was discovered.

Unfortunately, his life had never been that easy, all he had ever gained requiring time, effort, daring and, on occasion, blood. Regardless, he would do what he had been sent here to do, and it would not be his veins that spilled crimson.

Once again feeling the quake he had experienced when the lord of Wulfen had turned to search him out, he raised his right hand to eye level and, palm facing down, watched the twitching and shuddering of bones and flesh. As always, he was fascinated by his body's response to the prospect of bloodshed that ever proved his father wrong about his runt of a son.

However, Morris was not such a liar himself that he did not acknowledge there was something more to this quaking than excitement. Wariness, he once more named it, for it was possible the completion of his task would bring him face to face with the lord of Wulfen whose reputation preceded him as it did all those who bore the name of Wulfrith. But should it come to that, the big, slow-moving man would underestimate his opponent as many before him had done.

Morris dropped his hand to his side, expelled a long breath that ended on laughter. His life was about to take a turn for the better, for Sir Talbot had assured him that Lady Richenda would be indebted to the one who ensured her grandson lorded Cheverel—so much that she would grant him any number of things.

And the first of those things? Lady Susanna who, when this was done, would have no place to go but home. What she had long refused him and allowed others, she would refuse him no more. Such imaginings...

And they nearly proved his undoing.

He sat forward, swept his gaze over the wood that did not yet reveal what was felt and heard—riders, heading this direction, doubtless sent by Everard Wulfrith.

"Miscreant!" he hissed and leapt to his feet and ran.

24

THE TALE WAS told—as lightly as possible, but still Everard felt its weight, for until Susanna had come to Wulfen, he had believed it need never be spoken of, not even to his brothers. And nearly as discomfiting as the words that had flayed open his past was how often Abel's gaze drifted to Everard's shaved head. *That* had been left untold, but his brother was no fool.

Abel sighed and sat back in his chair.

Knowing his penchant for wry observation, Everard awaited the response that, he silently vowed, would not cause him to say or do anything he would later regret.

Abel frowned, looked to his hands that rested flat upon the table, turned up the scarred one that was no longer capable of wielding a sword. "I am sometimes astonished by the turns one's life takes," he said slowly, "the bad and the good—more, that the bad can lead to a far greater good than if that which cut us had not."

Everard stared at him, searched for a glimmer of mischief. Was it possible Abel had expended it upon his introduction to Susanna? Not likely.

His brother curled his fingers into his palm as far as they would go, splayed them, looked up. "I am sorry for all you have lost, Everard, and I do not doubt it goes beyond what you have shared, but mayhap this is an instance of good out of bad—that, in the end, you will gain more. Just as I did."

Still no glimmer. Was this what love had done to his brother who, before Helene, had been quick to jest and goad and wager, more often thoughtless than thoughtful?

"I know you do not wish to hear this anymore than I would have," he continued, "but I do not believe I overstep in saying 'tis past time you let go of your regrets."

This was not a conversation Everard would have expected to have with his younger brother. Garr, possibly, but not Abel. Still suspicious, Everard said, "I believe I have let go—or, at least, begun to."

There was the glimmer, there was the smile. "Ah, the lady, Susanna."

"What of her?" Everard asked so sharply that the light in his brother's eyes began to dance.

"If my son, John, can see it, surely I can," he said. "Of course, perhaps you do not, which is all the more reason to rejoice that I am here to point the way, eh?"

Everard narrowed his lids. "I think I liked you better when you were philosophizing."

Abel's laughter sounded around the solar. "Nay, you did not. It made you uncomfortable."

He could not argue that.

"And now, I must make you so again—for John's sake, mind you."

Now *that* was arguable, for Abel had found his stride and was enjoying it too much to merely play the helpful bystander.

"Speak," Everard barked.

Abel reached for his goblet and drained the last of its contents. "My son wishes to know if you intend to wed the lady."

Everard was not surprised. "As discussed, she came to me that I might aid her nephew. For that, she is here."

"Aye, but it does not answer my question. And 'tis a good one, for when we met outside the wood, Lady Susanna and you had just come from the falls, which is rather alluring this time of year."

Everard scowled. "She has been too long confined to the tower room. I but took her riding."

"Ah, the tower room." Abel's eyebrows rose. "That one better known as the consort room."

Everard deepened his scowl. As women were not allowed at Wulfen, at least not in any visible way, that room which could only be reached by way of the secret passageway had served the lords of Wulfen Castle as a means of discreetly accommodating a visiting wife—or, in the case of their father, the occasional lover.

Though Everard hated defending himself, he would not have his brother think ill of Susanna. Thus, he said, "It was necessary to place her there to ensure she remained out of sight and not become a distraction to our young men. Do not read more into it than that."

The humor about Abel's mouth faded. "I do not, Brother. I but test your patience—and find it to be a bit more movable than usual." He frowned. "You are changed, and 'tis not simply that you have more hair than I have seen in eleven years."

Everard curled his hands over the chair arms. He should have shaved days ago. However, as on the mornings past, he had not done so this morn, though he had briefly taken up the blade before setting it aside. But it was not only remembrance of Susanna—her mouth beneath his, her fingers sliding over his scalp, her withdrawal and sorrowful conclusion that his heart belonged to Judith—that had stayed his hand. It was the realization that his heart did not belong to another and had not for a long time. He had loved Judith, and he remembered that love well and how it had moved him and how deeply the loss of it had hurt, but it was a memory. Susanna was not. And his protests against his brother's conclusions about the ride to the falls were simply that. Protests.

"Ah," Abel said, "you cannot argue it, can you?"

He wanted to, for he was more accustomed to winning than losing where this brother was concerned. But in this matter, denial would only make his loss to Abel that much greater.

"Nay," he said, "I cannot."

Abel did not give a shout of triumph as once he might have done, though he did smile. "Women," he said, as if answering something that had been asked of him. "One thing we were not taught at Wulfen—or mayhap we were, though 'twas done subtly by the absence of women whom we were oft told distracted men from their purpose—is that the female may be the stronger sex."

Everard frowned. "This from you? Either you are more changed than I, or you are laughing behind your face."

Abel held up a hand. "I am serious. Much thought I have given this. Aye, we can better wield arms and physically subdue our foes and make ourselves heard above the roar, but women can change men—those same men who change the world. Consider Eleanor of Aquitaine."

King Henry's wife whose summons they awaited. A famed beauty and more than ten years older than her husband, she was said to be a force not only of words but action and that even Henry was oft in awe of her.

"For as long a shadow as the king throws," Abel said, "who can say how much is his and how much is his queen's?"

Everard knew he remained the subject of the conversation, but he was amused. "You *have* been giving this much thought, so deeply it makes me question if married life agrees with you."

"It does—perhaps too much for a Wulfen-trained knight, but..." Abel settled more deeply in the chair, slid down a bit, and thrust his legs out before him. "...though Helene and I do not always agree, I am grateful to have a wife for whom I wish to change when change is called for." He clasped his hands upon his chest, grinned. "Perhaps you will find such a wife yourself."

Deciding to ignore that last comment, Everard said, "I am glad you are content, Abel, and that I will soon have another nephew or niece."

"So you shall. Now tell me, how much does Garr know about Susanna and Judas de Balliol?"

Everard wearied of the conversation, but it was a reasonable question. "I sent a missive weeks past and informed him of the situation, though at the time, I did not have cause to go into detail as I have with you. Regardless, he understands 'tis a personal matter requiring an audience with the queen and that, when I am summoned, I may need him to take charge of Wulfen if you have returned to Baron Lavonne's service."

Abel was quiet a moment. "I am sure my lord—our brother-in-law—would not object if I remain at Wulfen longer than planned or, if the summons is a long time coming, return to Wulfen sooner than planned."

"Your wife may object."

That smile again. "That is the thing about marrying for love—much understanding, much forgiveness."

Everard nodded. "Then I shall call upon you."

"Good." Abel yawned. "'Twas an early start to the day, thanks to John who does not require as much sleep as I did at that age."

Everard did not gainsay him, though he could have, for he remembered well the little brother who had rarely required prodding to arise with the groaning and grumbling squires and pages before the dawn.

Abel sank further down in the chair. "If you do not mind, rather than seek my chamber abovestairs, I shall catch a nap here."

"Of course." Everard pushed his chair back and stood. "Rest as long as you like, for the morrow is soon enough to begin work with the squires." As he started across the solar, he said over his shoulder, "I shall see you at supper."

"Nay, you will see me before then," Abel said. "I need only an hour."

When Everard came out from behind the curtains, the lead squire of the patrol he had sent to the falls was conversing with Squire Werner who looked not a little uncomfortable. Everard might have thought it portended ill if not that John had fastened himself to Werner's side as he had done with Joseph during past visits to Wulfen. Fortunately for Werner, this visit would be different for John who would soon turn eight. Beginning on the morrow, while his father trained squires, he would begin training as a page.

Everard halted at the edge of the dais. "Anything?" he asked the young man who had sidestepped Werner.

"My lord." He dipped his head. "As ordered, we searched the wood near the falls and beyond, but we found no trespassers or signs of trespass."

That did not mean someone had not been there, for the area was regularly traveled during morning exercises and it would be difficult, if not impossible, to separate the presence of squires and pages in training from that of one passing through who may or may not be of ill intent.

Everard inclined his head. "Tell the patrol to remain alert."

"I shall, my lord." The young man turned and strode opposite.

A moment later, John stood where the squire had, face turned up, eyes wide. "Uncle? I am ready to begin my training."

"Are you? It was a long ride."

"I am not tired."

Of course he was not. Though one other than Abel had sired the boy, John had the spirit of the man who had claimed him as his own in taking the widow, Helene, to wife.

"Then you shall serve me the remainder of this day," Everard said.

The boy's face flushed with excitement, but he contained its loud, verbal expression as he had not been able to do even a year past. Though John Wulfrith would remain at Wulfen only as long as his father did, he was ready to take the first steps along the arduous path to becoming a man and a knight of England. Two years hence, his feet would be firm upon that path when he came to stay.

A glance at Werner confirmed what Everard sensed—the squire was not pleased, but like John, he knew how to conduct himself.

"Come, John," Everard said as he descended the dais. "There is much to do ere nightfall, and I am in need of assistance."

25

Too late, she wished she had not come. But she had and now, again, she was free of the tower room. Now, again, the back of the tapestry was before her. Now, again, she was about to set foot in the solar.

But this time she was fully clothed as befitting a lady, would not need to carefully pick her way over the rushes, would not find it necessary to pass so near Everard's bed. This time, she was expected.

"My lady?"

Susanna focused on Sir Rowan who had stepped out of the passageway ahead of her and held the tapestry back to prevent the torch's flame from tasting the tightly woven threads.

He smiled reassuringly. "There is only one way now, and that is forward."

Liking him even better for understanding her hesitation, she listened for voices in the solar and, hearing only the sound of those in the hall beyond who gathered for the evening meal, hoped she could settle in before Everard or his brother joined her.

Smoothing her hands down the waist of her bodice, then her skirts, she stepped from the passageway and followed the knight out from behind the tapestry.

And there was Abel Wulfrith before the fire that glowed and crackled and spat, hands clasped behind his back, gaze awaiting hers.

Outwardly, she did not falter. Inwardly she stumbled—and once more when he came forward and she noted the hitch in his stride. Another injury suffered during the battle that had damaged his sword hand?

When Sir Rowan halted at the center of the chamber, she drew alongside him and was twice over glad that she had taken extra care with her appearance, for she felt Abel Wulfrith's scrutiny and there was comfort in knowing she presented far better in bliaut and veil than tunic and chausses.

"Lady Susanna." He halted before them. "My brother will join us shortly. Until then..." He looked to the large table where she was to join them for supper, an invitation with which she was even less comfortable in the absence of Everard.

"I will leave you now," Sir Rowan said and, before she could form a protest that would not sound fearful or childish, he had turned toward the curtained entrance.

"My lady?"

She returned her gaze to Sir Abel and saw he offered the crook of his arm. Pulse quickening, she glanced from it to his face, back to his arm.

Stop this, Susanna. You have not lived eleven years beneath your brother's and his men's cruelty to now be fearful of a Wulfrith.

No sooner had she chastised herself than she almost laughed, for the Wulfriths' reputation was hardly founded upon harmlessness. There was far more reason to fear one of their family than a man like Alan de Balliol—

Nay, she did not think that was true, for if all the Wulfriths were as Everard, they did not prey upon women, the young, the weak, or the old. If one feared them, that fear would surely be warranted.

"Were my wife present," Sir Abel said, "she would assure you that though my teeth are sharp, I do not bite ladies."

Seeing the twinkle in his eyes, Susanna allowed herself a smile. "Of course you do not," she said and set her hand upon his arm.

He led her to the chair to the left of the one where Everard would be seated at the head of the table. Once she was settled, a platter and goblet before her, he strode to the opposite side and lowered into the chair across from her.

"I am glad we have this time alone before my brother arrives," he said.

Feeling her smile waver, she tightened it. "Oh?"

"He has told me your tale and his part in it, and the reason you and your nephew were granted sanctuary at Wulfen."

"For which we are grateful, and I assure you, we will not remain longer than necessary. As soon as the queen summons—"

He raised a hand. "I do not look for assurances, my lady. I trust my brother's judgment and am certain he did the right thing."

She frowned. "Then?"

"To put it more lightly than I should—and I hope it will not cause you too much discomfort—I am delighted to make the acquaintance of the one who, 'twould seem, has wrought welcome change in my brother."

Susanna struggled to hold his gaze, but as when she had braved her brother's lest he find the lie in her—and there had often been a lie—she did not look away. "That is kind of you to say, Sir Abel, but I fear you credit me with what I do not deserve."

"I do not believe that." He leaned forward, almost conspiratorially. "But there is work to be done, hmm? He is still much too serious." He winked, but not in any way lascivious as she had become accustomed to at Cheverel. This was mischievous, and it loosened something inside her.

Surprised by laughter, she caught her breath and pressed her lips together to prevent more from escaping.

"There," he said. "'Tis good to know you are not naturally serious yourself, my lady. But then, neither is Everard, for he was not always as he is now." He put his head to the side. "But I need not tell you that."

Despite the discomfort of knowing Everard had revealed the part she had played in his past, she said, "I remember." Everard had been of a more serious bent than some, but he could also be light of mouth, not only with smiles and laughter but words that had teased and cajoled and drawn her to him—just as they had drawn Judith.

"As told," Sir Abel said, "more work to be done."

And he seemed to believe it fell to her. "As also told, you overestimate my influence."

She thought he might gainsay her again, but he said, "I hope I do not," and moved the conversation in a different direction. "I observed your nephew late this afternoon while he tilted at the quintain—fairly impressive for one his age, though he certainly looks older than ten."

"He has always been of a good size. Though it means he is mistaken for being several years older and, thus, more is expected of him, methinks it better in a world such as ours to be large rather than small."

He nodded. "Certes, size has always served the Wulfriths well."

A moment later, the sweep of the curtain let in more of the din of the hall, announcing the arrival of another.

Susanna sat straighter, looked over her shoulder, and warmed when Everard's eyes shifted from his brother to her and a half smile drew up his mouth.

"I am glad you have joined us, Lady Susanna," he said as he pulled out his chair and lowered into it.

Yet another way he was trying to make things better for her. "As am I." Despite her initial unease, it was true. Though she knew better than to like anyone of such short acquaintance—that it created a false sense of trust—she liked his brother and that he genuinely seemed to care about Everard's wellbeing. Not even when she had been in Alan's good graces and he had, on rare occasion, spared her a kind word or tolerant smile, had she felt loved. And, obviously, neither had he when she had betrayed him with her silence.

With good cause, she reminded herself of how he had treated his first wives, as well as Judith previous to learning she carried his child.

"I trust Abel has not revealed all our family's secrets," Everard said.

Sir Abel chuckled. "I assure you, I revealed only those that might embarrass you."

TAMARA LEIGH

Though Everard's smile seemed genuine, there was a flicker of something else, perhaps sorrow or regret. "I am sure," he said.

The arrival of Squire Werner bearing a jug and basin, followed by John Wulfrith who had a towel draped over one arm, put an end to the conversation.

In silence, Susanna, Everard, and Sir Abel submitted to the squire who poured water from the jug over their hands into the basin, then John who came behind and dried their hands, all the while struggling to keep a grin from his face. Soon, both withdrew.

However, before talk could resume, the squire returned carrying a pitcher and a cup. He set the latter in front of Susanna and, as she raised it to her lips as had become habit before meals, she ignored Abel Wulfrith's curious regard and sipped the draught as the squire filled the three goblets with wine.

Once again, he disappeared and quickly reappeared, this time accompanied by Judas, both bearing platters of viands.

Had Susanna not seen her nephew earlier in the day, she feared she would have been too joyous to remain seated and would have embarrassed him.

His eyes met hers, he smiled slightly, and then he averted his gaze as if for fear of being distracted.

Squire Werner came alongside Susanna, balanced the platter on one arm, hesitated, then set a small trencher in front of her. "Boar soup, my lady," he said and moved to his lord's side to serve him.

Judas did not announce the items on the platter but set it between Susanna, Everard, and Sir Abel within reach of all. Upon it were slices of yellow and white cheese, pots of butter, thick slices of bread formed of alternating layers of wheat and rye, and a silver saltcellar that held precious, flavor-enhancing granules.

That last Susanna missed less and less these past weeks as she adjusted to the fare provided by the cook. Though she did not believe salt bore much, if any, blame for the state of her stomach, she determined she would not yield to its temptation, for she was growing fond of a stomach that did not roil or burn or retch up its acidic contents. Too, now that she was able to hold down greater amounts of food, she was not as prone to lightheadedness when rising to her feet, and though she knew she was yet too thin, she did not think she looked as gaunt. As Everard had noted, Wulfen *had* been good for her.

"I shall bless the meal now," a voice spoke between her and Everard, and she looked up to find that, while she had been lost in thought, a stout man clothed as a priest had entered the solar. And Judas had slipped away. "Let us pray," he said and bowed his head with its short, dark hair woven through with silver.

As Susanna lowered her chin, she marveled that Wulfen had its own priest, and marveled again that it should surprise her. But then, it was years since a priest had blessed any meal of which she had partaken.

After giving thanks for the bounty, the man of middle years said, "Amen," nodded at each of them, and turned away.

"Something is amiss, Lady Susanna?" Sir Abel asked when the priest was gone.

Feeling her frown, she cleared it. "I am sorry to admit it," she said as she watched him sink his spoon into his soup, "but I was taken aback to see a priest at Wulfen and, no less, for the blessing of the meal."

He raised his eyebrows. "We even have a sizable chapel. Surely you do not think us ungodly, my lady?"

"Ah, nay! 'Tis just that…" She glanced at Everard and saw he watched her. Wishing she had guarded her words, telling herself here was another reason to slowly warm to a new acquaintance, she searched for a way around the discomfiting truth that, following Judith's death, Alan had refused the local priest admittance to the manor house.

"Just that…?" Sir Abel prompted.

She shrugged. "I suppose one thinks of Wulfen Castle as a place dedicated to the intense training of knights who will more readily lay hands to arms for the shedding of blood than lay hands to prayer." It was a feeble explanation, and when she ventured another glance at Everard, his eyes told he knew there was more to it.

"So Wulfen is," Sir Abel said, "but all the more reason for faith to come alongside our charges."

Susanna inclined her head. "I am glad 'tis part of the training received here." Hoping that was the end of the conversation, she took up her spoon.

"It is not part of the training," Everard said. "Though our young men are required to attend mass each morning and show respect at the blessing of meals, we do not *train* them in faith. That is left for those destined to lives of prayer. Rather, we encourage them to avail themselves of the guidance of the priest and the comfort of the chapel as they deem necessary. And, by example, we reveal the place faith holds in the lives of those who wield arms to protect all who depend upon us to keep them safe—including those who pray."

"I see," Susanna said. "I apologize if I have offended."

He smiled wryly. "You have not. I but wished to clarify Wulfen's role in the lives of those with whom we are entrusted."

Sir Abel cleared his throat, nodded at his brother. "As told, my lady, much too serious."

Everard glowered. "I have the feeling I would not like what was said of me in my absence."

"That is a feeling you ought to attend to." Sir Abel grinned, scooped up a spoonful of soup, and slid it in his mouth.

As Susanna dipped into her own bowl, she reflected that she liked the easy exchange between the brothers—more, the tone of affection, disguised in derision though it often was.

"What was that?" Sir Abel exclaimed.

She looked up, saw him grimace.

"What?" Everard said.

"Whatever I just swallowed." He stuck his spoon back in the soup, pushed it around. "Have we a different cook? If so, I wonder that any of you are well enough nourished to lift a sword."

Only then did Susanna become aware of the scent of sage and sweet basil—more, of pepper so potent it tickled her nose. Recalling Squire

Werner's hesitation before serving her soup, she pulled her spoon from the bowl and said, "I fear there has been a mistake, Sir Abel, that you were given my soup."

He looked from her to Everard and back. "Truly?"

"Aye, my meals are prepared with few, if any, spices, which is why you find the soup so bland."

"You do not like spices?"

"I do, but as they unsettle my stomach, Lord Wulfrith was kind enough to ask your cook to omit them from my meals."

Once more, he looked between her and Everard, then said, "Very considerate of my brother, especially as it could not have been an easy thing to ask of Cook." He leaned forward. "The man is a bit of a tyrant. One has to be quite ill for him to accommodate requests for specially prepared food." He glanced at Everard who scowled, then reached his bowl across the table.

Susanna took it and passed her bowl to him.

During the remainder of the meal, most of the conversation was spent upon the business of Wulfen as Everard informed his brother of the measures taken to tighten the stronghold's defenses and updated him on training programs and the progress of particular squires.

To Susanna's surprise, she found it interesting. To her chagrin, her rapt interest became a source of amusement for Sir Abel who made a habit of suddenly smiling at her or raising his eyebrows.

She was pleased that when Squire Werner returned to refill their goblets, nothing was said about the mishap with the soup. And he redeemed himself near meal's end when he came bearing fragrant roast apples garnished with rosemary and sorrel, the latter absent from the apples he set before her.

A quarter hour later, as the din from the great hall rose, evidencing meal's end, Squire Werner once more entered with Judas and collected the dishes, leaving only the wine-filled goblets.

When Susanna's nephew passed by, she caught his eye, and he slipped her a smile before following the squire from the solar.

"And now, as promised"—Sir Abel retrieved his goblet and stood— "I shall join my son for the after dinner activities. I thank you for the company, Lady Susanna."

She nodded. "I enjoyed your company as well, Sir Abel."

He stepped to Everard's side and clapped a hand to his shoulder. "We will talk more on the morrow," he said and strode across the solar.

Susanna peered over her shoulder and, when he pushed aside the curtains and went from sight, looked around. "May I ask...?" Was it trespassing too far?

"You may," Everard said.

"Is your brother's limp permanent?"

"Aye, 'twas gained at the same time his sword hand was injured, but he has learned to compensate for it and is nearly as formidable as once he was—perhaps more so since many are quick to believe it makes him less of an opponent."

"He seems a good man."

"He is." He looked toward the fireplace. "Would you like to sit before the hearth?"

With him. She would, but because she wanted to, she should not. "'Tis growing late, and I am tired. Methinks I should return abovestairs."

He pushed back his chair and stood. "I will take you."

She had not considered that. Though she knew she need not fear for her virtue with Everard, she feared for her heart that might never recover if she continued to allow him so near it, for even the touch of his eyes was quick to bring it into play. But to be in close proximity with him...to be alone with him...to feel the touch of his hand...

Rising quickly lest he offer assistance, she said, "As you know, I have braved the passage by myself, but I thank you for the offer, Lord Wulfrith."

"Nevertheless, I will take you."

She considered the determined set of his jaw and sighed. "If you insist." As she stepped away from her chair, raucous laughter arose from the hall. "It sounds as if they are enjoying themselves," she said.

"Well earned. The days are long at Wulfen."

She glanced at the curtains and, to her surprise, Everard asked, "Would you like to see?"

She blinked. "May I?"

He gestured for her to follow him across the rushes. At the curtains, he drew back the edge and she stepped in front of him to peer at the scene.

It was a busy one, made up of dozens and dozens of squires and pages and knights, some playing games at tables, others upon the floor, some talking and boasting and singing, others gathered before the great fireplace. The latter was where she found Judas—and, to her surprise, Sir Elias who held the attention of all where he stood with his back to the fire, a hand raised to quiet them.

Susanna looked up at Everard, whom she had known was much too close but seemed even more so when he lowered his gaze to hers. "What is Sir Elias doing?" she asked.

"Telling tales." His breath fanned her face. "Since Sir Rowan, who usually entertains our young men with fearsome and fanciful tales of knighthood, has been occupied with watching over your chamber, your knight has filled the vacancy. And quite well, for he never wants for an audience."

Susanna looked back at Sir Elias and watched as he wove words, some of which carried above the din, and gestured with such dramatic sweeps and thrusts that he reminded her of the jongleurs and minstrels who had often performed in the great hall of Judith's family's home. Many an evening, she had watched with rapt attention and, afterward, been inspired to compose her own poetry and stories.

"You did not know this about him?" Everard asked.

She met his gaze. "At Cheverel, Judas oft mentioned Sir Elias was capable of spinning a good tale, but I never witnessed it myself—did not know he was this good."

"Perhaps he felt it safer that you and others did not know it about him."

"Safer? That makes no sense. 'Tis a rare talent to possess, one of which he ought to be proud."

"I agree, which is why it is curious that, in all his years of service to your brother, you were not made aware of this particular talent of his which, though he is passing proficient at arms, seems more a strength."

That was curious, but easily explained away. "I would guess that though family duty bound him to become a knight, his heart lies elsewhere."

"Perhaps," Everard murmured.

Holding his gaze, Susanna became more aware of how near he stood. Nervous, she looked higher and noted, as she had done while dining, that the light blond hair that had once sprung from his head in abundance seemed of a darker shade. But perhaps that was because it was so short and, given the chance to lengthen, would be lightened by the sun. Did he intend to let it grow? If so, why now?

"Sweet woodruff," he said low.

She caught her breath, just barely kept her hand from reaching to the pendant beneath her bodice that now held that which he had said better fit her than roses. Avoiding his eyes, she looked lower and saw his nostrils flared slightly as if he breathed her in. And that thought filled her face with heat.

Hurriedly, she stepped around him and, heading for the tapestry, said, "I am ready to return to my chamber."

Everard did not know what had possessed him, but whatever it was, it was becoming something of a companion. And not necessarily an unwelcome one. What *was* unwelcome was his next thought that, perhaps, Abel might offer insight. Doubtless, he would try—in between peals of laughter.

Everard retrieved a torch from a nearby sconce and crossed to where Susanna awaited him alongside the tapestry. He went ahead of her, unlatched the hidden door, and held it for her to pass through. As she did so, he said, "We go right this time."

She halted over the threshold, turned. "For what reason?"

"Your chamber lies in that direction."

Her brow rumpled. "You know it does not. 'Tis up the steps to the left."

"No more." He stepped forward, and she had to retreat to make room for him in the passageway.

As he secured the door, she said, "I do not understand, Lord Wulfrith."

By the light of the torch, he considered her troubled face, wished it did not bother him to be so formally addressed. "Trust me, Susanna," he said and turned and strode to the right, the main corridor by which all other rooms in the donjon were accessed.

There was silence behind him, but then he heard her slippers upon the stone floor. He passed by the first stairway to the left and paused at the second.

"As these steps can be treacherous in places," he said, "I would ask that you hold to me."

She lowered her gaze to the hand he proffered and, hesitantly, slid her fingers over his.

Everard closed his hand around hers. Silently acknowledging how well he liked the fit, he drew her up the steps. Though usually quick to ascend the passageway, he moved at a slower pace to allow her to lift her skirts clear. Still, it was not much more than a minute and a few turnings of the stairs before they reached the uppermost landing and there was no longer a need—or was it an excuse?—to hold to her.

He released her hand, fixed the torch in a wall sconce, and worked the catch. Before he pulled the door inward, he said, "Let us hope the priest is not at prayer."

Her frown showing he had once more baffled her, he opened the door. As there was no need for a tapestry on the other side, the passageway entrance being disguised as one of two side walls of an alcove, Everard swept his gaze around a room softly lit by candles and listened.

"There is no one within," he said and entered ahead of her.

When she stepped alongside him, he reached back and pulled the door closed.

"'Tis a chapel," she whispered, gazing at the altar.

"As my brother told, we do have one. You may avail yourself of it if you wish."

Her gaze swung to his. "I would like that. Very much."

He inclined his head. "I am sorry it has been so long denied you." As, he surmised from what she had told in not revealing the true cause of her surprise at finding a priest at Wulfen, it had been denied her at Cheverel.

"I thank you." The lovely curve of her mouth warranted too much contemplation.

"And now your chamber." He crossed to the doors. Once again confirming there was no one on the other side, he led her from the chapel into the torchlit corridor, to the right past two doors, and onto the winding stairs at the far end.

At the first landing, he halted before a single door and nodded at the stairs that continued upward. "Access to the roof. I but ask that you continue to be discreet."

She nodded. "Of course."

He pushed the door open and, pleased to find several candles had been lit and coals burned in the brazier as instructed, stood aside. "It was my sister's chamber three years past, and now 'tis yours for the remainder of your stay."

"Why was she here, a place women are not allowed?"

"Just as you required protection, so did Gaenor while my family determined if the man whom King Henry had ordered her to wed was worthy of her. Until then, we hid her here."

"Did he prove worthy?"

"Aye, Baron Lavonne is a good husband and father. 'Tis he whom Abel serves."

She smiled, peered into the chamber, then entered and crossed to the center of the room.

"It is much the same size as the other and similarly appointed," Everard said from where he stood just inside the doorway. "In addition to providing access to the chapel, come the morn you will see your view is much changed, that you will be able to see what goes in the inner bailey and, to a lesser extent, the outer bailey and training field beyond the walls. Too, Judas will be able to visit you here, though 'tis best for his training that he do so only occasionally."

He waited for her to respond, certain she would, but she remained silent and unmoving with her back to him.

"As for Sir Rowan," he continued, "since I still cannot allow you to move freely about the castle, he will keep watch outside your chamber should you require anything and, if you wish to visit the chapel, serve as your escort. Regardless, I trust your stay will be more comfortable."

Still she did not speak.

"You like it better, do you not, Susanna?"

"I do," she whispered.

Everard knew he should stay where he was, but he crossed the fresh rushes and stepped in front of her. "What is wrong?"

She lifted her face.

Tears in her eyes would not have surprised him, but the wonder he saw there did—so bright she seemed years younger.

"Forgive me," she said. "So many prayers have been answered that I am afraid to believe this is real. And ashamed to admit that if it is not—if it is all but a dream—I would rather not awaken lest I find you refuse to aid Judas...have set us outside your walls...still think ill of me...."

As he had done on the night past, Everard longed to pull her into his arms, but he had already tested himself too far by drawing so near when she had looked out upon the great hall, then in clasping her hand in his when he had drawn her up through the hidden passageway. What was this tightness in his chest? What was this want that made his hands ache with emptiness? Atonement, as she believed? Desire? More than desire?

Until he understood and made peace with what he felt for her, it was best—especially for Susanna whom he would not have hurt again—to observe the proprieties as much as possible.

"I assure you, it is real," he said. "The wrongs that can be righted have been and, God willing, will continue to be."

As she stared at him, her upper body swayed toward him as if she might step nearer. But then she eased back, and when movement at her sides drew his gaze, he saw she had also turned her hands into fists.

"I shall leave you now," he said.

"Aye, it is late. I need to make ready for—" She frowned. "Is my pack here?"

He looked around but, as he did so, realized it would not be found here. Though he had instructed Squire Werner to transfer her personal belongings to this chamber, there had been no time during the supper hour to do so and little time since for, with Abel's departure, the meal and conversation had ended abruptly.

"'Tis not, but I shall collect it for you."

Susanna opened her mouth to tell him it was not necessary, but closed it at the realization her protest would sound childish and might reveal its roots—that being in his company made her emotions teeter toward those befitting a girl eleven years younger, one who would not mind being *simply* anything to him as long as she was something.

"I thank you, Lord Wulfrith."

He turned away.

When she heard the last of his footsteps, she surveyed the chamber that had been Lady Gaenor's. It was nearly the same as the one in which she had spent the past—

How many weeks was it? Three? It seemed longer, each day having made its every hour and minute felt, even the dust of its seconds.

Would the days until the queen's summons arrived pass more quickly now that her circumstances had changed? Now that she wanted more than ever to be near Everard though such longing frightened her for the pain it could leave in its wake?

She tossed her circlet and veil on the bed and lowered into the chair alongside a small table upon which she hoped the chess set would soon reappear. If it did not, she would not complain, for she now had access to the chapel. Indeed, this night she would avail herself of the Lord's house to thank Him for so generously answering her prayers for Judas. And though she did not often spend prayers upon herself, she would thank Him for the change in her own circumstances. More, as Everard had encouraged, she would ask for forgiveness so she might be freed from guilt, as she would pray he was freed from his.

Dear Everard...

She closed a hand around the pendant beneath her bodice and saw again his face when it had seemed he breathed her in. "Stop it," she whispered. "You will only make all the days and nights after Wulfen longer."

Leaning back in the chair, she slid her gaze from the bedside table to the bed with its two mattresses that made it sit higher than the one she had passed so many nights upon, to the side table that was barren in the absence of writing instruments. Hopefully, Everard would also deliver those—

She gasped, leapt to her feet, and if ever it could be said she was capable of flight, it would have been at that moment. Still, it might be too late.

26

HE TRESPASSED. HE knew it. And yet, when he had slid the sheaf into her pack atop the other items he had placed inside and had once more glimpsed the sweeps and curves she had inked into several pieces of parchment, he had not heeded the voice that forbade him to read them. That which had recorded what he had guessed to be Sir Rowan's comings and goings was gone—likely by way of the brazier—but there were others in the form of verses.

One revered the silent raven-mantled sky resplendently torn through with bright lights too distant to do more than glimmer atop the tip of one's finger. Another extolled the passage of young men into knighthood as, dressed in snow-white garments, they put on spurs, swords, and daggers to defend faith, family, and country. But it was the one with its familiar final verse that, despite remorse over his trespass, he read through a second time.

If one could live without a heart
better it torn from the breast ere ever it knew love
If not that—aye, if not that
better it lay light within one's being, near forgotten
If not that—aye, if not that
better its beat unfelt, its coursing unheard
If not that—aye, if not that
better it moved by feelings far from love

If not that—aye, if not that
better it break over pain of sweet remembrance than bitter loss
If not that—aye, if not that
better one never knew the one who broke one's heart
If not that—aye, if not that
comfort me, dear Lord, for the days and nights of longing are long

The muscles of his neck tense, he kneaded them. If the beautiful, pained words were Susanna's, if they reflected what she felt, if those feelings were for him, if his unknown heart was in accord with hers—

He growled. If there were not so many *ifs*!

An instant later, a nearly nonexistent sound entered the chamber. It was the release of the hidden door's catch, and that other sense told him it was not Squire Werner who came onto the stairs.

Though he knew the easiest course was to slide the parchment into the pack and not speak of it, this time he heeded the voice that had first warned him against trespassing. He strode out onto the landing where the flame of the torch he had brought with him writhed amid the stir of air from the hidden passageway.

And there was Susanna half a dozen steps down, face flushed, hair loose upon her shoulders, skirts raised to her calves.

Her wide eyes met his, and widened further when they fell upon that which he held. With a sharp breath, she slapped a hand to the wall to steady herself.

Everard extended the parchment. "Will you tell me about this?"

Her eyes flew back to his. "You had no right to go through my belongings."

"I did not, and I will not attempt to excuse my unseemly behavior. I can only apologize."

The intensity with which she regarded him was almost unnerving, especially as she appeared more cornered than angered.

"Will you tell me about the words written here?" he asked again.

"Why?"

"They are lovely, and I remember your fondness for penning verses. Are they your own?"

She shook her head. "They are not mine."

Did she lie? And why was the possibility of a lie more appealing than what she had just told? "This is the parchment I sent you," he said, "so 'tis your writing."

He heard her swallow. "My writing, aye, but not my words."

"Whose?"

After a long moment, she said softly, "Judith's."

Everard was surprised, certain that if the verses were not Susanna's, or if they were and she refused to acknowledge them, she would have attributed them to a troubadour. "You are saying Judith composed this?"

Still she held her gaze to the parchment. "I am. They reflect what she felt for you—and her loss."

Why would she not look at him? Because she did, in fact, lie?

He descended the steps until he was only one up from where she stood. "Susanna, never did I know her to be capable of such verse, spoken or penned."

Her hand rose as if to snatch the parchment away, but she stopped herself and looked up at him from beneath her lashes. "You did not know her capable of it because you did not know her those last nine months when she was much changed and given to deep reflection."

"As, I am sure, you were," he pressed further, still searching for the lie.

Once again, he sensed about her the air of a cornered creature, but she put her chin high and said, "They are Judith's words. Thus, you should take it."

She lied, Everard decided. She was too nervous, too cornered, and there seemed nothing else that could have so swiftly stirred her from her new chamber than the realization he might discover her writings.

Everard drew a thumb across the final words. "Nay, this is something for the giving, not the taking, best bestowed by the one who felt deeply enough to compose it."

Her lips parted, and he thought she meant to remind him that bestowal was not possible in light of Judith's death, but instead she drew the parchment from his grasp.

He turned up the stairs and said over his shoulder, "I shall retrieve your pack and see you safely returned to your chamber."

Minutes later, Susanna once more ascended the passageway to the chapel, this time ahead of Everard, for the protection afforded her was nearly as good as holding his hand which, he had been certain, she would reject.

"May I remain here a while?" she asked as he secured the door behind them.

"You may. I shall deliver your pack to your chamber and, when I return belowstairs, ask Sir Rowan to await you outside the chapel."

Susanna braved Everard's gaze that felt too adept at peeling back whatever layers she pulled around her. Did he know? Had her protests been for naught?

A moment later, he strode past her. When the doors closed behind him, she crossed to the altar, sank down on the kneeling bench, and brought her hands together only to falter over the rolled parchment clenched in the right.

A sharp laugh parted her lips, and she muttered, "For what am I here?"

She had come straight from one sin to ask forgiveness for others. She had lied, willfully and nearly as thoughtlessly as she had done at Cheverel where she had been given far better reasons to do so. Though when she had written the verses, she had tried to convince herself she was but giving voice to what Judith had felt for Everard, the truth had been inside her all along and was more true now.

Love had written those words. Her love, not Judith's. But she had not claimed them as her own, could not bear the thought of Everard shouldering more guilt that might lead him to sacrifice himself in allowing her to ask more of him. And it was not only for his sake, but hers.

Better the ache of being nothing to him than simply Susanna, she had told herself when she stood below him on the stairs, the thought of him pitying her more than he already did making her nearly sick.

She expelled her breath. At the end of it, she felt so empty she sank back on her heels and bowed her head.

"My lady?"

She snapped her chin around.

Moving toward her was the thickset priest who had blessed the meal.

"Father!" She rose to her knees.

He held up a hand. "Stay, child. I but wish to offer counsel if you are in need."

At that moment, she was more inclined to retreat, but when he settled in several feet distant and clasped his hands behind his back, she did not move from the bench.

"I know you to be Lady Susanna," he said. "I am Father Stanis."

"I am glad to meet you, Father."

He inclined his head, and candlelight slid over his silver hairs among the black. "You seek the Lord?"

"I did, but...I should not be here."

"Of course you should. Here is where all should be no matter their burdens—especially if they are ready to have those burdens lifted."

"For that, I should not have come. I fear I have too recently added to my burdens."

Above eyes that were incredibly soft for a man, his thick eyebrows rose. "Will you tell me more?"

It could do no harm, could it? And it was so long since she had known the comfort of speaking with a man of God. She glanced at the parchment. "I told a lie, one that came so easily I am tenfold more ashamed to admit it."

"Shame is a good thing, and all the more reason you should be here."

"Even though I would likely lie again?"

He frowned. "You are not ready to own to the truth and ask forgiveness from the one who suffers from this lie?"

"Blessedly, he does not suffer. Indeed, the lie serves him as well as it serves me."

"You are certain of that?" Quickly, he added, "Not that it would make it right."

"I believe so, and yet..."

"Then you are not certain."

"Perhaps I just wish to not be certain, for there to exist the possibility, no matter how small—"

Wondering how she had let herself be drawn so far down this steep, crooked path, Susanna shook her head. "Regardless, I hate that I lied, and more so that I lied in nearly the same breath as that with which I now seek to be absolved of other sins. God cannot be pleased I am here—repentant on one hand, unrepentant on the other."

Father Stanis stepped forward and touched her shoulder. "My lady, no matter how hard you strain to live free of sin, rare will be the day when you are not tempted to succumb even in some small way. You will yield, you will sin, but that does not mean you do not come before the Lord to give thanks for your blessings and seek His strength in righting unrepentant sins alongside those for which you are ready to repent." He lightly squeezed her shoulder. "He is pleased you are here. Now He waits to hear from you."

Did He? She looked to the cross upon the altar. "I never feel worthy enough to be in His presence."

"There are others of my calling who might not agree"—he chuckled—"rather, who would *not* agree, but I believe those humble enough to question their worthiness are more welcome in the Lord's presence than those who believe themselves worthy."

She frowned.

"Be assured, my lady, He wishes to be your strength."

Did He?

"Would you like me to pray for you? To seek forgiveness of your sins and strength to come out from under the lie?"

She nearly agreed, but his time with God was better spent elsewhere. "Nay, my nephew is more in need of intercession—for his health and that justice be served in defense of his claim to his father's lands."

The priest's brow creased. "Surely you do not think the Almighty incapable of attending to prayers for you as well, my lady?"

"Of course not. I—" That *was* how it sounded.

"Lady Susanna, I will pray for you, as well as that fine lad."

She looked nearer upon the man. "You know him?"

"He attends morning services with the others. I should tell you that twice he has sought me out to ask for prayer."

That surprised, but what surprised more was when he added, "For you, my lady."

She stared at him.

He inclined his head. "As I said, a fine lad. And now, I shall pray."

He was right about the lifting of burdens in this place, for the weight upon her felt suddenly lighter. "I thank you, Father Stanis."

Without further word, he passed behind her, stepped to the kneeling bench on the opposite side of the altar, and lowered to it. When he bowed his head, Susanna started to do the same and found she yet held the parchment that was both her truth and her lie. She set it upon the bench and clasped her hands.

This time when she prayed, she did so without apology—absent the disclaimer of asking the Lord to bless Judas even if her sins were too great for her to be blessed.

A while later, she ended her prayers with the beseeching that Everard again find what he had lost, that he love again as once he had.

27

THE DAYS WHILED away, clambering one upon the other until their collective past amounted to a sennight and, at last, the summons arrived.

Susanna stared at the man before her, in whose presence she had not been since the night he had left her in the chapel. It was almost too much to be so near him again and see up close what she had known only from a distance when he had come within sight of her chamber window. But it was necessary, for he brought word that Judas's moment was near at hand and they would not be required to travel to London, a journey that would have taken days.

Since Queen Eleanor was touring the country to ensure it was properly administered in her husband's absence, she would pause at Stern Castle, the home of Everard's oldest brother, Baron Wulfrith, and there the matter of Cheverel's heir would be decided.

Susanna rose from the chair in which she had received Everard. Determinedly holding her gaze to his to prevent it from straying to his scalp that was less visible than the last time she had been so near him, she said, "'Tis of good benefit, is it not, that the queen conducts her inquiry at Stern?"

He loosely folded his arms over the dirt-streaked, perspiration-dampened tunic that evidenced he had come directly from the training field. "Most often," he said, "there is an advantage to meeting an enemy upon ground with which one is familiar, but though I do not doubt your sister-in-law and her mother will find it unsettling and believe it to be a show of favoritism, it is surely a matter of expediency. We still must prove to Queen Eleanor's satisfaction that Judas is the legitimate issue of your brother."

"Of course. When do we depart?"

"As the queen arrives at Stern three days hence, we leave Wulfen in two days."

When she would be gone from here as if she had never been. "I shall be ready."

Eyes once more tempted to his blond hair, she lowered her gaze to his booted feet, the muddied soles of which had collected bits of the rushes he had tread upon.

To her surprise, he stepped forward and halted near enough that the scent of his hard labor was unmistakable. Near enough that, if he chose, he could touch her.

"Worry not," he said. "As promised, if the queen denies Judas, he will return here with me and you shall remain at Stern Castle to serve as my mother's companion."

For one not entirely selfish moment, Susanna wished the queen would not find in favor of her nephew. Never had she known Judas to be as content and certain of himself as he had become at Wulfen. Not that he no longer wore the years of oppression like a great mantle, but during his two visits to her chamber this past sennight, he had been quicker to smile and converse, and she had even glimpsed what appeared to be happiness when he told her of his training and the areas in which he excelled. Too, for one who was better on his way to becoming a man, he seemed younger—nearer his age than his eyes told. As for the selfish part of that moment, Susanna could not help considering that, were she at Stern, she might see Everard from time to time.

"Susanna?"

She floundered for her place in the conversation. "Then your mother has agreed that I may come to Stern?"

"Aye, I received her reply several days past and would have told you sooner had you accepted one of my invitations to again join Abel and me at meal."

Having determined it best to remain as distant as possible so that her ties to him might be more easily undone when they parted ways, thrice she had declined.

"God willing, I will not have to impose upon her," she said, "but I am grateful."

He nodded and lowered his gaze over her. "You look well."

And felt well, her stomach having mostly made its peace with her, such that she had begun to drink only half of the draught before her meals. "As do you," she said—lamely, she realized when he raised his eyebrows and peered down his front.

In that moment, Susanna's eyes strayed as she had told them they could not and settled upon his blond hair. The sun had lightened it as expected. Doubtless, given the chance to lengthen further, one day it would once more tempt a woman's hands to thread fingers through its golden strands.

"'Twas unseemly to come to you like this." he said. "I apologize, but I did not think the tidings should wait, and I must return—"

His sudden silence jolted her, and she realized her gaze remained fixed upon his hair. Feeling herself warm, she lowered her eyes to the solemn depths of his own. Did he know her thoughts?

At the least, he knew the direction they had traveled. Thus, it seemed no further damage could be done by asking, "Will you not shave?"

"I will not."

"Why?" *That* she should not have asked, but just as her eyes had not consulted her, neither had her tongue.

"Eleven years is a long time," he said as if that were explanation enough, then he stepped near, laid a calloused hand on either side of her face, and tilted her head up to meet the descent of his own. "I have missed you," he said, the warm breath upon which he spoke all that separated their lips.

And how I have missed you. How heavy I feel at the sight of you coming and going so far below my window, ever looking ahead, never looking up.

This time he did not seek permission to kiss her. As his mouth covered hers, she mentally closed herself in with him to keep out the dissenter that warned she should not do this.

Taking in the salty male scent of him, an odor that should have offended but did not, she started to lower her lids—then sprang them wide. With Everard, she did not need to close her eyes, did not wish to blunt the memory of him as she had aspired to do with those who had come before him.

At least, not now. Later, when this can never be, you will wish you had.

As he coaxed her lips to part, she determinedly studied his face, for her lids were so long in the habit of covering her eyes that they kept trying to descend. His skin was tanned, somewhat weathered as was expected of one who spent his days out of doors, his jaw firm and bristled with hair darker than that atop his head, his cheekbones broad and defined, and the grey-green color of his eyes...

Unseen, for he had lowered his lids, unlike—

The memory twisted its way up out of her oily depths, and she saw again the man-at-arms who had first known her mouth. Horrified at the true cost of being let back inside the walls, she had stared wide-eyed at him as he pressed her hard against the gate, bruised her mouth and cut the insides of her lips against her teeth, made her bile rise and, throughout, stared back at her out of eyes better suited to a hideous, hungry thing than a human. For that reason—that vile memory that would not be pushed down deeper—she had learned to keep her eyes closed.

"Susanna?"

She caught her breath, which was more easily done now that Everard's mouth was no longer upon hers.

"You watch me," he said.

And you do not watch me. Do not see me.

Humiliated at having provided more evidence of how deeply she felt for one who could never feel the same for her, she took a step back. Only when he lowered his arms to his sides did she realize that, other than his hands upon her face and lips upon hers, his body had not touched hers. He had held himself apart.

So that he might not further offend her senses? To combat temptation? *Does it matter?*

Too weary to worry if her question would sound like a lie, she said, "Was I watching you?"

His lids narrowed. "Mm."

She shrugged, turned and crossed to the window, and settled her arms on the sill to peer out at the farthermost reaches of the training field beyond the walls.

Finally, she heard Everard's boots crush the rushes underfoot, but before he departed, he asked, "Will you again decline supper in the solar?"

She looked over her shoulder. "I thank you, Lord Wufrith, but I am content to take my meals here."

He inclined his head and turned away. When she could no longer hear the sound of his boots, she lifted a hand to her mouth and slid her fingertips over the places he had been. Memory enough...

"I should have closed my eyes," she whispered.

28

ON THE MORROW they departed, but this day was the same as the other six days of the week when pages, squires, and those who trained them commenced the day with a run through the wood.

Every morning since being given the front-facing tower room, Susanna had risen before dawn to watch from her window as they poured out of the donjon into the torchlit baileys and gathered outside the walls where Sir Rowan said they donned weighted belts before setting off. This morning, however, she watched from between the battlements, leaning into the embrasure as she tried to locate Judas among the many. She found him moments before he surged forward beneath the inner gate's raised portcullis.

Though it was impossible to know with certainty which of the young men was her nephew once they reached the outer bailey, she continued to watch and then to pray for him and the others—that their ventures into the dark over rough terrain and alongside the waterfall would be without mishap.

"Amen," she said and opened her eyes to set them upon the outer training field from which Judas and the others would shortly depart. Instead, a voice averted her attention, and she looked down upon the unmistakable height and breadth of Everard and his short blond hair of which torchlight seemed particularly fond. It was Sir Elias with whom he conversed on the lower steps of the donjon, but though the bailey was now empty save for the two of them, they spoke too low for her to catch their words. Then Sir Elias curtly nodded and strode toward the outer bailey.

Susanna watched Everard as he stared after the other man until he went from sight. When he turned and looked up, she nearly pulled back but stopped herself with the reminder that he could not see her in the shadows between the battlements. Still, she did not think it imagined that she felt his gaze—was certain he knew exactly where she stood.

As his torchlit eyes held her unseen ones, she felt the ache in her chest bloom. "I love you," she said softly, knowing it was the only time she might be able to speak the words to him, wishing he could hear them but glad he could not.

A smile curved his mouth, then he descended the steps and followed after Sir Elias.

Though Susanna meant to return to her chamber, she was drawn across the roof to those other battlements against which Everard and she had sat on the night she had told all and he had pulled her onto his lap and kissed her.

As she neared the door in the roof through which they had come, she felt a pang and, to her surprise, realized she missed the tower room below. It was silly, for she had felt more like a prisoner there and yet...

It was where she had become acquainted with Everard Wulfrith who had grown out of the young man with whom she had been besotted and into one worthy of far more than infatuation. It was where she had fallen in love.

She halted alongside the door, considered the wall against which she had sat with him, then turned aside. As she did so, she caught a glimmer at the base of the battlements.

Careful to keep it in sight, she crossed the roof. The moment she pinched it between thumb and forefinger, she knew what it was, for it was eleven years familiar to her. She held up the ruby, and moonlight passed through its crimson facets.

Everard must have dropped it when he had embraced her, just as she had lost hold of her necklace. But why had he not retrieved it? Even if impossible to find in the night, surely he could have found it in the day. Or perhaps not.

Determining she would once more return it to him so it could be restored to his dagger, she retraced her steps to the front of the donjon.

Shortly, she bid Sir Rowan a good morn where he had appeared outside her chamber.

He showed no surprise that she had been on the roof, for things were much changed since she had moved to her new chamber—so much that when he left his post to attend to personal needs, no one was set outside her door to relieve him.

He smiled at her now and said that her morning meal had been delivered to her chamber. She thanked him, hesitated, then stepped forward and wrapped her arms around him.

He stiffened. "Lass? What is it?"

She lifted her head. "You have shown me such kindness that I am saddened to know I shall see you no more after the morrow."

She felt his muscles ease. "It has been my privilege to serve you, my lady, though I would not be surprised if we meet again."

She nodded. If her fate was to become a companion to Everard's mother, it was a possibility. Lowering her arms, she took a step back.

"May I ask a favor of you?" he said.

"Anything."

"When you meet Lady Annyn at Stern Castle, would you tell her she is ever in my thoughts and prayers?"

Remembering his tale of the young woman who had been like a daughter to him—who had stolen into Wulfen Castle to kill a Wulfrith, only to steal his heart and have hers stolen in return—she said, "Most assuredly, Sir Knight."

He caught up her hand and pressed a kiss to the backs of her fingers. "You would make him a good wife, Lady Susanna."

She caught her breath, coughed to clear the saliva that sought her lungs. "Sir Rowan?"

He released her hand. "Now it remains to be seen if his wits are as sharp as his brother's."

She did not know how to respond to that, did not know if she was expected to. Thus, she forced a smile and slipped into her chamber.

"He means well," she whispered and set her thoughts elsewhere.

He could never get near enough. But this morn...

Morris looked up. This morn had enough unclouded moon that he was certain he would be able to pick Judas de Balliol from among the young men who ran the wood. Now all he had to do was wait.

Convulsively, he gripped the handle of the dagger that had last cut the throat of the plump hare he had eaten raw lest a fire drew the notice of Wulfen's patrol.

Disgustingly sure of themselves, the young men held to no discernible pattern that would have allowed him to relax his guard. He would have liked to think it a result of negligence, but he knew the reputation of Wulfen and was certain the patrols ran exactly as planned—never giving any of ill intent a moment's peace. Thus, he was exhausted and impatient, two states that would serve him poorly if he was not cautious.

"Come Judas, the betrayer," he muttered where he leaned against a tree just down from where the young men would cross the waterfall's upper pool. "Come and let us see you returned to the arms of your harlot mother that I might have my reward." The harlot Susanna de Balliol.

He chuckled. It was redundant to name either of them a harlot, for all women were of that bent, were they not? Certainly in his experience—

He stilled his hand upon the dagger and snapped his chin to the left whence came the sound of dozens of feet that would become dozens more before the one he sought came within reach.

With a satisfied sigh, he slipped to the backside of the tree so moonlight would not reveal him. And when the first of the squires who always outpaced the pages came into view, he looked beyond the tight group who vied to remain out front and muttered, "Be of good cheer, Judas, your wait is near over. As is mine."

The sound of feet, labored breathing, grunts and occasional shouts rising above the water's fall as the young men pounded past, he relaxed his shoulder into the tree's bark, knowing it would be some minutes before he could put his dagger to good use. One thrust would do it, more if any others got in his way.

As expected, moonlight revealed the boy. As not expected, the weakling whom Morris had caused to lose his breath nearly long enough to slip through death's door, was far from bringing up the rear which would have seen him seized and gutted. In fact, Judas de Balliol was so near the front of the pack that not only was he untouchable due to a lack of preparation, but it would have been impossible to separate him from the others without having Wulfen-trained young men turn on him. And he was not one for dying foolishly.

Muttering curses, he slammed his back against the tree and glared heavenward. "This time You did not do well, did You, Lord?"

Minutes later, when his prey and the other whelps were beyond his reach, he thrust off the tree and started back across the wood to where he would await his next opportunity. Or make it.

29

"THERE IS YOUR prey," Everard said low. "Bring it to ground."

Judas looked over his shoulder at him. Squinting against the early afternoon sunlight that shone through the leaves, he nodded, then turned to the one at his side. "I am ready."

"Let us go," Squire Charles said.

The two moved cover to cover, bows at their sides, arrows nocked the sooner to fly once the grazing deer was within range.

When they gained more distance, Everard would follow, keeping them in sight so that, regardless of the outcome, he could assess their strengths and weaknesses to aid in bettering their skills.

It was a good pairing, he reflected as he looked from the light-haired Charles, who could learn from Judas's stealth, to the dark-haired Judas who could learn from the older boy's bow skill. Together, their chances of putting venison on the table were well-favored.

When they reached the midpoint without alerting the deer, Everard left his cover and followed.

Nearer the young men drew, almost close enough to raise their bows and assume the proper stance. Shortly, they took aim. But before the lethally tipped shafts could be loosed, the deer's head came up and the animal bounded away.

Had it caught a sound, a scent, or a movement made by its pursuers? Everard pondered as Judas and Charles gave chase and he came after them. Or had another animal of the wood frightened it?

Though Everard had detected nothing untoward, it could have escaped him—that or the warning was exclusive to the deer's keen sense of danger.

While Judas and Charles raced ahead, Everard kept pace, maintaining his distance in the hope they would be afforded another chance. When they slowed, he slowed, when they crept, he crept.

And there was the deer where it had paused in a clearing, tense and watchful.

Go, Everard silently commanded and, as if heard, Judas and Charles moved forward.

Everard watched, listened, felt. And that last inconstant sense of his turned constant. Something portentous was here that could not be seen or heard and, a moment later, the deer turned its head in the direction whence that feeling came.

"Run!" Everard bellowed as their prey sprang away and a man—one not too distantly familiar—lunged from behind a tree.

The Cheverel knight, Sir Morris, faltered at the sight of Everard whose presence he had surely not expected, the same who had wrenched his sword to hand and now hurtled forward in the hope of reaching his charges first.

Lord, aid me! Everard silently shouted as the startled young men, who had yet to heed his order, swung around to face him. "To me!" he barked.

They saw the danger, then—the one who charged, the raised dagger that sought blood—and gathered their legs beneath them.

Judas's speed served him well, carrying him out of reach, but Charles fell behind. And the one who had become the pursuer, surely realizing he would require a shield to escape, seized the older boy and flung him to the ground.

The impact caused Charles to lose hold of his bow, but he quickly regained his feet. However, the deceptively slight Sir Morris moved with greater speed and dragged the squire in front of him.

Charles thrashed as he tried to retrieve his dagger, but even when it was taken from him and tossed aside, he went still only when his captor slammed his forearm against his neck and pressed a blade to the soft underbelly of the young man's jaw.

Everard slowed, though he did not halt until Judas had gained his side.

"'Tis him," the boy gasped, pointing with his bow at the one who had come to murder him, who had tried to ravish Susanna, who had just made the most perilous mistake of his soon-to-be shortened life.

Judas drew a shaky breath. "He is the one, my lord. He——"

"This I know," Everard rasped as he surveyed Sir Morris whose unkempt, begrimed state evidenced he had been long in the wood awaiting this opportunity. Doubtless, his had been the presence felt at the waterfall.

Everard looked sidelong at Judas. "Stay here."

"But Squire Charles——"

"Stay!"

Anger leapt in the boy's eyes, but now was not the time for lessons. Thus, Everard gave him a warning glare and strode forward with his sword before him. "Release him, Sir Morris!"

The knight leaned in and propped his chin on the squire's shoulder. "I thought you might remember me, Lord Wulfrith. Hence..." He swiftly drew back the dagger, causing Charles to suck air as a thin, red line appeared against his pale skin.

Everard stayed his advance, firmly planting his feet so he would not be tempted to rush the miscreant and cost the squire his life.

"I see we understand each other." Sir Morris's smile was a crooked, hunched thing.

"Release him," Everard growled.

He snorted. "You know I cannot do that. This fine Wulfen knight-in-training is my surety." He shifted his gaze to Judas. "Of course, I would have preferred it to be that slippery weakling but…" He shrugged. "… no matter since there can be no mystery as to that one's death now all that is left to me is to go into hiding."

It was true. He had been seen and, unless he could kill all three of them, those who had set him this grisly task would disavow him and whatever reward he had been promised.

The knight stepped back, taking Charles with him. "Your squire shall accompany me in the retrieval of my horse. And you, Lord Wulfrith, will stay where you are."

"Nay."

The man's eyes narrowed. "You shall, else I will gut him where he stands."

If Sir Morris was so fool—so reckless—to yield up his *surety*, it was better done here than to allow him to take the squire from sight where Charles might even more cruelly meet his end.

"Then all the sooner you will be mine, Sir Morris," Everard said and realized he wanted that very much as he felt bloodlust seep into his veins, gathering to surge as it had not done in a long time.

And would not do so again, he determined, recalling when his father had hard-heartedly doled out the lesson against allowing revenge to foul decisions made from the hilt of a sword.

Control! Drogo had snarled above Everard whom he had knocked face down in the dirt in the presence of all, his booted foot in the center of his young son's back. *Naught will better land the blow than control. Naught will better determine the outcome. Naught will better ensure the state of your soul.*

Everard had hated him for days after that, but had been forced to concede his sire was right when next he and his opponent met on the training field. Squire Jordan, three years older and accustomed to drawing blood that often required the physician's services, had fallen beneath the control exercised by Everard. That day, it was Jordan whose flesh had submitted to the plying of a needle.

Everard returned to the present. "Take him, Sir Morris, but I *will* follow, and the moment you determine your surety is no longer needed, I shall prove otherwise."

The man's gaze wavered. It was his only hope. If he could reach his horse with Squire Charles in tow, escape was possible. Here, absent a shield, death was beyond possible.

Pulling the squire with him, he began backing away.

Everard stepped forward.

Charles grunted, for the knight had cut him again, this time a long score near the great vein in his neck.

"Keep your distance!" Sir Morris warned.

Everard gripped his hilt harder. As he allowed the man to widen the gap between them to another fifty feet, he heard the crackle of leaves and glanced around to find Judas advancing on him, bow at his side, arrow loosely nocked.

Returning his gaze to Sir Morris, Everard said across his shoulder in a voice that would not carry beyond Judas, "Find Sir Abel where he hunts in the wood over the ridge, and tell him we head northeast." Even if Sir Morris changed course, there was none better at tracking than Abel. Not that Everard anticipated the need for help in taking down his prey, but he wanted Susanna's nephew safely away from here.

When the footsteps continued to advance, Everard growled, "Did you not hear me?"

Judas drew alongside. "I heard."

A glance at the boy showed his gaze was fastened on the two who were close to distancing themselves another fifty feet.

"Sir Morris tried to kill me," he said, "and now he intends to kill my friend."

Everard struggled for patience. "I will not lose any of my charges this day, nor will I see your aunt's heart broken." And it was possible, if not by

Sir Morris's foul play, then another of Judas's breathing attacks that could force Everard to choose between giving him aid or Charles. "Go!"

The boy shook his head. "I will keep my breath about me. I vow I will."

"Do as told!"

"I will not." Though it was said firmly, it was edged with fear. "I shall come with you, Lord Wulfrith, and you will just have to make this another of my lessons."

Such insolence was worthy of dire punishment, but the flint in Judas's eyes told it would be a waste of time to argue it further. "Then stay close," Everard barked.

For a quarter hour, they followed their prey, a slow progress since Sir Morris took no chance on becoming a target to an arrow or thrown dagger. Quickly, though surely not soon enough for the squire, they discovered how near they could draw before the young man suffered a cut. By the time Sir Morris's destination became apparent—a thickly wooded area where a horse was tethered beside a stream—the upper portion of Charles's tunic was steeped in the blood of a dozen dagger strokes.

"Stay close," Everard told Judas again and lengthened his stride.

As expected, Sir Morris shouted for them to maintain their distance and retaliated with a sweep of his dagger, this one to the shoulder. The squire's grunt of pain was met by Judas's grunt of anger.

Praying the knight did not slay Charles, that he knew he needed to draw nearer his horse to have a chance of escape, Everard began to run.

Two more cuts, the last one causing the squire to stumble and nearly take Sir Morris to the ground with him.

"I shall kill him!" Judas spat where he ran alongside Everard, his breathing audible but seemingly without strain.

Sir Morris dragged a bent-over Charles to his feet and continued his backward flight, but though his pursuers neared, he did not apply the dagger again, surely realizing that further injury would slow his retreat and might cause him to lose his shield altogether.

Time and again, Everard gauged the distance between the knight and horse until he determined the place at which the knight might risk relinquishing his surety in hopes of gaining the saddle. He was almost there.

The sun flashing on and off Everard's blade as he moved beneath the canopy of leaves, he increased his speed and found satisfaction in seeing desperation more deeply line Sir Morris's face as he peered over his shoulder and back at Everard. His horse was yet too distant, pursuers too near—the latter now barely fifty feet away.

Sir Morris halted. Bracing his feet apart, he dragged Charles close, laid the edge of the dagger across his throat, and once more set his chin upon the squire's shoulder. "Come no nearer, else his death shall be upon your head, Wulfrith!"

Everard heeded the warning and felt Judas's roiling when the boy did the same. "Do you kill him, Sir Morris," Everard shouted, "I will take you down like common game." He nodded at the bow Judas held. "Release him, and I will grant you the opportunity to die like a man, perhaps even kill me." He raised his sword higher.

The knight stole another glance at his horse, and the bitter smile that spread his lips revealed he recognized the hopelessness of his quest—and also told that he had made his decision. Death was at his door, but he would not be the only one standing there when the specter forced its way in.

Everard considered Squire Charles whose life was about to be sundered. The young man's eyes, dark with fear, bright with unshed tears, awaited his.

Once more stirred by bloodlust, Everard began to imagine the ways in which he would exact revenge upon this vile, godless—

Control, Everard! There has to be a way. Think! Observe! Find!

"You believe me a fool," Sir Morris called.

Almighty, show me ere the spilling of blood cannot be stemmed!

The knight shifted his weight. "Even if I slay you, and I assure you 'tis not beyond me, that whelp"—he jutted his chin at Judas—"will put an arrow through me."

Everard looked sidelong at Judas and saw in his eyes what Sir Morris knew. The boy would aim as best he could and wish his arrow all the way to its mortal target. Only ten years old...

It must not come to that.

Determined that Judas would not lose his friend, that he would be dealt no further emotional wounds that could push him over an edge from which he might never be retrieved, Everard focused on Sir Morris. And there, in the straddling of the miscreant's legs, in the lessons of the one held before him at dagger's edge, was the answer. A poor one since it could go horribly wrong, but the only one.

"Release him," Everard called, "else the squire may forget a lesson he found difficult to learn—one I would encourage him to set aside this one time." He shifted his eyes to Charles and watched a frown crawl across the young man's face.

"What say you?" Sir Morris demanded.

Understanding widened Charles's eyes, and it was he who answered his captor by once more embracing the fighting strategy to which he had often turned when he had first arrived at Wulfen. With a shout surely fed by every drop of blood cut from his flesh, he kicked his right leg back and up between Sir Morris's legs.

The knight howled.

Praying the dagger at Charles's throat would be displaced as the two fell backward, Everard lunged.

Flailing. Cursing. Scrabbling. Grunting. Then the flash of the blade. And more blood.

"Nay!" Everard bellowed as the squire, a hand to his neck, life trickling between his fingers, broke free of the knight. He made it to his knees, dragged a foot beneath him, and fell onto his side.

Almighty! It was all Everard had time to send heavenward before Sir Morris stumbled upright, transferred the bloody dagger to the opposite hand, and jerked his sword from its scabbard.

Despite the smaller man having been incapacitated by Charles's blow, one that put a bend in his back and shoulders, he was quick to deflect

Everard's sword. Then he was to the right, raising his blade overhead to ward off the next blow, thrusting his dagger forward in an attempt to pierce his opponent's heart.

Everard registered the sting long enough to also register that his control was slipping again. Forcing out all thoughts of Charles who might already be lost to them, he focused his awareness on every inch of his body in relation to the knight who had leapt backward and was positioning himself to transition from defensive to offensive. Then Everard charged.

He swung. He thrust. He parried. He relieved the miscreant of his flesh-seeking dagger. He gave no quarter, wasting no moment upon toying with his prey, divesting him of strength—and, ultimately, his sword.

The blade descended from the great height to which it had spun. When it met the ground, well out of reach of the panting, slick-faced Sir Morris, the knight threw his bloodied arms out to the sides and backed up against a tree.

Breathing hard, as much from maintaining control as exertion, Everard followed and pressed the tip of his sword to the man's throat.

Sir Morris glanced at the blade and a slow smile drew up his mouth. "I do not yield."

Everard narrowed his eyes. "Still, you are a coward. Still there will be naught left of you."

"Then do it! Put me through that it might be said I died at the hands of a Wulfrith."

Many did consider it an honor—the one consolation before they breathed their last. "I would not have that said of you," Everard said, "not when your death is best left to the king's executioner—be it on your knees with your head on a block or in the air with a rope 'round your neck."

Sir Morris bared his teeth, but before he could respond, Judas cried, "Do it!"

Everard shifted to the side to keep the knight in sight and looked to the boy who stood back and to the right.

Bow aloft, an eye trained down the arrow, Judas said again, "Do it, else I shall!"

"Ah, look!" Sir Morris called. "The wheezing little Judas thinks he can do a man's work." He laughed. "Loose it, boy!"

Everard pressed the blade harder, drew blood that caused the man to suck air. "Shut your mouth!"

"Or what? You will kill me?"

"I will do to you what you did to my squire—open you one piece of flesh at a time."

The knight cut his gaze to Judas. "I would loose it on you, boy! You know I would."

The next cut went deeper. As the man groaned, Everard returned his attention to Judas. "'Tis not for you to do, Judas."

"He is a murderer!"

"That he is." Everard struggled to keep anger from his voice. "One who deserves justice meted out by the queen. Now lower the bow so we might see to Squire Charles."

"He is dead!"

Everard feared it was so, but he had to keep the boy from crossing the line he was too young to be so near. "We need Sir Morris alive to aid in the defense of your claim to Cheverel."

"I do not care!"

Scraps of patience left to him, Everard said, "Lower the bow, if not for yourself, then for your aunt. She would not want this."

The bow wavered but held its aim. However, just when Everard thought there would be no reaching him, Judas dropped his arm and released the arrow into the ground. And Everard saw his face was wet with tears.

"Milksop!" Sir Morris choked. "Weakling! Misbegot—"

Everard slammed his fist into the knight's face, knocking his head back against the tree. Broken nose and mouth spraying blood, Sir Morris's eyes rolled up, then he sank to the ground and slid sideways into unconsciousness.

Knowing he would be some time in returning to this world, Everard ran to where Charles lay. As he carefully turned the squire, he felt the heart that beat beneath his hand and breath upon his face. It was something.

The numerous cuts on Charles's throat, collarbone, and shoulders were not responsible for the amount of blood that had felled him, but neither was it the great vein in his neck. The blade had caught him beneath the chin and sliced up over the jaw bone to the ear——one long, unbroken wound brimming with blood. Unless infection set in, it should not prove mortal.

Thank you, Lord.

Charles rumbled low in his throat and raised his lids. "There was honor in it, was there not, Lord Wulfrith?"

That his first words were spent upon concern over the means by which he had freed himself of Sir Morris brought further relief. "Much honor, Squire Charles. We need the miscreant alive, and the manner in which you acted made it possible."

"How bad am I?"

"You will live, and with a fine scar to show for your bravery."

Surprise widened his eyes, perhaps as much for the news his injury was not mortal as reference to his mettle. But then he gave a pained, apologetic smile. "Everything..." He cleared his throat. "All turned black."

"You yielded up a good amount of blood," Everard excused the loss of consciousness, determining it did not need to be told that shock——the belief the blade had found its deadly mark——had likely played a part.

He looked across his shoulder. "Judas!"

The boy did not move. Bow lax in his hand, his gaze was fastened upon Sir Morris.

"Judas!" Everard called again.

He lifted a shoulder toward his ear as if to block out the sound of his name.

Everard eased Charles to the ground. "Rest. I will return shortly." He strode to Judas who immediately dropped his chin to his chest.

Everard laid a hand on his shoulder. "Charles shall recover."

No response.

"We must needs get him on Sir Morris's mount so you might return him to Wulfen and see his injuries tended."

Judas flinched. "He is not dead?"

"Come see."

His shoulder grew more tense, suddenly sank, then the fingers slung lightly upon the bow released it to the ground.

Silent tears, but Everard felt their quake. He moved his hand to Judas's jaw and lifted the boy's moist, flushed face.

Judas sniffed hard, swallowed hard. "I am sorry," he whispered. "I know I should not..."

Everard bent near. "You are meant to feel this way. There is no shame in it."

Judas's eyes darted over Everard's face, and he took a faltering step forward. Only the one, and then he took it back, surely telling himself he did not need one who might offer comfort as his father had never done.

Everard himself was unaccustomed to offering much beyond encouragement, praise, and the occasional shoulder grip and back slap, for that was far and away enough to move one from boyhood to manhood. But this was different. Judas de Balliol was not just one of many charges. He was Susanna's nephew, his wretched upbringing the result of Everard's indiscretion.

With a sigh, Everard stepped forward and briefly clasped Judas. However, as he started to set him back, the boy wrapped his arms around him and, though his tears remained unvoiced, his shoulders jerked. It did not last long, and when he pulled away, his eyes were nearly as florid as his face, but for all that, his expression was resolute.

"I shall return Squire Charles to Wulfen," he said and snatched up his bow.

As he ran to his friend, Everard crossed to Sir Morris. The knight had not moved from his bloodied slump, but consciousness would not likely be denied much longer.

Having no rope with which to bind him, Everard used the man's sword belt, pulling his hands behind his back and cinching them tight. Then he returned to Judas and Charles and sent the former to retrieve the horse.

Shortly, with the injured squire on the rear of the saddle, Judas on the fore, the two set off across the wood.

When they went from sight, Everard returned to Sir Morris who was beginning to rouse, once more rendered him unconscious to speed the long walk to Wulfen, and hefted the man onto his shoulder.

"Ah, nay!" Susanna cried, curiosity over the commotion having drawn her to the window, the sight that gave rise to fear holding her there.

Judas, his tunic marked with blood, the young man at his back even more bloodied, reined in before the donjon steps. As the knights and squires who had followed them into the inner bailey gathered around to aid in their dismount, Susanna swung away. A moment later, she threw open the door and ran past a startled Sir Rowan.

"My lady!"

"'Tis Judas!" she cried over her shoulder. "He is injured!"

The knight caught hold of her arm, but hardly had she begun to struggle than she realized he did not pull her back but, rather, forward down the passageway. Then they were upon the steps, and she was grateful for his steadying hand.

Before they reached the great hall, the commotion outside came inside. When they came off the steps, Judas was moving swiftly across the floor ahead of the squire who was supported by two knights, one of whom shouted for the physician. The other was Sir Elias.

Susanna pulled her arm from Sir Rowan's grasp and ran. "Judas!"

His eyes landed upon her, and the serious set of his face momentarily reflected surprise, perhaps even dismay, but then he smiled tightly and called, "I am well!"

She faltered, torn between gaining his side to assure herself he spoke true and withdrawing so she did not shame him.

"Lady Susanna"—Sir Rowan's hand was once more upon her arm—"come aside. If any of it is his blood, 'tis very little."

So it seemed. She considered Judas who had gone to stand alongside the table upon which the squire was being laid. He did appear steady on his feet, his color was good, and there was no evidence of strain that might evidence he was in pain. Indeed, the only thing of note was something more defined about the face he lifted to one of the knights who questioned him. He looked more mature.

As for the squire, he was well enough to attempt to raise himself from the table—only to be reprimanded by a thick, grizzled man garbed in simple tunic and chausses who appeared at his side and pressed him down.

"Can you discover what happened?" she asked Sir Rowan.

"I shall." He guided her to a nearby alcove where she could watch without drawing too much attention. "Remain here."

As he turned away, Susanna was struck by the absence of one who ought to be present. "Sir Rowan!"

He looked over his shoulder.

"Everard—Lord Wulfrith—what of him?"

"I would know that as well," he said and strode across the hall to join the knight who questioned Judas.

For minutes that seemed hours, Susanna gripped her hands before her and moved her gaze between the squire and Judas as she strained to hear what was spoken. However, there was not enough substance to the words to make sense of them—until she caught the name that told all. Sir Morris.

It would have been easy to sink into hopelessness born of fear for Everard's fate, for surely whatever caused him to remain absent from the great hall had something to do with the Cheverel knight. She could only pray it did not prove mortal. And so she did pray until Judas came to her, showed he had spilled no blood of his own, and told the tale.

30

Susanna was here. Everard knew it before he set foot in the hall, for she had not been at her window where he was certain she would have stood had Sir Rowan been willing to confine her to the chamber.

His walk back to Wulfen cut short by the appearance of Abel whom Judas had come upon before exiting the wood, Everard had taken the horse offered him. Thus, though soiled by blood and dirt, those odors were not bettered by more than the usual amount of perspiration as would have been expected had he carried Sir Morris the entire way. Still, he was hardly presentable. But when he saw Susanna step out of the alcove and her anxious eyes roved over him, he did not think she would mind even if he perspired such that he looked as if he had come in out of the rain.

With long-reaching strides, the knight on his shoulder groaning, Everard crossed the rushes toward where the physician tended Squire Charles. Alongside a trestle table against the wall, he halted and, making no allowances for the knight's hands being bound behind his back, heaved him onto the wooden surface.

Sir Morris shouted out of a blood-crusted mouth, arched his body, and opened eyes rimmed with the purple bruising of a broken nose.

Everard bent near. "I would not fuss overly much, else you may tempt my men to behavior unbecoming a Wulfen knight." Catching movement out of the corner of his eye, Everard glanced at the one who drew near. "And then there is Sir Elias. I am sure you remember him—he who abducted Lady Susanna and her nephew."

Sir Morris glanced at his fellow Cheverel knight, gathered his cut and swollen lips together, and would have spat in Everard's face had his target not stepped aside.

"You have been warned," Everard said and, as Sir Elias set himself over the miscreant, crossed to Charles. "Rufus?" he asked.

The physician completed one of a dozen stitches that marched up the squire's jaw. "Naught dire, my lord. This brave young man shall yet see spurs fastened to his boots."

"Of course he shall." Everard met Charles's gaze and saw the glint in his eyes that bespoke determination to not cry out each time his flesh was pierced. Then he looked to Judas who stood on the opposite side of the table. "Have you spoken with your aunt?"

"I have, my lord. Her worry is eased."

"It appears, Lord Wulfrith," Rufus said, "you shall also require my needle."

"Later." Everard pivoted and strode toward where Susanna stood alongside Sir Rowan.

She stepped forward. Amber eyes more golden than he remembered, she said, "You are hurt."

"Not so badly I will not soon heal. Most of the blood is that which forsook Sir Morris."

To his surprise, she boldly touched the flesh beneath the gash across his collarbone. "This is yours." Her fingers brushed the slashed material centered over his heart. "And this..."

Everard folded his fingers over hers. "I am well, Susanna. Once the physician is finished with Squire Charles, he will stick me with his accursed needle and all will be mended."

As she stared up at him, Everard was tempted to kiss her. Here. In the hall. In front of those who surely watched even if it appeared they did not.

He released her hand.

She took a step back and said in a rush, "I pray you will forgive me for coming belowstairs. Sir Rowan is not at fault. I—"

"I understand."

She frowned. "You are not angry?"

"Under the circumstances, I cannot be. But now that you have seen Judas is unharmed, Sir Rowan ought to return you to your chamber." What he did not say was that the longer she lingered, the more likely she would come to Sir Morris's notice and suffer the man's foul mouth.

"Sir Morris," she said as if slipping inside his head. "Judas said you believe he will be useful when we stand before Queen Eleanor."

"For that, he lives." Everard motioned Sir Rowan forward.

The knight stepped alongside. "Come, my lady."

At her hesitation, Everard said, "As we depart for Stern on the morrow, see that your belongings are packed. I will send Judas to you later."

She inclined her head and turned with Sir Rowan toward the stairs.

"Lady Susanna!" Sir Morris called as she began her ascent. "Plying your favors here, too, I see."

"Gag him!" Everard bellowed.

"Doubtless, you have made many a Wulfen knight—"

It was Sir Elias who carried out Everard's order. With a fist.

As the crack resounded throughout the hall, Everard looked to Susanna where she had paused on the stairs. Back stiff, she did not look around and, when she remained unresponsive to what Sir Rowan spoke in her ear, the knight braced her arm with his and guided her up the stairs.

Though Everard was not in the habit of cursing others, and he managed to keep the words from his lips, they resounded through his thoughts and stirred up that bloodlust. Thus, he determined it best to leave Sir Morris to his men and seek the chapel where he would give thanks for the day's outcome and pray for strength to contain his blood-lust and forgiveness for his failings.

Such shame. Though Everard knew the truth of that to which Sir Morris alluded, Susanna had been pierced to have those crude words spoken in his hearing—her sins made all the more vivid and distasteful. And not only to him but the others, especially Judas.

At Cheverel, she had been discreet in the granting of favors, and though suggestive comments had sometimes been spoken in her nephew's presence, she had been fairly certain he was yet too unsullied to delve their true meaning. But one would not have to think deep to understand Sir Morris's taunt. The only way he might have bettered it was had he outright called her a harlot.

At the door to her chamber, she eased her arm out of Sir Rowan's hold and met his gaze. "I understand if you think poorly of me, but though I long for your kind regard, I am too tired to explain what Sir Morris told."

He raised his eyebrows. "My lady, you have my kind regard no matter what that knave tells. No explanation is needed."

Her throat tightened. "I thank you."

"There is, however, one thing I would ask."

She stiffened. "Aye?"

"That you heed the words I next speak, that you hear no condemnation in them, that you receive them as a daughter would receive words from her father."

Her eyes and nose stung more sharply. "Of course."

He set a hand on her shoulder. "Desperation breeds sin, but it is the one who breeds desperation who must first answer for those sins."

As his words wound through Susanna, joining with those spoken by Everard the night on the roof when he had said that what she had done to survive was between her and God, the chill that had settled over her began to recede.

"There now," Sir Rowan said, "let that be your comfort."

Oh, I shall miss you.

"I will," she said.

He reached around her and pushed the door open. "If you require anything, Lass, you have but to ask."

She managed a smile, stepped inside, and closed the door.

Her possessions were so few it did not take long to return them to the pack she had brought with her from Cheverel. Indeed, that which required the greatest amount of time was the one parchment across which she had written words of longing she had claimed belonged to Judith.

How she wished Everard had taken it. But he had said it was for the giving, best bestowed by the one who felt deeply enough to compose it.

"What do I do with you?" she murmured, lightly running fingers over the words that seemed composed more out of pieces of her heart than letters. Take it? Leave it? And if she left it, where? Here?

She sighed and turned her attention to the ruby she had found on the roof. This she must give to Everard, for he would surely wish it restored to his dagger. More, it would allow him to ever feel Judith's presence at his side. Surely a comfort.

Elias was no happier this eve than he had been this morn when Everard had first told him 'nay.'

"Unless you give good cause to remain at Wulfen," Everard said, "you will accompany us to Stern Castle on the morrow."

The man's mouth tightened, eyes darted around the solar as if a good cause might be found amid the furnishings. "My agreement with Lady Susanna was that I deliver her to Wulfen." He returned his gaze to Everard who stood with his back to the hearth. "That I did. Had you put us outside your walls, I would have aided her as best I could in gaining an audience with the queen. However, since she has you to deliver her, as well as speak for Judas—"

"This you have already told. And as I have told, it may be necessary for you to stand witness to what occurred at Cheverel. Now, unless you decide to speak in truth, your time would be better spent readying for our departure."

Elias startled. "Truth?"

Everard tired of the game. "You are passing proficient at arms, Elias"—he purposely divested him of his title—"evidence of knighthood training or blessed natural talent, but there is more to you that would not only explain your impassioned talent for telling tales but the desire to absent yourself from Queen Eleanor's presence despite your wish to be elevated to the head of Cheverel's household knights and see justice done for Judas de Balliol."

Other than twitches about the eyes and mouth, Elias had stilled.

Everard was about to send him away when the man heaved a sigh. "Shortly after our arrival at Wulfen, you said I sounded more a poet than a knight."

"You do."

Elias nodded. "Ere I tell the truth, first I would assure you I am of noble blood."

Thus, if he was not as his garments, armor, and sword proclaimed him to be, exposure and the accompanying shame would likely be the extent of what would be required of him to atone. "Continue."

"My name is not Elias Cant. It is Elias de Morville. My father, as much a brute to those of his family who defy him as to his enemies, holds lands from King Henry in Normandy. I am the second of two sons, held in reserve should ill befall my older brother. Thus, though I wished to pursue poetry and song, I was made to train for knighthood."

Everard gestured to one of two chairs before the hearth.

Elias dropped into it and Everard took the other.

"Eight years past," Elias continued, "at the age of ten and six, I fled the lord entrusted with my training. Realizing it would be impossible to pursue the life I wished in France without being dragged back to my father who would thrash me near unto death, I crossed the channel to England. Here, I joined a company of performers and, for four years, traveled town to town and castle to castle earning coin as a troubadour." He frowned. "The living was not as I had imagined, and there were times I regretted rejecting my life of privilege, but mostly I was content."

He turned silent, and Everard sensed a woman in that silence.

"Then I learned the folly—the true extent of helplessness—of being common. Our company was invited to pass the winter at the home of a great baron in the North, and there I fell in love with a serving girl, and she in love with me." He leaned forward. "I know this to be so, that Lettice felt deeply for me."

Everard waited.

"Her father had died the year before and her mother was more interested in grieving than seeing to the feeding of her children. It fell to Lettice to care for her family, but there was not enough coin. Thus, out of desperation she…" His hands closed on the chair arms. "…sold herself to clothe and feed her mother and sisters."

Everard recalled the night on the stairs when, in defending Susanna, Elias had claimed he knew what desperation did to women. His peculiar choice of words—that it beat women down until all that remained were unplucked petals too bruised to stay long upon the stem—had first told there was something about him that did not fit.

"I tried to save her," he continued. "I slipped her food, gave her coin, told that I would leave the company and remain in the North, vowed to wed her. At last, she agreed and set aside all others. Or so I believed."

Everard heard the grind of his teeth.

"A sennight ere we were to speak vows, I came upon her with a household knight. I knew it was ravishment, certain she would not betray me, but when I dragged him off her, she protested. Then the knight beat me." He was silent a long moment. "Barely able to stand, I was brought before the baron who refused to allow me to offer defense for having attacked his man. He had me beat again and thrown out. I made it to Lettice's cottage in the village and waited outside for her. When she returned, she said I had ruined all, that never would her lord allow us to wed. I asked why she had given herself to the knight, and she told that he had offered good coin with which she could buy her sister shoes. I told her I would have given her the coin out of my next earnings, and she looked at me as if I were a half wit and said it was only her body and there was no quicker, easier way to see her palm filled."

He closed his eyes. "I knew then that if we wed, she would not remain faithful—that there would be times when the quicker, easier way would win out over love for me." He lifted his lids. "She was broken."

As Elias had feared Susanna might be. But she was not. Nor would Everard allow her to be.

"For many," Elias said, "that is what it means to be common—sacrifice, lack of self respect, the realization you hold no value other than that of chattel. When I left Lettice, I determined to never again suffer the helplessness of a commoner, nor the beatings of a man less noble than I. Thus, I took up sword and armor and became a knight errant. Eventually, I sold my services to the lord of Cheverel."

Everard inclined his head. "How came you by sword and armor?"

"Stolen from the knight who beat me." He held up a hand. "I vow I did not plan it, nor did I kill him. As I recovered in a nearby town, he and others came for a night of drinking and wenching. Fortuitously, his loud boasting brought him to my notice. Thus, once he was sated senseless, I bestowed the favor of relieving him of all that extra weight."

It was hard to fault him for that. "You love this Lettice still?" Everard asked, his thoughts having touched upon Judith.

The man's eyebrows jumped. "Four years it has been. Though I feel for her, more, I ache that one as lovely and kind as she should be so ruined."

And for that, he had set himself as Susanna's protector.

"That is my sorry tale," Elias said, "and the reason I prefer to remain at Wulfen."

"You fear Queen Eleanor will recognize you?"

"Though I have never met her, I resemble my father, and then there is my given name that might jostle her memory. If I am found out, she will surely be angered that I deserted my family and claimed the unearned title of knight. Thus, not only do I fear for my neck, but my presence could prove detrimental to Judas, the words I speak in his defense rendered worthless."

Silence fell in which Everard thought on all that had been told and tried to determine if there was a way to negotiate the waters of Elias's deception. In the end, he accepted what always served best—honesty. But there was help for it, and he would give it even though it went against the reputation of Wulfen with which he was entrusted.

He stood and called to his squire.

The young man thrust aside the curtains. "My lord?"

"Send for Sir Abel and Sir Rowan."

Squire Werner inclined his head and departed.

"What do you intend?" Elias asked sharply.

Everard crossed to his chest atop which lay his sword. "You will right one wrong, Elias de Morville"—he pulled the blade from its scabbard—"and I shall lessen that wrong by righting the other."

Elias rose and warily eyed the sword as Everard advanced on him. "I do not understand, Lord Wulfrith."

"You will accompany us to Stern." Everard halted before him. "Ere the defense of Judas's claim to Cheverel, we shall seek a private audience with the queen, during which you will lay claim to the de Morville name."

The man's eyes widened.

"Queen Eleanor will be displeased," Everard continued, "but as *Sir* Elias de Morville, knighted at Wulfen, methinks it will go easier for you. More, any words you speak in Judas's defense will be better heeded if they do not stand in the shadow of deception."

Dread chased uncertainty across the man's face, but at last he said, "Very well." Then he sighed. "I think I am glad of it. 'Twill be good to finally come out from under fear of discovery."

A quarter hour later, in as seemly a manner as possible, Abel and Sir Rowan standing as witnesses, Elias de Morville received a blow that promised to leave its mark upon his cheek, then rose as Sir Elias in truth.

31

IT WAS SIR Elias who confessed all to Susanna when the Wulfen party paused before the nooning hour to water the horses. Standing in the shade of trees near the stream's bank, the knight touched his swollen cheek in response to the question she had waited hours to ask, and revealed the truth Everard had pulled from him.

Much of what she had thought she understood about the man upended, much of what she had not understood explained, she had marveled at the blessing that was Elias de Morville. She had thrown her arms around him to express her gratitude—and past his shoulder seen Everard and Judas and others watching. Sir Morris's taunt of the day past returning sharp as a slap, she had pulled away. But what was seen was seen, what was thought was thought.

Thus, when it came time to remount, she was not surprised to find Everard at her elbow. Recalling when last he had seen her and Sir Elias so near—nearer yet—she tensed.

"He told you," he said.

She moistened her lips. "He did. And I thanked him. Most inappropriately but—"

"I did not say that."

She turned to fully face him. "Will you not?"

"Certes, it could have been done better, but I understand." He smiled slightly. "My greatest concern was that Sir Morris might choke on his gag and render himself useless to our cause."

Our cause. If how it sounded was how he truly felt—that it was no longer merely guilt and obligation that roused him to Judas's side—Susanna had more reason to love this man. Unfortunately, it was harder yet on her heart.

She looked over her shoulder at where Sir Morris was bound to his saddle. Above the gag with which it had been necessary to once more stopper his insults, he narrowed his gaze upon her. "I am sure he would have much to say," she murmured.

"Naught of merit."

Though once more tempted to throw her arms around a man, she restrained herself, for it was more than gratitude that made her long to embrace Everard. "I am grateful for your understanding, and that you saw fit to knight Sir Elias. Though I did not think him a friend, he has proven one." She frowned. "I do worry, though, as to how he will be received by the queen."

"We shall know soon enough." He laid a hand upon her arm. "'Tis time we ride."

She gave herself into his care and, two hours later, when she gained her first glimpse of Stern Castle, she still felt the hands that had lifted her into the saddle.

Everard slowed the party, reined around, and guided his horse alongside hers. "It seems we shall know this very day how Sir Elias is received by the queen." He nodded at the gathering before the walls—raised tents, wagons, baggage carts, horses, pack animals, scores of people.

"Those of the queen's household who cannot be accommodated within Stern's walls," Everard said, "as well as others who wish to have their grievances addressed."

She glanced at Judas and Sir Elias who rode on the other side of her. The former's mouth was parted with wonder, the latter's tight with what was surely foreboding.

She swung her chin around. "But the queen is not due until the morrow." No sooner did she speak than she warmed at the realization her words sounded less like an observation than an argument that could be won—one capable of moving Queen Eleanor from the end back to the beginning.

Everard inclined his head. "That is our queen, and that is the reason we traveled this day and not the next. We can only hope Lady Blanche and her entourage have not yet arrived."

Susanna had assumed her brother's widow would appear on the morrow. Hence, the possibility the woman and her mother were already here caused her heart to lurch.

Everard's hand closed over hers. "All is well," he said low, then squeezed her fingers and released them.

"Do you believe I have a chance, Lord Wulfrith?" Judas asked moments later.

"I do. But regardless of the proceedings and the outcome, I expect you to conduct yourself as befitting one trained at Wulfen."

"I shall try, my lord."

"Do not try." Everard's tone had an edge to it. "Do."

Judas's hesitation was palpable. "And if Lady Richenda comes to Wulfen as well?"

"Be prepared that she and Sir Talbot will be here, Judas. Thus, you are to keep your distance and never find yourself absent the company of trusted others. Is that understood?"

With what seemed effort, he nodded.

"Susanna," Everard said.

"Aye?"

"I expect the same of you."

It sounded like an order, and she nearly took offense. But she knew his words were not meant to prevent her from inconveniencing him. "I shall be cautious."

He inclined his head, summoned two knights, and instructed them to take Sir Morris into the wood and remain there until the miscreant could be brought within Stern's walls without alerting others to his presence—specifically, any from Cheverel whom he would not have know the fate of their assassin.

"And now to Stern." Everard urged his destrier forward.

As they passed by the great gathering outside the walls and guided their mounts onto the drawbridge, men-at-arms shouted down from the gatehouse.

Everard acknowledged the enthusiasm with which he was greeted, and there was more to be had within the outer and inner baileys. When they guided their horses amid the bustle of the latter, the three figures who descended the donjon steps immediately came to notice.

The two women were garbed as only those of the nobility might clothe themselves, fit with lustrous head veils and beautifully cut and trimmed bliauts. The man between them, who held the arm of each, wore a richly embroidered and belted tunic against which the hilt of a dagger sparkled with gems that included the red of a ruby. Of near equal note was his size—taller and broader than Everard or Abel—and his hair. It was silver, a color she had never seen on a man younger than two and a half score. And yet Baron Wulfrith could not be much more than thirty and five.

As Everard swung out of the saddle, the older of the women hurried forward. She hugged him fiercely, and he lifted her off her feet and returned her embrace before setting her down.

Taking his face between her hands, she said in a softly accented voice that sounded of Scotland, "My Everard." She lifted her bright gaze higher. "'Tis good to see you are still as golden as the day I birthed you."

He chuckled, said something that made her smile, then she stepped aside.

The younger woman, a dark-haired beauty upon whose hip a child rode, stepped forward—surely Lady Annyn who had shorn her hair and breached Wulfen's walls all those years ago as told by Sir Rowan.

"Artur," she said, glancing at the boy who could not be much more than a year aged, "here is your uncle, Everard."

The child's dimpled hand that had been stroking and tugging at his mother's tresses, stilled. He frowned at Everard, then tucked his head beneath Lady Annyn's chin.

"He is shy," she said, "but give him a year and he will surely be as often beneath your feet as his brother, Jonas, once was."

Everard patted the boy's arm, leaned forward and kissed his sister-in-law's cheek, then he stepped past her toward his brother.

Susanna looked to the baron and found he watched her out of eyes the same grey-green as Everard's and Abel's.

The brothers embraced. It was a quick show of affection, but it seemed genuine. Then something was spoken between them that could be nothing good, as told by Everard's stiffening. And when he turned and crossed to where she and the others remained astride, a muscle in his jaw convulsed.

He lifted his arms to her. "I would have you meet my family."

She leaned toward him. When he set her to her feet, she whispered, "What is amiss?"

"Lady Blanche and her party arrived hours ago."

She caught her breath.

"Worry not," he said, then called, "Dismount, Sir Elias and Judas."

As they did so, Everard led her forward. "I present Lady Susanna de Balliol. Lady Susanna, my mother, Lady Isobel"—

She who had agreed to take an unknown woman into her household should Judas's claim to Cheverel be rejected.

—"my sister-in-law, Lady Annyn, and my brother, Baron Wulfrith."

He who was to have died at Lady Annyn's hand but had, instead, won that hand in marriage.

"I am pleased to meet you." Susanna kept her chin up in an attempt to cover her discomfort at how closely they regarded her. Even more worrisome was the bit of a smile upon the baron's face.

She looked to the two who came alongside her. "My nephew, Judas de Balliol, and our protector and friend, Sir Elias of Cheverel."

"We are pleased to welcome you to Stern," Baron Wulfrith said.

Susanna inclined her head. "I thank you for your aid in resolving the matter of my nephew's birthright. I know 'tis a great imposition."

"A welcome one," Lady Isobel said, "for it has delivered my son home where he has not been for far too long."

"Mother," Everard said, "there are matters that must be attended to, and I would confer with my brother. Thus, I ask that you see Lady Susanna settled into her chamber."

"'Twill be my pleasure."

Everard released Susanna's arm. "I shall see you at supper," he said and gestured for Sir Elias and Judas to follow him and his brother.

Catching her lower lip between her teeth, Susanna watched as her nephew strode behind the others toward the outer bailey. When she looked back around, Everard's mother was instructing two squires to unload the packs.

The lady turned to Susanna. "After your long ride, I am sure you are in need of freshening."

"I would be grateful, my lady."

As Lady Isobel led the way up the steps, Lady Annyn drew alongside Susanna, and the child on her hip came out from under her chin to observe the woman who ascended alongside his mother.

"This is Lady Susanna, Artur. Can you say Susanna?"

He pushed three fingers into his mouth, intently sucked them, then popped them out and said in a gravelly little voice, "Sanna."

Susanna stumbled on the step up to the landing. If not for the lady's hand that turned fast around her arm, she might have dropped to her knees.

"You must be tired," Lady Annyn said.

"More surprised than tired," Susanna said as the porter opened the doors ahead of Lady Isobel. "My nephew began calling me Sanna at about Artur's age. Of course, 'tis rare he does so now."

"Ah." Such a beautiful smile the lady had that it was impossible to imagine how she could have passed for a boy. Before Susanna could think better of it, she said, "How did you do it?"

"Hmm?" Lady Annyn murmured as she released Susanna's arm.

"Sir Rowan told me the tale of how you disguised yourself to enter Wulfen so you could—" Susanna closed her mouth. Artur might be only a year old, but such should not be spoken in his hearing.

The lady made a face. "You know far more about me than I know of you. We shall have to remedy that."

The prospect of female companionship sent a thrill through Susanna, for it had been woefully absent since Judith's passing.

Side by side, she and the baron's wife entered the great hall behind Lady Isobel, and Susanna found it awkward to put one foot in front of the other as she marveled at the overwhelming number of occupants.

"Mostly Queen Eleanor's entourage," Lady Annyn said, "though there are—"

"Sir Talbot," Susanna hissed and would have halted if not that the lady hooked arms with her and drew her forward.

"So 'tis." Lady Annyn tilted her head near. "And since he looks not at all pleased to see you, methinks you should gift him with a beatific smile, hmm?"

It was asking much, but Susanna pushed up the corners of her mouth as she held the man's narrowed gaze where he stood near the dais with two other Cheverel knights. And the bile rose, for here was the one who had conspired with Lady Richenda to leave Judas vulnerable on the training field in the hope of inducing a fatal breathing attack, the same who had led the hunt when Sir Elias had taken Judas and her from Cheverel, and quite likely he who had sent Sir Morris to murder her nephew.

"Nearly there," Lady Annyn said, and Susanna turned her attention to the stairs upon which Lady Isobel had paused. Moments later, they went from sight of those in the hall.

As Susanna breathed out relief, Lady Annyn withdrew her arm and wrapped it around her son who once more played with her hair. "I do not like that knight," she said. "He makes me itch to have a sword near at hand."

A soft chuckle from Lady Isobel, two steps up, told that the woman heard what was spoken behind her back.

In the midst of trying to imagine Lady Annyn wielding a sword, Susanna recalled the favor asked of her. "I have word for you from Sir Rowan, Lady Annyn."

Her eyebrows rose. "Do tell."

"I am to say you are ever in his thoughts and prayers."

The lady did not respond until they started up another set of stairs. "Those are glad tidings. And it says much about your character that my old friend entrusted you with such words."

"He was kind to me during my stay at Wulfen Castle."

"Ah, that most hallowed place where women are not allowed," Lady Annyn mused as Everard's mother led them down a corridor. She slanted a smile at Susanna. "I know I should not be so bold, but I am undone by curiosity."

"What say you, my lady?"

"My beloved brother-in-law has hair." She made no attempt to keep the words from Lady Isobel's ears, and Susanna wondered if she spoke for both of them. "Not much yet, but that is what makes it more interesting, for 'tis surely a recent development. As, of course, are you, Lady Susanna."

Obviously, she aspired to see something that was not there—

It is there. It is just not what she thinks.

But it was not Susanna's place to explain about Judith whom, she was fairly certain, was unknown to these women who likely wished Everard to have a wife and children as his brothers had not denied themselves. It was for him to reveal that his years of grieving were coming to an end.

As Lady Isobel pushed open a door, Susanna met Lady Annyn's gaze. "Apologies, my lady, but I cannot speak to Lord Wulfrith's reasons for no longer putting blade to scalp."

The lady sighed and nodded for her to follow her mother-in-law into the chamber.

As Susanna stepped within, the sound of children at play drifted through the open window.

"Would that I could offer you your own chamber, Lady Susanna"— Lady Isobel halted in the center of the small room that boasted a good-sized bed and several neatly laid pallets—"but all has shifted with the queen's arrival. Thus, you are welcome to share the bed with Lady Annyn and me."

It was custom for a lord to relinquish his private chamber to a visiting overlord, as well as other chambers to those of high rank in the entourage, but it was something with which Susanna had little experience, for Cheverel was of minor importance compared to other baronies.

Though relieved she would not be sleeping in the hall where Sir Talbot and the other knights of Cheverel would surely make their beds, Susanna's greater concern was for Judas. "I thank you for your generosity, but can you tell me where my nephew will bed down?"

"A pallet has been laid for him and one for Sir Elias in the chamber my sons will occupy next to this one."

Safe, then.

The lady gestured to a basin on a nearby table. "While we await the delivery of your pack, you are welcome to freshen yourself."

Susanna stepped past her, removed her mantle, and splashed handfuls of perfumed water over her face and neck. As she patted a towel across her damp skin, a gasp sounded from the window where Lady Annyn and her son peered downward.

"'Tis said *I* am bold," the baron's wife exclaimed.

In a moment, Lady Isobel was beside her daughter-in-law. She shook her head and looked across her shoulder. "Though I had thought you might rest ere supper, Lady Susanna, methinks you ought to accompany us to the garden."

"Now?"

"Aye, Queen Eleanor is there with her children. Unfortunately, in our absence, Lady Richenda and her daughter have happened upon her."

Susanna thought it likely the "happening" was intentional. Still, she said, "I would not wish to interrupt the queen's time with her children."

"It is already done." Lady Isobel stepped toward her. "Now we must ensure you are also known to our queen."

Susanna smoothed her wrinkled skirts. "Am I presentable?"

"You are." Everard's mother turned. "Come."

They had to pass through the hall to reach the garden, but though Susanna was certain she once more fell beneath Sir Talbot's regard, she fastened her eyes ahead as she walked between Baron Wulfrith's mother and Lady Annyn whose son had once more tucked his head beneath her chin and whose lids were trying very hard to lower.

Upon reaching the door that accessed the garden, Lady Isobel paused. "Prepare yourself, for Queen Eleanor is most formidable."

Not wanting Everard's mother to think her fearful or unversed in such behavior, Susanna said, "As is Lady Richenda."

Lady Isobel arched an eyebrow. "I believe you are right, but methinks you shall soon discover the difference between earned formidability and that claimed by grasping hands."

Susanna blinked.

"Be not troubled," Lady Isobel said as she opened the door. "You are among friends."

That she should be so quickly favored by Everard's family caused Susanna's throat to tighten. Then she was walking a path between trees, hedges, and clusters and sprays of flowers, the sound of children's laughter ahead, the figures of more than a dozen visible around the immense garden.

Nearly all present were noblewomen, as told by their fine garments. And there were three knights whom Susanna guessed were the queen's guard. But where was the woman who had earned the right to be called formidable? And where was the one who had not?

As the path curved to the right, they halted when four children hurtled from one side of it to the other—a girl and boy aged five or so, followed by a younger girl and boy nearer three years of age.

"Issie! Jonas!" Lady Annyn called.

The older, dark-haired girl halted and, as she spun around, caught the arm of the younger of the boys as he made to run past her. He was also dark of hair, and his large grey-green eyes snapped at the girl who had put an end to his fun.

"Artur's older sister and brother," Lady Isobel said. "The other two were the queen's children."

Looking up at Lady Annyn who had stepped off the path onto the grass, the girl said, "We are playing nicely as you said we should, Mother."

"Are you, Issie?"

Something sparkled in the eyes of Lady Isobel's namesake, and there was something of a smile about her mouth—not unlike the one with which her father had recently regarded Susanna. "Oh, aye. Though Lord Henry wanted to challenge me with sticks to see if he could best me this time"—she leaned forward as if to impart a secret—"which he cannot, you know, I told him that I am to behave the lady."

"I am pleased, Issie."

The girl sighed. "'Tis not as much fun, but Lord Henry and I are allowing Jonas and Lady Matilda to chase us and, I promise, we are not trying very hard to escape—just enough so they cannot catch us."

"I can catch you!" the boy exclaimed.

"Of course you can, Jonas." Lady Annyn ruffled his hair, then reached to her daughter and hooked a tress out of her eyes and behind an ear. "You think so too, do you not, Issie?"

The girl glanced at her brother, shrugged. "He is a boy, but 'tis possible."

It was hard not to laugh, especially knowing Lady Annyn's past, but Susanna contained her mirth.

"Are not my grandchildren beautiful?" Lady Isobel said near her ear.

"They are, my lady." It was true, for their mother was present in their faces, and there was evidence of their handsome father in the boy's visage.

"Go on, then," Lady Annyn said, and daughter and son disappeared in the direction of the royal children.

Lady Isobel resumed their course and, when they came around a great, square hedge, Susanna's heart beat so fast she felt it in her neck and wrists.

Though the backs of the two ladies who stood in the grass off the path were turned to her and veils covered their hair, the height and width of the one on the right told that here was Lady Richenda. And seated on a bench before Lady Blanche and her mother was a regal, resplendently-clothed woman who could be none other than King Henry's queen. Despite an age approaching two score and an expression more tolerant than pleased, she was stunningly attractive.

Lady Isobel halted, and Susanna and Lady Annyn did the same. One did not approach a queen without invitation.

"You would like to hold him, Your Majesty?" It was Lady Richenda, and when Lady Blanche took an uncertain step forward, Susanna realized that the infant, Alan de Balliol, was being offered.

As the queen held up a staying hand that sparkled with a great number of rings, her gaze shifted to the space between the two women and eyebrows arched as she beheld the three who awaited her summons.

"I thank you, Lady Richenda," she said, "but methinks there is one more deserving of such joy." Her eyes settled on Susanna. "The babe's aunt, Lady Susanna de Balliol, am I right?"

With great gasps, Lady Richenda and Lady Blanche turned.

"Aye, Your Majesty." Susanna curtsied. When she looked up, the queen's hand that had stayed Lady Blanche motioned her forward.

She had taken only two steps when Lady Richenda cried, "Oh, my dear Susanna!" and bustled forward.

Susanna halted and, a moment later, was face to face with the woman she disliked most in all the world.

She startled when Lady Richenda reached up and gripped her face between her hands. "We were worried about you, child."

Grateful for the folds of her skirts that hid her fists, Susanna said, "Your worry was for naught, Lady Richenda. As you can see, I am quite well. As is my nephew, Judas."

The woman's gaze wavered, and her smile tightened. "Good tidings, indeed, Lady Susanna." She withdrew her hands, lowered to her heels, and stepped aside.

Susanna resumed her advance, and Lady Richenda joined her. A moment later, she halted alongside her sister-in-law.

Lady Blanche, cradling her son who was trying to fit a wet fist in his mouth, glanced up. In that brief moment, misery and weariness were evident upon a face that seemed nearly as gaunt as Susanna's had been when first she had arrived at Wulfen Castle.

In spite of all, Susanna ached for this woman whose mother had made of her a puppet, who might have become a friend and companion had Lady Richenda not come to Cheverel.

"Lady Blanche," Queen Eleanor said, "do you not think your sister-in-law would like to hold her nephew after so long an absence from Cheverel?"

Susanna heard Lady Richenda's swift intake of breath.

"Of course," her daughter said and turned to Susanna.

The passing of the babe was an awkward thing, but once he filled the curve of Susanna's arm and his eyes stared wide at her, she was swept with memories of Judas in swaddling cloths. "Oh," she sighed, "he is lovely." She stroked the back of his wet hand, and he grasped her finger and pulled the knuckle to his mouth.

"Now, it would seem, you have two nephews," the queen mused.

Susanna was surprised by how intently Eleanor watched her. "So I do." The speaking of it giving rise to guilt, she determinedly turned it aside. It was not this babe's fault that Lady Richenda sought to deny his older brother his birthright. Though Judas had, for years, occupied the whole of Susanna's heart, there was room for another.

Especially if that other displaces the ache that will be left by Everard.

"Ah, Lady Susanna," Lady Richenda said for all to hear, "this is a sad, terrible business that brings us here, is it not? But I am certain our good queen will set everything to rights."

"Lady Richenda," Queen Eleanor said sharply, "as told, I am at my leisure and we shall not talk of these things. They will save for the morrow."

Lady Richenda mewled. "Apologies, Your Majesty, I forget myself."

"Do not do so again."

Susanna held her brother's second-born son several minutes until he began to fuss and Lady Richenda informed her daughter it was time to feed him.

Lady Blanche stepped near and, as she eased the babe into her arms, murmured, "I have missed you terribly." There was desperation in her voice that roused sympathy. It had been impossible to be close with her since Lady Richenda's arrival at Cheverel, but it must have been of some comfort to have another woman beneath the roof.

Susanna smiled, and Lady Blanche turned away.

Lady Richenda did not—until Queen Eleanor said, "You have my leave to accompany your daughter, Lady Richenda."

The woman jumped just shy of actually coming off her feet. "I thank you, Your Majesty." She hurried away.

When she was gone, Queen Eleanor said, "A babe looks good in your arms, Lady Susanna, and yet you are not wed and have never been, I am told."

It was discomfiting to know inquiries had been made of her. "'Tis true, Your Majesty."

"A broken betrothal?"

Susanna flushed. "Aye, Your Majesty."

"By whom?"

Though thankful it had not been asked of her in Lady Richenda's presence, it was no easy thing to be asked it with Lady Isobel and Lady Annyn attending to every word. "The decision was my brother's."

"And his reason?"

"He wished me to remain at Cheverel and serve as companion to his wife, Judas's mother."

"Did you wish it as well?"

Susanna felt tears at the backs of her eyes, and it angered her that she should be nearly moved to them. For fear the queen would see that anger, she lowered her gaze.

"Hardly how a loving brother behaves toward a loving sister," Eleanor said.

It was obvious she did more than guess. She knew things Susanna would have believed too far beneath the notice of one of royal personage.

She once more braved the woman's gaze. "In the end, it proved a blessing, Your Majesty, for it allowed me to give my motherless nephew the care he required."

"An honorable sacrifice. But tell me, in all these years, have you never loved?"

Susanna felt her eyes go wide. "Your Majesty, I do not mean any disrespect, but I do not see the relevance of—"

"You *have* loved. Now the question is, were you loved in return?"

That anger again, and not only directed at the queen but at herself.

Fortunately, she was saved from answering when Eleanor's gaze went to a place beyond Susanna and she called, "Come forward, Sir Durand."

The knight strode past Susanna and bent to the queen's ear. She listened, said, "I will meet with them," and offered her hand to the man.

He drew her to her feet.

Immediately, two ladies appeared and were instructed by their queen to deliver Lord Henry and Lady Matilda to the solar. As they hastened away, Queen Eleanor said to Susanna. "And so to business. Good day."

Susanna curtsied again. Then, relieved she had been saved from angering the queen, she watched the woman cross the grass with the knight following close behind. As Eleanor stepped onto the path, a curious thing happened. Lady Isobel narrowed her lids at Sir Durand and her mouth turned grim.

Wondering what the man had done to earn her displeasure, Susanna stepped forward and caught Lady Isobel's muttered, "She calls him her gallant monk!" Everard's mother shook her head and started back toward the donjon.

As Lady Annyn shifted a softly snoring Artur on her shoulder, she said low, "Would that I could explain that, but 'tis a confidence closely held by the family—an old hurt that, though the scab gets smaller with each passing year, it yet pains when torn away."

"You need not fear I will pry," Susanna said.

"I do not. Now, to rest, hmm?"

32

Eleanor was amused. At least, she appeared to be.

"Elias de Morville." She ran her gaze down the knight and back up, her lips curving a bit more as she considered his face. "Otto's lost pup." She nodded. "And heir."

Everard shifted his gaze from the queen who had granted them a private audience in the solar, to Sir Elias whose solemn expression transformed into one bent with confusion.

"Your Majesty," the man said, "I fear you are misinformed. I am not my father's heir. I am second—"

"Now you are first." She shifted in the great chair positioned with its back to the hearth. "I regret it falls to me to deliver grievous tidings, but your brother died from an injury received in tournament…" She frowned. "…three summers past."

Sir Elias took a step back as if to find his balance. "I did not know."

"How could you?" She reached a hand toward the lady to her left, and her fingers were fit with a goblet whose stem was wound around with colorful ribbons. "You did, after all, reject your noble blood and flee France to play the troubadour here in England, thereby abandoning your family and allowing them to believe you dead by foul means." She raised an eyebrow.

"It was wrong of me. My only defense is that of having been young and foolish."

"Indeed. And when you determined to be young and foolish no more, to take up the life of a knight—one unearned—why did you not seek your father's forgiveness and blessing?"

"Your majesty may not know my lord father, but—"

"I know Otto de Morville. Not well, but enough to assure you he would welcome your return. Especially now, for he is desperate. In the years since your brother's passing, he has vigorously undertaken the getting of another male child. Unfortunately for his young wife, she has yielded up naught but daughters, and I am told the birthing of the last was so ruinous that she will bear no more. Thus, you are his only hope since he, like so many, deem females unworthy of inheriting lands."

So spoke Eleanor who, surviving the death of her young brother, had become Europe's most eligible heiress upon inheriting the Duchy of Aquitaine, the largest and richest province of France.

She lifted the goblet and, over its rim, glanced to the right where Everard stood beside his brother, Garr. She sipped, lowered the vessel. "And so, Sir Elias, you are in a fine position to see yourself restored to your family, one made stronger by having attained knighthood at Wulfen whose reputation is without equal—to which I, myself, can attest." She nodded at the knight who stood unmoving to her right.

Sir Durand was well known to the Wulfriths. Too well known—blessedly, more the good of him than the bad. That is, providing one took into account all he had done to redeem himself since committing the terrible sin that Everard's mother yet struggled to see past. More, providing one forgave as all were called to do.

It had been a surprise to find the knight at Stern Castle, for after his aid in the rescue of the woman who would become Abel's wife, he had sought service with King Henry in France. According to Garr, he had distinguished himself such that when Henry had sent Eleanor to serve as his regent in England, Sir Durand was among those chosen to accompany her. That should have sufficed to attest to his return to favor, but the queen had gone further. During a conversation with Everard's mother on the night past, she had remarked that the Wulfen-trained knight was a rare man with whom she could trust her ladies, then called him her "gallant monk." That did not sit well with Lady Isobel who knew Eleanor was informed on the matter of what had occurred between the knight and her daughter, Gaenor. However, Everard was inclined to believe the queen had meant well.

Garr nudged Everard, and he found himself beneath Eleanor's probing regard. Doubtless, she awaited an answer to something put to him.

She cleared her throat and said, "Can you or can you not attest to the same, Sir Everard—that Wulfen's reputation remains without equal?"

He tensed. "I can, Your Majesty."

"Then we are pleased." She returned her attention to Sir Elias.

Everard had known the bestowal of knighthood upon Elias was a risk to his family's reputation, but it was necessary—for Susanna and Judas. Even Garr had grudgingly agreed when all was told, then given Everard a knowing look that brought to mind words spoken years past when the two had watched Abel struggle to overcome his injuries.

I know the lengths to which a man will go for the love of a woman, he had said. *Indeed, if ever you determine to wed, I believe you will go as far—mayhap farther.*

Everard had been quick to assert that his life was at Wulfen and he had no desire to grow a family of his own. He had meant it—then.

"As for the morrow, Sir Elias," the queen said, "I see no reason it should be known you are only recently knighted, nor that it was a Wulfrith who bestowed the honor, for it would call into question the verity of your testimony. As you know, my time is precious, and since you were found worthy of knighthood, all that matters is that *I* am content you speak in truth."

"Most assuredly, I shall do so if called upon, Your Majesty."

Her brow turned thoughtful. "As told, your Wulfen knighthood will raise you in your father's estimation, but even with him I would hold close its timing." She smiled lightly. "*That* is advice only. And now we are done."

Sir Elias did not move. "Your Majesty," he said urgently, "with regards to returning to France, I am not sure I—"

"Ah, but I am sure." She sat forward. "Thus, I withdraw Lady Susanna's offer of the position of head of household knights, not only because you will reclaim your place among the de Morvilles, but to ensure your testimony on the morrow is above the taint of suspicion. Do you understand, Sir Elias?"

He nodded.

"Good. That is all."

He pivoted and Everard and Garr made to follow him from the chamber.

"A word, Sir Everard," Queen Eleanor called.

He turned and she motioned him forward.

As the door closed behind his brother and Sir Elias, Everard halted before the queen.

"I have read your account of what passed between you and Lady Judith while she was betrothed to Baron de Balliol. I would ask but one question out of the hearing of others."

Everard glanced at Sir Durand and steeled himself, certain he would not like what was said but grateful it was done within the relative privacy of the solar.

"Should I acknowledge the infant's claim to Cheverel," she said, "will that be the end of your involvement? Will you wipe the dust of Lady Susanna and her nephew from your hands when you return to Wulfen?"

It could have been worse. "Nay, Your Majesty. I pray you do not think it an admission of guilt, but I have made provision for them both should the lie that I fathered Judas de Balliol prevail."

"What provision has been made for the boy?"

"He will continue training for knighthood at Wulfen."

"And Lady Susanna?"

"She will remain at Stern and serve as my mother's companion."

"That is generous of you and your family."

"It is not. 'Tis because of my wrong that Lady Susanna and her nephew are forced to defend what need not be defended."

"I am glad you acknowledge it." She took another sip from her goblet. "It gives me ease to know that, regardless of my decision, both will be provided for, especially as the lady seems genuine in her regard for her nephew."

He frowned. "You have met Lady Susanna?"

"Not an hour past in the garden. Of course, I would not speak to her of the morrow. Not that she pressed me, though I cannot say the same for Lady Richenda."

"She was there also?" he asked sharply.

Eleanor drew her head back slightly. "You are all concern, Sir Everard."

He was not sorry for it. "As you will learn on the morrow, I have cause to be."

She smiled faintly. "Aye, Lady Richenda was there, and her daughter with the babe. But worry not, your sister-in-law and mother were present throughout, and Lady Susanna conducted herself well."

Everard was versed enough with Henry's queen to know they were not idle words, but still he was gripped with the longing to confirm Susanna had not been overly affected at finding herself breathing the same air as Lady Richenda.

"I am thinking, though," Eleanor said, "that if I acknowledge Judas as heir, something will have to be done about Lady Blanche's mother, as I foresee that even with Lady Susanna wed, the woman will prove difficult."

Everard felt cold, sharp steel as if he had taken a blade to the back. "Lady Susanna wed?"

The queen's lids narrowed, and she stared at him before saying, "It seems a good solution, for not only will her nephew require a protector to administer his lands until he is of an age to do so himself, but the lady has long been denied the comfort of a husband and children of her own. Certes, I shall find someone worthy for her." To his further displeasure, she turned to her knight and said, "Were I not so loath to give you up, Sir Durand, I might consider you."

He inclined his head. "I am glad you are loath, Your Majesty."

She laughed, a brief husky sound, and looked back around. "Was ever a man so reformed?"

Everard tensed further.

"Though Sir Durand oft distracts my ladies, especially those who like a challenge and seek to tempt him, he wants naught to do with them outside of his duty to me."

Her *gallant monk*. Everard glanced at the man and saw from the firm set of his jaw that he was not pleased with the conversation's direction. Neither was Everard.

"Of course," the queen continued, "wedding away Lady Susanna is simply talk since one cannot know if her nephew will prevail, hmm?"

Everard inclined his head. "So 'tis, Your Majesty."

She gestured toward the door with her goblet. "We are done, Sir Everard."

He bowed, turned, and crossed the solar, the possession of which could not be soon enough returned to his brother.

"Linger a moment, Sir Durand."

Durand broke the stride he had hoped was long enough to see him from the solar before he once more came to the queen's notice. Mindful to keep his face as expressionless as possible, for he was too fresh from her comments to the Wulfriths about his reformation and Eleanor was too sharp-eyed, he turned. When the door closed behind the other knights, he bowed. "Your Majesty?"

"You know Everard Wulfrith well?"

Durand glanced at her ladies who moved toward the chairs at the hearth. "I knew a younger Everard Wulfrith fairly well, Your Majesty."

"What do you believe the older Everard Wulfrith thought of my proposal to find Lady Susanna a husband?"

Durand did not like being put in such a position, especially with regard to the Wulfriths with whom he had done his best to make amends, but he also knew Eleanor was not seeking information she lacked. "Methinks he did not like it, Your Majesty."

She inclined her head. "That is troubling. Indeed, it does little to dispose me toward his testimony."

Meaning it would hardly be objective. Knowing he was watched as carefully as she had watched Everard Wulfrith, Durand continued to keep control over his expression.

"Of course," she continued, "if it is true he is opposed to the lady wedding another, one must question whether feelings for her or a desire to himself administer Cheverel make him so."

In this, Durand had to defend Everard. "From what I knew and know of the man, Your Majesty, if he wants the lady for himself, 'tis because he has feelings for her. Too, as he is lord of Wulfen Castle, the added burden of administering a distant barony would surely hold little appeal for one charged with so great a task."

The queen was not slow to smile. "I was thinking that myself. In which case, he will not be overly disappointed should I determine Lady Richenda's grandson has a better claim upon Cheverel, hmm?"

In that a husband would not have to be found for Lady Susanna. Did the queen already lean in that direction? Or was Eleanor simply being Eleanor?

She sighed. "In the end, we can only hope Lord Wulfrith honors his family's name by speaking true and giving none cause to suspect he is biased toward Lady Susanna. But we shall see what the morrow brings."

Durand steeled himself further, for he knew she was not done with him.

"As for you, Sir Knight, though I am partial to your guard and your company, I may, indeed, have to find a wife for you."

And what of her *gallant monk?* Though Durand had been surprised to discover he liked serving the queen, on this matter, he did not like it at all. "I would rather you not concern yourself over my marital status, Your Majesty."

"All the more reason, Sir Durand." She waved a hand. "You may go."

He bowed and strode from the solar. Now to find Everard.

So this was jealousy. Wanting someone as he had wanted no one in a very long time and feeling the cruel twist in his chest at the prospect of being denied.

I want what Eleanor would gift to another.

But this was not the angry sort of jealousy that tempted one to hatred of that other. It was not what he had felt all those years ago when Alan de Balliol had claimed Judith for his own. This jealousy was far more grounded in sorrow and regret. And though, like that other one, neither was there light at the end of it when he tried to peer down its length, it was darker yet.

I want Susanna. For my own. Not to atone. To love.

Everard stared at the darkened ceiling above the bed he shared with his brother who was no more asleep than he, as told by the rhythm of Garr's breathing that lacked the depth of Sir Elias's and Judas's who occupied the pallets.

Everard turned his head and asked low, "Is there something you wish to say, Brother?"

Garr's eyes glittered. "Only if there is something you wish to ask."

Everard grunted. "Would that I had the words."

Silence, and then Garr said, "I watched you during supper."

"I am aware."

A short release of breath, almost a laugh. "I saw how you watched her."

And it had made Everard uncomfortable. But to ensure Susanna and Judas were not bothered where they dined among the masses gathered for the evening meal, he had borne the scrutiny of his brother—he who claimed the eyes were the seat of emotion from which truth could not hide. Fortunately, Lady Annyn had ensured that those from Cheverel were placed distant enough to cause no trouble. Too, the meal had been half as long as it might have been had the queen presided over it. Instead, Eleanor had sent word that she and her children would take their meals in the solar.

Grudgingly grateful his brother awaited an invitation to elaborate, Everard said, "And?"

"It seems you regard her as once I regarded my wife when I thought her beyond my reach. Do you believe Lady Susanna beyond your reach, Everard?"

It was a conversation he had never expected to have, one he had been certain he would not want to have, and yet relief began to peel away his jealously guarded layers.

He listened, confirmed Sir Elias and Judas yet slept, and said, "She has feelings for me, but I have given her good cause not to trust what I feel for her. Indeed, until this day, I was not certain I trusted it myself. I feared, as she does, that my emotions were more heavily weighted by guilt and the need to right wrongs. But even were I able to set aside the longing to atone, still I would want her. And were she absent, I believe that ever would I feel the emptiness she left behind."

"You will tell her?"

Would he? If he did, would she yet think him motivated only by those things she thought had roused him to kiss her? And were she to believe him, would it not be all the worse for them both if Judas was acknowledged as heir and the queen wed Susanna to another? But if Judas was denied—

Nay, he would not wish there. Judas was heir to Cheverel, and Everard would do all in his power and at prayer to see him acknowledged as such—including taking to heart Sir Durand's warning that he hold close his feeling for Susanna when he gave testimony.

Garr spoke again. "Our father told that a man should love nothing save his destrier, sword, and shield—warned that always a woman turned a man from his purpose. What he did not tell, likely did not know, was that such purpose is best tempered by the love of a good woman." His hand gripped Everard's shoulder. "Tell her. Do not wait 'til it is too late as it nearly was for Annyn and me."

"I thank you for hearing me, Brother," Everard said, "and I shall consider what you have said. However, much depends on the morrow."

He thought Garr might press him further, felt the unspoken words in the space between them, but his brother released his shoulder and said, "Then sleep, for there is much to do to prepare the boy to stand before Henry's queen."

So there was. And, Everard knew, Susanna would not like it.

Determined to settle his mind, he turned onto his side and sent up a prayer that Judas would be heard and justice done.

33

"He says I must marry him, but I do not want to. He is too pretty."

Issie Wulfrith's words lacked the petulance one might expect from a child who had not yet attained the age of six. There was no whine to them, no hint that another should intervene. It seemed only the expression of an opinion.

Susanna felt the constriction in her chest ease. After four hours of standing in the alcove watching the queen's man call forth the petitioners who sought redress, she embraced the diversion offered by Baron Wulfrith and his daughter. The queen having called for a break in the proceedings and exited the great hall, the dark-haired girl had raced through the throng and met her father as he descended the dais.

Now as they neared, her hand clasped in the baron's, he said, "Lord Henry may be pretty now, but he will make a handsome man, just as you will make a beautiful woman—like your mother."

"Still I do not think I will want to marry him."

"Then 'tis good he is betrothed to the daughter of the king of France."

She gasped. "Oh, that is good. But has no one told him?"

"I am sure he knows, Issie. Mayhap he just finds a girl with a sword, even if only a stick sword, more interesting than one without. I did."

Susanna smiled, and in that moment, the baron's gaze lifted from his daughter's upturned face to hers. Though certain his destination had been the inner bailey to take in fresh air after the press of too many bodies that summer's heat had turned foul, he altered his course.

A moment later, he stood before her.

"Lady Susanna, you have met my daughter, Issie?"

"Not formally." Susanna moved her smile to the girl. "I am pleased to meet you, Lady Issie."

The girl considered her, and Susanna felt as if she were being measured. Then, bright as sunshine punching a hole through the clouds, Issie Wulfrith smiled. "I am glad to meet you, my lady. I am sorry I did not greet you in the garden yesterday, but my brother..." She sighed. "Boys can be difficult, do you not think?"

As on the day past, Susanna was once more tempted to laughter, but though she longed to allow that rare emotion to roll through her, she said as solemnly as possible, "So they can be, Lady Issie."

The girl looked up at her father and raised her eyebrows as if to prove herself right on the matter.

He looked back at Susanna. "I trust your observations of the proceedings have provided insight into what to expect?"

Though his mother had informed Susanna that, unlike most of the other petitioners, her presence in the great hall was not required until the matter of Cheverel was brought before the queen, Susanna had ventured belowstairs to be better prepared for what was to come. Such a relief it was that Lady Richenda had not done the same.

She inclined her head. "It has provided good insight."

"Some of it troublesome?"

Did it show on her face, or had he also been bothered by several of the decisions handed down? "Mostly, I think the queen is wise, but there are times her determinations seem more a result of whim."

"I fear that is the prerogative of royalty." He must have sensed her rising unease, for he added, "I do not believe the matter of Cheverel will be so lightly dealt with, and for that it saves for last."

She blinked. "Does it?"

"Another prerogative of royalty, though this one is welcome since it means the hall will be cleared of spectators."

Welcome, indeed, the prospect of a large audience such as that which attended the proceedings this day with their tittering, rude asides, and foul gestures, having unsettled Susanna. The fewer in attendance the better, not only for Judas's sake and hers, but Everard's. In defending her nephew's claim to Cheverel, he would be flaying open his past.

She frowned. Had Baron Wulfrith arranged it thus? She nearly asked, but his daughter exclaimed, "Uncle Everard!"

Susanna followed the girl's gaze to the one who strode toward them and felt her heart convulse. It was the first she had seen of him since supper on the night past when he had been seated at the high table amongst family. He looked more grave this day. And deeply fatigued.

"Little Lady Isobel," he acknowledged his niece with a smile that, though it appeared genuine, was strained.

"Issie," she corrected. "That way you do not have to say 'little,' which I am no longer."

"Apologies, Lady Issie." He looked to his brother. "We are next?"

"It has not been spoken, but I would make ready."

A shiver went through Susanna. This was what they had long awaited, but now that it was upon them...

"I will leave you and Lady Susanna to prepare." The baron started to turn away.

"I thank you, Baron Wulfrith," Susanna said.

He considered her, then said, "You may call me Garr, my lady."

She inclined her head. "Thank you, Garr."

He turned to his daughter. "A ride, Issie? Or are you too big?"

"I am not *that* big!"

He chuckled and swung her up and onto his back.

When they passed through the doors, Susanna looked back at Everard.

He held out a hunk of bread. "Eat."

That one word spoken by him after all these weeks momentarily squeezed the breath from her. He was as firm as when he had commanded the same of her so that he would not be inconvenienced by her infirmity, but there was more to it now.

She turned her hand around the warm bread. However, as her fingertips brushed his palm, he closed his fingers around hers and said, "I remember, too, Susanna."

Tears rushed her eyes, but though tempted to avert her gaze, she held. "Much has changed."

"And will yet change." It was said with the intensity of a promise, then he released her.

"I thank you," she said, "and for the consideration at supper last eve." Nothing had been spoken by the serving girl who had placed a trencher before her, but her meal had been as absent sharp spices as those prepared for her at Wulfen.

Everard nodded and, as she broke off a piece of bread, said, "There is something we must needs discuss," and stepped into the alcove alongside her.

"Aye?" She popped the piece in her mouth.

"When we go before the queen, you will serve as a witness."

She chewed, swallowed. "Of course I shall."

"A witness only. You will not present Judas's claim to Cheverel."

She frowned. "You will?"

"Nay, I also will serve as a witness only."

"I do not understand."

"Last eve, Judas told that he wishes to be the one to defend his claim. Thus, Sir Elias and I have been preparing him—"

"Nay!" She dropped the bread and took a step toward him. "What are you thinking? He is but ten!"

"In years, Susanna. Though I also had doubts, he presents well—"

"Before you, mayhap, but before the queen—"

"Susanna"—he lowered his hands to her shoulders—"hear me."

She did not want to hear him. What she wanted was to find Judas and make him see sense. She did not count herself an orator, but she was an adult and more capable of ensuring she was heard, especially above the voices of those from Cheverel. And—oh!—what perverse glee would pulse through Lady Richenda if Judas was the one against whom her grandson's claim must be defended.

Realizing how quickly her breath came and went, knowing Everard was prepared should she try to break free, she drew on years of experience with repulsing advances and drew a deep breath. Upon the exhale, she let her shoulders slump and lowered her chin.

Everard eased his hold.

She twisted out of his hands, but as she set foot outside the alcove, he hooked an arm around her waist. He pulled her to him and pressed her against the side wall.

She snapped her chin up. "Release me!"

His eyes drifted to her mouth. "Would that I could, Susanna, for now is not the time to be thinking of you in any way other than as Judas's aunt."

She stilled.

"Now listen. I know Judas is yet a boy in many ways. However, his circumstances and the attempts upon his life have thrust him nearer manhood than one his age ought to be. He knows it and is determined to do this—to be done with peering out from behind your skirts while you defend him and take his blows."

She drew a sharp breath. "He said this?"

"He did, and he will not be argued down from it."

"Perhaps you did not try hard enough."

"In the beginning I did, but then I saw the good of it."

"Good?"

Everard laid a calloused palm to her jaw and, despite her churning, she was tempted to close her eyes and savor his touch. "Judas will not be alone," he said. "We will be near. And do not forget that, unbeknownst to those who would steal Cheverel from him, we have Sir Morris. If he can be made to talk, it will greatly aid Judas's defense."

She pulled her lower lip between her teeth. "Do you think he will talk?"

"'Tis all in the timing."

She wanted to know more about that timing, but before she could press him, he continued, "If Judas can do this for himself, I believe it will be a balm to all he has suffered."

"And if he cannot?"

"Then he shall return to Wulfen, nearer manhood for having made the attempt."

Oh, Lord, let it be so. Should Judas lose Cheverel, let it not break him.

This time there was no feigning acquiescence. Lowering her tense shoulders, she said, "I will not argue it, then."

Everard drew the pad of his thumb across her lips, lowered his head. For a moment, it seemed he might forget to think of her only as Judas's aunt, but he stopped while there was yet space between their mouths. "No matter the outcome, when this is done, I would speak with you."

"About?"

"Us."

Was there another word of so few letters that held as much meaning? That had the potential to so beautifully remedy the state of loneliness?

Only in its purest form. Only if it does not spring from a need to atone. Was it possible with Everard? Was it too much to hope that even if he could never come near to loving her as he had loved Judith, he might feel enough for her that there would be some happiness for them?

"Susanna?"

She nodded. "We should speak. Too, I have something I must needs give you."

He drew his head back, but though she expected a frown, his expression held a smile. "I am glad to hear it." He released her.

He could not know she had found the ruby, could he? But if not that, it had to be the poem to which he referred. If so, would he truly be pleased for her to give it to him—to reveal the truth of her feelings?

"Lord Wulfrith, Lady Susanna."

She turned with Everard to face the knight who had come to Queen Eleanor in the garden on the day past.

"Sir Durand?" Everard said.

"I am to tell you the queen will hear the matter of Cheverel when she returns to the hall a quarter hour hence."

Susanna's mouth went dry.

"We shall be ready," Everard said.

Sir Durand inclined his head and strode opposite.

"Come." Everard took Susanna's arm. "I will see you abovestairs so you might freshen yourself."

She was grateful for his escort and, when they parted outside her chamber, she was more grateful for the words he spoke near her ear.

"I will be with you."

In that moment, she knew it was time to repent of her lie—no matter the consequence.

34

ALL WAS SILENT as Judas stood erect before the queen who had called forth those representing the claimants to Cheverel. A stride to his right was Lady Richenda who had been first to answer the summons and whose head had snapped so quickly around when Judas came alongside her that it seemed impossible she could not have broken something in her neck.

"What is this?" Lady Richenda squawked.

"That, Lady Richenda," Eleanor said, "is the one you hope to set aside in favor of your grandson."

From where Susanna sat alone upon a bench against the wall, across from the bench upon which sat Lady Blanche with her babe and, beside her, Sir Talbot, she heard Lady Richenda gulp. And then the woman rushed to words with, "Forgive me, Your Majesty. 'Tis just unseemly, do you not think?"

Susanna was surprised by her vehemence, certain the lady would be delighted at the prospect of matching wits against a boy she deemed incapable of offering up a good defense.

At the queen's silence, Lady Richenda continued, "What I mean is that he is but a child—"

"I am not a child," Judas said. "I am my father's heir."

She gave a short, sharp laugh. "That is for our queen to decide, and I am sure she—"

"You are sure of naught," Eleanor said, "especially the mind of your queen, Lady Richenda."

"Of course, Your Majesty. I did not mean to offend. I only—"

"Enough!"

In the quiet, Susanna ventured a look at where Everard stood at the entrance to the kitchen passageway.

How she wished him nearer, but he had positioned himself at a distance. It was for the best, though, since it would not do for him to appear any more partial to Judas's claim than he already appeared to be.

He gave her his gaze, and all of her warmed over love for him. When this was done—regardless of how it was done—she who had felt deeply enough to compose the poem, would bestow it upon him. And if he offered to share his life with her, she would accept.

What if his offer whispers of atonement?

Better than it scream of atonement. Thus, another reason to pray Judas's claim was acknowledged, for Everard ought to feel he had made reparations enough that he would only be moved to take her to wife if his feelings had true depth.

A moment later, Sir Elias appeared at his side, but Everard kept his eyes locked with hers and tilted his head toward the other man who spoke in his ear.

"Do you believe you are capable of defending your claim, young Judas?" the queen asked.

Susanna returned her attention to her nephew.

"I do, Your Majesty."

"Do you expect that, because you are ten years of age, my sympathy will be roused such that I will look more favorably upon you?"

Susanna caught her breath. This was the reason Lady Richenda had not rejoiced to find Judas alongside her. Though he looked much older than ten, it was poignant that a boy should take upon himself a matter of such grave importance.

"Nay, Your Majesty," Judas said, "I have no such expectations. I but wish to do this myself."

"Does your aunt approve?"

"I do not think so, but still I will do it—if you allow it."

"I shall, providing you understand that should I find against you, it is of your own doing."

"Agreed, Your Majesty."

Susanna stared at her beloved nephew who stood so tall and determined.

"Then we begin." The queen motioned to an elderly man. As he had done with the other cases, he stepped forward and handed her the missives sent ahead to request an audience.

She accepted them, the ends of which curled over one another in an attempt to return to their rolled state. "I am in receipt of your two missives, Lady Richenda, the first in which you assert your grandson's claim to Cheverel based upon circumstances and speculation that young Judas is not the son of Baron Alan de Balliol. The second in which you attempt to offer proof of Judas's illegitimacy by asserting it was Lord Everard Wulfrith who fathered him."

Lady Richenda nodded. "As you can see, 'tis most clear this boy—"

"Naught is clear until I say it is, Lady Richenda."

Movement on the other side of the hall drew Susanna's regard, and she saw Lady Blanche press the back of a fist against her mouth as if to keep words from bursting from it. Doubtless, she would not be averse to securing a better future for her son than that of playing brother to the baron of Cheverel, but she clearly liked none of this.

"Young Judas," the queen said, "why are you named such?"

Susanna clenched her teeth. There was only one answer for that, and it would not aid his defense.

But he did not react in any way that indicated the question distressed him, and Susanna guessed his calm was a result of the time Everard and Sir Elias had spent preparing him.

"My lord father," he said, "embittered by my mother's love for another man previous to her marriage, further embittered by my birth that caused her death, determined to mark me with the name of the betrayer."

Though Lady Richenda kept her mouth closed, the corners turned up.

"Then," the queen said, "it is reasonable to conclude he had doubts of having sired you."

"It is, Your Majesty."

"There!" Lady Richenda cried. "There 'tis!"

"Lady Richenda! Such outbursts will not benefit your grandson. Indeed, they dispose me toward finding in favor of young Judas. Thus, keep your tongue fastened to your palate or you will be removed."

Lady Richenda lowered her chin.

The queen narrowed her gaze on Judas. "Are you aware that Baron de Balliol oft claimed he had been cuckolded?"

"I am, Your Majesty—when he had partaken of too much drink and usually after I had shamed him with one of my breathing attacks."

She frowned. "One would not guess you suffer from such."

"Less and less the older I grow, Your Majesty."

She returned her attention to the parchments. "Since he never sought to disavow you in writing, one must question how greatly he doubted you were of his loins."

A groan escaped Lady Richenda.

The queen looked to her. "On this you may speak, Lady Richenda."

"My son-in-law but waited to learn the sex of the child my daughter carried ere formally setting aside the boy. Unfortunately, the baron died ere the babe's birth."

"What say you to that, Judas?" the queen asked. "Do you believe he would have named your brother his heir had he lived?"

"It is possible."

The queen slowly nodded. "But possible does not make it so, does it?"

Lady Richenda's hands at her sides opened and closed.

"Lady Susanna," the queen called. "Stand."

She rose. "Your Majesty?"

"You believe Judas to be your nephew by blood, fathered by your brother?"

"I do."

"Have you a means to prove it?"

She tried to moisten her lips, but her tongue was too dry. "The morning after sheets. As is custom, they were hung out to attest to Lady Judith having come to the marriage bed a maiden."

"But that is not always a certainty. There are ways…" The queen glanced at Judas, grimaced. "What else would you offer in support of your nephew's claim?"

"I was close with Lady Judith, and never did she indicate my brother had not fathered the babe she carried."

The queen laughed, and it was like a dagger to Susanna's breast, and the blade twisted sharply when Lady Richenda's shoulders shook with unspilled laughter of her own.

"You may have been close with your sister-in-law," Eleanor said, "but I assure you that she knew well you were her husband's sister. Have you anything else to add?"

As her belief in Everard's word would hardly suffice, she said, "I know in my heart that Judas is a de Balliol."

Lady Richenda tried to disguise her snort by coughing over it.

"Does your nephew resemble your brother?" the queen asked.

Struggling to ease the tension in her jaw, Susanna considered his profile. "They have much the same coloring."

"A not uncommon coloring. The question, Lady Susanna, is if one sees Alan de Balliol in your nephew's countenance as well as his build. Was your brother a large man?"

Feeling the stirrings of bile, Susanna wished she had eaten more of the bread Everard had brought her. "He was of a good height."

"That does not a large man make, such as your nephew promises to be—and as all evidence suggests the Wulfriths were at his age." Eleanor nodded at Baron Wulfrith where he sat at the far end of the table.

"Our father," Susanna said, "was nearly as tall and broad of shoulder."

"That is something. Have you any more to say, Lady Susanna?"

"I would share with you the reason my nephew and I fled Cheverel with the aid of Sir Elias—"

"That is not relevant. You may sit."

"But it is—"

"Not at this time, Lady Susanna."

Clenching handfuls of her skirts, Susanna lowered to the bench.

The queen drew a parchment from beneath the others. "I am also in possession of a missive sent from Lord Wulfrith of Wulfen Castle." She looked up. "Come forward, Lord Wulfrith."

Everard leveled his shoulders, gave Sir Elias the nod he awaited, and strode forth. Though grateful the hall was clear of spectators, averse as he was to opening himself wide to the world, his gratitude was more for Judas's sake. He was confident the boy would conduct himself well, but it was more easily accomplished amid the calm.

As he neared the dais, he ignored the temptation to look toward Susanna, for the queen's regard was keen, and he would not have her see anything that might cause her to think his testimony was any further biased. He halted to the left of Judas and bowed.

"Let us begin with the most vital question, Lord Wulfrith. I assume you know what that is."

He inclined his head. "I did not and could not have fathered Judas de Balliol, Your Majesty. At no time did I have any such relations with his mother."

Lady Richenda harrumphed.

"Yet is it not you whom Baron de Balliol believed to have made of him a cuckold?"

"I fear 'tis true."

"What led him to think such?"

"I served Lady Judith's father ere she wed Baron de Balliol. We fell in love, and he witnessed a kiss we shared." There was no advantage in telling it was Susanna who had revealed that. "Before the nuptials, I attempted to persuade the lady to flee with me, but she refused, and I left her father's home and did not see her again."

"She made a fool of you."

Everard ground his teeth. "She did not. Though I know I did wrong in pursuing another's betrothed, I loved and was loved in return. In the end, Lady Judith determined she would do her duty to her family and honor her betrothal."

The queen flicked her gaze to Judas. "And nine months later, a child was born."

"That I was told."

"And never did you see the boy until he and Lady Susanna sought your aid to prove he was of legitimate issue?"

"Never did I see him."

Eleanor put her head to the side. "If you did not sire young Judas, why grant him and his aunt protection? Indeed, why admit them within Wulfen's walls, the likes of which are closed to women?" She glanced at Garr. "Well, most women." Mischief lingered in the gaze she returned to Everard.

"I did it for the love I once bore Lady Judith, and it was the means by which I accepted responsibility for that which led Alan de Balliol to question his wife's chastity."

"Generous, especially after the passing of so many years."

Lady Blanche's mother muttered something.

"Lady Richenda," the queen said, "I grant you permission to repeat your words in my hearing."

"Self serving," the lady bubbled over. "That is what I said Your Majesty, for surely Lord Wulfrith would wish his son to hold a barony. Indeed—"

"That is all, Lady Richenda." The queen returned her attention to Everard. "What convinced you they were in need of protection, Lord Wulfrith?"

"They were pursued by those from Cheverel who passed near the castle shortly after they were admitted."

"What cause did they give to fear those from Cheverel?"

"Your Majesty," Judas ventured, "may I answer?"

"You may."

"A fortnight ere we departed the barony, I overheard a conversation in which Lady Richenda suggested to her daughter that should I not arise from one of my breathing attacks, my death would ensure her grandson was named the heir."

Lady Richenda drew a sharp breath.

"How did Lady Blanche respond?" the queen asked.

"She protested, and though I did not see, I heard her mother strike her."

"Your Majesty—"

"Seam thy lips, Lady Richenda!" Eleanor waited for the woman to comply, then said, "That is concerning, Judas. Still, it may have been speculation only."

"It was hoped, but while I was training at swords, my aunt was summoned to the manor house, and Sir Elias and another knight entrusted with my care were called away by Sir Talbot. I was left with Sir Morris, and though I tried to leave the training field, he forced me to engage at swords with him. He pushed hard, and when Lady Richenda appeared upon the field where never had I seen her, I guessed he meant to cause me to lose my breath."

"Did he succeed?"

"He believed so."

She raised her eyebrows.

"I feigned an attack, Your Majesty."

Another sound of distress from Lady Richenda.

"When only my aunt came to my aid, having realized I was in danger, I knew my death was planned. Thus, with Sir Elias's aid, we fled Cheverel."

Everard was glad the boy had spoken up, for he told it convincingly. This morn, when Judas had related the incident that had prompted him and his aunt to ride on Wulfen Castle, Everard had felt a flicker of anger that Susanna had not shared it, but he understood she had withheld it in the beginning because Judas had wished none to know of his affliction. Afterward, it had surely been an oversight.

"What say you to this allegation, Lady Richenda?" the queen asked.

"A great work of imagination and cunning, Your Majesty. Though the boy did appear to lose his breath, and I was present with the others, none knew how to aid him."

"You did not instruct Sir Morris to push the boy beyond his limits?"

"Most assuredly not, Your Majesty! The knight but did a kindness in training him."

"I would speak with this Sir Morris."

Peering across his shoulder, Everard saw Lady Richenda's face flush.

"Would that I could produce him, Your Majesty, but he left our service some weeks past."

Since Sir Morris had not returned with word of having accomplished the task set him, she was surely prepared for such a request, and here was her means of disavowing knowledge of the miscreant's foul deed. Doubtless, she hoped the knight had either died in the attempt to take Judas's life or abandoned the plan and moved on.

It seemed a good time to incite the assassin. "Your Majesty," Everard said, "permit me to speak again."

"Permitted, Lord Wulfrith."

"Two days past, Sir Morris made another attempt upon Judas de Balliol's life in the wood near Wulfen Castle."

This next gasp from Lady Richenda was more shrill than her earlier expressions of shock.

"The tale grows more interesting." Eleanor folded her hands atop the missives and leaned forward.

"You speak true, Lord Wulfrith?" Lady Richenda asked.

This time she was not silenced, and the smile hovering near the queen's lips told she would be allowed this outburst.

"Sir Morris attacked Judas and one of my squires," Everard said, "causing grave injuries to the latter."

"Vile, ignoble knight!" The woman clapped a hand to her upper chest. "Sly be his name, for never did he give reason to believe he disliked the boy enough to harm him. Ah! If 'tis true murder was his intent, mayhap he did, indeed, seek to cause the child to lose his breath."

"I say again, I am not a child!" Judas growled and took a step toward her. "You lying—"

"That is enough, page of Wulfen," Everard warned. Until now, the boy had been quiet and watchful as instructed, but Everard had known it would not last, for he had felt Judas's boil. The surprise of it was that he had contained it as long as he had.

"Enough, page of Wulfen," Everard repeated when the boy continued to hesitate over the reminder he was of that esteemed brotherhood, that in the short time he had been at Wulfen he had gathered into his being those who trained him and those with whom he trained, that it was not only his character that would be measured.

At last, Judas took back the step he had advanced on Lady Richenda.

"'Tis good to see you have learned to respect authority, *Judas*," the woman said.

"And good that he escaped harm," the queen submitted. "Would you not say, Lady Richenda?"

A simpering smile creased the woman's face. "It is good he was not harmed, Your Majesty." Her chin came around, and she raised her eyebrows at Everard. "Whereas Sir Morris...?"

Did she feel the stickiness of the web she tread? "He did not meet with a good end," Everard said.

Her lids flickered, and he knew she savored relief.

"You are certain you knew naught of his intentions, Lady Richenda?" he put to her.

"How would I be privy to such ungodly plans?" She tried to stand taller. "If this is an attempt to sully me—the grandmother of Cheverel's true heir—in hopes the queen will find in favor of one likely born of you, Lord Wulfrith, 'tis most un-Christian."

Everard dipped his chin. "Apologies, my lady."

She sighed deeply. "I certainly shall not mourn Sir Morris. Indeed, it is tempting to rejoice that such a knave received his due in full."

"*Did* he receive his due in full, Lord Wulfrith?" The queen's voice held a note of mischief.

"Not yet, Your Majesty."

"What say you?" Lady Richenda demanded. "You told that he died."

"I did not. I said he did not meet with a good end."

"He yet lives?"

"He does." As her mouth went lax, Everard shifted his regard to Eleanor. "Your Majesty, you said you would speak with Sir Morris. Shall I produce him?"

"I think you must, Lord Wulfrith."

Everard turned, briefly met Susanna's gaze where she sat forward on the bench—eyes wide, face flushed—and called, "Sir Elias!"

The knight stepped from the kitchen passageway. Sir Morris came behind him, drawn forward by a rope bound to joined wrists. Gagged, this time to ensure his presence was not too soon revealed, his seething eyes stuck to Lady Richenda who stared at him over her shoulder. He had heard every word Everard had meant him to hear. And he did not appreciate the murder attempt being laid solely at his feet.

"Lady Richenda," the queen said, "I do not think this knight will be content to impale you with his eyes only. Rejoin your daughter. And you, Judas de Balliol, gain your aunt's side."

The boy's name in full—not merely Judas as she had previously named him—portended well.

The two obeyed, moving opposite one another. Then Sir Morris stood before Henry's queen.

"Ere we hear from Sir Morris," Eleanor said, "I must ask of you, Sir Elias, if all you have heard told by Judas, Lady Susanna, and Lord Wulfrith is true."

"It is, Your Majesty. Every word."

She looked to Sir Morris. "I shall hear him now."

Elias wrenched the gag down around the man's neck, and the knight spluttered and coughed.

"So this is the good end with which Sir Morris did not meet," Eleanor said as she considered the broken, heavily bruised face that Everard yet felt in his knuckles.

"This *ignoble knight*," Sir Morris spat, "did not act alone." He jerked his chin to the right, spreading his hatred from those who had thwarted him to the ones who had set him the task that would see him dead.

Though Sir Talbot and Lady Richenda stiffened further, Lady Blanche appeared equal parts confusion and fear. Unfortunately, the babe sleeping on her shoulder would not likely remain thus much longer.

"I would hear your account, Sir Morris," Eleanor said.

The man was slow to respond, but when he returned his attention to the queen, his words poured like water from a pitcher.

"'Tis true I sought to cause that whelp to lose his breath, just as it is true the task was given me and I was well paid though the end result was not the desired one."

"I am sure you would like to tell us who pressed coin into your palm."

He jerked his chin to the right. "Sir Talbot."

"He lies!" The knight thrust to his feet—only to drop back to the bench when two of the queen's knights moved toward him.

Sir Morris's mouth bent as near a grin as his swollen, cut lips allowed. "Of course, I do not doubt it was that vile, ignoble Lady Richenda who first pressed coin into *his* palm."

She yelped, and Sir Morris said, "Sly be *your* name, lady."

"What of your attack upon Judas de Balliol in the wood, Sir Morris?" the queen asked.

"More than coin was promised me if I succeeded."

"Tell."

"Sir Talbot said Lady Richenda would be indebted if, by my actions, her grandson gained Cheverel."

"How was such a debt to be paid?"

This time he looked to the left, past Everard whose every muscle tensed. "I was to have the Lady Susanna when she returned to Cheverel after her nephew met with an unfortunate death."

"You were to *have* a lady, Sir Morris?" The queen's words were so dangerously spoken that, had he a chance of living much beyond this day, he would have been wise to heed her tone.

"Aye, what she long refused me—what she willingly gave others." He scoffed. "The woman is more harlot than lady, Your Majesty."

His words sliced through Everard, its path so blue with heat he was certain it must be what it felt like to be struck by lightning. Despite having endured numerous battles and challenges throughout his life, many life-threatening, this seemed the greatest of all, for he absolutely must heed Sir Durand's warning. He could not take Sir Morris to ground and feel the satisfaction of knuckles against bone, nor could he defend Susanna. He had to stand here as if his heart were not present and let the words spoken against her pass. And, throughout, he could not even send her a reassuring glance for what it might reveal to the queen who watched him.

He held, and finally she returned her attention to the knight. "I do not thank you, Sir Morris, for you are unworthy, but I am glad to know your tale. And now, lest one of those at hand determines to steal from the hangman the right to dispatch you, you are dismissed."

She knew. Had he held his tongue and fists for naught?

"We are not done!" Sir Morris shouted as Sir Elias took hold of him. "There is more."

She raised her eyebrows. "The tale is scandalous enough."

"Ah, nay." He laughed. "I can do better."

She swept the air with a hand, and Sir Durand took charge of the knight and began to drag him away.

"Neither was Lady Richenda's grandson fathered by Baron de Balliol," Sir Morris screeched over his shoulder. "Look to Sir Talbot for that bit of betrayal."

With the exception of the babe's soft whimpering, there was silence, and then Lady Richenda set to weeping and moaning and babbling over the lies she was made to suffer.

Susanna could only stare, just as she had done since the aspersions against her had fallen upon the ears of all present and she had silently beseeched God to stay Everard's hand.

"Aunt Sanna?" Judas asked softly, the reassuring hand he had laid upon her arm when Sir Morris had named her so vile a thing now trembling.

She glanced at him, shook her head to let him know she was as lost as he, then looked to Lady Blanche who slumped over her child and Sir Talbot where he sat unmoving and unprotesting. Was it true? Was little Alan de Balliol not a de Balliol? Or was this Sir Morris's revenge upon those who had tried to heap their sins atop his own?

Suddenly, the queen laughed. "Henry will be most intrigued," she pronounced, then called, "Come forth, Judas de Balliol."

Her summons caused Lady Richenda to go quiet.

Susanna turned to face her nephew. "Whatever she decides," she whispered, "you cannot lose, Judas mine."

He nodded, released her arm, and strode toward the dais. As he passed Everard, Susanna glanced at the man whose roiling she had felt when he had denied himself the satisfaction of adding to Sir Morris's cuts and bruises, the man who would ever hold her heart.

Determinedly, she shifted her regard to Judas who had halted before the dais.

"You are called by your full name, Judas de Balliol," Eleanor said, "because it has been decided that, regardless of whether or not you and

Lady Blanche's babe share your father's blood, you are the acknowledged De Balliol heir. Cheverel is yours."

As Lady Richenda cried out as if someone had stuck her with something sharp, Susanna was swept with relief so intense that she was grateful for the support of the bench beneath her.

Dear Lord, thank you!

It was over. Judas and she could go home. Far away from Everard...

Unless he truly feels for you, hope whispered. Might he?

Judas bowed. "I am grateful, Your Majesty."

The queen inclined her head. "Regarding the charges leveled at Sir Talbot, Lady Richenda, and Lady Blanche, though I believe it possible they are not without merit, we lack sufficient proof and must consider it may be vengeance at work." She narrowed her gaze upon those from Cheverel. "Thus, I caution all to give no cause for this matter to be revisited. That said, all that remains is to entrust someone with the administration of Cheverel until its heir is of an age to fully assume his responsibilities. Thus, I propose we find a husband for Judas de Balliol's aunt."

It was a blow for which Susanna was unprepared, and she could not keep her eyes from flying to Everard who had not moved his gaze from the queen. Had his shoulders been as square, his jaw thrust so far forward when last she had looked upon him?

"I will think on it," Eleanor said. "We are done."

"Your Majesty!" It was Lady Blanche. She had taken to her feet so abruptly that her babe returned to fussing where he lay in the crook of her arm. "I would speak to what Sir Morris told."

With a cry, Lady Richenda bounced to her feet and gripped Blanche's arm. "You need not defend yourself, Daughter. All know—"

Lady Blanche wrenched free with such violence her babe squealed. "I shall not defend myself. 'Tis the truth I will tell."

Her mother grabbed at her again, but she evaded those hooked fingers and, a moment later, Lady Richenda was held by one of the queen's knights.

"You are certain you wish to do this, Lady Blanche?" the queen asked.

"'Tis the only way to free myself and my child."

"Then I shall put the question to you. Is your babe of Alan de Balliol's loins?"

Amidst her mother's moaning and groaning, Blanche set her chin high. "It is possible."

"You cuckolded your husband."

"I did as my mother commanded so I might give my husband the son he desperately wanted."

"If the father is not Alan de Balliol, is it Sir Talbot, Lady Blanche?"

"It is." She peered across her shoulder at Judas. "I am sorry. Truly, I am. I hated what I did, but…" She shook her head. "I wish to go home, Your Majesty."

"Under the circumstances, methinks Cheverel may not be—"

"Nay, home! My home. I would live under my brother's protection." She pointed at her mother. "Without her."

"That can be arranged," Eleanor said, then to Blanche's mother, "I believe that if you have any hope of saving your depraved soul, you shall require years of solitude, reflection, and prayer. Thus, you shall be removed to a convent."

As Lady Richenda took to screeching and straining, the knight who held her began drawing her away.

"As for you, Sir Talbot, you will have to sell your sword arm to another, for you will not return to Cheverel. Nor will you ever again venture near Lady Blanche. And now we are quite finished." She stood and swept out from behind the table.

Near numb with relief, foreboding, and shock, Susanna watched as Eleanor exited the hall.

Then Judas was upon her. He embraced her and pressed his face into her shoulder as his body gently convulsed with the release of emotion.

She wrapped her arms around him and pressed a kiss atop his head.

"We did it, Aunt Sanna. We did it."

"You did it, Judas mine."

"And you. And Lord Wulfrith."

"So we did." She lifted her gaze to Everard who watched from a distance, who had said he wished to speak to her regardless of the outcome. But he could not have known that Judas's acknowledgement as heir would also see a husband provided for her—one of the queen's choosing, which surely would not include Everard whom some might yet believe had fathered her nephew.

Judas raised his head. "Are you very sorry you shall have to wed?"

There had been occasions over the years when he had asked the reason she lacked a husband. Refusing to burden him with the truth that her betrothal had been broken as punishment, always she said it was because she had found no one to love who would love her in return. He had been baffled, for he had seen no love between his father and Lady Blanche, but always Susanna had called herself silly and changed the subject.

She tried to smile. "I suppose it is past time I wed, hmm?"

"Even though you may not love or be loved?"

"Even though."

He frowned. "I know Sir Morris lied when he called you a…" He growled, shook his head as if to empty out the terrible word. "Do you think Lord Wulfrith—?"

"He has been very good to us, has he not?"

His frown deepened. "He has done right by me."

"So he has." She glanced at Everard whose brother had joined him and Sir Elias. "He has made everything right."

"I must needs thank him." Judas released her, pivoted, and hastened toward the men.

Having promised Lady Annyn and Lady Isobel she would deliver tidings of the queen's determination where they waited in the chamber abovestairs, Susanna turned away. As she ascended the stairs, she was stabbed with sorrow that the steps would not be further worn down by years of her passage upon them. Soon she would leave Stern and once more make Cheverel her home. And there she would marry a man not of her choosing.

35

STILL HE HAD come.

Unable to move her eyes from Everard where he filled the doorway, Susanna rose from the chair she had been ushered into a quarter hour past.

"Lady Susanna has shared the good tidings," Lady Annyn said where she held the door she had opened to her brother-in-law. "We are heartened to know justice is done."

He inclined his head and looked to his mother who had also arisen from her chair. "Forgive me, but I would speak with Lady Susanna alone."

Though Susanna felt Lady Isobel's sidelong glance, she held her gaze to Everard.

Shortly, he closed the door behind the two women. "How do you feel, Susanna?"

"Blessed. Relieved. Joyful." She sighed. "And yet, as if I am days without sleep."

His brow furrowed. "Perhaps we should speak later."

She took a step toward him. "Pray, let us do this now, for I do not think I will rest until I have heard you. And you have heard me." That last was the hardest to say, but it would be harder to do.

His brow cleared. "Very well. But let us begin with what you wish to give me."

She stepped to where her pack lay on a nearby table. "This." She drew out the linen packet and opened it to reveal the ruby.

His eyebrows drew close. "That?"

"I found it on the roof and knew you would wish to—"

"I should not have left it there," he said brusquely, "but it was no oversight."

She blinked. "Was it not?"

He strode forward and halted before her. "That night when I held and kissed you, Susanna, I put Judith behind me. How far behind, I was not certain, just as you were not. But I am certain now, and I was made even more so on the day past when Sir Elias and I were granted an audience with the queen and she told that if she found in Judas's favor she intended for you to wed."

He had known?

"And I do not think I have ever been so jealous."

Then…? Was he saying he loved her?

"I know what I want," he said, "and, I vow, it is not out of a need to atone."

Susanna forgot her circumstances long enough to savor joy. Then she remembered she was to wed another and hoped Everard did not, in fact, feel strongly for her.

"'Tis good this is recovered"—he turned the linen over the ruby and set it on the table—"but I had hoped you meant to give me the poem."

And how I wish you had not.

"I do not believe they are Judith's words," he continued. "I believe they are yours. I believe they are what you feel for me. And I would have you know I welcome them, for they are a match for what I would speak were I capable of composing such myself."

Feeling tears gather, she held her breath for fear its release would cause her emotions to scatter.

"Tell me they are your words, Susanna."

She was tempted to let the lie stand in hopes it made it easier for them both, but she could not. Slowly exhaling, she drew the parchment from her pack and held it out. "For the giving, not the taking," she repeated what he had spoken over a sennight past, "bestowed by the one who felt deeply enough to compose these words."

Without moving his gaze from hers, he closed a hand around it.

"I am sorry I lied to you," she said. "When I wrote it, I told myself it was surely what Judith felt, for she did love you, but they are my words, Everard. My feelings. My..." She looked down. "...ache."

He hooked a finger beneath her chin and lifted her face toward his. "Ours has a different ending. There will be no days and nights of longing."

The last verse...

"I love you, Susanna de Balliol. Will you have me?"

Tears causing his features to waver, she shook her head. "You know that is not possible. The queen says I am to wed a man of her choosing—"

"So you will. We must only persuade her I am that man and would make a worthy husband capable of administering Cheverel for Judas until he is grown."

"But surely she will not allow it since 'twas thought you might have fathered Judas. It would not look right."

"All that matters is that it look right to the queen, and after Sir Morris's revelations, I believe it will."

He sounded so certain. But, then, he was a Wulfrith.

"Will you have me, Susanna de Balliol?"

Daring to believe it was possible, she laid a hand on either side of his face. "I will have you, for you I have loved, Everard Wulfrith. You, I shall ever love." She drew his face down to hers, his mouth onto her mouth, and watched for his lids to lower. They did not. Amid the sweetness of their kiss, he looked into her as she looked into him.

Then he drew back, so slightly that when he spoke, his lips brushed hers. "You watch me again."

"Because you are the one I wish to kiss." She frowned. "Do you not want me to see you?"

"More than anything. 'Tis simply natural to close one's eyes when so near another, when one is feeling."

Was it natural? For this had he closed his eyes before? For this did her lids grow heavy each time they kissed?

Embarrassment crawling through her, she drew her head back. "I did not know. Always I…"

"Tell me."

Naught of which to be ashamed. Naught of which he would have you be ashamed.

"Always I closed my eyes tight so I would have fewer memories of those with whom I bargained." She dragged her teeth across her bottom lip. "But I want memories of you, Everard. I want to see you, to have no doubt it is you who kisses me."

His smile was gentle. "It will only ever be me, as it will only ever be you."

Only ever…She glanced at his fair hair. "What of Judith?"

"I loved her and shall not forget her. But though she was the love of my youth, you, Susanna…"

"Aye?"

"You are the love of my life."

In that moment, had she words to express the depth of her own love, she did not think she could have spoken them.

"Now," he said, drawing her near again, "close your eyes."

She lowered her lids and felt his splayed hand move from her waist to the middle of her back.

"Who holds you, Susanna?"

"Everard."

His hand slid higher, caressed her neck. "Who touches you?"

She smiled. "Everard."

His fingers skimmed her jaw. "Who gazes upon your lovely face?"

A breath of laughter escaped her. "Everard."

His lips touched hers. "Who kisses you?"

She sighed. "Everard."

He lifted his head and pressed kisses to her closed eyes. "Who do you see there in the dark?"

"The one I see in the light." She raised her lids, and there was her reflection in his grey-green eyes. "Everard Wulfrith, the man I love."

"Just as I see you, Susanna. Only you."

Epilogue

Stern Castle, England
July, 1160

HIS NAME WAS Judas. Not Judas of the Bible, but Judas de Balliol. And he was his father's heir.

As Susanna watched him where he stood across the great hall amid the revelers and alongside his friend, Charles, her full heart made room for more. Had ever a journey so dire and distant ended so well? Judas was safe and would be baron, she was loved and the wife of Everard Wulfrith whose hand rested upon the curve of her waist, whose ring upon her finger he had placed there scant hours earlier.

He chuckled over something Abel said, and she lowered her chin to consider the amber gem upon her hand that winked gold each time it caught the light—the same as her eyes, Everard said. For that, he had chosen it from amongst the gems his mother offered to mark the occasion of their marriage. Its twin, also removed from the necklace that had been given to Lady Isobel when she was young, shone from its place upon his hip. Where once a ruby had been set, pried free, and gifted to a woman he had loved, there was amber for the woman he now loved.

Susanna shifted her gaze to Garr's and Abel's daggers. Above each scabbard, the hilts into which gems were set were identical, a ruby at the intersection of cross guard and grip. As for Judith's ruby, Everard had ordered that it be set in the Wulfrith dagger forged for Elias who would soon depart England to be reunited with his family in France. And to further ensure Susanna's friend was well received by his father, Everard had spent countless hours personally training him in the weeks since Queen Eleanor's visit to Stern Castle. Though it had meant she and Everard had little time together, the hours had passed quickly, filled with becoming acquainted with the family Susanna would marry into.

It had been a gradual introduction, the first ten days mostly spent with Annyn and her children and Lady Isobel. Then the others had begun to arrive in anticipation of the marriage of the last Wulfrith sibling.

First had come Everard's sister, Lady Beatrix, and her husband Lord Michael D'Arci. Susanna had liked the petite woman almost immediately, for there was so much joy about her despite a head injury that sometimes caused her to struggle over words. Five months pregnant with their first child—*finally,* she said—she frequently stopped mid-sentence to grab the nearest hand and lay it upon her belly to share the stirring of her babe. As testament to the bond the sisters-in-law were forming, Susanna's hand was often the nearest, and she exclaimed with Beatrix on the occasions she was able to feel the flutters and light taps of the very tiny babe within.

Now Susanna turned her face away from the men who made up half the gathering of kin and looked to her right where the beautiful, golden-haired woman stood beside her.

Beatrix greeted her with a bounce of delicately arched eyebrows. "Soon," she whispered. "I am c-certain of it." She patted the small bulge beneath her hand, then looked to her sister on her other side. "Be ready, or you shall miss it again."

Lady Gaenor smiled, and the turn of her lips and show of teeth was so striking it was as though an unusually pretty woman had traded places with a relatively plain one.

A taller woman Susanna had not seen. Indeed, the lady was close to the height of her eldest brother, Garr, and not much shorter than her husband, the even more imposing Baron Christian Lavonne.

Susanna glanced at the man where he stood alongside Abel and once more entertained the thought that the Wulfriths must have searched far and wide to find a man who would not be looked down upon by their sister. Blessedly, husband and wife seemed devoted to one another, the sweet, brief meeting of their eyes and hands speaking well of their hearts.

"I am ready," Gaenor said. "See, here is my hand."

Beatrix grasped it and set it upon her belly. "Just to be sure." She laughed, as did Gaenor.

In personality, the older Wulfrith sister was also different from the younger and, at first, Susanna had been wary of her, for Lady Gaenor had seemed unapproachable. However, though harder to know than Beatrix, being of a quiet and reserved disposition, she proved every bit as kind.

"Do you think my sister is just a little excited, Lady Susanna?" This time, it was Susanna at whom Gaenor directed her smile, and the distance between the two women seemed to diminish further.

"Quite excited," Susanna agreed. "Beyond happy."

"Are we not all?" Beatrix exclaimed. Then she gasped, snatched up Susanna's hand, and pressed it alongside her sister's. "There is my babe."

The movement was slight but more strongly felt than before.

"Ah," Gaenor murmured, "there your babe is, indeed."

"A lovely sight," Lady Isobel called in her soft Scottish accent.

All three looked up as the mother of the indomitable Wulfriths returned to the gathering, and behind her came Annyn and Helene. Though the latter, Abel's wife, was too soon into her own pregnancy to yet show that the Wulfriths would continue to grow in strength and number, Susanna noted the hand she lightly laid upon her abdomen.

I wish that, too. Pray, Heavenly Father, bless Everard and me.

Lady Isobel halted alongside Gaenor. "From the smile you wear, Daughter, you have, at last, been formally introduced to your new niece—or nephew."

"I have. But, alas, the babe has once more settled." She lifted her hand from Beatrix's belly, looked to Helene. "I hope my Lyulf gave you no trouble in seeking his rest."

THE LONGING

The lovely, auburn-haired woman with whom Gaenor was obviously close, shook her head. "He hardly stirred, even when I laid him to bed."

"The same cannot be said of that rascal, Jonas," Lady Isobel said, "but methinks he has met his match in Sir Rowan."

Susanna looked about, but she did not see the aged knight who had come from Wulfen Castle to give her in marriage to Everard. It was he who, a half hour earlier, had scooped up Annyn's disgruntled son while the boy's mother carried little Artur away from the joyous din.

"Is Sir Rowan yet abovestairs?" Susanna asked.

Annyn blew a breath up her brow. "Aye. Issie has convinced him she is much too old to rest her eyes while the sun yet shines. Thus, she has claimed a perch upon his knee and a tale for her ears."

It was said lightly and with fondness for which Susanna was grateful. When she had told Annyn that she wished Sir Rowan to present her at her wedding, the pronouncement had not been received with the enthusiasm of one soon to be reunited with a dear friend, but with weighty hesitation. But the lady had said it would be done, and the awkwardness with which Sir Rowan and she had first greeted one another had resolved over the past few days. There was a tale there, but Susanna knew it was not hers. She was only glad its ending—perhaps better called a new beginning—found Sir Rowan and Annyn once more easy in each other's company.

Lady Isobel sighed. "I am sure Jonas strains his ears to hear Sir Rowan's story."

"Indeed." Annyn raised her eyebrows at Susanna. "As I believe you have discovered, my children are not fond of sleep. But be forewarned, 'tis not an uncommon trait among the Wulfriths."

Susanna hoped there would be such a day when the trait passed to her own children.

"Will you dance with me, Wife?" Everard's voice tickled her ear.

She looked around and found his face so near hers that, were they alone, she would have drawn nearer and closed her eyes so she could feel his kiss all the way through. "I will."

He moved his hand from her back to her arm and guided her among the gathering to the floor where celebrants danced to the sedate but joyous melody birthed by the musicians in the gallery above.

"Sweet woodruff," he murmured as he drew her into his arms.

She had worn the pendant for her wedding day, this time on the outside of her bodice, and the petals and leaves wafted their lovely fragrance between them.

"I am happy," she said, "as I never thought to be."

He touched his lips to her brow. "As am I."

"I fear you will miss Wulfen."

"I shall, but you I would miss more if I did not loosen my hold upon my lordship, and there is much to be done at Cheverel to ensure it is fit for the baron our nephew will become."

Our nephew. There could be no sweeter tears than those that filled Susanna's eyes. Everard would remain the Lord of Wulfen, but it had been decided amongst the brothers that until Judas assumed his title in full, the duties of training young men into knights would be divided among the three of them. Everard would preside over Wulfen during spring and autumn, Garr would take winter, and summer would fall to Abel. All that remained to be settled was Annyn's proposal that wives be permitted to discreetly visit their husbands in their seasons. At first, the Wulfrith men had rejected the idea, but Annyn had proven persuasive enough that it remained under consideration.

"Have you thought any further on Lady Annyn's proposal?" Susanna asked as her husband guided her over the floor.

He raised an eyebrow. "Have she and Lady Helene tasked you with prodding me whilst I am at my weakest?"

"Weakest?" She smiled. "Can such a word be applied to a Wulfrith?"

"Certainly on his wedding day that much too slowly approaches his wedding night."

Though Susanna felt the pink in her cheeks, she also felt bold. "Then for this, women ought to be allowed within Wulfen's walls."

He laughed. "You may be right, dear Susanna." He drew her closer and she laid her cheek on his shoulder. As he moved her, she saw they were no longer the only Wulfriths in one another's arms. There was Garr with his Annyn and Michael his Beatrix. And when Everard turned her, she saw Christian with his Gaenor and Abel his Helene.

I am part of this. This is my family. So like a dream…

She drew back, met her husband's gaze, and slid her fingers into hair that was nearly as golden as Beatrix's. "Are you truly mine, Everard?"

He lowered his face near hers. "My beloved is mine." He lightly kissed her. "And I am hers. Now and ever."

Excerpt

LADY OF EVE

A "Clean Read" rewrite of the 1994 bestselling
Virgin Bride from Bantam Books
Available Summer 2014

Arlecy Abbey, England
Early Autumn, 1156

Of what benefit was it to be a vision in virginal white if one's groom was
not of one's choosing?

Hoping to calm her racing heart, Lady Graeye Charwyck lifted a
hand and pressed it between her breasts. She loved the Lord, but she did
not believe He was any more pleased to have her as His bride than she
was to have Him as her groom. If it was true what she had been taught,
He knew her heart. He knew she did not want this. He knew there was
no worth—nothing precious—in vows grudgingly given.

"Dear Lord," she breathed and bowed her head to stare at the toes of
her shoes peeking from beneath the skirts of her bridal habit.

"Be still!" the novice mistress reprimanded, her deep voice jolting
her charge's slender frame.

Graeye lifted her head, stiffened her spine with well-learned obedience, and sighed—a lack of deference for which she immediately
repented. Though not of late, she had more than once felt the sting of

Mistress Hermana's strap, for that part of her spirit which had not been broken picked the most inopportune times to declare that this life was not of her choosing. Of the three vows she was about to take, she knew obedience would be the most difficult to keep.

Digging her short nails into her palms, she slid her gaze up the black-clad woman. She need not have gone farther than that square, unmoving chin to know of the novice mistress's displeasure, but she did.

With a snort of disapproval, Hermana reached forward and tugged on the wimple where it passed beneath Graeye's chin up to the stiffened band around her forehead.

Heart sinking further, Graeye lowered her eyes and forced herself to be still. Over the years, she had become painfully accustomed to such ministrations—a vain attempt to conceal the faint stain marring the left side of her face. Starting just shy of her eyebrow, the mark faded back into the hairline at her temple. Though it was not very large or conspicuous, it might as well have covered her entire face.

The mark of the devil, Hermana often pointed out. Always, the devil in Graeye was responsible for the trouble she got herself into. What might otherwise have been viewed as simple, childish pranks or the foolishness of youth, the superstitious woman attributed to evil. When the other novices skipped matins or devised tricks against one another, their punishment was a verbal reprimand and prayers of repentance. For Graeye, it was that and more—a strap across the back, hours on her knees scrubbing floors and pulling weeds, and, always, humiliation before her peers.

Though she did not believe the devil was responsible for her penchant for trouble, she knew well the curse her physical flaw afforded. It was, after all, the shape of her destiny thus far.

Her father, unable to bear the sight of her any longer, had dedicated her to the Church when she was seven, only days following her mother's death. The handsome dowry he had provided the convent at Arlecy had ensured her acceptance no matter what mark she bore. And no matter her own feelings. Now she was to wed—not to a mortal as she might have wished, but to the Church.

On this, the day of her Clothing, she would become a nun, her profession made, hair sheared, a black habit her only garment. It burdened her, but still there was a blessing in it, for her passing into sisterhood would finally free her from Hermana's dominance. Though the woman was not a nun, for she had once been wed and her chastity forever lost, she had held the esteemed position of novice mistress for as long as Graeye could remember.

Now Graeye would have a kinder master to serve—the Lord.

If only I could rejoice in that and be content...

When the faint sound of music from within the chapel indicated the commencement of the ceremony, Hermana snapped, "Eyes forward!"

Graeye began a mental recitation of her prayers—not those devised for a novice preparing to take the veil, but her own pleading that she be freed from this obligation.

Minutes later, the large oaken doors to the chapel groaned inward.

Squaring her shoulders, Graeye pressed her bouquet to her abdomen, gripping it so tightly her fingers crushed the delicate stems and leaves. But though she commanded her legs to take that first, fateful step forward, she could not.

Hermana had the solution. She always did, in this instance, a sharp nudge that would likely leave a bruise.

"Halt!" The command sliced the cool morning air.

As if joined, Graeye and Hermana whirled around to search out the intruder.

Though the half-dozen knights who emerged from between two of the outlying buildings came disarmed, as was the only permissible entrance to this holy place, a small group of clergy were vainly trying to halt their advance.

"You dare enter consecrated ground without permission?" Hermana demanded as she hurried forward to place herself in the intruders' path.

"Forgive us," a tall, thin knight said, though he sounded less than repentant. He withdrew a rolled parchment from his belt and handed it to the novice mistress. "I carry an urgent message from Baron Edward Charwyck."

Graeye sucked in a breath. A message from her father? Had her letter of appeal brought a change of heart? Biting her inner lip so hard she tasted blood, she watched as Hermana turned to put the sun at her back to better read the missive.

The woman's thick eyebrows drew closer, ever closer. Then she lifted her eyes to stare over the top of the parchment at her charge.

Suppressing the desire to wrap her arms around herself, Graeye shifted her gaze to the right. There, a young, fair-headed knight stood beside the messenger, eyes intent upon her. She lifted a hand to the wimple, ensuring the mark remained covered.

The crackle of parchment broke the silence, then Hermana traversed the stone walkway and ascended the steps to the chapel. The abbess stood at the top, having come outside to discover the cause for the delay.

The exchange between the two women was hushed. While the abbess, a woman Graeye regarded with affection, listened, the other began to gesticulate wildly. The abbess raised a hand to quiet Hermana, took the parchment, and examined it. Shortly, more words were spoken and the novice mistress descended the steps.

Venturing a look past the stern-faced woman approaching her, Graeye was startled by the abbess's serene countenance. Though she could not be certain, she thought the woman's mouth curved toward a smile.

When Hermana stopped before her, Graeye met her gaze.

"'Tis your brother, Philip," the woman began, her voice strained as if weighted by emotion. "He is deceased." As the words passed her thin, colorless lips, she crossed herself.

Graeye could only stare. Then, remembering herself, she also made the sign of the cross.

Philip dead. There was an odd fluttering in her chest, but she felt little else.

Contrite over her lack of deep emotion, she offered up a silent explanation for her un-Christian reaction. She had hardly known her half sibling, for he had been quite a bit older than she, and her few remembrances of him were seeped in pain.

She had seen little of Philip while he had been in training, first as a page, then a squire, at a neighboring barony. However, she had seen enough to dislike the loud, foul-mouthed boy with whom she shared a father. He had taunted her about her "devil's mark" and played cruel pranks on her when he caught her out from behind her mother's skirts.

God forgive her, but she could not mourn one whose memory dredged up old pain, and whom she had not seen for nigh on eleven years. He was a stranger, and now would forever remain one. Still, she would pray for his soul.

"Your father has requested you attend him so that your brother might be given a proper burial," Hermana went on, her voice choked, eyes moist.

Graeye wondered at the woman's peculiar behavior. She had never known Hermana capable of any deep emotion other than anger and displeasure.

"And as you are now his only hope for a male heir," she continued, "'tis not likely you will return to us."

Leave Arlecy? Forever? Graeye's heart swelled as she stared into that wizened face, her hand reflexively opening to release the ravaged bouquet. With a soft rustle, it dropped to the cold stones.

My prayers have been answered. I am freed.

In the next instant, she suppressed the smile that tried to bend her mouth into a shape with which it was mostly unaccustomed. Why had God waited until the last moment to grant her desires? Had He been testing her? Had He—?

"You are to depart immediately," Hermana said. "I will have your possessions packed and sent on later."

"I must change," Graeye whispered.

"There is to be no delay," the woman snapped. "You are to leave now so you might complete the journey ere nightfall."

Graeye had no intention of arguing. Atremble with excitement, she lifted the skirts of her bridal habit clear of her feet and walked quickly to the knight who had delivered the message.

The man was much older than he had appeared from a distance. In fact, he looked well past two score years, every telling groove in his hard face stark against his chalky complexion.

"Lady Graeye," he said, "I am Sir William Rotwyld, Lord of Sulle, vassal to Baron Edward Charwyck." His eyes shone with a coldness she feared to fathom.

Inclining her head, she clasped her hands before her. "Sir William."

"Come." He grasped her elbow. "Your father awaits you at Medland."

Stealing a look behind, Graeye swept her gaze past Hermana and settled it on the abbess. This time there was no doubt that the woman smiled.

2

Medland, England
Autumn, 1156

A BROOM IN ONE hand, a dirty rag in the other, Graeye took a rest from her labors to cast a critical eye over the hall. Through her efforts this past month, the castle had seen many changes inside and out, but none were as obvious as those found here.

Gone was the sparse, putrid straw that had covered the floor and upon which she had slipped on her first day at Medland. In its place were fresh rushes that smelled of sweet herbs. Immense networks of cobwebs and thick layers of dust had been swept away. Dirty, tattered window coverings had been replaced with oiled linen that held back the night's icy draught and let day's light spill beams throughout. Trestle tables and benches that had threatened to collapse beneath a man's weight had been repaired, though they did not look much better for all the effort. Even the threadbare tapestries had been salvaged by days of cleaning and needlework.

Still, no matter how hard she worked, the donjon would never be grand, Graeye conceded with a wistful sigh. But at least it was now habitable. And it was the castle folk she had to thank for that. Determined as she had been to set Medland right, she could not have accomplished most of it without their help.

It had taken persistence and a considerable show of interest in the reasons behind the sorry state of the demesne before the people set aside their superstitions over the mark she bore and revealed what had transpired these past years.

Four years earlier, her father had relinquished the responsibility of overseeing Medland to Philip, and it had been a poor decision. Unconcerned for the welfare of his people, the young lord had squandered time and money.

By the second year, his neglect had led to diminished stores of food for the castle inhabitants. Hence, he had appropriated livestock and grain from the villagers to meet the demand within the walled fortress. That had weakened the once prosperous people and resulted in winter famine.

Philip had been a cruel master, too, doling out harsh punishment for minor offenses and using his authority to gain the beds of castle servants and village women. There were even whispered rumors that his cruelty had extended to the taking of lives when he was displeased—that his late wife had met her end in such a fashion.

Graeye had chosen not to delve too deeply into that last matter. Instead, she set to righting the wrongs, and it was that which brought the castle folk and villagers to her side. It had taken courage she had not knowns she possessed, but she had opened the stores of grain her father hoarded and distributed a goodly portion among the people. Though Baron Charwyck and his men had grumbled over her actions, none had directly opposed her.

When she had toured the village and fields outside the castle walls, she was relieved to discover the villagers' crops were in better shape than their lord's, though she kept this to herself for fear her father might again lay claim to the harvest.

Through her efforts, the harvesting of the lord's sparse crops and the plowing and sowing of the fallow fields were set in motion, though not without a great deal of prodding. Still, she knew that even if the fields yielded late crops, it was unlikely there would be enough to last through the long winter that the brisk autumn winds promised. Though the changes she had wrought were considerable, there was still much to do.

With that reminder, Graeye drew the back of a hand over her warm, moist face. She was tempted to remove the stifling wimple but squelched the impulse. Several times during the past week, she had contemplated discarding it altogether, but she was not ready to expose herself to greater curiosity than that which she had endured thus far.

"Lady Graeye," a man's voice called.

She propped her broom against the wall and turned to face the one who crossed the hall toward her. It was the young knight who had caught her notice at the abbey—Sir Michael Trevier. During her first days at Medland, he had been instrumental in helping her gain acceptance among the people and implementing changes. He had been all smiles for her then, always at hand to assist in whatever task she undertook. But that was in the past.

A fortnight earlier, he had issued a challenge to the knight her father had chosen to be her husband. Sir Michael had wanted her for himself and had been prepared to do battle to win her hand. However, Edward Charwyck had remained adamant that Sir William Rotwyld, the messenger who had retrieved her from the abbey, was to be her husband.

Angered, Sir Michael had hurled insults at William, pointing out that his great age might prevent him from fathering the heir Edward badly wanted.

Although Graeye would have far preferred marriage to the kind young knight than the repulsive man of Edward's choosing, in order to avoid bloodshed, she had declared that she was content to wed William.

Though she had been successful in preventing the two men from taking up swords, Sir Michael was no longer her champion. He had no smiles for her, nor warm words to ease her misgivings. He had become conspicuously scarce, practically a stranger. She missed him.

"There is a merchant at the postern gate who says he has cloth for you," he said when he halted before her.

"Cloth?" Graeye frowned, trying to remember when and for what purpose, she had ordered it. "Ah, for the tables." She gestured toward their bare, unsightly tops. "Do you not think coverings will brighten the entire hall?"

Mouth set in a grim line, he turned away. "I will send the man to you," he tossed over his shoulder.

Once more pained by his indifference, she hurried after him and caught his arm. "Sir Michael, do you not understand why—?"

"Perfectly, my lady." His gaze was stony.

"Nay, I do not think you do. Will you not let me explain?"

He shrugged her hand off. "A lowly knight such as myself deserves no explanation."

So he thought she had rejected him because of his rank. "You are wrong. I—"

"Pardon me, but I have other tasks to attend to." He bowed stiffly and walked away.

Graeye watched him go. Though she could not say she loved him, he was every bit the brother she had once imagined having. Perhaps love would have grown from that, but she supposed she would never know.

"He is the one you want, is he not?"

She spun around to face Edward. "F-father," she stammered.

His lips twisted into a knowing smile.

Trying to gauge his mood, she took in the sour smell of alcohol that ladened his breath, the sound of his shallow, labored breathing, and the gray, sagging features set with reddened eyes. It was a common sight, for he was more often drunk than sober, but she had yet to become accustomed to such a state.

His mood was harmless, she decided. Blessedly, with each passing day, he became more genial, but it had not been like that when she had first arrived at Medland. Then he had been half-mad with grief over Philip's death, had called her the devil's daughter, had—

She did not want to think on that first night, for it chilled her to relive the memory. Fortunately, now he mostly named her *Daughter of*

Eve whenever he was displeased. Not that she liked being blamed for the sins of man alongside Eve, but it was better than the alternative.

"The cloth has arrived," she said, hoping he would not pursue the matter of Sir Michael. "By tomorrow eve, the tables will all be covered."

He glowered, then slurred, "William will make you a good husband. That pup Michael knows nothing of responsibility or loyalty. And, I assure you, he knows little of breeding."

Graeye blushed and averted her gaze. "Aye, Father."

"But still you want the young one, eh?"

She shook her head. "I have said I am content with Sir William."

"Content!" he spat. "Yet you would choose Sir Michael if I allowed it. Do not lie to me."

Reminding herself of the vow she had made weeks earlier not to cower, she lifted her chin. "It is true Sir Michael is young and handsome, and he is soft of heart, but—"

"He is a weakling, that is what he is. He has no property and very little coin."

Though Graeye knew it was unwise to defend the knight, she said, "He is still young, and what would William have if you had not given it to him?"

Surprisingly, Edward did not anger. "True," he mused, "but he earned it. That, Sir Michael has yet to do. If ever."

"Methinks he will."

"Not with my daughter. Nay, I want an heir, and soon. Your union with William will ensure that."

"How can you be certain?"

He grinned. "William made seven boys on his first two wives—not a single girl child." He let that sink in, then added, "It is a son you will bear come spring."

Then it was not the knight's possessions, nor his years of loyalty that had decided Edward. It was his ability to produce sons. She suppressed a shudder at the thought of the man making an heir on her.

Edward turned and surveyed the hall. "You have done well, Daughter."

He had changed topics so abruptly that it took her several moments to understand he referred to the improvements made to the hall. Relieved, she abandoned all thoughts of her future as William Rotwyld's wife.

"I thank you," she said. All the hard work was worth it for just those few words of praise. Had he also noticed the improved foodstuffs that graced his table, or had drinking numbed his sense of taste?

"Methinks I shall have to reward you."

"'Tis not necessary," she said.

"Of course it is not necessary! If it was, I would not do it."

Realizing he teetered on the edge of a black mood, Graeye merely nodded.

Edward grumbled beneath his breath, studied the floor, smacked his lips. "A new wardrobe! Aye, it would not be fitting for a Charwyck to go to her wedding dressed as you are." Sneering, he slid his gaze down the faded bliaut she wore.

Graeye smoothed the material. Having no clothing other than what she had worn as a novice at the abbey, she had taken possession of the garments that had belonged to her mother. Though aged, they fit well, for she was nearly the same size as Lady Alienor had been, only a bit shorter.

"I would like that," she said, imagining the beautiful fabrics she might choose.

"It will be done." Edward swung away and stumbled in his attempt to negotiate the level floor, sending the rushes beneath his feet flying. Somehow, he managed to remain upright.

Graeye hurried forward and caught his arm. "You are tired," she said, hoping he would not thrust her away as he often did when she touched him, averse as he was to being near her—as if he truly believed the devil resided in her.

He looked down at her hand but did not push her away. "Aye, I am tired."

She urged him toward the stairs. "I will help you to your chamber."

The wooden steps creaked alarmingly beneath their feet, soft in some places, brittle in others, reminding Graeye that she needed to set some men the task of replacing them.

Up a second flight of stairs they went, down a narrow corridor, and into the lord's chamber where Graeye tossed the covers back from the bed. "I will send a servant to awaken you when supper is ready," she said as her father collapsed on the mattress.

"Supper," he griped. "Nay, send me a wench and ale. That will suffice."

Making no comment, Graeye pulled the covers over him. He asked for the same thing each evening, and each time she sent a manservant to deliver him to the hall. It was bold, but thus far he had allowed it.

As she straightened, Edward caught hold of her hand. "A grandson," he muttered. "'Tis all I ask of you."

Pity surged through her as she gazed into his desperate, pleading eyes. He was vulnerable, pained, heartbroken. Here was a man of whom she was no longer frightened—the one who should have been her father these past eleven years. Perhaps it was not too late.

Graeye knew she should not entertain such thoughts. After all, had she not been Edward's only chance for a male heir, he would never have sent for her. Knowing this should have been enough to banish her false hope, but she could not help herself.

She bent, kissed his weathered cheek, and whispered, "A grandson you will have. This I vow." When she lifted her head, she saw that his eyes shone with gratitude amid brimming tears.

"I thank you," he said, his fingers gripping hers tightly. Moments later, he fell asleep.

Graeye withdrew from his chamber and quietly closed the door. She had taken but a single step toward the stairs when a sound caught her attention. Chills pricking her skin, she slowly turned to face the small chapel situated at the end of the corridor. As no torches were lit beyond Edward's chamber, she squinted to see past the shadows, but they were too deep and dark.

Though she longed to return to her chores belowstairs, she knew she must eventually face the memories that had haunted her dreams since that first night at Medland. Thus, she squared her shoulders, drew a deep breath, and walked forward.

What had caused the noise? she wondered, refusing to allow her imagination to believe it had anything to do with her brother's death. A rat, perhaps, or a breeze stirring the rushes about the chapel.

As she drew near, the sound became that of scratching and quick, shallow breathing.

Heart leaping, Graeye halted and peered into the shadows. "Who goes?" she demanded, hating that her voice should shake so.

Silence, then a deep groan. An instant later, a large figure bounded out of the darkness and skidded to a halt before her.

Mouth wide with the scream she had nearly loosed, she stared at the great, mangy dog. "Oh, Groan!"

Tongue lolling, the dog wagged its tail so vigorously that its backside jerked side to side.

Graeye sank to her knees and slid an arm around the animal. "You are naughty for frightening me," she scolded and turned her face away when he tried to lick it.

As she stroked his head, she remembered how frightened she had been of the beast when he had introduced himself during her first meal at Medland. She had rarely been around dogs, and certainly never one of such grand proportions, and had shrieked when he had laid his slavering chin upon her lap. That had gained her nothing but humiliation, for the dog had not moved, and her father's men had roared with laughter.

She had succeeded in dislodging him by tossing food to him, but always he returned to her and Edward had advised that if she beat him rather than feed him, he would not bother her. Such callous words had replaced her fright with a need to protect him.

Since that day, Groan—as she had named him due to his penchant for making that horrible sound—had attached himself to her side. And he had more than once proved valuable.

Recalling the night, a sennight after she had returned to Medland, when Sir William had cornered her as she readied to bed down in the hall, she shuddered. The vile man had taunted her with cruel words, and his hands had bruised her as they made themselves familiar with her cringing body. Though he was to be her husband, and she had known it was unlikely she could prevent the ravishment he intended, she had fought him. It had not deterred him. In fact, he had seemed to enjoy her resistance. Even as he had torn her bliaut and laid hands to her flesh, he had threatened that if she bore him a child with the same mark she carried, he would kill it himself.

That had frightened her more than the inevitable violation of her body. She had been about to scream when Groan had appeared. Snapping and snarling, he had circled William, bunching his body as he readied to attack.

The man who had thought nothing of exerting his greater strength over a frightened woman had retreated, leaving Graeye to offer profuse thanks to her unlikely champion.

Conveniently forgetting her resolve to face the memories that had been birthed within the chapel, Graeye straightened. "Come," she said. "I will find you a nice morsel."

The dog looked over his shoulder, back at her, then bounded to the chapel door and resumed his scratching and sniffing.

Graeye pulled her bottom lip between her teeth. Sooner or later, she would have to go inside and brave her fears. She supposed it might as well be now.

"Shall we see what interests you, Groan?" she said and stepped forward. When she pushed the door open, Groan rushed in ahead of her.

It was not like that first night when a profusion of candlelight had greeted Graeye. Today, the chapel was dim, its only source of light that which shone from the small window that had been opened to air out the room.

Crossing herself, Graeye stepped inside. Instantly, her gaze was drawn to the high table that stood against the far wall. Her brother had been laid out on it that first night, his ravaged, decomposing corpse emitting a horrible stench. She could still smell it. And found herself reliving when Edward had brought her here. She had been unable to cross the threshold for the smell that assailed her, and so he had thrust her inside.

"I would have you see Philip with your own eyes," he had said, "that you might know the brutality of his murder." He had pulled her forward and swept aside the covering to reveal the festering wounds and Philip's awful death mask.

"See the marks on his hands and chest?" He had run his fingers over the stiffened corpse. "These he survived. 'Twas the arrow that killed him."

Battling nausea, Graeye asked, "Arrow?" She saw no evidence of such a wound.

"Took it in the back!" Edward's face turned a horrid crimson as he stared into his son's sightless eyes.

Anxious to withdraw, Graeye touched his sleeve. "Let us speak elsewhere. This is not the place—"

"That accursed Balmaine witch and her brother did this to him!"

Graeye's head snapped back. Balmaine? Was that not the family under which Philip had completed his knighthood training, the same whose properties bordered those of Medland?

"I do not understand, Father. The Balmaines are responsible for this?"

He looked up from the body, the hate upon his face so tangible it gripped a cold hand about her heart. "Gilbert Balmaine challenged your brother to a duel, and when Philip bettered him, his wicked sister put an arrow through his back."

Graeye gasped. Though her familial ties were strained by the long years of absence, she was appalled to learn such an injustice had been done her brother.

"Why?" she whispered.

Edward gripped her upper arm. "'Twas the Balmaine woman's revenge upon Philip for breaking his betrothal to her."

Graeye had not known of her brother's betrothal. Despair over the lost years gripped her. Perhaps things would have been different had her mother lived and Graeye had been allowed to grow up at Medland.

"Why would Philip break the betrothal?" she asked, and flinched when Edward's fingers bit into her flesh.

"She was a harlot—gave herself to another man only days before she was to wed Philip. He could not wed her after such a betrayal."

Graeye clenched her hands. What evil lurked in a woman's heart that made her seek such means of revenge? "When did he die?"

"Over a fortnight past."

She glanced at his corpse. "Why has he lain in state so long?"

"He was returned to me nine days past over the back of his horse," Edward said, the corners of his mouth collecting spittle.

"Whence?"

"One of the northern shires—Chesne."

"The north? But what was he—?"

"Be silent!" Edward gave her a shake. "The Balmaine is my enemy—ours! Do not forget what you have seen here, for we will have our revenge."

"Nay, we must forgive, Father. 'Tis not for us to judge. That is God's place."

"Do not preach at me!" He drew his arm back as if to strike her.

Graeye stared at the hand poised above her, shrank from him.

Abruptly, he released her. "I will have my revenge," he barked. "And you, Daughter, will pass the night here and pray Philip's soul into heaven."

She shook her head. It was too much he asked. If there was not yet disease in this chamber, there would soon be. She pulled free, spun around, and ran for the door.

Graeye dragged herself back to the present. She did not need to relive any more of that night to exorcise her memories. There was not much else to them other than endless hours of prayer. Locked in the chapel, she had knelt before the altar and prayed for her brother's soul and her own deliverance until dawn when a servant had let her out. Since then, she had not come near this place.

Groan's bark brought her head around. "What have you found?" she asked.

Crouching low, he pushed his paws beneath the kneeler and swatted at something that gave a high-pitched cry.

"Is it a bird?" No sooner did she ask it than a bird flew out from beneath the kneeler and swept across the chapel. Groan chased after it, but it was too fast.

It was a young falcon, Graeye saw as she rushed to close the door so it would not escape into the rest of the castle. Had it slipped free of the mews?

It took patience and effort, but between Graeye and Groan chasing it about, the falcon finally found the small window and its freedom. Gripping the sill, Graeye watched the bird arc and dip its wings in the broad expanse of sky.

How would it feel to have wings? To fly free and—

She chastised herself for such foolish yearnings. There was nothing she had wanted as badly as to come home to Medland and assume her place as lady of the castle. In spite of the obstacles encountered these past weeks, and that she was to wed a man she loathed, she had never known greater fulfillment.

With the abbey forever behind her, her future was assured. That, no one could take from her.

3

THERE WAS TO be no more discussion of Graeye's marriage to William Rotwyld. Simply, there was to be no wedding.

An air of import surrounded King Henry's knight as he strode into the hall five days later, his armed retinue following close behind and spreading out to position themselves about the room. Clothed in chain mail, they wore no smiles nor congenial air that might mistake them for visitors simply passing through.

Realizing something serious was afoot, Edward ordered all, except his steward and William, from the hall in order to receive the king's missive in private.

Graeye did not have long to learn what news had been brought to her father, for his explosion was heard throughout the donjon. She hurried into the hall and stumbled when she saw the half-dozen knights clamoring to hold her red-faced, bellowing sire from the messenger.

Shot through with fear, she searched out William and saw he stood beside the steward, his expression reflecting the other man's. Shock, disbelief, outrage.

She moved forward and halted before the messenger. "What has happened, Sir Knight?"

His gaze swept her faded bliaut before settling on her face framed by its concealing wimple. "Who are you?"

She dipped a curtsy. "I am Lady Graeye."

His eyes narrowed. "Sir Royce Saliere, here by order of the king. You are a relation?"

Graeye glanced at her father. "I am the baron's daughter."

Surprise transformed his dour face, but he quickly recovered. "No longer baron." He gave what seemed a token shrug of regret. "By King Henry's decree, all Charwyck lands are declared forfeit and returned to the sovereignty of the crown."

Edward roared louder, raising his voice against God as he struggled to free himself.

Feeling as if she had been delivered a mighty blow, Graeye shook her head. It could not be true. The king would not take from the Charwycks that which had been awarded the family nearly a century past. This had to be some kind of trickery by which another sought to wrest her father's lands from him now that he was without an heir.

"Methinks you lie," she said.

Sir Royce's eyebrows arched. "Lie?"

"King Henry would do no such a thing. My father is a loyal subject. He—"

"Can you read?" Sir Royce's tone was patronizing.

"Of course," she said and took the document he thrust at her. Immediately, her gaze fell upon the broken wax seal. Though she had never seen the royal signet, she did not doubt this had, indeed, come from the king. Heart sinking, she unrolled the parchment and read the first lines. And could go no further.

"Why?" she croaked, reaching for something to hold to but finding emptiness. If the Charwyck lands were lost, what was to become of her father, an old man no longer capable of lifting a sword to earn his living? And what of her? She would not be needed to produce a male heir—of no value since William would not wed her without benefit of the immense dowry she would have brought to their union.

"For offenses committed by your brother, Philip Charwyck," Sir Royce said as he pried the document from her fingers.

Graeye swayed but remained on her feet. "I do not understand," she said. "Of what offenses do you speak?" She stole a glance at her father who had quieted.

"Murder, pillaging..."

Remembering her brother's disposition, the accusations should not have surprised her, but they did. "Surely you are mistaken." Desperation raised her voice unnaturally high. "'Twas my brother who was murdered. Why do you not seek out the perpetrator of that crime?"

The man raised his eyes heavenward as if seeking guidance from God. "As I have told your father, Philip Charwyck was not murdered. His death is a result of his own deceit."

"What did—?"

Sir Royce held up a hand. "I can tell no more."

"You would take all that belongs to the Charwycks and refuse to say what, exactly, my brother is accused of having done?"

He folded his arms over his chest. "Your fate rests with Baron Balmaine of Penforke. 'Tis his family the crime was committed against, and King Henry has given the care of these properties to him."

Graeye barely had time to register this last shocking news before her father erupted again and renewed his struggles. "Curse the Balmaines! With my own sword, I will gut the miscreant and his sister!"

Sir Royce grunted, signaled for his men to remove Edward.

Graeye rushed toward her father. "Nay!" she cried, following the knights as they half dragged, half carried Edward across the hall. Her efforts to halt their progress were to no avail, for she was thrust aside each time she stepped into their path. Neither William, nor the steward, were of any help. As if great pillars of earth, they remained unmoving.

She hurried back to Sir Royce. "Where are they taking my father?" She touched his sleeve. "Surely he has committed no offense."

"He must needs be held whilst he is a danger to others." He looked at her hand upon his arm.

She dropped it but continued to stare into his unmoving face. "He has been dealt a great blow. Not only has the king taken everything he owns, but he has given it into the hands of my father's avowed enemy."

The man considered her, then ran a weary hand through his cropped, silvery hair. "Lady Graeye, I do not fault your father for his anger. 'Tis simply a measure of safety I take to ensure Medland passes into Baron Balmaine's hands without contest."

"He will be coming soon?"

"A sennight." He turned and strode to where his knights were gathered near the doors.

So many questions swirled about Graeye's mind that she thought she might go mad, but she knew it would be useless to pursue the matter. She turned and looked at William and the steward. "All is lost," she said.

At their continued silence, she withdrew from the hall. Without benefit of a mantle to protect her against the lingering chill of morning, she set out to discover her father's whereabouts. Not only did she know the precipice upon which his mind balanced and worried for his welfare, but she needed to know if she would be allowed to remain at his side to care for him, or if he intended to return her to the abbey.

It was no great undertaking to discover where Edward had been taken, for with expressions of concern, castle folk pointed Graeye to the watchtower.

Along the way, she became increasingly uneasy about the great number of the king's men positioned around the walls. They were alert, ready to stamp out any signs of uprising. That unlikely possibility made her smile bitterly. Not only had the number of Edward's retainers been depleted from Philip's foray to the north, where he had given up his life for a cause as yet unclear to her, but few would be willing to challenge the king's men for their lord. They disliked him so.

At the watchtower, a surly knight halted Graeye's progress. "You would do well to return to the donjon, my lady. No one is allowed to see the prisoner."

"I am his daughter, Lady Graeye. I would but look to his needs."

He shook his head. "My orders are clear. No one is allowed within."

"I beseech you, let me see him for a short time. No harm will be done."

He did not waver, though she thought his eyes softened. "Nay."

Even as Graeye told herself she should not, she snatched up her skirts, ducked beneath the man's arm, and managed to make it up the flight of steps before encountering the next barrier. The first knight tight on her heels, she came to a halt when faced with the two who guarded the room where her father was surely imprisoned. They had heard her advance, for their swords were drawn and trained upon her.

The knight behind need not have gone to the trouble to seizing hold of her, as she could go no farther, but his hand turned around her arm. "You——" He snapped his teeth closed on his next words.

Tears flooding her eyes, she peered up at him. "Just a moment," she choked. "'Tis all I ask."

The angry color that had flooded his face receded and, miraculously, he said, "For a moment only."

He released her and motioned for the guards to move away. After a brief hesitation, during which Graeye feared he had reconsidered the wisdom of allowing her to see her father, the knight threw back the bolt and opened the door.

With a murmur of gratitude, she entered the cold room. She had expected to be granted privacy with her father, but it was not to be. His great bulk shadowing the floor, the knight positioned himself in the doorway as she crossed to where Edward huddled in a corner of the room.

She lowered to the floor beside him.

Forehead resting on arms propped on his knees, he seemed not to realize he was no longer alone.

Graeye's heart swelled with compassion for the pitiful heap he made. True, he had often been unkind, had never loved her, had not inquired as to her welfare at the abbey, but he was her father. He was a man who had lost everything—his son, the grandson who would have been his heir, his home, and now his dignity. Everything gone. Would the remainder of his mind go, too?

Though she longed to embrace him, she knew she risked much by simply laying a hand upon his shoulder. "Father?"

He did not move.

She spoke again, but still no response. She moved nearer and tentatively slid an arm around his shoulders. "Father, 'tis I, Graeye."

He lifted his head and stared at her. Then he came to life. "'Twas you who brought this upon me!" He swung his arm, landing it so hard against her chest that she fell over. "Spawn of the devil!"

With her back to the cold floor, Graeye drew a shuddering breath.

"I should have left you to the Church!" Edward lurched upright and set himself over her. "For this offense, I am to be punished to everlasting hell."

Graeye glanced at the knight who had not moved from the doorway, then slowly rose and took a step back. "I have come to see to your needs."

"My needs?" Edward thrust his face close to hers. "What else have you come for?"

She held his stare. "I would know what is to become of me."

He laughed, a loud, raucous noise that died abruptly. "And what do you think your fate should be, Daughter of Eve?"

"I would stay with you."

"Me?" he mimicked her voice. "Of what use are you now that all I possess has been stolen?"

"I would care for you. You will need—"

He seized hold of her. "I do not need the devil on my shoulder."

"'Tis not true—"

"Know you that twice your mother bore me sons? Sickly things that lived no more than a few days. Then she bore you with the devil's mark full upon your face—strong and healthy. Then no more."

This was the first Graeye had heard of it. Never had her mother spoken of those children who had come before. It explained much of her father's treatment of her, but now that she knew, perhaps she could do battle with it—find a way to reach him.

"Nay," he continued, "you will return to the abbey. As the Church has already received your dowry, your place there is secure. *That* Balmaine cannot take from me."

She pulled free of his hold. "I do not wish to return."

"Think you I care what you wish?" He advanced on her again. "Many a daughter would vie for the soft life of a nun, but not you. 'Tis the devil in you that resists. Thus, as my final offering to God, you will return."

"You need me!" It was no lie. What would become of an old man alone in a world so changed from what he had known? And what of her? She could not simply wander out into the world without a man to protect her.

"I need you?" he scoffed. "Nay, I needed your body. Blood of my blood. A vessel for the heir you would have made with William. Now"—he gave a short laugh—"you may return to the abbey or go back to the devil whence you came. That is your only choice."

The air of hate upon which his words were delivered cut deeply and Graeye backed away.

"And do not let me see you again without your nun's clothing!" he yelled.

She was surprised when she came up against the knight in the doorway. Wordlessly, the man drew her outside and closed the door on Edward. There was silence. Then a great clamor arose as the old man threw himself against the door, his curses vibrating through the wooden planks.

"My lady," the knight spoke to her bowed head, "'twould be best for you to return to the donjon." At her nod, he gently guided her forward.

She was grateful for his support. Otherwise, she did not think she would have made it down the steep stairway, so blurred was her vision.

At the bottom, she expected him to send her on ahead, but he led her past the curious stares of the soldiers and castle folk and did not relinquish his grip until they stood within the hall.

She tried to smile, but it was useless. "My thanks, Sir...?"

"Abelaard," he said with a small bow.

"If you will wait but a few minutes," she said, stepping away, "I will gather blankets that you might deliver them to my father."

A thick silence followed that had her turning back around. Too late, she realized it was beneath the knight's rank to perform such a duty for her.

"My apologies," she said. "I will send a servant."

Looking relieved that he did not have to refuse, he offered an uneven smile. "My sister is a nun," he said gruffly. "'Tis not a bad life she has."

Graeye stared at him, watching as he grew uncomfortable with the effects of his poorly timed, though well-meaning disclosure. "I fear you do not understand, Sir Knight," she said, then turned away.

It was difficult to find privacy where she could vent her distraught emotions, and in desperation she returned to the small chapel abovestairs.

Kneeling before the altar, she clasped her hands to her breast and tried to offer up prayer. However, there was no room for such devotions. All of her hopes were dashed by the coming of the treacherous Baron Balmaine. She gave a shuddering sob, then cried as she had never cried—and vowed she would never cry again.

About The Author

TAMARA LEIGH HOLDS a Master's Degree in Speech and Language Pathology. In 1993, she signed a 4-book contract with Bantam Books. Her first medieval romance, *Warrior Bride*, was released in 1994. Continuing to write for the general market, three more novels were published with HarperCollins and Dorchester and earned awards and spots on national bestseller lists.

In 2006, Tamara's first inspirational contemporary romance, *Stealing Adda*, was released. In 2008, *Perfecting Kate* was optioned for a movie and *Splitting Harriet* won an ACFW "Book of the Year" award. The following year, *Faking Grace* was nominated for a RITA award. In 2011, Tamara wrapped up her "Southern Discomfort" series with the release of *Restless in Carolina*.

When not in the middle of being a wife, mother, and cookbook fiend, Tamara buries her nose in a good book—and her writer's pen in ink. In 2012, she returned to the historical romance genre with *Dreamspell*, a medieval time travel romance. Shortly thereafter, she once more invited readers to join her in the middle ages with the *Age of Faith* series: *The Unveiling, The Yielding, The Redeeming, The Kindling,* and *The Longing*. Tamara's #1 Bestsellers—*Lady at Arms, Lady Of Eve, Lady Of Fire,* and

Lady Of Conquest—are the first of her medieval romances to be rewritten as "clean reads." Look for *Baron Of Blackwood,* the third book in *The Feud* series, in 2016.

Tamara lives near Nashville with her husband, sons, a Doberman that bares its teeth not only to threaten the UPS man but to smile, and a feisty Morkie that keeps her company during long writing stints.

Connect with Tamara at her website www.tamaraleigh.com, her blog The Kitchen Novelist, her email tamaraleightenn@gmail.com, Facebook, and Twitter.

**For new releases and special promotions, subscribe to
Tamara Leigh's mailing list: www.tamaraleigh.com**

Made in the USA
Columbia, SC
21 March 2020